The Divorced Lady's Companion to Living in Italy

Catherine McNamara

First Edition: The Divorced Lady's Companion to Living in Italy

First published in Great Britain in 2012 by:
Indigo Dreams Publishing Ltd
132 Hinckley Road
Stoney Stanton
Leics
LE9 4LN

www.indigodreams.co.uk

Catherine McNamara has asserted her right under the Copyright, Designs and Patents Act 1988 to be identified as the author of this work.

ISBN 978-1-907401-73-2

British Library Cataloguing in Publication Data. A CIP record for this book can be obtained from the British Library.

Designed and typeset in Minion Pro by Indigo Dreams.

Cover design by Annie K. Hannigan

Printed and bound in Great Britain by Imprint Academic, Exeter.

Papers used by Indigo Dreams are recyclable products made from wood grown in sustainable forests following the guidance of the Forest Stewardship Council

For S. and D. in that great KitKatClub in the sky

ACKNOWLEDGEMENTS

Thank you to my publishers Dawn Bauling and Ronnie Goodyer of Indigo Dreams Publishing who decided to give this manuscript the go-ahead.

Thank you to my readers who supplied grammatical wisdom, opinions and support: Emily Booth, Paola Cecchetto, Rachel Chu-McNamara, Anne Hallihan, Stuart Rosewarne.

Thank you to the generous Chris Manby for her cover comment.

Thank you to Diana and Kevin, Kay, Arrigo, Omar, Georgia and Finley.

And finally, thank you to my editor, John F. Griffiths, who has been a pleasure to work with.

Catherine McNamara

Contents

The Divorced Lady's Companion to Living in Italy

1. LONDON

An old friend of mine named Jean fell through a tear in her marriage and landed on her feet. One autumn, Jean met a solicitor from Milan on a singles trekking tour in Peru and packed her bags. She sold the house with its clutch of hydrangeas. Her adolescent children learnt Italian with ease. It was reported that, at forty-four, Jean gave the Milanese man a chubby male love-child.

Jean wasn't really a close friend of mine, though we had married the same year and our children were the same wretched ages. The parallel in our stories narrowed one quiet Sunday afternoon in the kitchen when my husband Peter informed me he had fallen in love with a woman named Danielle and was moving to a flat in Shepherd's Bush. His words exerted visceral, slow-release punches. I realised he had been naked in the arms of another woman. The first person I thought of was Jean in Milan, framed with dabs of gold from a painter's brush and a corona of religious spurs. At that moment Jean became my patron saint.

In the aftermath, I dropped a stone in weight while waiting for my outrage to burst like rotten fruit on cement. It never happened. Rather, I was curious to know of Danielle's hair colour and whether her neck already had faint train tracks; if she blew her nose in public and where she bought her shoes; whether her ovaries were better kernels than mine. I asked Peter. He gave me strained, sideways looks. He refused to include me in any sort of 'threesome' and I quickly became the lone mare put out to pasture, the *divorcée*. I walked woodenly through the streets and couldn't understand how the brand had come to be on my forehead, but it was now.

Everything that I had taken as given in my life had been swept away.

Several weeks into the summer, I took a leaf from Jean's book and joined a tour group. I didn't fancy a long plane journey and my idea of a trek was an aisle-by-aisle supermarket excursion, so I folded away the Andes, Himalayas and Kilimanjaro brochures. I also wasn't keen on declaring myself a *single*. That had a discarded, forty-something ring to it and I was terrified of ashen widowers called Ted with yellow teeth. I might have known: my group in Rouen consisted of three young nuns from Tanzania, a haggard gay couple in toupees and crumpled lapels, and the inevitable New Zealander. The tour guide, Sylvie, was bonking the New Zealander by the second night.

I felt a deepening heaviness on returning to the house – had Jean felt like this before she had unearthed the man who'd reset her life? Days later, Peter came around in a hired truck to collect the last of his things. I watched him carry out his university papers from the attic and a deck-chair in the garden that a great-uncle had carted off a P & O liner. He took the bosomy Henry Moore-style sculpture, inherited from his bohemian aunt, from our living room. The new lovers were ready to decorate, he said. I figured that 'bosomy' was the flavour of the day.

Later, his guard was down in the sunshine and he suggested I prepare a cup of tea in the garden, where we sat down with new, blinking formality.

'You know, you've done wonders with this patch of ground.' He looked around with detachment at the trellises we'd put up together, as though he'd never seen them before. His lower lip had become more sensual and pronounced. 'So how was the history trip to France? Did you meet anyone? We're all keen for you to … you know, move ahead. I've spoken with the children. They want you to savour life. You have a right to it all, Marilyn, remember that.'

I was alarmed to feel that Peter was prodding about my soul with his poker. Peter bought foreign programmes for a huge television network. He had spent years sorting the sheep from the goats and dangling carrots before his audience. I was now seeing the invisible side of Peter I had never known. He was trying to sell me the new Marilyn reality show: *Here's Marilyn sobbing on the Channel crossing. And here she is crying into a très, très grand bag of French crisps.*

He drove off in a fine mood and I shut the front gate under the Queen Caroline roses. I ate a greasy bar of chocolate I found in my daughter's pocket and turned on a documentary about Mussolini with his harsh, captivating face and his thwarted escape to Switzerland. Mussolini and his lover were brought back to Milan and hung upside down like fowls.

Whatever Peter had said to the children about Danielle, it clearly hadn't upset them. School recommenced and they came home bickering from the station, emptying the refrigerator as voraciously as ever and wandering distractedly and untouched to their rooms. For years our family life had provided book-ends for Peter's heavy working week. Now that he had removed himself from our lives for good, I waited for Vanessa to break down or for Eddy to come sniffling into my bed – but I hugged myself under the covers alone.

In fact Peter had been quick to install a new schedule so that no one missed a beat. Every other weekend he drove the children down to Brighton where Danielle, whose name bobbed about like an apple in a bucket, had a place. On Sunday night they were dropped off and burst shrill and clear-eyed into the house.

After suffering this for a while, I called Peter. 'What do you mean, I'm dismantling you?' he cried. 'We're all trying to give you some time to yourself. Some time to rebuild. You need some personal space around you, you know, now that you're on your own,' Peter said with ugly clarity. 'Read up, spend some time online. Go into the city. Be open about it.'

But I didn't feel like opening up any further, any more than I had already been split apart. On one of those first weekends alone I brought out our wedding album plus a couple of boxes of photographs. Seventeen years ago we looked like a pair of intercourse-driven sods. Peter's career hadn't taken off and I was swimming with nausea from our daughter's tiny seed inside of me. Peter's gestures – an arm beckoning me, a disarming clutch – were those of the man who used to say he wanted to die in my arms. What had happened? I put aside the series of awkward, non-art house photographs he had taken of my stretching belly, which revealed the fright and embarrassment in my eyes. Then there was Vanessa, my shrieking cub, my downy pink alien in a home-knitted blanket. I combed through masses of baby photographs with their limpid physical cadences: the first smiles, the first steps on soft summer grass. Oddly, I came across an unfamiliar photo of my neighbour Jean Harper and I holding onto our toddlers down by the river, surrounded by ducks. It was an unexpected surprise. My patron saint was reaching out from her new life to speak to me. Try as I might, I could not recall who took the photograph or what we might have said to each other that afternoon, as I never took my children to the river and I hated ducks.

After that I used Jean's photograph as a bookmark. I went for a job interview at a local sports clinic and returned to work as a physiotherapist. Nearly four months down the line, it seemed I had turned the first corner in my new single life. Each day it gave me immense pleasure to use my hands to deliver relief to other people in pain. I came home exhausted, arms and shoulders aching. I worked with a young girl who had just had the pins removed from her broken leg and an elderly woman who told me my hands were like angels' wings.

But one morning, only weeks into the job, the street was buzzing with police cars and the clinic was sealed off. I watched my boss Mrs Giles being frogmarched into a vehicle, blood all over her tunic. Apparently Mrs Giles had displaced Mr Giles' head with a hunting rifle after she found him canoodling with a nurse called Sheneen. I drove home, stunned, in my crêpe soled shoes and blue uniform. The postman was zigzagging at the far end of the street. Some travel company had obviously anticipated my unemployed status and the letter-box was stuffed with a fresh batch of brochures for singles tours: The Missionary Trail in Coastal China, Cro-Magnon Man in the Swiss Alps, Rock Wallabies in Tasmania ....

Peter commiserated briefly about my job and then, out of the blue, asked if I were ready to meet Danielle. So far, according to our family and few communal friends, it had been a seamless separation. I listened to my ex-husband's upbeat voice. He sounded as though he was headed to a restaurant with candles on wonky tables, and a jazz concert afterwards; he sounded as though he had just had fantastic sex. I began to shake all over, thinking of quiet Mrs Giles raising the gun to her husband's head. Then, bang! – all the splattered mulch on the walls.

I cut him off and threw away the phone. I cursed Sheneen and Danielle and wept into the couch.

Probably the person I have always relied upon most is my close friend Pamela, who is a clairvoyant. Pamela and I grew up in identical council terraces, both of us possessing mothers with foreign accents that were often lightly mocked by shopkeepers. My mother was Hungarian with robust bones. Pamela's mum was Irish with a mild pale face. The two women mistrusted each other's food and ways and never got along.

But Pamela and I stayed friends for years. She hadn't moved from our old neighbourhood, which had grown quite classy now, and had five children with three different fathers. One of her sons was a monk in Burma. One of the girls sang with a pop group that had hit the charts. Pamela had a massive tattoo all over her back from the early days before Buddhist mantras and barbed wire biceps. She didn't give a toss. Every two or three months she would come all the way to my house from the city in her pompous old Bentley and we would moan to each other and have a laugh before getting blind drunk.

A few days after the clinic was shut down Pamela's car appeared on the drive. I had known this was coming. Ever since Peter had walked out I had avoided lifting the phone and calling her, and dodged her calls for weeks. I drew across the curtain and saw her lighting a fag on our garden path. I tiptoed to the door.

'Why on earth didn't you tell me?' she said. 'He's taken off, the bastard. You're getting *divorced.*'

I realised that our intimacy and her creepy intuition had joined hands. She pushed past me into the house and I saw a little bump pushing through her sweater where I guessed she'd finally had her nipple pierced.

'So he's left you for some gorgeous young girl?'

I began to dissolve into tears.

'Not to worry,' she muttered. 'They won't last.'

She went to her usual sofa and pulled down a Greek souvenir ashtray from the bookshelf. Pamela was the only person who smoked in my house. I looked at her fuming my way.

'Why didn't you want to tell me?' she snapped. 'Stop standing there and go and get some of that Chenin blanc he hides out the back.'

I brought out one of Peter's bottles and uncorked it mechanically, then fumbled around for some glasses. I slopped some wine in them and began to weep.

'There, there now.' She came over and soothed me. 'I know I needn't have been so cross, but that's what I've come to say. You see, I've been having the oddest dreams about you … and Peter, God curse him. It's been going on for weeks: people speaking foreign languages; you looking as though you're more than half-drunk; some perky-looking girl and a Chinese guy in a coat.' She broke off and smiled at my sobbing face. 'Did you know I had my nipple pierced?' She whipped up her jumper and pulled down her bra to show me. It looked like a fish-hook trapped under the skin. 'Eric's done one too so we'll both be setting off the metal detectors.'

I blubbered into Peter's Chenin blanc. Pamela rattled on about her spot on one of the breakfast television programmes that morning, where she had an on-and-off job ever since she forecast the flooding of New Orleans in a local newspaper. She told me about the makeup woman crying over her failed IVF, while she was certain the woman's womb carried a tiny fertilised seed. And then she talked about the blond interviewer, very famous and rude, who'd had sex with three men the night before. Pamela sat back puffing, one nipple sticking up like a tin soldier under her old Vivienne Westwood jumper. 'Look love, I know you're blocking me out, you always have done. So we won't go there, okay? Meantime, what about a sandwich, or even some Hungarian leftovers. I have an appetite to murder.'

I turned on Annie Lennox and brought out cheese, salami and dark bread. Later, I opened the bottle of grappa Peter and I bought on our trip to Venice the previous winter. We'd made love a few times in the tasteful sponge-painted hotel room. On the cheap flight back, there'd been so much turbulence over the Alps that we held hands. Peter's moist fingers had fastened and unfastened on mine as the violent blue sky tossed us between air currents. I had savoured the way he clung to me. But then I remembered the way he had trailed off into the terminal with his phone cupped to his cheek. That was when the grappa turned as sharp as knives.

I don't know how Pamela drove home that evening, or what I prepared for the children for supper, or how I propelled them to school the next day. I know I was dragged to the computer that morning by a strange force, where I signed up on a dating site and within moments began to chat to a man named Brett. Brett was over from Hong Kong visiting his sister (people speaking foreign languages?) and had nothing to do that day. I showered and dressed.

We met in Leicester Square and ventured into Starbucks, ordering twin cappuccinos. He too was divorced. His ex-wife worked in a merchant bank in Hong Kong. Tall and crisp-looking, he reminded me of a Chinese detective from a crime film. His cropped greying hair was plugged thickly into the top of his forehead. I had never seen such determined hair growth except on dolls. Brett spoke at length about internet dating and how I shouldn't take any type of risk, even chiding me for meeting him so readily. I felt glad of his protection. He told me how he had flown to Mexico to visit a woman he had chatted with every day for six months. I was disappointed, picturing tall Brett meeting a woman with Frida Kahlo allure.

Brett's tone fell to a more intimate register and I realised we had been talking for nearly two hours and I was famished. We moved on to Chinatown, where it seemed that many of the restaurants had emptied for the afternoon. Brett said he had some Cantonese friends who would serve us, so we began to wander down side-streets, a discreet cut-out of safety space running between our bodies. People still streamed everywhere so I sensed no alarm bells ringing as I occasionally glanced at the handsome couple we made, reflected in the shop windows.

But then Brett's hand came to rest on the small of my back. I guess I reacted badly. He quickly removed it and stepped backwards, hands raised.

'I'm so sorry,' he said, bowing his head. 'But this is the restaurant. You see? To the left here. Of course, if you'd rather not go in ....'

It was the type of dive one of Peter's cronies might have sent us to, urging us to try the Peking Duck. A surge of nausea rose from yesterday's grappa and I stood dehydrated, my will buzzing, unable to free fall towards the foreign man. The street was empty. I felt a twang of fear. Up on the main street I saw an older woman behind a pushchair. In a shaft of afternoon light it looked like Jean. In fact at that moment I was certain it was Jean.

Brett's lips opened hungrily and with a spicy taste over mine, his tongue plunging inside with a big randy wetness. I jerked away and ran towards the street screaming.

Days later at the local shops I heard from a neighbour that Jean had indeed returned for a quick visit. One of her mother's sisters had passed away – breast cancer again – and she'd flown across for the funeral. But she hadn't brought the baby. Teething and on bottled milk, the baby had stayed in Milan with her lover's mother. Now it was apparent that not only had Jean found a good roll in bed and the licence to reproduce, she had located a mother-in-law who loved her like a daughter. How to explain this fluke after marvellous fluke? How had Jean, high up in the Andes, fallen upon the solicitor from Milan, rather than seedy Brett? Had they sat together in the searing air, wordless? Had they warmed each other's frozen feet in a wind-lashed tent?

Everyone who saw Jean said she had been more forceful and trim, despite the family's loss: radiant, healthy-looking, with beautifully tailored clothes. I wished I'd known Jean's aunt so I could have gone to the funeral and seen her for myself. I worked out she hadn't even been in the country the morning I met Brett, so it couldn't have been her pushing a pram in Soho, exercising the powers of the patron saint.

Within days, she had gone, rushing back to a new job in Milan. They said she had opened a small language school and her brother was moving over there to help kick it off. Apparently the whole Italian nation had taken to studying the English language and Jean's enrolment books were full.

Over on the high street, a flyer with an Italian flag was taped in the newsagent's window. In a dashing, robust typeface I read about the *English NOW Language Institute* in glamorous Milan, offering teaching positions to enthusiastic undergraduate students. My heart did a quick somersault. Jean must have bustled in and attached it herself. I tore off one of the little paper tails with the international number printed on it. Of course I had no intention of calling – it seemed beyond the pale to take jobs away from youngsters. Perhaps if I booked the Churches of Rome tour I could travel north and breeze through the glass doors of Jean's school. Perhaps the talents of the undergraduates would fall short and Jean would be begging me to brush up my clauses and antonyms.

Feeling ragged, I called Pamela.

'Hello love,' she answered promptly. 'I've been thinking of you. I'm just having a massage here with my girl Sally, who is still singing with the Honeyguns. D'you remember how she was, little blond Sally? Well, Sally just told me she's up the duff with the drummer. What on earth are you doing chasing Japanese men?'

'Pardon? He was from Hong Kong, actually.'

'Ha! Don't try and ruin my signals. For Christ's sakes, Marilyn. Don't go courting danger on Peter's account. You'll be travelling soon anyway. Think blossoms, think strong coffee. Now I have to turn over. This pierced nipple thing is killing me and I'm far too noxious to become a grandmother.'

Blossoms? Coffee? For years Pamela had been on the verge of having her own show but each time she took the mickey out of some pink-faced executive and was sent packing. Was she taking the mickey out of me now? Had she always known, through our years of shoulder-pads and dancing to Cyndi Lauper, that my marriage would fall to bits?

As I finished the call, the phone rang again with its stupid electronic melody. It was my ex-husband. Suddenly, I was seized by the awful feeling that both he and Pamela had somehow witnessed me being kissed by a wet-lipped Chinese detective from a dating site. I shrieked, 'Shut your damned trap, Peter. I'm leaving for Italy next week.'

2. MILANO

Though there had been the brief interlude in Venice last winter, by the time I touched down in Italy I was ready to admit that my sexuality had been spiralling downward for years. We certainly didn't have any of Pamela and Eric's raciness. Peter and I used to make love on occasion, but it was a slippery, innocuous affair, concluded with separate showers and a rub on the back. We had left off with tongue-kissing an age ago, and when Peter looked at me penetratingly, it was probably because he was remembering a phone call he had to make on LA time. If I saw he had a hard-on in the bathroom in the morning, he dispensed with it while I prepared his coffee in the kitchen. I couldn't even remember the last time I had gotten down on my knees.

The plane touched down on the runway. I was at Malpensa Airport outside Milan, staring at the passport on my lap. As I blinked away my tears, I scanned the passengers filing down the centre of the plane, worried someone would turn around and see that I was newly single and bereft. I heard the Italian language thrown back and forth by men with messy grey hair in elegant jackets carrying pink sports newspapers. I saw the woman who had never shut up the whole flight finally disappear under the 'USCITA' sign. For a moment I worried I would remain strapped in my seat belt forever. I looked outside at the broad, low bus, now filled with people, and at the driver with his shaven head and Magnum moustache in his iridescent safety uniform.

Inside the airport, a cranky older woman snapped open my passport. It didn't matter that the woman had a menial job flipping open EU documents and glancing at faces all day, the woman was as busty and feisty as Sophia Loren, with rich dark hair and vivid purple fingernails. Her heavy eyebrows flicked up when she caught me looking over the furrows and relaxed pores of her face. She said something to me that I couldn't understand,

and then made a comment to the young, tanned officer I hadn't noticed leaning against the wall behind her. They both laughed. I quickly pushed myself out into the luggage hall. I wandered between the idle conveyor belts trying to remember when I had last sniggered with a young man like that, a man with dirty thoughts. It reminded me of a film I'd seen, where a nuclear meltdown had gone on scorching downward like a hot coal dropping through the earth. That was how Peter must have felt when he was waiting at the station fantasizing about Danielle, or ten minutes after they'd had sex and his thighs were still weak. I looked around for the carousel with my flight number. Everywhere my eyes travelled there were men touching women they loved, and women turning to them with trilling eyes. I slumped against a bloodless marble pilaster.

'*Sta bene, signora?*' said a foxy policeman with a German shepherd swishing its tail.

I knew enough of Italian to smile and say, '*Sì*' awkwardly.

'*Sicura?*' he smiled, using the endearing tone he probably used with dithering pensioners. His eyes were wide apart and brown, deeply set below the peak of his dashing cap, framed with eyelashes to die for.

The wolf-like animal sniffed my hand and the officer's smile expanded.

'*Vuole venire con me, signora?*'

'Pardon?'

As he gently dislodged my side from the marble pilaster I realised it was the first male contact I had had since Brett's wild kiss and a rough hug my son had felt inspired to give me at my departure. He passed his arm under mine and the warmth flooded through my shirt directly into the starved tissue. I felt hot coals forming instantly at my crotch, fusion racing through my body. The conveyor belt nearest to me jumped to life and people closed together, a couple of them staring at me being led away.

The officer took me to a type of staff room, pushed some coins into a coffee machine, murmuring to the dog which dropped to the floor next to him and crossed its paws.

'*Ecco, signora,*' he said distinctly, as though trying to gauge the well-being of a senile aunt. '*Quanto zucchero?* How many sugar?'

He placed the cup in front of me, while I tried to halt the tears filling my eyes.

'Two, *grazie.*' I fumbled through Italian numbers in my head. '*Due, per favore.*'

My first consecutive words in Italian! He shook a sugar sachet into my cup and smiled as he began to stir. It felt like Pavarotti had strolled into the room and burst into song.

The coffee scalded my lips and carved a path into my chest. Instantly, my brain seemed lighter and clearer, and somehow even the skin of my face felt tighter as the concentrate of energy blasted along my nerves. Everything around me bore a sheer, atomic outline – from the officer staring at me to the poster on the wall advertising a vibrant pistol and a bright clutch of drugs. Even the dog's huge paws seemed to be buzzing on the gleaming marble floor with its ruddy flecks.

Afterwards, the officer retrieved my suitcase and accompanied me to the airport bus. Giddy, I bought my ticket, found a blue-cushioned seat, and waved him goodbye. I sat back as the bus pulled onto the autostrada, relishing the still-warm imprint of his fingers around my inner arm. I glanced at my co-travellers, chewing away my smile. Many were lone businessmen who all wore looks of remote sexual voltage before they plucked out their mobiles and began to broadcast into them. Then they sounded like B-grade actors starved for a crowd. A few Euro-youngsters had their iPods wired to their ears. I glanced back and saw the Sophia Loren official flipping through a paparazzi magazine two seats behind, her ankles crossed above stiletto heels. She was dressed in casual gear now and leaned across the aisle to show her friend a photograph. As she moved I saw curlicues of lovely white lace cupping a pair of tanned boobs that were tucked into her shirt like small pets. Then she must have felt me staring. She glared in my direction and I whipped around to the front.

We pulled up alongside the *Stazione Centrale*, a massive white elephant in the midst of city buildings, and were spilt out with our bags. I looked up and saw a row of Roman centurions and their steeds peering down from the roof through clots of pigeons. Still giddy, I rounded the colossal flank and met a steady stream of people dragging trolleys between staunch white columns, while more cocky young policemen were stationed about the taxi rank with dogs. I saw Sophia Loren walk past and slide into a taxi, comfortable with an entire crowd of men peering at her bust and legs. Further on, towards the piazza, an agitated crowd frayed around corners and filed underground to the city trains. A man waved blood-red scarves in the air on a corner. An old druggie extended a yellow criss-crossed hand. I looked up to the damp grey Italian sky, identical to the sky I saw day after day at home. To my delight, it now pulsed with mystique.

I'd told Peter I would only be passing through Milan, with a view to enrolling in a foreign language course in Perugia. But I had no intention of repeating the Rouen experience on a grander scale with *penne all'arrabbiata*, and I had a feeling that Jean Harper's presence here in the city was a distinct call to remain in Milan. Peter had generously offered to take the children until the end of term, which was when I'd told him I would make my decision whether or not to come back. 'I admire that sort of spirit,' he'd said. 'Kids are hardy little creatures.'

It also hadn't escaped my attention that my mercenary children were enjoying the honeymoon with Danielle: a new leather jacket had shown up in Vanessa's wardrobe plus a pair of cropped black boots; Eddy had a new stash of games. I no longer felt curious about the state of Peter's lover's neck and what shoes she wore, whether she had big ears or blond highlights. Pamela had brushed it off saying they wouldn't last but I knew Peter was full of post-sex charity every time I saw him. 'Put yourself first, Marilyn. That's the way from now on.' Even his lunch-box looked big and rank in his jeans.

These heavy thoughts hauled me directly back into miserable *divorcée* land. The thrill of the coffee had abandoned me and I tried to relocate the lifeline to my loins. But none of the goatee-chinned policeman here looked ready to catch me when I fell. They stood in groups, guns on slings over their shoulders, eyes trained on the good-looking women thronging by.

'Marilyn? Marilyn Wade?'

A petite woman who somehow knew my name stepped out of the crowd and walked straight up to me.

'You are Marilyn, aren't you? Peter Wade's wife? We met at the award party last summer. D'you remember? It was that terrible survival show where they all lived on grilled beetles.'

I took a step back and tried to bring the English-speaking woman into focus. She had a strong Australian accent, copper-toned hair in lively springs, a laptop bag under her arm and a pretty patterned dress scooped in at the waist. I heard bells ringing and it wasn't the local cathedral. She'd been at Peter's side all evening pawing his arm, while he whipped his hand around her shoulders at every possible occasion. She was Fiona Miller, a sassy Australian girl who'd sold Peter a horrific television series that became a national hit.

'I thought it was you,' she continued. 'My name's Fiona Miller, I'm from Sydney. Have you lost someone? You over for a dirty weekend? Look, Peter told me you guys have split up.'

'Peter told *you*?' I gawped.

'Sure, we keep in touch. It's Danielle, I knew it was. She's quite a goer. Oh, don't worry, my darling hub left me for a French actress when I was four months preggers and I lost the baby. And the girl only did commercials, with a voice-over I expect. I think Danielle at least does scripts. Awful ones.'

Despite her heels she was still quite shorter than I was and I raised my eyes above her hair, trying to wish her out of my panorama.

'Are you okay, dearie? Where are you staying? Sorry to say, but you look awful. How about crashing at my place till you get your bearings? It's just around the corner and there's a spare bed and you can take a Panadol and lie down.'

'I'm sorry? There's absolutely no need.' I pulled away, just as I realised the energy required to hunt down a hotel was not going to present itself and I needed a very strong cup of tea.

'Come on, Marilyn,' insisted Fiona. 'I bet you took off without even booking a hotel and you haven't thought to eat in hours.' She smiled dazzlingly.

I looked at this perky, overfriendly woman who had singled me out in central Milan. She was right, I was on my last legs. And yet I couldn't believe I was stalled here, actually beginning to contemplate her offer.

'That's it then, you're coming with me,' she announced. Then, without waiting for my agreement, the woman who'd sold my husband the prize-winning beetle-eating show turned on her high heels and began to tug me into Milan.

We headed away from the station. Fiona chattered tirelessly about everything under the sun. About Peter. About living in Milan versus living in Rome where she'd also stayed. She saluted shopkeepers and men in news-stands, wedging her handbag under her arm and urging me to do the same. She wasn't even shy of the topic of Peter's hussy, Danielle. She was keen to shed light upon the type of predator my ex-husband had fallen for, while I struggled to batten down my ears.

'I'm not saying Peter wasn't up for it – you'd be surprised by what they call a day at the office – but Danielle knows how to dig in her claws. I can't think how many families she's ripped apart … I'm sorry, is this too tough for you?'

She leant across and took over, pulling my suitcase as my limbs went to water. I didn't like her insider's version of events. Nor the fact that Fiona Miller, who had probably crossed Peter's turf, was now trying to make a mission of me. I put on my most stringent look.

'I'm quite fine, you know,' I said. 'I was on my way to leaving Peter myself. I am almost grateful to that woman.'

'You're kidding me. Well then – gosh!' Fiona frowned. 'Then I guess I have it all wrong.'

'And I would appreciate it if you could choose something else to talk about.'

I let my abused Good Samaritan put that in her pipe to smoke as I lifted my tear-filled eyes along the boulevard. Graceful apartment buildings extended into the late afternoon. Sad autumn greys traced the window cornices and balustrades. Glossy boutiques and bars alternated along the footpath, filled with women browsing through clothes and men watching women waltz past with shopping bags. Many eyes stopped on Fiona, who seemed not to notice as she walked with a pleasing lilt.

'It's not the most glam end of town,' she said cheerfully. 'But I'm only on a short contract in Rome. They practically overlapped and I couldn't be bothered setting up down there again. Too many bad vibes, you know? So I've settled for the train trips where you can get some work done. Just amazing I've run into you, isn't it?' I was surprised by her staggering friendliness.

'Besides, I'm pretty well looked after in Milan, in certain departments. It would be a shame to chuck it all in. Now that I think of it, if you are staying in Italy, the lease is all paid up for a good three months. You could stay a while if you're interested. I might just have to take off for a new series. D'you have plans to stay?' she asked, a little too eagerly for my liking.

I had no plans of any sort and this woman was certainly not about to become my sounding board. Then I heard myself saying in a chilly voice, 'I suppose you could say I may be working for a friend, an English friend. She has just opened a language institute.' I had no idea I would bring Jean's name into play.

'Oh right, the language institute scam,' Fiona replied. 'Be careful, they pay their teachers rat shit.'

'I'm quite sure it wouldn't be like that.'

'Yeah, right … Here we are then. This is us.' She tapped a code into a keypad on a wall and two heavy wooden doors drew apart. Inside, after a section of rosy flagstones, we passed into a second, dingier courtyard and then climbed a stairway to the left with Fiona helping me drag my suitcase. Three flights later she swung the door open onto a dark, sweaty apartment that smelt of unwashed sheets and sharp socks.

'Phew! What a whiff. Sorry about that, we really need a change of air in here.' She snapped on a lamp and lunged towards a thick belt in the wall which jerked up a window blind. Thin afternoon light scrolled out over an apartment that made my teenage daughter's room look immaculate. Fiona opened the window in a kitchenette and a wave of fried meat came over in a crosswind from the air shaft between buildings. I suddenly wished I taken an about-turn at the station. The idea of a thrifty hotel room reeked with allure.

'Oh God,' she sighed, 'bloody Giampietro and his *spezzatino*.' She cleared the divan of a pile of clothes. 'Oops! Had a friend over before I left and he must have left these.' She held up a pair of crumpled men's boxer shorts and waved them at me. 'Here, have a seat.'

She was talking to herself as she bundled the clothes up and took them away to the bathroom, where I hoped the washing machine hadn't lain idle for too long. I clutched my handbag, inhaling my unexpected landing pad in Italy. Fiona came back and switched on the television set, perhaps thinking a pair of go-go girls jiggling their assets might clear the air. Everywhere I looked I saw tabletops piled with magazines, bottles of juice, wineglasses and food wrappers. Not to mention a classy pair of Ugg boots kicked under the coffee table with whatever else lurked down there.

'You're lucky I have a spare bed,' she said as she careered about. 'Look, you've caught me at a rather messy point in time, Marilyn. Just try and feel at home if you can. Park your suitcase in there. That's the bathroom next to my room.'

At home? I wonder if Peter, who liked his socks in coupled rolls, knew his Aussie mate as well as I did now.

'God, you look a wreck,' Fiona said encouragingly. 'Why don't you drop that bag and eat something, Marilyn? There must be some cheese and olives in the fridge. I'm not sure I would trust anything else.' She threw off her shoes, then stood still for an instant in her sad little hallway and took me in. 'Look, I'm really sorry love but I have to take off now. I have this prior engagement.' She rolled her eyes. 'Now get some rest and we'll do some retail therapy tomorrow.'

She whipped into the bathroom and I heard her rattling her makeup, then from her room I heard the sound of tissue paper being removed from a pair of shoes. My heart softened a little. Fiona came out in a pair of teetering cut-off boots, looking smashing. Then the front door slammed and she was gone.

I stood there for some time until I realised that every sound had been erased except for the natter of the TV. I was used to a quiet home, but not a quiet corner of a big city. It felt bizarre. I released the grip on my bag and took a couple of hesitant steps into her living room. How dare she call me Marilyn, as if we were the best of friends? I turned around and slowly walked over to the air shaft with the fried meat smell and could see four other window openings. I heard a shower tap turned on; a naked foot stepping off a bath mat onto tiles. That felt way too intimate. From above, a woman's voice pitched into the empty volume like a voice in a play. She was complaining. But whoever she was complaining to must have heard it all before. Then the silence came again, filling the shaft. I drew away feeling like some sort of voyeur.

I found some aspirin in a bathroom cabinet crammed with lavish creams and makeup – this girl spared herself nothing. I also found a drawer full of condoms. I picked up one packet with a racy couple on it and felt a spike of envy. There were little yellow haloes in wrappers scattered all over the bottom of the drawer and I wondered if she had grabbed a handful for the evening's escapade. I had no doubt Fiona was a woman who had sex, *miles* of it. Grimly, I made myself a jam sandwich in the kitchen then took it into the living room where I noticed a signed photograph of George Clooney on a bookshelf stacked with fashion magazines – George Clooney?

I walked over and it was George Clooney all right. With his crushed black opal eyes and gritted teeth smile. He didn't look too happy to be spending the night.

'Hello George,' I said softly. 'Nothing planned? Poor old you.' I went over to the spot Fiona had cleared for me on the couch and sat down. I gobbled the food, not realising I was famished. Then I sat back for my first evening of Italian TV. There was a quiz show with a tiny bald presenter and a big-breasted black girl in silver hot pants. The camera grazed over her near-naked curves and occasionally she smirked. The game show was irrelevant. It was all about the promise of the big-breasted girl's smirk. I switched over to the news programme.

The tanned newsreader dressed in gallant orange seemed to be hawking a more mature version of the same thing. I was shocked. This wasn't written in my guidebook. Whatever happened to Michelangelo and centuries of raising cathedrals from the earth?

Later, I found an old Charles Bronson film dubbed in Italian. Here the voices lagged behind the actors' lips and only the gunshots rang out on cue. I was soon dozing off to cowboy music. Without venturing anywhere near Fiona's shower, I pulled myself off to the spare bedroom and threw my fully clothed body on the unmade bed.

An hour later, the afternoon's strong coffee and a sense of overwhelming strangeness were still keeping me wide awake. I tried to tease out the day's good points, touching the zone along my inner arm where the young officer had grasped my flesh. I thought of the coffee-fuelled clarity that had sizzled through my organs all the way into Milan. I thought back to my becalmed house in England, resting in its dark cul-de-sac. *Did you hear Marilyn Wade's left her children and taken off to Milan? Who would ever have thought?*

As I lay there I shed my clothes onto the floor, too tired to maintain my concern about Fiona's dubious sheets. My thoughts began to zing from the young policeman to the black girl in silver hot pants, to the racy couple on Fiona's condom packet. Where on earth was my new life headed? And why was there a signed photograph of the delectable George Clooney sitting on this messy woman's shelf?

Three hours on and I was still wide awake.

When I finally heard a key in the lock, I was about to get up to speak to Fiona. All I wanted was to hear another human voice. Then I realised she had a man in tow and they were grappling with each other. I could hear whispers and groans. I lay back mortified, clutching my naked body, which somehow implied I was a third desperate party in on their act. The night was so soundless or my senses were so razor-edged I thought I could hear the fabric torn from her body and the rasp of the man's jeans along his thighs.

I listened to them bonk until daylight.

'How did you sleep, Marilyn?' asked a fresh-looking Fiona in the kitchen. There were no signs of the raspy-thighed man.

'Er, very well, thanks,' I replied. My throat felt like chalk and my eyes blistered. 'Thank you so much for helping me out. I'll find myself a hotel this morning.'

'No way! I'll have no such thing, you're not ready for downtown Milan at all. Your immune system is probably shot through with all the stress you've been up against. I spent two years on every sort of drug under the sun after my hubby left me. Although what you need is semen. Good old-fashioned spunk. Full of zinc, they say. Antidepressant. Coffee?'

'Oh no, not right now, thanks. Are you sure?'

'Semen? Oh yes, oh God yes.'

'No, I meant about staying here. I'm sure you have such a busy life.'

'No way! It's flat as a pancake, just work and more work. I'm back in Rome again tomorrow for the day. They're doing test runs with an audience, and the dubbing is through. But today I'm off. If you get your act together I'll take you on the divorcée's shopping round of Milan. Do you have Peter's credit card?'

'Well, yes, but I'm not what you would call a shopper.'

'Excellent.' She pushed over a tiny espresso cup of black treacle and spooned in sugar, then topped it up with a nip of grappa. 'Rocket fuel from my Veneto buddies. Throw it back.'

I felt a sizzle behind my left ear then the top of my head blew away. Meanwhile, something fiery shot through my chest. It made yesterday's elixir seem like a drink of milk.

'Not bad, eh?'

Fiona downed hers and began tapping her imaginary watch as I leaned against the kitchen sink, every nerve-end alight. Finally I lumbered off to the spare bedroom and dressed. Within ten minutes we were out on the street.

Fiona frowned at my jeans and grey sweater. 'Pack in a hurry, did we? Never mind. We'll soon fix that. I always wondered what these executives had for wives and girlfriends.'

Fiona wore a black light-wool dress with a narrow ruffle along the low neckline, and a choker with a red amber ring set in antique silver. She had big hoop earrings popping through her soft coppery curls, and rich dark red nail polish and lipstick that made her pale skin look edible.

'I know what you're thinking. That I look as far from being Italian as you do from Elle Macpherson – no offence to Elle. But let me tell you it works. You know, rattling a different drum. Men get tired of the Mediterranean look. Oh, you'll see it everywhere, it's the local hallmark, but anything else is exotic and just what Mamma told them to run a mile from. How's that for the best drawcard in the book? In this country all you need are tits, and yours would be fine if we could give them a bit of a hoist.'

'Do you *mind?*' I stared at her as she took a long sideways glance at my chest.

A pair of handsome men in suits passed, chuckling at us, as Fiona skilfully unglued her eyes from my bosoms and met their gaze. I watched a meticulous collusion taking place. The men slowed down and savoured her, eyes skimming her pretty face and working along the line of her legs, while Fiona put a slyness into her smile I hadn't seen before, and dropped her eyelids a fraction. I couldn't believe I was watching such unchecked flirtation at ten o'clock in the morning, with shoppers and babies in prams rolling past. Then Fiona expertly laughed off their attention and swanked into a shop with a line of G-strings on rotating dummies in the window. She dragged me in her wake.

'Sorry, guess I didn't have enough breakfast,' she giggled.

But it wasn't over yet. One of the chuckling men stood in the doorway and looked through me to her,

'*Volete venire a bere un caffè con noi, ragazze?*'

'*No, grazie.*' Fiona beamed. '*Un'altra volta molto volentieri.*'

'Now.' She turned to me. 'We can't go off drinking coffee with strange men. We have to get your boobs happening. Right?'

The man backed away amused and Fiona pulled me further into the shop. She spoke to the salesgirl who brought out a delicate underwired brassiere made of black petals. And then a shred of accompanying cloth with the same motif in the front, although this diminished to a twist of thread at the back. Fiona saw my look. 'Never mind the G-string, let's check out this piece of work. Now go on.'

She pulled the curtain across. I turned over the delicate garments in my hands. Never in my life had I even contemplated wearing anything like this. This was the sort of thing Madonna wore to breakfast. Outside I heard Fiona and the girl laughing together. I removed my sweater and hung up my old grey bra, sliding the shiny new black straps up my arms. My breasts fell into the embroidered cups that barely screened my nipples, and when I clasped the hooks at the back the structure gently pushed the flesh upward in pearly shimmering plateaux.

I was stunned. It was so beautiful.

Then Fiona whipped the curtain open.

'Geez! They didn't call you Marilyn for nothing.'

I blushed as the salesgirl craned to see, and a girl and boy holding up an orange G-string peered across the shop. I was half-naked public property. Fiona picked up the black shred and shook it at me. 'Here, put this on. We're taking the lot. They'll itch at first but then you won't be able to do without. Put 'em on.'

Fiona had laid three more bra-and-panty sets on the counter by the time I cautiously came out. 'Let's kill three birds in one shot. What do you prefer? Black-black-black? Or some hot purple or this silky grey?'

'Oh,' I stammered. 'Just black. Black is fine.' I pulled out Peter's credit card and watched the girl begin to wrap the other items. As she ran a scissor blade along the ribbon to produce a scroll, I couldn't help wondering whether my ex-husband had ever shopped for underwear for Danielle. Was she the bouncy braless type or did she prefer a spot of slinky European lingerie?

'Here, why don't you take this as well? You know, to pad around the house in.' Fiona showed me a sheer black negligée. For an instant I saw myself leaning in a doorway, hand on hip, in a Sophia Loren pose. But then I stalled. No matter what I wore or didn't wear, no one would ever see me. And my sordid ex-husband would be tearing off Danielle's G-strings and C-cups and devouring *her*.

'Oh, will you stop thinking about him and his tits-and-arse,' Fiona scolded. 'Let's keep that card burning'

The girl deftly wrapped the negligée and I followed Fiona onto the street. Ten paces later I couldn't resist the urge to scratch my bottom, given I had a length of sandpaper lodged in the middle, working up and down with each step. How did Madonna stand it?

'Marilyn, stop that. You're walking like an ex-pole-vaulter. Here, let's nip in for a quick coffee.'

We turned into a narrow bar with a swarthy man going through the noisy process of producing twin thimbles of espresso coffee. He disengaged the percolator, slammed the old coffee into a chute at his hip, shoved it into an upturned funnel where a fresh portion of coffee was pressed in, then whacked the percolator back into the machine and supplied two new crisp white cups before the hot black trickle commenced.

'Ciao, Fiona.'

'Ciao, Federico. This is Marilyn.'

'*Ciao,* Marilyn, *come stai?*'

This was all spoken through the mirror as the coffee coloured the bottom of the tiny cups. The man had a beautiful broad back showcased by his tight T-shirt, with scrapings of black curly hair along the nape of his neck. Before he even began to turn I knew he was Fiona's male friend from last night, the man with the rasping thighs. Involuntarily, I felt my nipples contract within my saucy new bra.

There was no further conversation between the lovers as Federico was called down the other end of the bar by a woman waving a white sandwich stuffed with rosy prawns. She was complaining about her *tramezzino.* Fiona downed her espresso while I hesitated, wincing as a minor atomic explosion took place in my brain.

'D'you need some grappa in that?'

'Oh no, not at all.'

'Well, drink up, I know this great boutique around the corner. You'll never want to wear your old gear again. Hang on, let me pop into the loo.'

Fiona slipped down the aisle at the back and I noticed Federico abandon the complaining lady to follow her. They emerged five minutes later, Fiona looking identical and Federico returning to slam the coffee percolator against the black chute.

'Rule number one,' she said. 'There are no public toilets in Italy. Never forget to go at a bar. Although most of them stink.'

I noticed that a tiny fabric-covered button remained open below her waist, exposing a patch of vulnerable underbelly like that of a sleek white bird. I wondered about the skin there beginning to stretch with the baby she had lost. She saw me looking and buttoned up.

Fiona handed me a clutch of dresses and headed back out to look for some more. Undeterred by the merciless light in the booth, I stripped down to my new knickers and stood there rocking my breasts in their black balconies. No one was ever going to beg me to pose for an underwear ad, but I felt grand. I tried on Fiona's first selection, a printed wraparound dress that was not my style at all, and let my boobs snuggle in the deep V. Fiona charged back and was impressed. She shoved a softer grey thing at me that had the opposite effect: breasts covered in draped fabric and an indulgent dip at the back. I had to admit she had quite an eye.

'That's great,' said Fiona. 'It'll be well into autumn before you'll need a proper coat. So we'll have to work on that later, assuming you're still here then.' She looked at me with her eyebrows arched.

I let it hang there and she steamrollered on.

'We ought to do something with your hair, though. I guess that's for after lunch. Oh, and jewellery. You'd be surprised what you can still get away with.'

We carried my bags over to a shoe shop close by where Fiona selected a batch of five-inch heels. My jaw dropped. Surely I was tall enough already? I pointed out that not even Nicole Kidman went out of her way to be a giant, and that perhaps I should stay with a pair of classy flats à la Carla Bruni. But Fiona said, 'This country *glorifies* tall people. All the aristocrats are tall. Milan is full of thirteen-year-old Russian models who are six feet tall, haven't you noticed? If you've got it, *tower.*'

We came out with a pair of new season boots, some patent pumps and a pair of impossible bronze stilettos (last season's Dolce e Gabbana with the price slashed). Peter's credit card was red-hot. I wondered if I would be wearing silver hot pants within the week.

Over lunch Fiona's phone began to ring crazily. The first few times she went outside onto the footpath to speak to whoever it was, but then she began to frown as the phone kept ringing, until she turned it off when our Milanese cutlets arrived. Fiona had told me I could say goodbye to foreign food while in Italy, as the only decent food was local.

'And rule number two: *don't eat pasta,*' she said. 'Or you'll no longer be able to identify your waistline in a matter of months. Sophia Loren says she lives on pasta but it's not true. They all eat meat and salad to keep their figures. Otherwise you'll end up looking like somebody's mother-in-law. Remember that.'

Immediately I thought of Jean and how she might be faring after pregnancy on the generous national diet, and the dimensions of the lover's mother who babysat the love-child. Fiona continued giving me pointers throughout the meal, as if she had given great consideration to the idea of living in this country but had still had not decided either way. As she talked I began to warm towards her. She seemed like such a vulnerable battler, so far from home. I couldn't help wondering if there were days when she woke up without her verve.

'Fiona ….' I realised I was speaking my thoughts out loud. 'Did you ever sleep with Peter?'

'Wha-at?' she slurred. 'Well,' she said, looking down quickly and glancing towards the kitchen door. 'Well, yes. Yes, I did, Marilyn.'

The waiter stepped forward with the pair of chilled ricotta cakes we had ordered and placed them on the table. They looked grey and made without love.

I couldn't speak to her.

'Oh, don't get all shirty, Marilyn. Peter's a rat fink and you ought to know it. It wasn't even great sex. The other day he phoned me and asked me to watch for you and make sure you got the right train for Perugia. It looks like you've missed that one.'

She looked at me appealingly but all I could see was a cheap Australian hussy who knew how to peddle her survivor programmes. Her charms rattled to the ground. I could even see her and Peter at it on an office desk after work, or in a city hotel room. It didn't matter if it hadn't been great sex. It had still been sex with my husband, the man who came home to my bed.

'And what about that signed George Clooney photo?' I asked scornfully. 'How on earth did you get that?'

'What? What has that got to do with anything?'

'The one on your bookshelf – where, I might add, there is hardly a single book.'

'Last year I went to the première. His translator spilt red wine on my dress and the photo came with the dry cleaning. Marilyn, listen to me a bit. It was totally lightweight with Peter. When you work intensely with someone, very stupid things happen.'

I had no intention of listening to her anymore. I thought of George Clooney's clumsy translator and suave George Clooney with his pen poised to sign yet another photograph of himself.

'Look,' Fiona said, 'how about we wrap up this conversation? We're not going anywhere with it now. How about coffee then? With a splash of grappa?'

'No.' I shook my head. 'No more of that stuff.'

Fiona ordered two espressos and pushed mine towards me. She made the guy leave the grappa bottle on the table, tipping some into both our cups. I was glad she'd finally shut up.

After I'd drunk mine, Fiona took up the neck of the grappa bottle and filled the empty cup. I felt it corroding downward as I drank. Down, down, down to where it made a pool of warmth. How long was it going to take? How many Fionas had there been? Out in the street, afternoon shoppers pressed on and public buses rolled past. Many handsome men walked along, all dressed in suits, their eyes ferreting out cleavages and good sets of legs. Fiona looked at me with quick-thinking despair.

'I wasn't going to lie to you if it came out, but I could have, right? I'm not here to waste my breath tattling about Peter. Other women can do that.'

'Other women?'

'Marilyn, I just wanted my show to take off and get my boss off my back. For God's sake you're in Milan right now, free as a bird. What do you care if that dickhead went through the whole documentary department?'

I noticed a tall man with wavy grey hair walking slowly past. His eyes couldn't get enough of my cantilevered bosoms nestled into my new dress. Drunkenly, I hoisted them upward, and thought I saw a sliver of moisture at the corner of his mouth. But when his eyes travelled to my lank hair and blotchy face he leapt away and his pace quickened.

'Fiona,' I said, gasping slightly as I tried to align my G-string along my bottom. 'What time was my hair appointment?'

The hairdresser was not far around the corner. Fiona flounced in, saluting everybody, introducing me as though I were a cherished friend. While I had my hair done she read paparazzi magazines. I glanced at her occasionally, noticing the way they held her attention. Once she looked up at me and winked. The girl poured warm water on my scalp and squirted out a huge blob of cool shampoo. She rubbed and scrubbed and massaged until the skin burned and tingled. I had a warmer colour put in – it was Fiona's idea – and afterwards, looking in the mirror, I realised it was close to the tone I'd had as a girl. For all these dull years I had subtracted the boldness from my chocolate eyes.

We went home to dress up, caught a taxi to a new glamorous bar in the Brera and drank until they closed. At some point I remember I told her about finding Brett on the internet and she gave a wild whoop as though she had done the same thing. She grew misty-eyed over her wine and said that she had been trying to forget her ex-husband for five years and couldn't manage to fall in love. She said she missed her dead baby, she hated her job and she had never been truly happy in her life.

3. VIA VITRUVIO

Sorry darl, I've had to leave and couldn't explain to you last night. I've taken the show to South Korea and we are hoping for a new release. Federico (landlord's son, works in bar down the road) wants to marry me and it is really out of the question. All the best in Milano, the rent is paid up for three months. Let her rip! Love Fiona.

I found the note the next morning by the coffee percolator. Hours ago we had been drinking water at the sink, laughing together. I stood by the window in my new black negligée gripping Fiona's yellow post-it. A grey-looking man was leaning out of his bathroom window opposite with his mouth open. I shouted the rudest words that had ever formed in my mouth.

I ran into Fiona's room. The bed sheets were hardly disturbed. She must have spent ten wild minutes deciding which clothes to pack. Half of them lay abandoned on the floor with a good share of her astounding shoes. In the bathroom her stash of creams had vanished. I shivered in panic. I heard an aeroplane scoring the sky. Was that Fiona headed for Seoul?

I wandered from room to room in disbelief. How could she do this to me after all that tricky work yesterday? I read the note again. So it had been serious with Federico, the raspy-thighed man, or for Federico it had. *Let her rip!* – I assumed that was Australian lingo telling me to make the most of my three months in central Milan. I dropped the post-it and ran a hand through my new honey curls. I realised I knew nothing about Fiona except that she had lost a baby when her husband had taken up with a French woman who did commercials, and that she had slept with mine.

I was preparing a fresh coffee when I heard my mobile phone in my handbag breaking into its electronic song. I rushed over, spilling ground coffee all over Fiona's note. I hoped it might be Fiona herself so I could give her a piece of my mind. But as I answered I realised this was impossible as we had never even exchanged numbers. It was the man of the moment, my ex-husband Peter.

'Hello darling, how are you? How's Perugia? We've all been worried sick,' he cried.

Darling? Worried sick?

'I'm fine thanks, Peter,' I replied coolly, planting my other hand on my childbearing hip. 'I'm still in Milan staying with an old pal of yours, that Australian girl Fiona Miller. She told me all about how intensely you two worked together. Very chatty girl, although she hardly ever shuts up.'

I heard Peter gulp. 'Just checking in, dear,' he said. 'Er, would you mind terribly if I called you later?'

I stalked back to the kitchen as the coffee began to gurgle. I half-filled an espresso cup and sloshed in some of Fiona's grappa. Across the air shaft a stout woman's silhouette moved into the bathroom, the wife of the grey-faced man I presumed. As I stood drinking, the frosted glass window flew open and the woman began to shout at me just as the vile drink took force. I yelled back louder than I have ever yelled before. The woman slammed the glass and I slammed Fiona's kitchen window even harder.

I paced out to the living room and threw myself onto the couch. The coffee threaded out from my temples and I regained some mental keel, not that this was required before an episode of 'CHIPS' dubbed into Italian. The two cops in dazzling cream jodhpurs rode their huge motorbikes along LA's cement highways, chit-chatting like a pair of Roman bartenders. As I watched the dry desert sky my thoughts returned to Fiona. Yesterday had been one of the most vital days of my recent life. I remembered how timidly I had stepped off the plane and joined the other passengers in the bus. I had been invisible, an invisible blubbering woman scorned by Sophia Loren. I remembered slouching against the marble column and my rescue by the young policeman, how he had saved me with his tiny cup of jet fuel. I remembered wandering out of the *Stazione Centrale* and how Fiona had appeared on the glamorous landscape and tugged me into the city with her short, perky steps.

I trembled to think I was alone in Milan without Fiona, without her sassiness and her credible Italian. How would I find a supermarket? What on earth would I eat? Wave after wave of cold shock travelled through me. I had left my children. I had spent masses of money yesterday. I hadn't a clue what I was doing here.

In the midst of some family serial I dropped off to sleep again. Hours passed. I woke up famished, my sense of time eroded. The television was cranking out canned applause and snazzy music. A towering blond was flipping over letters on a huge panel, letters she probably couldn't even read. Outside the light had dimmed and over on the bookshelf George Clooney looked like he needed a drink. I wondered if Fiona might be chatting up a businessman on the flight to Seoul.

I showered, went into my room and pulled out the patterned wraparound dress with its dusty tones. I twirled round before Fiona's full-length mirror. Already my body seemed tighter and better defined. My honey curls bounced. I chose a pair of shoes I was pretty sure would kill me after ten minutes, so I looked about for some plasters to help out my poor feet. I started opening Fiona's drawers in the bathroom. Beneath the racy condom drawer I found shampoo sachets and waxing strips and nail polish remover, but no plasters.

Then I paused. I trod back into Fiona's bedroom. I wasn't normally a nosey type but I began rummaging through her dresser. I poked around, overturning theatre tickets and bank statements and phone numbers written on shreds of paper. Still no plasters. Strangely, I found her mobile at the back of the top drawer. How could she have left that? I went through her underwear, tossing lacy bits this way and that, her slinky T-shirts and sweaters in the next drawer, and what must have been her gym gear – track suit trousers and swimming goggles and costumes. Then I hit the bottom drawer.

I gasped. I knew what the tangle of penis-shaped coloured toys were, but I had never *touched* one. I sat back on my haunches, reaching out towards their Day-Glo colours, averting my eyes until frankly, I stared. She had all the happy extensions of the universe it seemed, carelessly interlocked. I was curiously contented. From the start I had suspected she was sex-obsessed. I slammed the drawer shut.

It was chilly in the streets. Despite my Day-Glo discovery I soldiered along the footpath wishing Fiona were still by my side, frowning at my bosoms and scanning men. Without her I felt like a wordless dummy and I made a note to memorise the lone grammar book I'd seen sitting on the shelf next to Mr Clooney. The shops were brightly lit and full of people, and the footpaths crowded with unintelligible conversations. The girl from the underwear shop stood just outside the door smoking a cigarette. She called out something that sounded like sisterly approval, and a couple of people walking turned around and stared at my new graceful curves. I didn't even have the time to blush before I realised I was smiling with a cheeky smile I hadn't used in decades.

As I had foreseen, the new leather bit into my toes and the high heels were murder on my back. After resisting for about fifteen minutes, I sat down outside a bar and deliberated on what drink to order. A smart youngster came up and I asked for a *prosecco* in beginner's Italian, stunned stupid when the boy added another question. A man reading a newspaper at the next table helped me out.

'He wants to know if you'd like some olives.'

Did Fiona's diet include the consumption of olives? Then I thought, *god-dammit!* I wanted the alcohol to go straight into circulation. I shook my head, I was growing to like the smudging of personal barriers these days.

'Oh, no thanks. I'll be fine with the drink. *No, grazie,*' I said. '*Prosecco, per favore.*'

The boy sashayed away and the man seemed too intrigued by his newspaper to keep the conversation alive. I felt a little peeved he wasn't stalking me with his restless eyes and even began to tell myself that his concentrated reading was a ruse. I thought I smelt a subtle woody scent from his direction as I glanced at his messy grey hair and tanned, well-governed features. I raised my chin in the air, sensing his nostrils contract at the scent of my own perfume, and wondered nonsensically if this man could ever become the love of my life. When the first bubbly *prosecco* tickled the back of my throat I thought I might give Fiona's approach a try.

'Are you American?' I tapped his sleeve. The article showed the current crop of Italian political figureheads, all with their mouths open, shouting.

'No, I'm Swiss and I run a modelling agency,' he said, his face direct and close as he removed his arm from my radius.

His gaze abandoned me as a translucent sylph glided from inside the bar and came to rest on the chair next to him. All heads turned, all jaws dropped. The girl's face shimmered with excruciating beauty. The Swiss man folded away the newspaper on the tabletop and the angry politicians seemed to shut up. He took her hand between his and a *frisson* took place. But the girl looked too exquisite to kiss or defile and made me want to cry for a deep and inscrutable reason. I pulled my head and shoulders away, and tried to conceal myself behind a couple of loud, smoking women. In a while the Swiss man rose with his companion and the crowd parted for them. I submerged myself in *prosecco* bubbles.

I hoofed home in agony and ripped open Fiona's drawer full of vibrators and dildos. One by one, I extracted them and felt their smooth plastic shapes, so close to children's toys in their shameless honesty and logic. I chose a dark purple one with a deep-nosed kink, inserted batteries and listened to its cheery buzz.

I awoke to the sensation of a cool hand whispering along my thigh. I thought it was the tangible end sequence of a dream until I felt down for the hand and grasped a solid set of chilly knuckles. I jerked up and rammed Federico in the chin. I had left the lights blazing and the sex toys littered around me. Federico reeled back swearing the only bad word that I knew – *Cazzo!* – and I leapt away from the bed as the vibrators rolled onto the floor in a series of soft bumps.

I ran into the bathroom clutching my negligée to my front, at the same time trying to shield my bottom with my other hand cupped behind me. It was one thing to play with coloured battery-driven toys but another to smell a man's pheromones in the same room. Federico ran after me, fully-dressed, thankfully, no arc-shaped intentions leaping from his jeans. I was petrified. I tried shutting myself in the cubicle but he blocked the door, watching as my arms wrestled with the negligée. I waited for the studded belt to be unbuckled and for him to overwhelm me.

But he pushed a hand into the doorframe and rubbed his chin. In an instant I had the negligée on and my first ring of defence was intact.

We stared at each other, our energy fields jostling in the tiny space. We were so close I could see hairs quivering in his nostrils. He had clear blue eyes with black pupils tightening in the centre of each. His forehead was dense and looming, ridged by a whopping mono-brow Fiona might have thought to pluck. His nose was broad and the cartilage looked as though it had taken a blow or two, while his lips were two plump cushions Fiona must have kissed to bits. Rather than handsome, he pulsated with a slightly scary darkness, and I wondered if that was why Fiona had left him for Korea.

My eyes roved down his body, snagging on the bump indicating his apparatus. I thought back to that interminable first night when I'd heard Fiona moaning and Federico's laboured male cries. Then I visualised how Federico had discovered me ten minutes ago, with a purple implement clutched in my hand like a sweaty bag of sweets. My face went up in flames.

'*Cazzo, mi hai fatto male!*' He rubbed his chin, his face mottled with soreness.

'What?'

He looked very cranky now and I wondered how I might make amends. Next, I registered an uncharacteristic mercenary prickle, remembering the useful things in Fiona's note. Federico, who harboured marriage hopes, had been dumped without knowing it. Federico was the landlord's son. Fiona said the rent was paid up for three months. I stood there realising that the same freaky good luck that had brought George Clooney into Fiona's living room had just dealt me a marvellous hand.

'Can I get you some ice, Federico?' I said kindly. 'I'm sure Fiona has some.'

I hurried out to the kitchen and he followed holding his jaw. I spotted Fiona's note covered in ground coffee on the bench and quickly scrunched it into a ball, tossing it under the sink. He slouched against the fridge, a picture of male loss.

'I want Fiona,' he moaned. 'Does she have 'nother boyfrenn'? Tell me.'

I cracked out some ice cubes and rolled them up into a tea towel with a printed kookaburra, resuming maternal activities I hadn't been hounded to do for entire days. It was like riding a bike. Federico put the ice to his chin and I smiled at the thought of the scorching persona starring in my ex-husband's new hit show: *Today Marilyn is wearing a classy black negligée while she soothes a muscled young bartender.*

'*Fee-ona!* Where is? Why she no answer her phone? Does she haff new boyfrenn'? *Chi cazzo sei tu?* Who the fuck you think you are?'

'Er,' I started, 'Fiona had to go to London urgently – a problem with work. She told me about you, she's crazy about you. Your English is very, very good. Have you travelled a lot?'

He puffed up and smiled. 'No, I never leave Italy. I travel to Roma once. But in Roma too many *terroni* from the south. My uncle go to Australia and have big farm. I dunno where, they grow banana. Are you Fiona sister?'

I was staggered by the question. Between Fiona and I the only common trait was that we were both bipeds.

'Y-yes. We are. She is my little sister.'

'You see! I know. I tell my father. He think you are big sister.'

Outside, a light switched on in the black vault and the grey-faced man leered into the void yelling, *'Figli di puttana! Andate a letto! C'è gente che dorme! Guardati! Sempre a scopare con le puttane straniere!'*

Federico leant out over the sink and boomed back. I looked at the curves of his buttocks and the fretwork of his spine and shoulders. I listened to his shouting without understanding whether it was in my defence, or his own, or whether they were simply swearing for the heck of it. When did Federico sleep if he worked all day and followed Fiona at night? He turned back grinning, well aware I had been studying him, he was used to women's eyes trained on his back.

'This is my *zia*'s husband. He never sleep, just television all day and always *hungry.*'

'Hungry?'

'You know, *arrabbiato*, he yell always.'

'You mean *angry*.'

'Yeah, whatever. You make me *caffè?* Your name is? So Fiona big sister like to fock like Fiona? She also like that plastic thing when she can't have me. When I have exam, you know?'

'You are a student? What are you studying?'

'I study *agronomia*. I ate it. I have only fifteen exam to go.'

'How long have you been studying?'

'Oh, like eight years. But my father give me job in bar. You got boyfrenn' or you like toy?'

He came closer and I didn't like his tone. I have a high regard for agronomy, a brother and uncle who work in the field, and couldn't imagine a more ill-suited apprentice.

'Well, yes.' I thought at the speed of light. 'I am visiting him now. He is Swiss, he runs a modelling agency. He's amazing. We're very much in love.'

'You like *svizzero?* Ha! They have sex with cow. Why you not with him?'

'I was before, we were drinking. But he works so much. He works very hard.'

He looked at me uncertainly and I knew he was seeing the half-naked woman sprawled on Fiona's bed clutching naughty toys. There was nowhere for me to hide. I grappled with the coffee percolator.

'You know, I like you, Fiona big sister. When Fiona come back and we get marry maybe we fock at wedding party like when you drunk, and I make you cry baby for more.'

He threw down the tea towel with the kookaburra and the ice clattered into the sink. The uncle from across the way yelled from a distant room. Federico's promise hung in the air so that a chill zigzagged over my back. Somewhere in the outside world a clock struck three.

'You know, I love Fiona, she is my woman. I know she older, but none of my brother get woman like that. *Nessuno.*'

He swung around, making his way to the front door which he slammed, and went off to wherever he slept.

I tossed and turned in a coffee funk until morning. The clocks had gone backwards at midnight, as I had understood from a diagram on the front page of the Swiss man's newspaper last night, so I spent half an hour fiddling with Fiona's various clocks throughout the apartment. I hunted down her mobile tucked at the back of a drawer, knowing exactly what I was searching for in the grey autumn morning. I saw her battery was low and plunged it in the charger nearby. I saw she had twenty-seven missed calls from Federico, and a handful from Peter. I felt a cold, clean *crump.*

Should I go into her messages? Throughout Peter's lengthy liaison with Danielle and whoever else, I had chosen not to delve. For instance, the day after we grasped hands over the Alps and he walked off into the terminal holding his phone with relief, Peter had forgotten his mobile on the kitchen bench. All morning I had sat there staring at it. There were five calls from a letter 'L' (Lily? Leah? Linda?) A couple of messages had come through. I saw the screen light up, but I couldn't take it in my hands and look at them. Then Peter had rung on the house phone around eleven in a wild panic: *Darling, you haven't seen my mobile anywhere? Has it been ringing? You mustn't answer it, love, they are international calls I'll pay the earth for!* I had finally picked it up when the 'L' number rang once more, my thumb over the little green button that would release my husband's lover's dirty voice. Then the ringing had stopped and the phone had jumped out of my hands onto the kitchen tiles.

This morning I scrolled shamelessly through Fiona's messages. There were many texts from Federico in a pastiche of colourful English, like a teenager given free rein with an erotic dictionary. He had a predilection for the C-word, which I found jarring, combined with every known expression for the male ornament. Then there were breasts and nipples, the entire rear area to the knees, and several references to toes and feet. He had an admirable linguistic vigour which I presumed found limited expression in the field of agronomy, though I couldn't work out whether *Your cunt is like a big cappuccino* was a turn-on or a translator's joke.

To my relief there were no messages along the same lines from my ex-husband to Fiona. However, there *were* calls. I saw Peter's number more than once in the list for the last few days. Supposedly Peter had asked Fiona to keep an eye out for me in Milan. But why so many other calls to his little Australian lover? Peter had called Fiona the day I had arrived. He had called her twice last night. What was going on here? Was Peter already betraying the woman who had torn my family to bits?

In my past life I used to drag myself to a couch in my sewing room upstairs. Something about the coordinates of the room made me fall into an impenetrable slumber, after which I would wake with woolly memory loss and go down to prepare dinner. Deep in my gut I'd always known Peter was a philanderer, but he still came home to me, he still kissed me on the cheek. Until Danielle there'd never been an uneasy announcement in my kitchen on a Sunday afternoon. Until Danielle I'd never realised he could cruise out the front door of my life.

I crawled back into Fiona's spare bed and tried desperately to drift off. But I knew it wasn't going to work. I knew the overheated messy rooms and Fiona's evil admission yesterday were not going to let me rest my head. I stumbled out to the kitchen and drank a gallon of water. Above the grimy air vent it was a crisp clear day, the air agitated and chill. I knew there was only one thing I could do if I wanted to begin to free myself. I retreated into Fiona's bathroom and looked at the shower glass fringed with mould and the toilet which faintly smelled of pee. I pulled out Fiona's cheapo cleaning products and a good rag. I squirted and scraped and sponged. Afterwards I had the hottest shower my skin could bear.

An hour later I buttoned down Fiona's black wool dress with the ruffles, which I had found stashed under the divan. I didn't question my desire to have her smell next to mine. Obviously, I filled the dress more abundantly. I put on her amber choker which I found thrown on the dresser. I brushed my hair, pawing through what was left of her makeup, using a pencil to draw around my eyes like the girl at the underwear shop. (Yet, staring at the English panda in the mirror, I had a sudden thought of the translucent sylph accompanying the Swiss man yesterday, how her skin had been the work of a gentle god. I resisted an inexplicable surge of tears and wiped it all off.)

Outside it was freezing and with my light autumn jacket I was severely underdressed. I turned away from the direction of Federico's bar and followed commuters heading underground to the nearest *metropolitana* stop. Down here it was warmer and the floors were covered in stippled black plastic like a designer facility, and the walls were fixed with panels of fine blended pebbles. On the map I saw that the green line forked onto the red line, which would take me to the Duomo in the centre of town. I bought a ticket and was thrust forward through the gates. I saw a policeman in red epaulettes with a dog. He was staring at women walking past as his fingers drummed on a big black gun.

The trains were newer than those I was used to, crammed with more men in suits and short Filipino cleaners and, every so often, one of the Russian models Fiona had talked about, whose aura demanded a ring of exclusive space. There were plenty of women from the Sophia Loren team, watching each other with cruel, vivacious eyes. Occasionally one of them took me in, from my hairline to the bulges in my toes, and I felt every flaw cracked open, every effort of mine nakedly exposed. They stared with wide flexed eyebrows and highlighter pencilled into the corners of their eyes. They wore new season boots as an army, and carried handbags fit for heads of state. I clutched my purse, valiantly concentrating on deciphering the adverts above their heads.

4. LA MADONNINA DI MILANO

I ascended the steps of the Duomo station and came out along the pale flank of the cathedral dusted in fumy morning light. The stonework stretched upward in tiers of ever-tightening pinnacles, that made one want to weep with their divine force. I thought of the construction: men on ladders tied together with rope; men with chisels. I thought of women in strange head garments looking up at the fandangled building at the end of the street. Wispy stone spans bounced between the spires, and the spires themselves looked plastic. A vendor came up to me with a concertina of postcards and I pulled away, anxious not to have him tagging along with me to the main façade around the corner. I walked briskly into the piazza reinforced by pangs of faith.

But the cathedral front was curtained in scaffolding and cloth. Embossed on great sheets of canvas, the strenuous architecture rippled in the city breeze, looking like a nasty photocopy. Tears of exasperation burst into my eyes. I knew I was overtired and choked with coffee but it was like finally reaching Machu Picchu and seeing only clouds.

Nevertheless I marched past the tent flaps and was ushered through swinging doors by a woman with greasy white hair and a pair of fissured eyes. She was selling rosary beads that looked like lozenges of chocolate, and faded holy cards with a thin Madonna who had never held a microphone in her life. Directly inside, a denim-clad man with a pony-tail was at work with a vacuum cleaner. Its fringes flicked around under a big disc that whirred over the immense flagstones. I trod around him into a long side aisle which smelt of polish as much as incense and ceremony. My shoes clipped over Latin inscriptions on the floor and every so often I stepped around a long-dead face engraved in the stone.

My pang for prayer abandoned me and was replaced by a type of creepiness. I walked past chapels with marble picket

57

fences. Inside, behind each fluted altar, was a procession of seductively lanced saints and aching women trapped in paintings, as well as ranks of angels blessing dour patrons, and cherubs lobbed onto gilt. Rather dizzying after a while. I looked across the width of a football field to where the light trickling through the surrounding buildings now pierced the church, so that a second dawn struck the grey bones of the structure and splintered out through the stained glass. I thought of the ladies in strange headgear waiting for this, and their collective gasps.

I put some change into a brass box and lit a candle at one of the more austere chapels. But even here my mind wouldn't settle. I looked above the altar to the kneeling woman with a gold corona and flames about her scarred feet. The outstretched arms of the Madonna were just about to snatch her to safety. I moved to the right and looked at the woman's profile from another angle. It couldn't have been – but it was. It was my icon Jean touching the sublime. I might have begun to weep, but the pony-tailed cleaner started whirring up the aisle behind me. The flame of my candle began to dance. Then I breathed heavily and the candle went out. I looked up again to see Saint Jean being airlifted to safety, leaving me in the Valley of Milanese Darkness.

I swept outside and crossed the busy piazza. I saw a girl on a mobile phone who looked just like my daughter Vanessa, walking into the big Zara shop. It was as though Madonna had slapped me on the face. How had I taken off and left my two children with a pair of fornicators? I blotted my eyes with a tissue as I pulled out my phone. Vanessa had become a big moody teenager now, with asymmetrical dyed hair and a face full of piercings. But I had a quick vision of my little girl's face smeared with jam.

'Mum? Gawd! Is that really you?' I swallowed the smell of incense at the back of my throat and wept. 'I'm at the station Mum, the train's late. We're at the far end, under the bridge.'

Vanessa was used to giving me location reports to stopper my worry. I felt that stopper dislodged now and my panic galloped loose.

'Is Eddy with you?'

'He's fine, Mum. We're both okay. You're not crying are you?'

Only three days had passed and suddenly I felt a truck-load of guilt. My heart stopped beating and I lost the wiring to my senses. 'Just a bit love, but I'm fine,' I stammered. 'Milan's really beautiful. I've just seen the cathedral. How's your dad?'

'Well, they had a big fight last night. Really something. She works a lot and he didn't cook anything. Neither did Eddy or I. She lost it. Dad had to cook pasta and it was way overdone. Bet you're eating good pasta over there.'

'I suppose so. Yes, it's really good.' I couldn't think back to any food that had passed my lips besides Fiona's Milanese cutlets and the chilled ricotta cake when she confessed she had been my husband's lover. 'The other day I bought some new clothes with a friend.'

'Who's that? Do you mean Jo Harper's mum – Jean? Don't they live in Milan? Can you speak Italian yet? Oh shit, the train is coming Mum. Got to leave you.'

I heard the rumble of the train before the phone clicked off. Guilt streamed down my face in murky tears. I had been a fool to let Peter cushion me into thinking he could tide over my absence with his bosomy lover, and even more foolish to think that I could sample an iota of Jean's extraordinary good luck. I turned back to the cathedral façade wrapped in its massive photocopy jostling in the wind. On the very top of the wispy stone trestles was the gilded *Madonnina* I remembered reading about on the flight. This twelve-foot high lightning rod was twinkling and flashing for all she was worth. I knew what she was telling me: she was telling me I should be on the next plane home.

I buttoned my jacket and wiped away my tears. There were so many people bustling back and forth that no one bothered to stare at a loitering, sobbing mother. Around the piazza the major fashion shops were stationed on every corner, while banking and insurance companies declared their religions in neon logos atop the lavish buildings. To the right was the spectacular Galleria Vittorio Emmanuele, a luxury shopping arcade funnelling through to the famous opera theatre, La Scala. I walked under the high glass vault criss-crossed by iron girders, pausing beneath the opaque dome with its wintry light. A shiny black Porsche was cordoned off on a pedestal and a girl in gold hot pants handed out brochures with a high octane smile. Pedestrian traffic meandered in every direction. Two overweight American men in crumpled jackets shuffled along with cigars, drawn to the sassy girl. There were endless men in suits striding with karmic disinterest. Some had the swishing and timely trench coat. Despite an undercurrent of vendors with football scarves and the unsightly presence of a McDonald's on a corner, all actors were meticulously rehearsed and I was grateful that Fiona had pooh-poohed my old jeans. I touched the choker I'd borrowed from her, wondering if it would be warm or cool in Korea.

Outside in the next piazza, the morning sun infused the mustard building façades and traced a dignified statue in the centre. I paused in front of La Scala, where Pavarotti had dragged his great weight onto the stage and sung like a god. My stomach was grumbling now as my eyes filled with operatic sadness. I decided that a shot of espresso would set me back on track.

Away from the main hubbub I found a little bar in a side-street, next to a shop window filled with watches on twirling stands. As I sat down at a table on the footpath a Chinese man with stubbly grey hair came out to take my order. I reacted horribly, recalling Brett in the passageway in Soho, pushing me towards the orange ducks and clamping his mouth on mine.

'No! Get away from me,' I shouted, almost upsetting the aluminium table.

The poor man retreated inside the bar and I sat there mortified, my terrible gaffe watched by several passers-by. A pretty young Chinese girl came out and I ordered a coffee and brioche. Then I hunched down with the free city newspaper. The girl brought out a tiny gritty coffee and a pastry roll on a plate, which sat there like a parked bus. I gulped down the coffee and left the pastry there. I put some euros on the table and attempted to give a reassuring smile to the bar owner, who scowled at me through the window. I paced back inside and apologised in English, trying to explain how I had met a man from Hong Kong on the internet and had been attacked in Soho. The Chinese man understood nothing. I pointed behind him and asked for a grappa which he poured into a small glass on the counter. The fumes rose between us like fuel for a small jet. Before I could apologise any further he shooed me away with both hands, as though I were a mad goose.

I hurried outside past the twirling watches on stands. Glancing at my reflection in the next shop window, I saw a naked model being dismembered and fitted into a red dress. I stayed to watch as the warm flood of the alcohol caught me in its arms. I began to wonder about what Vanessa had said earlier, about Peter's mistress losing it when she arrived home from work. Unlike his saucy sex kitten, I was no stranger to the blank stares of the hungry plonked in front of the television. And Peter was about as useful with a pan as I might be in a pair of hot pants and thigh-high boots. I felt a thrill to think that the lovers had argued over a pot of soggy spaghetti.

I walked into an underwear shop and looked about. My eyes roved from rack to rack, from colour to colour, trying to imagine the woman I was supposed to become. Would I ever possess any of Fiona's calm sense of choice? I pulled down a gorgeous bra set in ruby red. I knew my size in Italian now, but I didn't have the patience to try it on. I placed it onto the counter and rummaged through my purse. The girl began wrapping the items in gossamer paper, folding in the corners with grace. But this time I didn't want her ribbons and scrolls. I shoved them into the fancy shopping bag and handed over my credit card. She looked at me as though I were a crackpot and quickly swiped.

I marched outside, breathing in short sharp riffs. After years in the serene skin of Marilyn Wade, mother of two, I didn't recognise this heady shopper dashing through the streets. I hadn't as much as dashed to the letterbox in an age. At the end of Via Dante (who I knew I must look up), there was a huge medieval castle blocking the street. I stopped for a moment, trying to take it in. Standing there between McDonalds and Footlocker it was impossible to visualise a world throbbing with anything other than fashion and food.

And yet this structure had stood here for centuries, long before Dolce e Gabbana's great-grandfathers were off the breast, and way before the wispy Duomo down the road had been engineered to life. Who knows, downtown Milan may have been a muddy field rutted with donkey trails and this bulkhead looming over the landscape. Tiny window slots were dug high up into walls made of unthinkably huge russet bricks. Archers would have flung arrows from the turrets, and cauldrons of boiling oil would have been launched upon the screaming foe. After murderous battles I imagined madrigals sung by youths in bell sleeves and maidens groped by men with salad-bowl haircuts, with everyone wearing hand-stitched slippers made for elves. I clutched my bag of underwear and negotiated several blocks in a single-minded haze, ready to leave the fashionista streets in my wake.

Inside the walls the grounds were vast. They had been home to thousands, from the courtly royals to those living on slops. But now the series of football-pitch-sized courtyards where Old Milano used to be had been emptied out, planted with grass and crossed by gravel paths, with the occasional park bench for contemplation. From here, the russet walls looked impenetrable, like the end of the world, the muffled unknown expanding under the sky outside. Some wings were now museums and I saw a short suit of armour standing in a window. The faceless man would have come up to my chest. I tried to imagine the knight and frothing steed pounding over the moat, with flags flapping and flashing armour. Instead, there were tired ice-cream vendors and a Bangladeshi man with an unfathomable writhing toy.

I walked through section after section until I reached the final, external wall. Beyond the complex lay a huge park with twisting paths and slashes of red trees. I stood at the entry gate. My legs and feet had begun to pulse. I turned back to the castle and through the series of aligned doorways there was a peep-hole back into the modern city. The Bangladeshi man began running towards me waving a toy. I hobbled away from him, thirsty and fatigued. I saw a jogger disappearing into the foliage and followed him down a path. All around, big gold leaves lay on the ground and the trees showed their bald limbs ready for winter. I turned back. The Bangladeshi man had given up the chase.

I threw myself onto the first bench I came across, secretly easing off my heels. The bird calls made me think of the peacefulness of my own garden back at home, there was even a woodpecker at work. I plumped up my handbag and lay down for a moment, letting the blood flow along my exhausted legs. There was no one to see me curled up like a drunkard. I closed my eyes as the autumn sun warmed my face.

I woke up as the metal clasp tore across my cheek and my handbag was wrenched from under me. I caught a faint whiff of polish as the man jerked away, the shopping bag of underwear bouncing against his jeans as he charged into the trees. I called out, holding my stinging face, struggling to my feet. I looked down in shock at my destroyed feet surrounded by pebbles.

The bastard had taken my shoes.

I collapsed onto the bench. I caught a last glimpse of my shopping bag flashing through the trees. I saw he had a pony-tail and a denim jacket, not very unique traits in a hip metropolis. I opened my lungs and screamed. Two joggers with their legs moving in unison looked across at me for an instant, then paced away.

Everything was quiet again, but now the park felt like a risky, unsavoury place. How could this have happened? How would I get back to Fiona's place from here without cash? How on earth would I cancel my credit cards?

My eyes dropped to my big wounded feet and my shy elongated toes, carbon copies of my father's. Tears dropped onto my sheer stockings. I contemplated walking in bare feet across a city full of women wearing Prada jackets.

'Nooo …!' I howled.

I sat there willing a solution to present itself, longing to be back on Fiona's couch watching CHIPS with George Clooney. In the distance I saw a woman with two dogs approaching. My heart surged. She was like myself in my past life: no makeup, wearing an old track suit and leading two scruffy dogs. Perhaps she too had been dumped by her philanderer husband?

When she was a few metres away I turned to her, and tried to put together some Italian words, eventually resorting to a muddle of half-English. Her eyes skirted me and she did not alter her pace. She muttered something that sounded like Russian. I slumped back on the seat and cried.

A while later two teenage lovers came along, both dressed in black with tattoos seeped into their skin and silver piercings dotting their faces, which did not put me off in the slightest.

'*Scusate,*' I said, a begging mother.

They took this as a cue to open their mouths and poke out long pierced tongues like two trained monkeys at the zoo. They dragged each other off laughing and I wondered what my semi-Goth daughter would do if approached by a shoeless tear-streaked wreck in a park. Of course, I'd taught her to run a mile.

As I sat there my hunger kicked in and accelerated my thoughts. Perhaps there was a *metropolitana* station nearby. Perhaps I could swing over the gate as they did all the time at home. Perhaps on that whirligig train map I could sort out a path back to the house, to which I no longer possessed any keys. I imagined the feel of bitumen on my bare feet as I laboured through the crowds. My eyes filled again. I sent a prayer to Saint Jean of the Andes who I knew was somewhere in Milan with her lover and child, begging her to transport me to safety.

At that moment a broadly-built African vendor appeared from nowhere, babbling to me in weird, bouncy Italian, carrying a big black sports bag with his wares. He too looked as though he were having a terrible day, every cadence in his voice speaking of rejection and fatigue. I understood *signora* this and *signora* that, while he pulled out sets of cheap socks and handkerchiefs and waved them in the air. Then he eased back on the bench next to me and exclaimed, 'God, Mary and Jesuss!'

'What was that?'

'I said God, Mary and Jesuss. Excuse me, Madam. You are not Italian?'

'No, I am English and I have just been robbed.' I told him about the handbag and the new underwear, and the very shoes from my feet. Incredulous, he bent under the bench.

'No shoes? Ah, Madam, this one be bad. Even in Lagos this be bad thing. But this park be full of bad people. Why you sleep here if you have good clothes and watch?'

I stared at the saviour Saint Jean had zapped to my side. 'I – I don't know' was all I could manage. 'I walked too far. I fell asleep.

How on earth do you carry that heavy bag around all day?' My thoughts began to unwind.

The Nigerian laughed. 'The bag be nothin'. And the money is nothin' also. What is your name then? I am Christian Abolegbe from Lagos, living in Milan for three months now.'

'I'm Marilyn Wade. I have to cancel my credit cards. You don't have another pair of shoes in there, do you?'

'No, Madam. I do not.'

My eyes travelled down to the grubby pair of trainers at the end of his jeans. I couldn't believe I was even considering this. I looked back into his weary face which was now turning out a very cheeky smile. Our eyes locked together and I knew we were whittling down the same thought.

Ten minutes later I set out in Christian's oversized trainers minus my watch and Fiona's choker. Christian may have been a tough deal-broker, but I felt kissed by the universe. He tossed in three pairs of cotton socks made in Vietnam, which he gave me in a thin plastic bag. The shoes were far more comfortable than the heels I had been wearing, and I wished interminable suffering upon the female whose feet they would eventually adorn. Christian had given me a fairly good idea of how to head towards the *Stazione Centrale* area, where I hoped I might stumble upon Federico's bar and put an end to this ghastly epic.

As I walked, sultry women with refined black hair homed in on my flapping shoes and raised their perfect eyebrows. They craned their necks after me, sometimes releasing a cruel, disbelieving laugh. Several of the handsome grey-haired men in suits began eyeing me until their faces fell gobsmacked upon my shoes. I tried to walk close to the shopfronts out of the main channel of posers, but there was a cross-flow of women popping outside carrying shopping bags, whose eyes naturally careered downward. I veered over to the emptier strip along the roadside, in between the rubbish bins and the occasional beggar, only to provide a freak show for passengers staring down from public buses. I saw two tart old ladies pushed against the glass, whose yellow knuckled fingers had found something to point at.

Down in the *metropolitana* (Christian's deal included an unstamped ticket), I felt a degree of relief. The platforms and carriages were so crowded that my shoes escaped observation. But resurfacing was hard. I passed the Swiss man and his sylph sitting in an outside bar in the late sun. They were holding hands, two *prosecco*-filled flutes gracing their table. The older man's eyes dropped to my foot attire as though I had defiled the cradle of fashion. The girl looked at me with steel-tipped eyes.

A while later – it was an entire fluke – I stumbled into Federico's bar. I might have knelt down and kissed the floor tiles. I had wandered past a hundred underwear shops until I recognised the same girl Fiona had been chatting to the other day, in the doorway smoking a cigarette. She raised her arm to wave, until she saw my footwear and her hand clamped her mouth. She tossed the cigarette and went quickly inside.

'Hey, Fiona big sister!' Federico's gorgeous back was turned to the coffee machine. 'Your baby sister come home? You know I been hard all day long. She no call me, notin.'

He swung a *prosecco* onto the counter. I was drunk in an instant and my whole agonising crusade felt like a silly mishap, one that might have happened to any of the women gliding down the street. I began to laugh at Federico, pointing to my huge ratty shoes. He looked at me open-mouthed as I babbled on.

'*Ti hanno rubate le scarpe? Ma che cazzo facevi a Parco Sempione?* What you do in *parco? Ma anche la borsa e tutto?* How can? *Ma come si può essere così imbecille?*'

He ran around the counter to my side, holding my arm, tracing the nasty scratch on my cheek. 'But you are okay? *Dobbiamo pulire quel taglio. Cazzo!* You walk all this way here? *Ma no! Ragazza vieni qua.* Come to Fede.'

He opened his arms so wide and appealingly that I gulped down a sweet whiff from his underarms and banked myself against him. I felt what Fiona was probably missing lodged between his legs. I lurched backwards giggling and his arm tightened around my shoulder. If this were a rescue, then I ought to find myself a disaster every morning.

'Please, could you take me up to the apartment, Federico? I really must shower.'

'Of course, *piccola*,' he said, even though I was a good six inches taller. He shouted something to the girl out the back and strode out arm in arm with me.

Upstairs, I guzzled a jug of water and the nosy grey-faced uncle came to the window. I had stripped off the woollen dress and pulled on the negligée, waiting for the boiler to crank out some hot water for a shower. Federico lingered about behind me and I no longer cared if he saw me half-naked or not.

'You know, I have exam tomorrow, after work I must study hard. Tomorrow I go to the *facoltà*. You know you got great breast Fiona sister, she little but you big like Sophia Loren. You know one time we gotta talk. You tell me about your family and these things. I wanna know all Fiona family. Maybe we even get wedding fock early or somethin.' He laughed. 'No, only joke, maybe you get offensive. Okay, I am going downstair now.'

He left and I enjoyed a long shower. I was tempted to throw Christian's ugly trainers into the air shaft but then I tucked them under Fiona's bed. They had brought me home anyway. Next I went back into Fiona's drawer and pulled out her mobile. She'd received several messages but I was more intent on calling Peter and having my cards cancelled before the pony-tailed thief went and bought a new Ferrari or some property on Lake Como. I called Peter, still damp in one of Fiona's towels.

'Darling,' he purred. 'Couldn't you wait to see me? When are we getting together? Why are you on this number again?'

'Peter, it's Marilyn. Your ex-wife in Milan. Fiona left her mobile here.'

'Oh *shit.*'

'Peter, I've had my bag stolen with everything inside. You might want to cancel your credit cards quite quickly.'

'Marilyn, it's not what you think. We are just a pair of old friends, you know, ships at sea. Fiona's just popped up here for a couple of days for work. As a matter of fact, I called your number today and a man replied in a very strange language, maybe something Slavic. I'm sorry, I genuinely thought you were having some fun.'

I cut the line and fell back on the bed, the wind knocked out of me. Peter called again and I let it ring for the next half hour. I sat looking at Fiona's designer clothes still strewn all over the room, breathing in her faint smell. But I wasn't angry with the woman who made my ex-husband purr, whether or not she popped up between his legs for a spot of work. I had decided I liked Fiona and besides, hadn't I heard her cat cries with Federico here in the hall?

Back in the kitchen I made another jam sandwich and turned on the television. I put my feet up and watched two entire films dubbed in Italian. The first was an action film with Bruce Willis and his shaven egghead. He spoke in a high-pitched Italian voice and there were lots of noisy blow-ups on the screen.

Next, I watched a soft porn film from the eighties set in the Hollywood hills. Each morning, after waving her husband off to work, a young pretty housewife drove up to a lavish mansion behind iron gates. Here, she shed her shoulder-pads and became a busty call-girl in white lingerie. Her boss was a striking woman behind a lacquered desk, whose assistant was a tall man with an eyepatch. Each scene was misty and tense. The call-girl stiffly fondled another woman on a white settee. They kissed, tongues fluttering and eyes shut.

As I watched, I heard Federico's keys in the hallway. He lowered himself onto the couch, eyes straying to the television. Then he slid over to where I was sitting and snuggled close, inhaling me in exaggerated draughts. I started to laugh, worrying that a Brett scenario would evolve and he would be chasing me about the apartment like the other night. He paused as the call-girl now straddled the fully-dressed man with the eyepatch, in the most potent shot of the film. The young woman pulled out a gun. The door closed suddenly and we heard a hollow shot. I turned to Federico and opened my nightshirt to his mouth.

5. L'AGRONOMO

As a young woman I was bolder. But somewhere along the way my marriage turned a corner and I became another woman, a woman who could park a big family vehicle in the most stringent parking space, a woman who sat in the garden with mugs of tea. A woman who pretended to be asleep when her husband entered the bedroom.

When I first met Peter I treated him very badly and he fell desperately in love. I'd learnt the ropes with a work colleague of my father's and had many years of schoolgirl sex behind me, whereas Peter was a shy only child from a distinguished family. He had been watching me from afar. That was when I was boisterous, going to pubs in tight jeans and taking the pill. I overlooked Peter and invited drunken men home, men whose fingers were dirty and swift. Sometimes Peter's phone calls arrived late at night when I had another man wrapped around me and I would pull away and drag the phone into the hall, realising he was the first man who had bothered to fall in love. I liked his apprehension and the way he rode his nerves. We spoke for hours.

At first our sex was stilted and very bad. Later, making love became an unfolding, calibrated communion. I burned when I was away from him, and my thinking was ragged. If I look back now, I realise I was the one who gave Peter access to his stormy power. For a while our roles reversed, and I saw him flaunting this power with other women, leaving me aside with a calculated wrath. But he came back to me and we married when I was throwing up with Vanessa.

We took off to Venice to celebrate but it was a bad week – in the middle of *carnevale*, when the city was crammed with festive people wearing masks. I was devoured by fatigue. When Peter paused in front of yet another church with a bleached façade and a pair of statues gesturing from corrugated seashells, I would push the doors open and toss myself on the first damp pew. That was my rapport with Venice. There was even a photo of me dozing down by the Grand Canal, mouth open as I propped myself against a statue plinth.

I remember we made love quickly in the afternoons before I fell asleep, as other guests in the cheap hotel slammed doors along the hallway and tourists churned along under the window outside. Peter cupped the warm area where we thought our tiny prawn lay in my belly. I went to sleep savouring the strange country outside and the language of my husband's hands.

Somewhere in the morning I felt Federico disengage himself and slip out of Fiona's bed. I sensed him standing naked beside me. I didn't want to speak to him, just watch his strong bottom and soft groin before they disappeared, probably forever. I made a muffled sound and he paused, his member not far from my nose, with its musky, animal smell. I was so proud of myself. I turned over and bore down under the sheets, hearing his breathing recommence. I expected him to whisper *Cazzo!* and stride off, but he put his hand in my hair and ruffled it, whispering something I couldn't understand.

I nearly grabbed his hand and wept. He moved away, retrieving his clothes here and there. I smiled as I glimpsed his boxers travelling up his thighs. My mind started scrolling through what those thighs had done last night. Federico had unlocked a woman who had been caged inside of me for years. It had felt glorious, starring in my own minor porn flick. These were going to be the dirtiest memories I ever hoarded.

When I heard the door slam I called Pamela. She was driving her Bentley through traffic and she whooped when she heard me.

'I'm so happy for you,' she exclaimed. 'You have the world at your feet. This has been written on your forehead for months.'

I suddenly missed her tattoo fronds creeping out under her shirt and her pierced nipple bump on her boob, and wanted to tell her every single thing Federico had done to me.

'Is this your new number? Believe me girl, I know he went where Peter's never been.'

'Oh Pamela,' I said suddenly, surprising myself. 'I'm not coming back. I've decided to stay here.' I walked into the kitchen and found the grey-faced uncle leering out of his window. I gave him a fabulous smile. I was stark naked and jubilant.

'I had a feeling this was coming,' Pamela said.

'I'll get a job, that'll be easy enough. I already have a place where I can stay and I can have the kids come out at Christmas break.' I was amazed. Doors were opening before me and ideas were coming fast. The sex had thrust me into a new realm of conviction.

'When do you think you'll be going to Rome?' she said suddenly. I heard her beeping the Bentley's horn.

'I'm not going to Rome, I'm in Milan. I'm staying in *Milano.*'

'Of course, sweetheart,' she said, sounding flustered. 'You just stick to yer guns. Got to go dear, there's an idiot in front who thinks we have till January to cross these lights.'

I felt a little miffed Pamela hadn't swerved into an alley to hear all about my lovemaking, and I laid the phone down next to the sink. My neighbour was still leering out of his window. I waved him off and went back into Fiona's room. The sheets were still strewn every which way and I filled my lungs with the sweaty smell on the air. In Fiona's cupboard I found a post-copulation kimono which I threw around my shoulders, tying it loosely around my waist. Would Fiona have minded me bedding her discarded boyfriend? I thought with a mild start. But hadn't Fiona slept with that mediocre lover we now shared, the lecherous Peter? And besides, who was to know whether Fiona was trying out a new lover in some hotel room in Seoul?

Fiona's phone started ringing out in the kitchen and I stalled in shock. With a best friend who was a clairvoyant, I knew that telepathy jumped continents and phone circuits. What if Fiona had sensed I had slept with her lovesick boyfriend? What if she had changed her mind and wanted him back? But the name on the screen was 'Leonardo'. I saw that the battery was low and swiftly plugged in the charger in her room. Leonardo could only be the name of another jilted admirer. I'd hit the jackpot. Now it was time to work through Fiona's long list of sexual cast-offs.

'*Pronto! Buongiorno!*' I said cheerily.

'*Carissima! Finalmente ti trovo! Perché non mi rispondi mai?*'

'I'm sorry, but this is Marilyn. I'm Fiona's, er, big sister. Fiona's flown abroad for work. Do you speak English? Do you understand me?'

'I don't believe this.' He switched to a nasal American twang which threw me off. There were no kinks and he was speaking my language. 'Who the hell are you? Where is Fiona? I need to speak to her now. This is Leonardo.'

The man sounded as though he wasn't used to being contradicted and I sensed my voice was starting to give way. Had Fiona kept them all on their toes?

'I'm really sorry, Leonardo, that's all I can tell you. Perhaps, er, you could email her and explain your problem. Fiona's a busy woman and I'm sure she'll soon be back.'

I cut him off. Fiona's fake big sister? I was shaking. Leonardo called again and I put the phone under a pillow. I left the room to make coffee and go back to thinking about Federico's thighs.

The other thing was that I had to learn Italian. I'd begun a course several years ago, so some of the words felt familiar in my mouth. But I'd grown tired of the long drive to night lessons and given up on the interminable verbs. Now, as I took Fiona's grammar book down from the shelf, I had no idea whether I had enough brain cells left to tackle a second language. I read the book cover. 'Italian Language for Beginners'. Then in smaller case: 'Learn Italian in One Month.'

Inside, the book had been scribbled on in pencil and many of the exercises had been completed. In the margins on most pages were doodles of the male implement, like those you see in spray-paint along railway station walls or gouged on bus seats. Going by recent experience, I would have bet a great many of them belonged to Federico, except the ones that were lovingly shaded in black. I shook my head, trying to contain a spurt of envy. Now I was beginning to understand what made the world spin so hard.

I started my lessons: *Italian is a phonetic language which may be read aloud in the first instance. Try reading the following sentences phonetically.*

Il Duomo di Milano è un esempio di architettura gotica.

The Duomo of Milan is an example of Gothic architecture.

Io mi chiamo Priscilla Blakely.

My name is Priscilla Blakely.

Sto bene, grazie.

I'm fine, thanks.

No, preferisco il vino rosso.

No, I prefer red wine.

It seemed vaguely familiar. I thought of Jean and her new lover in the Andes, frozen toes interlocked:

Io mi chiamo Jean.

No, my husband never made love to me like this.

I found a dictionary and looked up Italian words:

bed – *letto*

shoe – *scarpa*

shower – *doccia*

brassiere – *reggiseno*
sex – *sesso*

I looked up a series of dirty words like a teenager and discovered that Federico's preferred exclamation, *cazzo,* meant penis. Penis? I could not understand why Federico called out 'penis' whenever he was upset. What on earth was hidden in this language of priests and popes? I returned to the grammar book for some basic verb conjugation. At high school I had studied French and never liked the way French women pursed their Brigitte Bardot lips. Italian seemed so much more lavish and corrupt:

I drink a coffee – *io bevo un caffè*
you drink a glass of *prosecco* – *tu bevi un bicchiere di prosecco*
he/she drinks a glass of red wine – *lui/lei beve un bicchiere di vino rosso*

It almost looked too easy …
I go to the bar – *io vado al bar*
I eat a sandwich – *io mangio un panino*
I make love to Federico – *io faccio l'amore con Federico*

Wonderful! I switched on the television to see how much of the language had seeped into my brain. It was an old episode of 'Happy Days', circa 1975. I watched the credits and settled down to decipher the tricky talk. I figured that once I caught onto a few verb structures and remembered some vocabulary, it wouldn't be much harder than wearing a new pair of shoes.

Wrong! Apart from Fonzie emanating an uncool slurred sound as he flagged his thumb, Potsie and Ritchie ran their words together mercilessly and I couldn't make out a thing. Every so often a word sprang free, but I was clueless. The Italian language was impenetrable. How had Fiona picked it up in months?

I went out to top up my coffee and saw Federico's uncle in his bathroom shaving. His eyes veered over to me and nearly popped out.

'*A me piace il cinema,*' I called out tentatively. (I like the cinema.)

Half-shaven, he leant out on the window sill and began wagging his shaving brush. He started a long monologue which I presumed included his thoughts upon Italian cinema, given I caught a couple of key words: Sophia Loren and *seno* (breast). My question had unleashed a torrent, but I couldn't understand a thing.

'*A te piace il sesso, scommetto?*' He leant forward and said this in a sly intimate tone. I was beginning to figure out that he had asked me something about sex when his wife pushed into their bathroom and clapped him on the ear. She yelled over towards me and I shrugged my dumb foreigner's shoulders. The frosted window slammed.

Sometime early in the afternoon Federico burst into the apartment in high spirits. He leapt onto the sofa and hugged me.

'*Cento dieci e lode!* I pass exam! *L'ho passato! Mi hanno dato cento dieci e lode.* They give me one hun'red and ten.'

I grasped that he had gone well in the exam and asked him what had been the topic.

'Oh, this one is not too hard. Irrigation technique in Pavia in *cinquecento e seicento.* I already study hard. I speak in front of six examiner.'

He gulped down some coffee and appeared to have mislaid any recollection of what had happened last night. I wondered if I had provided a springboard for the study of irrigation techniques. As cruel and haughty as it felt, I didn't believe him. I didn't believe Federico knew which way to hold up a book.

'I know what you thinking.' He read my expression. 'Fiona she think the same thing too, that I am stupid *truzzo milanese.*

But is not true. I am like my uncle, the one who grow banana or something in Australia. I study your country. I go there and build big farm with camel.'

A deep, carnal part of me wanted to lash out and lick his clenched fingers and fill his palm with kisses, but I rose and went to the kitchenette to rinse his cup. I unscrewed the percolator, emptied the coffee grounds and glumly began to prepare fresh coffee. He was probably right about everything except the camel.

Federico started flipping through my grammar book. He called out, 'So you study *italiano* now? You know Fiona say we do wedding in *italiano*, here at Santa Maria dei Miracoli. Fiona she is my *miracolo*.'

I felt a sudden subsiding at the sink. All of our blissful lovemaking had been me standing in for cheap, perky Fiona. I thought I would die if he made no reference to it.

He came in towards me and I involuntarily glanced at the bump in his jeans. He smiled. 'I go to work now.' I turned off the coffee gurgling on the stove. '*Vedi*, we are like family now,' he said. 'Very big family. You must come meet my father and mother. They love Fiona. They want plenty grandchildren. Maybe you meet my big brother Gino and have a *storia*. He have lot of women from America. Blond women like twenty-eight but he not mind that you older. Where is your Swiss boyfrenn'? Maybe you bring him here for Swiss fock?'

I tipped a good helping of grappa into my coffee and pulled my kimono back together. I didn't want to unravel his fine mood but I was perplexed and wounded. What if, in the big picture, Fiona was trying to oust Danielle and return to Peter's side? What then? When would darling Federico realise that whatever she decided to do, Fiona was never coming back?

'Yes, my boyfriend is coming tonight, so perhaps you'd better not pass by here. I would love to meet your parents. Was it you who helped Fiona learn Italian so well?'

'Oh yes, we fock in *italiano*, she love to fock in *italiano*. Then we have lesson after and I give her ass slap if she make mistake. In the beginning she make plenty and her ass very red.'

Way to go, I thought. Ouch!

'Federico, I need to find a job. Then I can stay here and be close to my boyfriend. And I want to wait for my sister to come back. You don't know of anything around here?'

'Well, yes, of course. My uncle pass in the bar yesterday, he at *fiera* selling to Japanese and don't understand English. He is very stressed. You want I call him? Come to bar at nine o'clock tomorrow *mattina*.' He downed his coffee and gave me an enormous blank smile. I was clueless. He rose to leave.

'You want I give you *italiano* lesson like your liddle sister?' he asked as though asking if I wanted a glass of water.

I stared back, goggle-eyed. 'Yes, *per favore.*'

I tidied the kitchen and retrieved my shirt and panties from under the couch in front of the television. I found a couple of Fiona's G-strings – scrags of netting and dental floss – and a pair of printed boxers, presumably belonging to the young agronomist. I smelt them. Yes, they were his. Then I held the underwear at a distance, shocked. How was it that I had come from being Peter's benign wife to a woman who thrust underwear into her face? I tossed them into the washing basket and took a long, soothing shower. I selected one of the new bra sets and began to go through Fiona's dresses thrown on the floor. Nothing seemed quite right so I pulled out the new printed wraparound dress I had bought the day before. If I ever found a job I would need some high-powered clothing, which meant I ought to check whether Peter had sorted out my credit cards. Reluctantly, I picked up Fiona's mobile, searching for Peter's number. But Peter's was off. I didn't leave a message. I sniffed trouble. Perhaps he had gone to join Fiona in Korea. Perhaps

Danielle had come at him with a battleaxe. I called Vanessa even though it was a little early and she was probably still in school. But she answered.

'Mum? Is that you?'

'Hello love, this is my new number.'

'Are you all right? Dad said you were robbed and they took everything. What a bummer! He's fixed your cards. Well, Danielle really, she was mugged last month. He's going to text you everything so you can pick up the new ones over there.'

'Why aren't you in school?'

'We're all at Brighton today, we skipped school. It was Danielle's idea. She was going crazy and said we should spend a day away from town. We had fish and chips on the beach.'

'Where's your father?' *(Shagging, shagging, shagging.)*

'Oh, they went back to shag after lunch. Eddy and I are on the Play Station … No, Eddy! What did you kill him for?'

I heard my son's voice, and in the background I thought I heard a grown woman's hearty laugh mingling with Peter's smarmy tones. I cut the connection and let the mobile drop to the floor. Every step I had taken away from my old life shrank to a cutting pain. I felt a cold hand reach deep into my chest and squeeze my heart hard.

I made a cup of strong tea and sat awhile in the kitchenette. In truth it was a fairly pleasant space. Each cupboard door had a ceramic handle with tiny printed flowers. A tall glass spaghetti jar stood empty by the sink. I couldn't imagine Fiona ever eating spaghetti, much less throwing it into a colander with the steam rising into her face. And yet, despite shacking up with a woman who had slept with my husband, I was grateful to have my budding life here and not in a nasty hotel. I began hanging up her clothes in the wardrobe and making some room for my own. Whether I wanted to or not, it looked like I would be staying quite a stretch while my life continued to fall apart.

That day I moved the rest of my things from the spare bedroom into Fiona's space. I didn't think she would mind. Her room was wider and cosier and I pulled up the blind she had left closed. The afternoon light drifted inside. I leant over the sill on this side of the building. Below was a long narrow courtyard where a single ruddy tree stood spilling its leaves. The refuse of the hot Milanese summer was still strewn about: rows of thin tomato plants and string beans, punctured footballs and a faded beach umbrella leaning against a wall. An old woman stretched to unpeg a row of big men's knickers. She had a clothes peg in her mouth. I felt calmer watching her, and was surprised when she looked up carrying her cane washing basket and called to me.

'*Buongiorno, signora,*' she said. *'Bella giornata, no?'*

'*Buongiorno, signora,*' I replied and waved.

The next morning my alarm roused me for a shower. The cool autumn sun was up early. Down in the courtyard my elderly neighbour had already pegged up a row of men's shirts. I dressed. I found a discarded handbag of Fiona's and put in some of the cash I had hidden away in my suitcase. As I drank my coffee I said words to myself in Italian: *A me piace bere il caffè la mattina* (I like to drink coffee in the morning); *A me piace Federico la notte* (I like Federico at night).

Down in the bustling city street I sensed glances in my direction. I may have been destroyed again, but I knew I looked good. Hadn't grand old Mae West said, 'It is better to be looked over, than overlooked?' And whether or not Peter and Danielle shagged until kingdom come I had made love to the spicy apprentice agronomist with his knowledge of ancient irrigation techniques. Not even Danielle could boast a young strapping lover like that.

As usual I passed the girl smoking a fag outside the underwear shop. This morning she smiled at me once again, cautiously peering at my shoes. I passed the Swiss model agency director grumpily reading the newspaper as he drank his morning espresso. I presumed his sylph was throwing up in the toilet inside. I turned around again and, finding his eyes travelling over me, couldn't help but smile. Would he ever know that this far-from-slim divorcée had claimed he was her Swiss-fock boyfriend?

I reached Federico's bar and threw back a *caffè corretto*. The same belligerent woman was at the far end of the zinc counter, waving her *tramezzino* at the poor bar girl. Federico's back flexed as he whacked the coffee grounds down the chute. I felt his tendons as though they had flinched under my fingertips. I guess when he turned around he saw me as Fiona's sister, and his eyes shirred for a second. I felt a sting of guilt for leading him astray in front of the soft porn film. He obviously loved her valiantly.

'You are lucky,' he said with a quick smile. 'My uncle he no find no one, so he need you at *fiera*. Right now.'

'Federico, what is a *fiera*?'

'You no look? What you have dictionary for?' He had a new irritated tone to his voice and I worried I might end up with a very red ass. 'It is like trade fair. Where Japanese and American and French come and buy things for shops. My uncle he marry woman from Arezzo and they make hat, a good one. He sell to Japanese. You catch *metropolitana* to Rho. Here, he write everything. You understand?'

He looked over the counter at my long legs in delicate high heels. 'By the end of day my big sister will be *distrutta*.'

6. LA FIERA

I carefully folded Federico's piece of paper with its unintelligible scribble and hobbled to the *metropolitana*. So far, so good. I realised how desperately I wanted to prove myself in Federico's eyes and felt foolish. How excited I was by the prospect of Italian grammar lessons delivered harshly on the rump! If I succeeded at the *fiera*, doing whatever Federico's uncle required me to do, I would be employable, with a more valid reason for staying in Milan. I imagined Fiona and myself having a great laugh in the cranky Swiss man's bar, recounting our tales of naughty language immersion and stints of comical labour. I imagined Federico's uncle would be nothing short of swooning and gracious, pawing me secretly while his long-suffering wife was turned away.

Over an hour later I met Gustavo's wife Alberta at the turnstiles to the trade fair, where she snapped over my pass and berated me for not arriving sooner. I had gotten seriously lost on the way. Four people had turned over Federico's uncle's note every which way claiming it was not even written in Italian. Finally a woman said the word *fiera* which I cottoned on to, and it was discovered I was on the wrong branch of the red line, so I hurtled up and over the stairway once again in my stilettos, just short of keeling over from the soot fanning into my lungs. Outside I caught the wrong bus, hailed down a taxi, and finally found myself badgering a Bangladeshi man holding leaflets in front of pavilion fifteen.

Inside, I couldn't see Alberta extending the family olive branch. She was short and yellow-skinned with viciously dyed red hair. Her voice snagged on smoker's phlegm. She raised her eyebrows at my footwear and pitched into the crowd as I careered after her bobbing head. The pavilion was filled with aisle after aisle of booths displaying bright summer clothing collections and all manner of accessories. Young models posed along the way, bronzed navels and shoulders luring buyers onward. Many of the stalls were crammed with people wearing heavy winter clothing, poring through the colourful, lightweight fabrics. Very quickly, I realised these were not shopaholics looking for karmic hits but seasoned buyers selecting products, writing down orders in niches of concentration.

Alberta hurried along, shaking her head, before she veered out of the river of people into a booth full of exquisite, straw-scented hats. She scowled as I hobbled to a stop. Her eyes led mine to the young model with a tanned midriff and cowboy hat standing next door, showing me how expressly she felt short-changed. She turned to a man reading a sports newspaper on a small table at the back, who raised a face with a delightful shadow of Federico about the eyebrows.

Alberta snarled, *'Ma hai visto che scherzo ti ha fatto il tuo nipote di merda! Ti avevo detto che è un buono a nulla! Andare in giro a scopare le vecchie puttane!'*

I had no idea what she had said, but it sounded as though she was furious with Federico for sending an old hag to do a young woman's work. Damn her!

Federico's uncle looked me over, glancing at the girl next door to confirm the comparison and shut the woman up. I tried to counter my shortcomings with an appropriate smile, one that might bridge the gulf over to Federico's flesh and blood. But Federico's uncle's eyes came to rest on mine listlessly, before dropping back to the newspaper.

Alberta thrust an order book and black pen into my arms and took off in the direction of a big yellow exit sign on the rear wall, cigarette case and lighter in hand.

'*Io sono Gustavo, lo zio di Fede.* Federico uncle.' Alberta's husband finally stood up and walked over. He offered me his chafed hand, while he took in a measure of my hip as he helped remove my coat. I loomed over *zio Gustavo* in heels. I smiled, waiting for conversation to flower, keen to be on the receiving end of some Milanese charm. Gustavo smiled back warmly but his face peered at some point behind me. I turned to see a chick with glossy black hair doing a Paris Hilton wave through a gap in the crowd. She was wearing wildly low cut jeans which looked like an anatomical fitting, and a tiny Sergeant Pepper's jacket with big gold studs. I turned around and stared. Her long exposed trunk was oddly proportioned, with the nether regions both front and back scored by diligent waxing. If she weren't a lap dancer by night then my name was Cindy Crawford.

'*Mi scusi, solo un attimo. Saluto un'amica.*' Gustavo lunged across the thoroughfare to the beat of summery disco music.

I stood rigidly amongst the hats. I don't think I had ever felt so explicitly cast off in my life, apart from Peter disowning me in my own kitchen. I watched Federico's short uncle swoon up to the half-dressed girl, his hand coming to rest on her flank. She had thick black eyeliner and a nasty smile, with a fake diamond pocking her front tooth. Behind her two haggard blond women were hawking skinny torn-to-bits denim jeans. I figured the Sergeant Pepper's lap dancer would have no trouble nailing their target market.

I retreated primly among the Tuscan hats, trying to smell a whiff of cypress trees on a sun-drenched hill. Each hat had fine ivory tones and immaculately stitched ridges. They floated on metal stands like spring butterflies. It was impossible to think of either Alberta or Gustavo as being the authors of such beauty. I touched one and it spun dizzily on its axis. What on earth would I do if a client came in and ordered a dozen container loads for the Far East?

I peered up and down the aisle to see if Alberta's fiery hair was coming back. Masses of foreign buyers moved past, eyes registering the hats, many of the stern faces ignoring the tawdry girls and staring seriously at maps of the facility. A British woman stopped to ask the way to the toilets and I felt a surge of power as she attempted to speak the local language.

'*Scusi la* toilet, please? *Dove?*'

'I think they're by the entrance. I'm sure I noticed them as I came in earlier. Why don't you try going back that way?'

'Oh, my goodness, you're English! I'm sorry I was convinced you were Italian. Thanks so much.'

I felt a warm smugness as I watched the woman bundle off with her bulky raincoat and armful of sample bags. *I was convinced you were Italian* had sounded like Vivaldi to my ears. I took up one of Alberta's hats, tipping the rear so that the brim lay low over my eyes, and waltzed up to the mirror on the back wall. I looked like a pre-plastic surgery Faye Dunaway from Bonnie and Clyde, minus cigarette and sub-machine-gun.

A red flash appeared at my shoulder. It was Alberta's filigree hair full of smoke.

'*Ma come si permette!*' As she whipped off the hat, the furrow dividing her forehead looked as though it might split apart. I staggered backwards away from her.

After an hour of hopping from one heel to the other while Alberta relished the view from the only chair, a group of Japanese paused to consider one of the items at the front. Gustavo had failed to return. Alberta tensed. The foreigners appeared to be converging inward, but then the ringleader with thick glasses withdrew, saw something ahead, and they all bowed away. Alberta's grimace ravaged her yellow face. Other stalls filled and emptied with buyers, but for a long time it seemed no one was interested in the meticulous Tuscan hats. Occasionally Alberta stared at me with distaste, as though I had brought upon the commercial lull. I avoided eye contact with her, and continued shifting from one heel to the other next to the river of people.

Midway through the afternoon I glimpsed Gustavo and his prey at the end of the aisle. How could Alberta not have known?

Under the thumping music, Gustavo stood on tiptoes to whisper sweet nothings into the lap dancer's multiple-pierced ear. People milled around them and they stood like a comedy duo acting out a pair of lovesick teens. I remembered the black girl in silver hot pants and the balding TV presenter and thought I could only be witnessing a national dynamic at work. Perhaps lovely alabaster Fiona had done well to vanish to Korea?

Shortly afterwards Gustavo breezed into the booth to collect the staunch little man bag that had been sitting on the table. As I half-wondered what might have been inside I caught the scent of floral perfume on his clothing and stared. Alberta must have seen me studying her husband with judgement, because as soon as he left she spoke across to me in a harsh voice. I guess she wanted to tell me she knew her husband had cuckolded her as many times as he had read the sports newspaper.

But it was much worse than that.

'You are *divorziata*, no?' she began tonelessly. Was it still written on my forehead?

I nodded, given my jaw had gone numb. There, before the stream of people and the panoply of the fashion show, I felt like a foggy-minded sheep about to be slaughtered. Alberta's slight sneer inferred I had run my life badly all along.

'My *nipote*, Federico, the mother she have ....' Here she made a wide arc where her breasts should have been, while staring at my knockers.

What? How dare she? I turned a mottled wine colour, clasping my chest. Alberta's face came as close to a smile as it ever would. She raised her eyebrows with cold joy. Not only was she was informing me she knew I had consumed her young nephew in bed, but she was accusing me of stepping into his mother's shoes – and her brassiere – in the most vulgar manner. She perused my jacked-up curvy body and must have seen through to the wretched abandoned wife inside.

'Your *marito inglese*,' she said. 'He leave you, no?'

I stared into the passers-by, looking for an answer to her cruel question. Faces floated along. I saw the dowdy British woman walking with a dowdy man. They laughed together. I stood there wanting to bawl.

'*In Italia,*' Alberta stated, laying down the laws of the flock. 'The *matrimonio è sacro*. The marriage is *sacro*. A woman *sa tenere il suo uomo*. Woman know how to keep man.' As she peered at me I thought I saw a flicker of helplessness quickly swallowed in her eyes. Then she stared at me as though I were a halfwit. '*Qui,* a woman know how to keep man,' she repeated.

I wasn't going to cry in front of her. I wasn't going to look like the only loser in a landscape where even an acidic, betrayed Tuscan wife could declare herself a winner. I finally turned away from her. My damp eyes followed a group of Indian ladies in delicately coloured saris, looking like a packet of sweets.

Alberta clutched her cigarettes and left the booth. I watched her slip through the crowd towards the exit, hating her. But she was right. She had kept her man, everybody kept their husbands here. Everyone knew that foolish Gustavo would never leave the roost. I wondered how Alberta had been an age ago, when she was the bewitching black-haired girl with a tiny waist who had taken Gustavo into her arms with young love. I wondered how many times her heart had been broken to make her become this scaly-skinned monster.

By the time Alberta came back I was in a tizz. A slick American gentleman had come in and begun delicately perusing the hats. He oozed class, gay class. Alberta quickly switched to polite business mode and showcased what I realised were their high-end favourites. From her determined gestures, I saw he was that gold nugget all were here to unearth, the new international client. But the man brushed off her cobbled English and glanced over at me.

'Ah, do you speak English, perhaps?' I heard a Boston twang and saw his eyes had a luring, enticing quality, although the look he gave me was bland. 'My name is Roderick Brighton. I've just set up a hat shop in downtown Provincetown, and I'd really like my partner to see these. May I try?'

'Certainly.' The brisk Bostonian took up a Truman Capote-style brimmed straw hat and wore it slightly askew, admiring himself in Alberta's mirror with brief, innocuous familiarity. There was quite a lot to admire. He was tanned with large relaxed bones inferring a capacity for subtle and powerful movement. His skin was lined and complete, and his eyes were full of casual self-esteem.

'Ah, my partner should be around any moment now. We glanced at your product early this morning and were keen to come back.'

Alberta handed him a stream of appropriate items which the refined man placed tastefully on his head, avoiding any sort of movie star pose as each hat enhanced the sultry line of his jaw. He made quick decisions, placing the chosen items aside on Alberta's polished table while she served him with sour glee. The idea crossed my mind that maybe he was somebody famous I failed to recognise, and then Brett the dreadful internet kisser I met in London turned a corner and stepped into the booth.

'Ah, here you are, Brett. I think I've made a good selection. Would you like to give it a run through?'

'Of course, Roderick. What about the straw quality? Are the rims double-stitched?'

I began to wobble. Thankfully the two buyers ignored both Alberta and myself and began to investigate the hats. Then Alberta thrust a new slightly racier model towards them.

They both nodded, and I thought Brett's eyes momentarily slowed over my face. In fact he concentrated upon me and spoke: 'You wouldn't have this model in black, with an ivory band?'

We were face to face, his hand loosely folded over Roderick's arm while my eyes were glued to the undeniable doll's hair plunged into his hairline. I felt the wetness of his lips and saw a stippled orange duck. Then nothing could save me from imagining the pair of them in a grinding male rapport in Alberta's matching hats.

'I'll just see,' I said jerking back into anxious Alberta.

'*Cosa?* What they want? *Dimmi deficiente,*' she snarled.

'Black, ah, *nero*. The same hat in black,' he said. Same *cappello* but *nero,*' I blabbed, thanking the Lord for the few insights I had gleaned from Fiona's book.

Brett swung around helpfully to Alberta. 'She's right,' he said, indicating me. '*Nero sombrero. Este blanco.* Or ivory. *Como elefante,* you know?' he pointed to the sleek ribbon around the hat. Aside to me he said, 'You see, I spent some time in Mexico. The Spanish words are about the same.'

I glowered with heat. Mexico? That was where he had communed with the Frida Kahlo look-alike after six months of creamy internet sex. The two men moved together again, fingers grazing over the products, the pair of them swiftly and coolly trying on models, looking as though they were soul-branded intimates who had worked together for years. Alberta stooped into a cardboard box under the table and I wondered what would happen if I reminded him of the coffee in Leicester Square Starbucks and the suggestion of a late Cantonese lunch. Then I thought I how stupidly I had charged off, bolting like a three-legged horse because his tongue had wrestled into my mouth.

The men concluded their order with Alberta, whose grimace loosened marginally as she placed her stained yellow hands in each of theirs. They both turned to salute me.

'Excuse me, er, Brett, you don't remember me?' I said as casually as I could with my heart knocking against my ribs. The two men glanced over me with bewildered looks.

'We chatted on the internet one morning last month, then met up at Leicester Square. You suggested lunch at Soho.'

Roderick let out a resonant chuckle and Brett looked puzzled.

'Oh *Christ*, Brett darling, and they are *still* cropping out of the woodwork.'

On Brett's face a visible struggle was going on and, more than ever, he looked like a Hong Kong cop trying to figure out a complex crime.

'Well?' Roderick said, his twang suddenly stronger. 'Make an apology to the poor little lady and you'll spend the week in chains, you Cantonese scoundrel.'

They turned away arm in arm beginning to laugh, with Roderick giving Brett an edifying smooch on the cheek. I felt like an utter fool as I watched them blend into the crowd.

The heating system kicked in throughout the rest of the afternoon and people shuffled around carrying coats and wearing maps of perspiration under their arms. Gustavo abandoned any pretence of work and left. Ten minutes later the lap dancer waved off the two crusty blonds. Alberta's foul mood cleared when two different groups of Asian buyers crowded into the small stand, and the Tuscan hats travelled out among their hands. She could neither understand them nor keep track of the hats and kept muttering about the *cinesi* (Chinese). But Chinese they were not. One set of buyers came from Korea, Fiona's destination, while the others were slightly miffed, formal Japanese. A line of defence extended through the tiny booth, and both groups pretended the other was not there. Alberta assigned the Koreans to me and I spent a good while excusing myself between customers to fetch hats and check prices. I tried on an endless succession while the unruly customers stared and reached into bags for snacks. The Japanese remained in a secretive cluster, one young funky girl making quick sketches of each item selected, while the male boss fingered the merchandise and might have been making an atom

91

count. I sweated, and suspected that I was reeking like a horse, and then nearly keeled over when the Korean boss belched a potent onion cloud into the confined space. The Japanese contracted further to one side in shock.

Alberta watched the tension with a pragmatic verve. She had hardly taken an order all day and I could see her itching for the climax. Finally, the selection was made. Order forms were filled out and the bowing began. The Japanese buyers withdrew and I noticed Alberta gasping for breath. She marched off for a victory cigarette. By now my head was spinning in the airless pavilion, and I was feeling dangerously faint. The Koreans spread out and a couple of the women removed their shoes and handed around a gaily printed thermos. Then they asked to see every single hat in the collection another time.

At the end of the day Alberta ordered me to stack the merchandise. Revived by the nicotine, she pulled out flattened cardboard boxes from behind the table and crankily showed me how to insert one hat inside the next with a wad of tissue paper, which I would have liked to push down her throat. I laid dozens of crisp ivory hats to rest in this way, allowing the country scent to waft some calm into my body. I hadn't eaten for hours and my feet were so consumed by pain I could no longer feel a thing. As Alberta perused her paperwork I sealed the boxes and gathered the metal stands together. She had some pimply delivery boy carry off the merchandise to their van, then took her last scornful look over my indecent curves and inappropriate footwear. She handed me a garish straw hat I hadn't seen all day.

'Here,' she said. '*Mio marito* and I, we say *grazie*. For your *lavoro oggi*. Your working at *fiera*.' She provided the most unflattering smile I have ever seen on the face of a woman. I dumbly took the hat instead of stomping upon it.

She collected my pass for the event and gave a silly laugh, as the pimply delivery youth was joined by a tall Senegalese co-worker and the two cleared the deck. I stood on the empty platform holding the cheap dyed hat.

'*Non le piace?*' she teased. (You don't like it?)

I grabbed my coat and stumbled backwards into the crowd. I couldn't believe that young, beautiful Federico had sent me to be exploited by these despicable people. I thought back to Federico's thighs wrapped around my own and the softness of his breath on my neck. Then I recalled the way he had cradled my breasts so lovingly. I saw Alberta's arms tracing an arc over her flat chest and shivered. Somewhere in the city there was a woman slightly older than myself, who had raised sons and surrendered them to busty girlfriends. I threw Alberta's hat in a rubbish bin, sick to the core.

Outside it was raining but I limped forth, hair soggy and face dribbling. I was in agony. As I swayed I saw shopfronts in bulbous pixels and the rain fell in fat drops before my eyes. Just before I headed into the dry *metropolitana* passage I saw a taxi set down a passenger and, despite cries from an old man advancing with a walker, I plunged inside like a diver from a cliff.

Several days later the urge to hunt down my young lover overpowered my shame. I just wanted to hold him in my arms. I also wanted to throttle him for sending me to his horrible aunt. I woke up clutching the cool sheets one morning, quite determined to pace around the block to the bar where Federico worked.

But once there I walked straight past Federico's bar without stopping. My feet hadn't entirely recovered and I felt a twinge along one thigh. I glimpsed him staring sadly out of the window, his eyes absorbed by something that I knew was not the night we had spent together. Oh Federico! His *tristesse* plunged deep inside of me and I felt wetness tingling at my crotch. But I didn't want to become the busty mother-substitute Alberta had seen like a big wrinkled baby rocking in his arms. I crossed the street further down, pushed around a corner and paused to ease my legs.

There was a man braced against a doorway. At first I assumed that he was seeking relief from the crowds. I was admiring his stylish trench coat when I realised he was clutching his heart. He turned to me with shock on his drawn face. It was the Swiss model agency director, the one with the vomiting sylph normally shimmering at his side.

'Are you all right?' I gasped, nursing being the last of my capabilities.

'What do you fucking well think?' He burst brutally out of his trance. The same woody scent leapt into my nostrils. But he had such a sharp twist in his eyes that I pulled away. After the day with Alberta I could stand no more nastiness, not even an arresting woody whiff of it. I left him there and hurried off, not even turning back to see if he had collapsed or was lying convulsing on the ground.

Afterwards I sensed that a fracas had broken out behind me, and when I was a block away I heard an ambulance ringing through the streets. But I was finished with cruel people. I flopped down into a bar for a drink and began to sob uselessly, choking and spluttering to a Duran Duran medley which made my condition feel interminable and deserved.

I received no consolation from my potential grammar teacher. It seemed as though Milan had given me the cold shoulder. I half-slept on Fiona's divan, listening to the sounds of my neighbours' lives coming from the air shaft until they dissolved in the night. I switched on the television and saw Bruce Willis' bald head. Perhaps it was a sign. Perhaps after the explosive film there would be some misty Californian porn and I would hear Federico's keys in the lock. I waited. My head fell back and I imagined my shirt being torn away, and Federico's hot lips pressed to my skin. Perhaps I needed to wait a little longer. I lay out on Fiona's bed, my hand tracing Federico's path. But it was no use. My body lay bulky and nude on the bed. I couldn't even trick myself into falling asleep.

Days later, I nearly died when I saw him in the neighbourhood. I was just about to enter a bookshop looking for a soppy English romance novel and saw him through the window with a pretty young blond. I tripped up the stairs as I wrenched myself backwards. She must have been about nineteen. I ran across the road, peering at them from behind a potted hedge. My lover, who I still suspected didn't know which way to hold a book, pulled out a spine and opened it for her. She leant towards him, and the skin of her neck was fresh and crinkle-free. I waited and yes, they kissed. First gently, and then full-on in Federico's thrusting twirling style. I stood there hyperventilating. A pharmacist in a white coat stepped out and shooed me off, the way one would shoo a pigeon. I stumbled on along the footpath. Inside my body I could feel a tangible shutdown. I felt my lust shrink away into a tiny knitted cocoon.

At home I yearned for Fiona. I wondered if she really were in Seoul strolling the city streets, eating warm soups with a new lover. Or if she had ridden Peter into the bed at home. One day her mobile began ringing and ringing. At some point in the afternoon I lifted it up from the table by her bed. Squinting through tears, I saw the name 'Leonardo' on the screen. I remembered his pushy American voice from before. Poor Leonardo might have to be told that Fiona had taken off.

'Yes?' I said tiredly. 'May I help you? This is Marilyn.'

'*O Cristo!* Look, this is Leonardo from Rome. I think we spoke several days ago. Your, er, *sister* Fiona seems to have changed her email address and I'm afraid it's rather fundamental that I speak to her.'

'Fundamental? And what would that mean?' I said carelessly. I breathed in deep and tried to send my tears back to base.

'Well, this is quite difficult,' he said. 'And rather unusual. Are you sure you don't know where she is right now?' His rich baritone gradually became a little calmer. 'You know, I've been calling this number all day.'

'I apologise, I've been busy.'

'I'm also quite curious, you know. I don't remember Fiona ever mentioning a sister.'

'Oh, we tend to crop up when we're least expected.'

'You have quite a way with words.'

'Pardon? It's called English.'

'As I was saying, I don't remember Fiona ever mentioning a sister, as such. I'd be very curious to know if you've inherited the family fault line,' he said, sounding a little devious.

'Fault line?'

'Well, it's rather private. Fiona used to joke about it. Of course, I can't speak of such things without looking a woman in the eye.'

I laughed. 'Really? I must say I agree. You had better back down, dear Leonardo, or I'll tattle to my sister.'

'Certainly. But how strange, if you don't mind me remarking, that you don't seem to have any of that endearing Australian accent of Fiona's? How on earth did you iron that one out?'

'Leonardo,' I said with a flutter of nerves. 'As you said yourself, there are some topics that must be discussed face to face, no? And you're being far too curious for this hour of the day.'

There was a moment's pause. That was when I realised I could probably learn to enjoy my role as gatekeeper for Fiona's many abandoned lovers. If I worked through their ranks, I was bound to get over losing Peter – and Federico – before the year was out.

'Let's just assume,' I said rather more playfully, 'that Fiona doesn't want you to know where she is right now. Perhaps she's just run off. You know our girl, she likes a bit of latitude.'

'Granted, but as her *sister*, she must have dropped you a line or sent you some sort of signal. The pair of you must be thick as thieves. Look, it really is imperative that I speak to her. Or, perhaps you'd like to hear what I have to say yourself.'

'And why on earth would I want to hear what you have to say?' The conversation was becoming tricky.

'Look, I'm not keen on spending useless time on the telephone. Given you won't reveal Fiona's whereabouts, why don't you hop on a train to Rome? It may not be so unpleasant to spend some time together.'

'Well, if you twist my arm a little harder ....' I could think of nothing more smashing than slipping away from my disgraces in Milan and trying on a new city.

'Aha, I see. Like your *sister* you prefer a little pleasure with your pain.'

'Sorry?' Whatever that meant I was far from caring. I suddenly wondered whether Leonardo was as good-looking as his rich voice promised.

'How about this then? There is a *Eurostar Italia* leaving the *Stazione Centrale* at three-twenty,' said Leonardo calmly. 'I believe you could be on it without too much of a rush. I'll be waiting for you at Roma *Termini*.'

'Okay, Leonardo,' I heard myself say as I rolled away from the phone. 'I'll be on it.'

Moments afterwards, my ex-husband Peter called up and I responded dreamily.

'Marilyn? Is that you?'

'Huh? Who are you?'

Peter wanted to talk to me about the arrangements for Christmas. I was absolutely perplexed. By Christmas time I could be wearing gold hot pants and whipping a chariot around the Coliseum.

'Well,' he said carefully. 'I think we need to come up with a realistic plan. Danielle says – and I think it's a great idea – that the children might benefit from some time abroad. And we were, well, thinking of making a short trip. You know, just us. We're tossing up ideas, you see. Maybe to Wales, or perhaps New York. Danielle would like to make some bookings. And, er, I was quite sure you would like some company over Christmas. I know how you've always made the occasion so special. So how about if the kids pop over to you for Christmas in Milan?'

I thought of how many times Peter had promised to take me to New York, which I had given up all hope of seeing. And I thought of Christmas, that trying time of gift-wrapping and strenuous cooking and masses of leftovers; the Christmas tree lights from the box of busted Hungarian trinkets that I now hooked up on my own. Now he and his bird wanted to dump the kids on me while they flew off to New York.

'I'm so sorry, Peter,' I replied, keeping my hurt on a short, tight leash. 'Frightfully kind of you to think of me, but right now I have a train to catch.'

7. ROMA

The original trip to Venice with Peter also included a dash to Rome in a blue Renault 2CV, which was like driving a cardboard cut-out powered by a hair dryer. The vehicle took every corner with pizzazz, tipping over on its springs. We took turns driving, with my attention span limited by bouts of parasitic fatigue. I fell asleep with maps spread out over my face. Peter smoked in those days and his smoke filled the tiny capsule until he unhooked a window flap and let the chilly air inside. We drove down the spine of the country, over the plains with their foggy rivers and wet grass, then climbed through the rugged hilly country further south, stopping briefly in Florence where Peter ate a seafood dish and was violently sick. In my hormonal stupor I spent a night wiping down his feverish temples. We made love like clams must do: a quick and warm secretion.

I remembered little of Rome however. It had been a windy and gritty maze of cobbled streets and by that time we were tired homesick tourists, upon whom the magic had worn thin. We came home on the cheap and over the next few months I put on a lot of pregnancy weight. Peter's workload increased. One morning sorting through the washing I pulled out a striped blue shirt with lipstick on the collar. I will never forget that. I spent the day in paralysis sitting on the washing basket. A grotesque pain worked along my thighs and buttocks and I couldn't move. When Peter came home he was all warm stroking hands. He manoeuvred me onto the floor and massaged me on my side, staying by me for hours as the pain dwindled. I never asked him about the lipstick.

After Vanessa was born it was Peter who took trips abroad. I slowed down, penned in the house with its screaming, wriggling new member. I was intrigued by her dainty growth and stark dependence, the exactness of her baby eyes and the knowledge unfurling within. I loved my little girl and grew fat in the kitchen with her. In my heart I knew Peter slept about with glamorous childless women in the city. But the hurt had softened. It grew quiet. I wanted another baby and soon found myself expecting one.

Now, seventeen years after that first trip to Italy, I sat back primly in my second-class *Eurostar Italia* seat. I was wearing a suit I had found in Fiona's closet which was more my size than hers. I wondered if she had bought it a little oversized when she had been pregnant. I wore one of her frilly scooped blouses and now regretted rashly handing over the amber pendant to Christian, my Nigerian life-saver in the park – it would have sat so nicely around my neck. I put my fingers into one of the pockets just above my hips and found a gold necklace with a ringlet of crystals pulled together like a bunch of grapes. As stealthily as possible, given I had an older man and woman opposite watching my every move, I took the two ends of the chain and clasped them under my hair, feeling the cool minerals touch my skin. Somehow I knew the chain was a gift Fiona had chosen to leave behind. Now I was convinced she had worn this suit when she was plumper with the child she had lost, and I was certain that the chain had come from the horrible man who had left her for the French woman who did commercials.

As the train rocked into a long tunnel and passengers' faces doubled up along the black glass, it suddenly clicked: Leonardo was Fiona's dastardly ex-husband. I was swimming into his den as the miscarried child hovered in limbo above us. How awful! I nearly ripped the crystals from my throat. The man and woman opposite, now eating home-made salami sandwiches, sensed my vehemence and stared.

In Rome I strode along the platform searching for the man who had ruined my Australian friend's life. I was on Fiona's side now. In my mind Leonardo was a smarmy, enigmatic creep wearing Armani. I clutched my handbag and launched into the station building. Smarmy, enigmatic types were on call today and I peered brazenly into the tanned faces of dozens of men. Then I realised neither Leonardo nor myself had a clue as to what the other looked like, and I thought that to the male Mediterranean population I was being a tad unfair. Finally, I felt tentative fingers at my elbow and swung around to face a cheerful non-Italian-looking man with curly ginger hair and a white-flecked beard. He wore old jeans, a chunky hand-knitted sweater and an amused smile.

'Hi, I'm Leonardo.'

'What?'

'Sorry, but I recognised that suit. And the chain you're wearing. They're Fiona's, aren't they? So you're Marilyn, are you? Fiona's sister?'

'Yes, yes I am,' I said, telling a fib longer than my thigh.

He took me in without shifting his eyes, extended his hand and said, 'That's interesting.'

I tensed my spine to stop my knees knocking under me. He continued, 'I'm a very old friend and I know Fiona is an only child. I was curious to check out who has been posing as Fiona's sister up in Milan.'

'That's a bit rich from an ex-husband who made her lose a child.'

'Lose a child? Are you mad?' (I caught a flash of tension on Leonardo's face.) 'Fiona's never been near having a baby and there was never any husband. What are you talking about?'

'But she told me ....'

He threw his arm around my shoulder and began to walk me towards the exit. I couldn't help feeling tearful and utterly confused.

'*O mio Dio*, Fiona is adorable in tiny spoonfuls but you mustn't believe her. Did she say she was going to Korea?'

'Well, yes,' I said, holding back on the tears. 'To sell her TV show. My ex-husband has worked with her in the UK.'

'You mean they had an affair?'

I nodded.

Leonardo shook his head as he walked. 'Okay, that's how she usually gets around it – "the French woman doing commercials, crap ones".' He did a pretty credible Australian twang. 'Then I'm afraid we have a long, long evening ahead.'

We emerged from the terminus building and began walking over cobbles. Leonardo veered over to a row of Vespa scooters.

'Ever been on one of these?'

I shook my head.

He turned a little key in the rear hump of one and pulled out two helmets, one of which he handed to me.

'That's the one Fiona likes. Here, you clip it under your chin like this.'

'I looked at Leonardo as the clasp made a click-click under his chin. Could I trust this man? Should I let myself be smooth-talked into the splendid city on the back of a wonky motorbike? I stood still for a moment, looking around at the old shuttered apartment buildings smouldering above street lamps, cars passing full of carefree handsome men and a transsexual with rugby thighs in a mini skirt. Above, pale stars trailed over a length of inky sky, the same stars that had shimmered over Hadrian and Caesar, many of the Popes, and the exceptional Marcello Mastroianni. I ignored my giddy indecision and buckled the helmet under my strong Hungarian chin.

Leonardo straddled the bike and kicked it to life, pushing it back to where I stood and urging me to hop on. Feeling like a cartoon character with a goldfish bowl stuck on my head, I bent towards him and slammed into his helmet. I tried sitting side-saddle but my big behind wouldn't fit when it was rammed perpendicular to his, so Leonardo bent over and brazenly hitched up my skirt just under my knickers. That was when another Vespa flew past honking madly at my naked legs. I climbed on, shyly sliding my crotch into Leonardo's rear.

Only now that our genitals were twinned on the seat, I was suddenly full of panic. What if Leonardo were a bearded serial killer in a cable knit? What if I were bound and tossed into the River Tiber?

The vehicle took off and I clamped my arms around him in fright. Leonardo turned to me, a grin hiding beneath the helmet and the ginger beard. I could feel two solid sets of ribs under his sweater and a cosy pair of love handles. The Vespa pottered into the traffic and Leonardo tried a running commentary. Our goldfish bowls clunked together and I couldn't hear. I tried to relax my grip around his middle without bouncing backwards onto the cobbles, but each time we bumped I gripped the strange man harder. We swept onto a busy roundabout with a half-opened ancient Roman vault made of millions of ruddy bricks. I smelt a wave of damp air as from the bottom of a garden. We tore down a main boulevard with a run of glowing shops and fluted church façades, and every so often a lazy southern palm reaching upward.

Leonardo plunged the Vespa into a series of steep crooked lanes before banking to a halt. I nearly flew over his shoulders. Wriggling my bottom back into place, I could only gasp. The spectacular Coliseum stood before us encircled by wild traffic, porous and violet and lit like a gladiator set. Leonardo turned around, cocking his head towards the monument.

He took off again in a slow, puttering circle, as close as possible to the massive building. The stone was so vividly sculpted it looked as though it had been knocked together last month. It was easy to imagine a crowd of feisty Sophia Lorens rocking up in their chariots and roaring tigers ripping Schwarzenegger-style gladiators to bits. From here the Roman

Empire felt like just another football series, tangible and testosterone-driven, with howling Christians instead of wailing WAGs; togas and grapes instead of jerseys and chips. I had a quiet laugh to myself as the marble bones of the Forum pushed into view.

Later, Leonardo smoothly brought the vehicle to a halt outside a restaurant in a side-street. I wobbled off and tugged down my skirt, my bottom stinging and numb. He helped me remove the helmet, nearly taking my ears with it, while I tried to revive my hair. He moved around me with a male gentleness which I couldn't decide was standard chivalry or budding interest. We had just had our thighs clapped together, as it were.

'Don't worry.' He nudged me inside, ahead of him. 'You look great the way you are. Besides, this place is no big deal. It's Fiona's favourite.'

I was beginning to feel disturbed about being slotted into Fiona's place, given he knew we were far from being sisters. Where was the mischievous Leonardo going with this? What was the fundamental truth he had wished to reveal? Leonardo indicated a table by an engraved stone column in the middle of the room. He eased me into my chair and then sat down comfortably. We were given tall menus on rippled card, hand-written for the evening. Leonardo rattled off in confident and lax Italian to the waiter, failing to realise he was the most underdressed male in the room. A couple of women watched him as he spoke, maybe tuned to the richness of his voice. He spoke to me. 'I hope you don't mind me ordering for you. It looks quite fancy, but the cook's a friend of mine. He'll probably come out and say hello soon enough. You do drink wine, don't you?' he said as the waiter poured the obligatory taste sample which Leonardo let swill in his mouth.

I sat back, compelling myself to take three deep breaths before succumbing to the alcohol's generous warp. Halfway through the first glass I had a glimpse of our bodies entwined on mauve bed sheets. I just wasn't sure about the texture of Leonardo's lips through his beard. I refused to nibble at the *grissini*, knowing that one of Fiona's canons was the avoidance of unnecessary carbs. But Leonardo began spooning marinated vegetable *antipasti* into my mouth. I sat there like a young bird in a nest, my mouth swooning for more, my hands placed girlishly over my breasts.

'Mmm,' he mused. 'I'd forgotten the beauty of stirring a woman's appetite.'

My mouth clamped shut. I wasn't going to be brought around as easy as that. Gripping my wineglass, I pitched backwards.

'And yet ....' He grinned. 'One must save oneself for the main course.'

Leonardo smiled coolly as our food arrived – succulent meat and more vegetables from heaven. Involuntarily, my entire body prepared for the kill. The first slivers of flesh I tried sent a salty, seasoned rush through my system and the tension in my body quickly cleared. Leonardo watched me consume it all with satisfaction, refilling my wineglass as I ate. I had never tasted food as magical.

'When you stop for a moment, you'll tell me what you think of the meal,' Leonardo chided.

'Oh, oh!' I paused. 'It's just wonderful. Wonderful. I'm sorry, I was quite starving.'

'Well, if you listen to any of Fiona's diet advice, I'm not surprised. Girl lived on coffee and gumption. Before we speak of our common friend – which I promise we will – why don't you tell me how you two came across each other? I'm sure there's quite a story there.'

'Oh, not at all. It was just through another person, a collision really.'

'You mean your esteemed husband? With whom she had the affair? Okay, I won't press you on that while our food's still warm. Do enjoy your meat.' He ordered more wine, helping himself to a long gaze into my cleavage. It occurred to me that just a few months ago my ex-husband had dumped me in my own kitchen, and here was I in Rome, stirring a foreign man's appetite.

'I'm rather curious,' he continued. 'It's obvious you are not English to the core.'

'My mother was Hungarian,' I replied between mouthfuls.

'And, let's say, you are recently divorced. With one, or perhaps two children, teenagers maybe?'

'Did Fiona tell you this?'

'No, she didn't. I know nothing of her friends and life in Milan. Nor yourself.'

I broke free of his stare and swept the heel of bread over the meat juices and scrubbed the plate clean. I wished I could say I was a war baby, but I had never known food hardship. This was just a blessed dinner.

'*Che buongustaio!* We call that *fare la scarpetta*. You make a little shoe to polish off your food. You make us half-Romans look like we have forgotten how to eat.'

'So you are half-Roman?'

'Well, much of it was acquired on the way. My mother was an Irishwoman who thought she was Audrey Hepburn in Roman Holiday. She not very innocently fell pregnant while studying here, and fled to cousins in New York. She died prematurely in a car accident leaving her childless cousins with an unsought-after burden. They brought me up. I first met Fiona over there when she was a chubby blond sporting an early Madonna look. She was a young and hardy television producer on the rise.'

'And you loved her?' I said boldly, barracking for the early Madonna Fiona.

'I don't dispute that we were involved.' I sensed he was skilfully changing tack. 'You know, Fiona has a habit of picking up strays, that's why I invited you down. I wanted to see who has moved into her life. She can be overly generous, and mildly silly. So why Milan? Are you looking for work there?'

I peered into my red wine. I realised I was more relaxed than I had been in months. I hadn't even noticed they had taken my plate away. I felt time and my surroundings had stilled around me, telling me that this would be a clarifying moment in my life. I wasn't thinking about whether I would sleep with Leonardo any longer. I needed to talk to somebody and the stranger in front of me was all ears. Suddenly I wanted to tell Leonardo everything. That I had gone to Milan because my old neighbour Jean had found love in the Andes. That I was a trained physiotherapist and that my clairvoyant friend said I would end up in a place where I would argue a lot. I wanted to tell him about my husband walking around with a package in his jeans and taking the Henry Moore sculpture from my house. I wanted to tell him that my being here, sitting in front of him, was part of a journey that wasn't going the way I thought it should have been, not in the slightest, and I hadn't a clue where I was headed next.

'Long story, eh?' Leonardo said kindly.

I took a couple of deep breaths as panic seized my vocal chords. How could I tell him any of this? Next, I cleared the deck and jumped into free fall.

'Well, no actually, it's not what you might think. After my husband's philandering I left him for a Swiss guy who has a model agency. We've just had a tiff and I've walked out. He's begging me to come back. Fiona's been wonderful.'

'Oh, really?' he spluttered into his *cabernet sauvignon*. 'So, no teenage kids then?'

'Kids? You're joking?' I couldn't believe I'd said it, expecting a lightning bolt to crack down from Jean-in-Heaven above. It was one thing to abandon your children to your husband's shag-happy lover, but another to deny you had ever given birth. I didn't know what I was doing, but I didn't want to tell him my pathetic story and break down in front of him. I drank up and continued twisting in the air.

'Fiona and I know each from work circles. I was a child actress in Hungary in a big TV show. And then I moved into production. I've been buying foreign material for our major station for years.' (Could that work, a Hungarian Jodie Foster moving into Peter's job?)

'Really?' Leonardo's face was busy realigning. 'I could have sworn you seemed more – if you don't mind me saying so – homely.'

'Oh, I think I'm homely enough,' I said with my most seductive chortle. Surely this was better than weeping into my napkin with crinkled, agonised eyes.

Leonardo seemed a little uncertain. I couldn't work out whether he was impressed or disbelieving. I had never whipped up a greater fib in my life.

'Dessert?' He pulled over the menu. 'Shall I order for you? Or you'd prefer to do it yourself?'

As he called the waiter an older, stooped man emerged from the kitchen in a white mandarin jacket and came across to salute Leonardo. They spoke together in Roman dialect and the cook looked at me with a startled expression saying, '*Veramente?*'

I delicately carved away portions of my *tiramisù* and asked Leonardo what he did for a living. I could feel the raw egg folded into the creaminess and the dappled cocoa powder tickling the roof of my mouth. I felt giddy with my new unchallenged persona. A Hungarian child TV star? Who would ever have thought?

'*Io?* I own an electronics shop over near the Pantheon. It's where the tourists buy adapters and phone chargers and politicians bring in their burnt-out shavers. Nothing like the glamour of you young ladies.'

'Believe me, it's not so glamorous,' I assured him. I heard my phone ringing in my bag and looked to see who was calling. It was Vanessa, the daughter I had just claimed never to have had.

'Oh!' I jumped. 'It's just my boyfriend,' I stammered, groping into the bag and stalking off. 'Please excuse me.'

I marched into the apricot Ladies' bathroom and gripped the phone, already in lather of worry. 'Darling? Darling? This is your mum. What's the matter? Is everything okay?'

I could hear her sobbing at the other end and saw her trapped near a Tube station by a group of thugs on crack brandishing pipes.

'I lost my phone, Mum, with all my messages. Danielle bought me a new one and I have the same number but I lost everything, all my texts from Thomas and David and Ricky.' I listened with relief to the sound of Vanessa heaving over her nonsense and realised this was the sound of my lifeblood. I calmed her down and saw her flawless skin and bright thick hair, the piercing she'd slid through her upper lip that I'd had to save from infection. We had a long talk where she boldly informed me that her father had always treated me like 'shit' and that he was getting his just desserts with hysterical Danielle, who would never transform him into the 'cool dude' she thought she had taken on board. As I listened I loved my daughter so much it hurt.

I went back outside to the table and saw Leonardo's concern. 'Everything okay?' he asked.

I sat down, both embarrassed and reluctant to send off the Hungarian child TV star into the sunset. 'Well, Leonardo, that wasn't really my Swiss boyfriend.' I sighed and began to tell him the truth. I told him it had been my sixteen-year-old daughter Vanessa on the phone, upset because she'd lost all her text messages, whose father Peter (Fiona's ex-lover) had dumped me for a younger sexier model after a string of liaisons during our marriage. I told him about following my icon Jean to Milan and cluelessly bumping into Fiona, who had dragged me to her house. I babbled on and on. About Brett from the dating site turning up with a gay mate at the trade fair, and clairvoyant Pamela with tattoos all over her back. About my miserable day at the *fiera* with Alberta's hats, and all about Fiona's vibrator collection in her bottom drawer. I laughed and sobbed into my plate and Leonardo ordered us chunky glasses of whisky as he listened at length.

Later we rode the wobbly Vespa into the night, all the way to the little electronics shop with its dirty roller door. Here, he parked the bike and told me he had booked a room for me at the hotel across the street. Though I was puzzled, I was relieved. After everything I had told him, the lure of sex had fallen away and I wanted to be alone. Leonardo explained where we were, and assured me he would drop by tomorrow morning before work. He offered me his hand and then pulled me to him in a tight warm hug. Our breathing was in sync for a stretch. Apart from Pamela, I had never spoken so much to another human being.

Leonardo kick-started the Vespa and clicked his helmet strap somewhere under his beard. He waved at me, puttering down the dim ancient street.

The next morning I awoke early and found that my bill had been settled and saw that the roller of Leonardo's shop remained closed. I had known he wasn't going to turn up for coffee. I just hoped he hadn't sent off an email chain-letter to the family saying Fiona was hosting a complete nutter. I found out when the evening train left for the north and went for a stroll. I set out around the girth of the ancient Pantheon rising in ruddy shadow, and discovered it was set in an undulating piazza surrounded by jumbled buildings. The cafés were opening and a few tourists with their cameras stood dwarfed before the dramatic marble columns rising from the podium at the front.

I stood breathless for a few seconds. The building hovered somewhere between the other-world and a blockbuster film set. Inside the huge vault there was a circle of chilly alcoves, each of which originally housed a Roman god. My eyes lifted from the half-dark to the punctured dome opening onto the sky, through which pearly illumination fell in a defined shaft. Peter and I had skipped the 'sights' on our unhappy visit and I now walked around slowly, observing the rich contrasting marbles, my heels clicking where the Roman public had gathered two thousand years ago wearing togas and leather sandals.

It was almost too much. I flaked out in a nearby café which charged the earth for a thimbleful of espresso. Then I looked back enthralled at the remarkable building, grateful that Leonardo had allowed me this discovery. Hadn't Pamela said I would find myself in Rome? The sun heaved up over the cluttered rooftops and I glanced into an apartment where an old man stood by the window smoking a cigarette. In another building I saw a cleaner wiping down window frames, inside and out, and begin to spray the glass. I smelt strong morning espresso all around me and the smell of yeast from a pastry shop wafting from an alley.

It came as no surprise to learn that Leonardo was not the owner of the tiny electronics shop behind the Pantheon. The woman raised her eyebrows and said she had never heard of him. I found his number on Fiona's phone and wondered if I should call him, outraged, demanding that he tell me the truth. But that was a bit tall from Fiona's fake sister, the ex-Hungarian child television star. I studied Leonardo's number for a moment and then deleted it. Leonardo disappeared.

I walked on through the tiny streets of shops and church façades all crammed together, stumbling upon the fabulous *Fontana dei Trevi* where Anita Ekberg had swept into the water with her extraordinary cantilevered bosoms in that black velvet dress. I had seen her interviewed forty years after La Dolce Vita. She was a stringy-haired giantess with a cawing laugh, like the mad lady stashing cat food into her coat at the back of the supermarket. Today the Bangladeshi men were out in force with their incomprehensible writhing toys and armfuls of plastic gladiators, football flags and T-shirts, beaded purses and peaked caps. Gay priest calendars fluttered in the wind and Audrey Hepburn on a Vespa smiled from a fridge magnet. Hungry women tourists knelt to the fake Chanel and Gucci handbags laid out on sheets over the cobbles. Chinese and Senegalese sellers called out in crooked Italian as I walked.

I found a trattoria I liked the look of in a tiny piazza with a delicate baroque church. The warm mustard sun seeped into my body. I didn't have a job yet, nor a reason for prolonging my stay in Italy, but I took the menu from a handsome waiter and ordered lunch.

8. GRAMMATICA ITALIANA

'Ouch! Ah! Stop!'

'*Cazzo! Mi vuoi ancora parlare in inglese?*'

'*O sì!* Oh no! *Smettila!* Stop! Please! *Ti prego! Ti prego Federico!* That hurts! *Non farmi più male!*'

'*Bene cara. Bravissima.*'

'Oh, thank God.'

Slap! … Slap!

'*Cosa osi dire? Ma non mi hai capito?*' (What do you think you're saying? Didn't you understand me?)

'*O sì! Ti capisco, ti capisco perfettamente. Italiano, parlo solo italiano.*' (Oh yes! I understand you perfectly. In Italian, I'll only speak in Italian.)

'*Bene.* Good. You very fast student, Fiona's sister. Almost good, like marvellous. Is good, what you do to me before.'

'Federico, I said I wasn't exactly Fiona's sister. Remember?'

'Oh yeah, whatever.'

Arriving with an aura of Roman serenity had not saved me from my first grammar lesson with Federico. He was fiddling with the television set when I got back to the apartment.

'We have electric storm. All the television set no working. Except yours. Your TV just fine. Just look at Pippo Baudo, he look twenty-five on your TV set, not eighty.'

I laughed grimly. I had made the quantum leap from mad, milling Milan to ancient Rome and realised with disappointment it would take me about five seconds to grovel back. I viewed Federico's lovely shoulders and the last knuckles of his spine exposed below his T-shirt begging for immediate attention. But I lingered on my lonely precipice.

'I'm just in from Rome, you know. It was wonderful.'

'*Sì?* Why you run away like that? Gustavo come knocking here and no find you. He want to thank you for *fiera*, he say you make big sale to Korea, biggest sale they ever make. He say the Japanese cancel everything and Alberta go crazy. Gustavo think you *fantastica.*'

'Gustavo?'

'Only Alberta – you see they always fighting – she say you steal some hat from her and I say, "No, Fiona sister never steal nothing."'

'What? Me, steal?' I was apoplectic. That wretched senile witch.

'I know you no steal. I tell her to shut the fock up. Oh, and I catch thief who take your things at the park the other day, you know your *reggiseno* and new shoes.'

'What do you mean? How?'

'You tell me you think pony-tail guy clean at Duomo. I find him and beat him up. He say you give him things for his wife and sister, so I beat him up again with my little brother. Then he bring me bag from behind *altare*. Big *bastardo*. Here, look at ….'

I took the bag and found my new crumpled underwear and the implausible shoes I had been wearing across the park.

'Now you can give black guy back gymnastic shoes and quit going to dirty park. Now get undress for grammar lesson. *Subito!*'

After the lesson I lay back panting and the first thing that came to mind was the blond girl I had seen Federico with inside the bookshop the other afternoon. I wanted to ask him. I wanted him to tell me it was his cousin from Trentino. But I pushed my face into his chest hair and whispered, 'No.'

'What "no"?'

'Nothing, I just said no to something to myself.'

'Tell me. Tell your *professore.*'

'No, it was just something silly that a grown woman doesn't need to repeat.'

'Grown woman? Grown woman who laugh like this?'

He began to tickle me on my right ear, reducing me to a giggling, begging mess. I rolled away onto my stinging bottom and sprang back involuntarily in pain, meeting him full on, our mouths an inch apart.

'*Dimmi,*' he said. (Tell me.)

'The blond girl in the bookshop,' I struggled.

'*Che cosa? Parlami in italiano.*' (What? Speak to me in Italian.)

'*La ragazza – b-bionda nel – nel negozio,*' I stuttered. (The girl – the blond girl – in the bookshop.)

'That,' he said solemnly, 'is someone who like me a lot. But I prefer my two sister in bed.'

He fixed his eyes on my face like a devotee and I began to liquefy. Then, out of the blue, he said, 'So you ate Alberta's guts?'

'What?'

'You no understand? Fiona tell me you say this one in Australia. You ate someone's guts,' he explained.

'You mean you *hate* someone's guts,' I told him, laughing. 'Do I hate Alberta's guts? No, although she's quite difficult.'

'*Che bella stronza, quella lì,*' he said, shifting me more comfortably into his arms. 'She have daughter in Venice who she fight with and they never talk for ten year. She never see her twin granddaughter. You want you work for them again?'

'No! I mean thank you, but no. She didn't even pay me. It's all bollocks about the hat – she gave me some horrible old thing that I threw away. I'm sorry, but I really never want to see her again.'

'So what you do in Australia for work, baby?'

Baby? I started to giggle. It was an age since I'd been called that. I couldn't help thinking of Peter cooing with Danielle in bed, calling her new raunchy names alluding to their wild sex. And here was my grammar teacher/lover calling me *baby*, the corniest and most adored one in the book.

'I've never been to Australia, Federico, I told you that. In England I worked as a physiotherapist until my divorce. You know what that is, don't you?' I wriggled down and began to massage his right hamstring, probably a neglected football injury which I'd noticed had gone tense at some point during our lesson. As I moved the burning skin on my rump made me wince. Federico 'ahhed' and showed his appreciation immediately, in the robust male form several inches to the north.

'So you work in massage joint? *Mio Dio!* Fiona's sister work in sex place. No wonder your husband leave you.'

'Not at all. More like a clinic, Fede, full of arthritis and sports injuries. I went back to work after the divorce but it all fell through and I came to Milan. Now I'd really like to work again, but I'm not sure how. Otherwise I ought to go home to my children.'

'Bring your children to Milan. Here there is football and fashion. Milan have everything. Look at London, everyone eating sandwich from plastic box. Here we have *Il Duomo* and *Via Montenapoleone.*'

'But no, Federico, it's been wonderful but I think my time is up. I'm not Fiona, you know. Fiona had a proper job, one might assume, but I am very far from that.'

Federico clasped me hard. 'You, Marilyn, must get my Fiona back. I no let you leave if Fiona no come back to marry me.'

For a moment I was terrified of the fervour in his eyes and had a vision of myself chained to the bath tap languishing for his visits, while Fiona danced her life away over the globe and Peter and Danielle took up golf. Then he smiled. 'I know you think I am bad *fidanzato* but Fiona she understand, you keep me good man for her. I work and study and fock Fiona's big sister, that is all I do. I am a good man, *si lo sono.*'

After this we made love slowly with Federico showing off his most tender and articulate side. I fell away declaring I would never go back to London. Then Federico went back to work and I showered at length, putting cold cream on my poppy-red buttocks. I eased onto the couch in my black negligée, irritated by the fabric on my skin and the pressure of the cushion. I was just going to have to toughen up. Next, I picked up my phone and the piece of paper I had torn off outside the supermarket on the high street so long ago, bearing Jean's number in Milan. My thumb hovered over the numbers. I might have missed the plane to the Andes, but I was a world away from the woman Peter had offloaded that Sunday afternoon.

I rang the number with butterflies in my stomach and tried to concentrate upon Jean-the-young-mother-in-the-duck-photograph, not Jean-the-seasoned-woman who had found real love. A female voice answered in sturdy but accented English.

'*Pronto?* Good evening, this is the English Now Language Institute, how may I help you?'

I felt dashed. I had prepared a few lines to help reintroduce myself to Jean, and had imagined our warm exchange in conversation balloons above my head. Instead the sturdy English speaker was waiting for a response.

'Er, I wish to speak to Jean Harper, the Director of the Institute. I'm an old friend from England.'

'I am sorry, but Signora Jean is not here right now. May I know who is calling English Now?'

I cut the line, trembling. Jean had a partner, a business and a love-child. I had Federico, Fiona and a red bottom. I sat there with burning eyes. Ten minutes later the phone rang again with its bright, stupid tune. It was Pamela and I felt a hot teary rush.

'Hey love,' she said in her deep smoker's voice. 'Everything okay? Just felt like checking up on you.'

'Oh fine, just fine.' I struggled to find some words. I didn't know where to start, so it was better to keep a lid on it. Where had all my Roman calm vanished to in my hour of need?

'There you go again,' she said in a soothing tone. 'Trying to push me away. It's all right, love. You'll be fine, the best part's still coming and I have a feeling it won't be half as tricky as you think. Don't mind me, but I think you should wear red.'

'What?' I gasped. 'You know I never wear red.'

'See you next week, dearie. Cheers!'

I switched on the TV and for the next hour watched Chuck Norris's lips moving to another man's suave sexy Italian. Next week? Red? Pamela had lost the plot.

Contrary to what I'd said to Pamela I ended up buying a red dress that afternoon. I told myself that I needed fitting attire to show up at Jean's language school (I would clean toilets, empty waste-paper bins, anything Jean threw my way) and saw a simple fawn dress in a shop window downstairs, with slightly bell sleeves and a clever cut on the bias. It was a shop Fiona had not taken me to so I stepped inside a little warily, expecting to be sprung for pretending too hard to be elegant, not traditionally my neck of the woods. The helpful older assistant – meaning not a flawless twenty-something with her tanned belly on show – said that the only dress left in the large size was red. I immediately shied away. But she urged me deeper into the shop and pulled out the soft, blood-red garment. There was an old Blondie song playing, one that had been everywhere when I was a secretive teenager on the pill meeting my father's colleague after work. I felt a shudder as I realised he would be hitting seventy now.

It wasn't the dress I had been looking for, but it had clearly chosen me. I pulled my shoulders apart and inhaled, pressing my tummy towards my spine and twirling around to see my fine (and sore) rump, twirling again to see my elegant cupped breasts. I still had my mother's clear milky skin on my chest and neck and despite years of laziness the tone was not too bad, although my neck etchings might have been put up for sale. But I wasn't sorry that my youth had vanished for good, nor that age had crept this far along my face. I reached out and took a light trench coat with a belt and big lapels – very Jacqueline Bisset – tied it over the dress while humming to Heart of Glass. I looked great. I began rummaging in Fiona's old handbag for my reissued credit card before my courage faded.

Out in the street a light drizzle had started and I pulled up my wide lapels and walked. The days were shorter now. The footpaths had been cleared of summer café tables and early evening drinkers gathered inside bars with smouldering lights. I chose a place in the next block that didn't look too crowded. Inside I saw a table and chair by the window and as I entered I decided to order a glass of local *cabernet* rather than my regular *prosecco,* given the new chilly weather. I removed my trench coat. A waiter appeared, extending long olive-skinned arms to take the garment. A dozen male and female eyes along the bar were watching me. I checked behind and it really was *me* they were looking at, not some young model who had wafted inside on a draught of air. Without thinking, I raised the glass that had materialised on my table in a general toast, barely wondering how Fiona would have handled the situation.

'*Saluti!*' I called gracefully. A line of glasses joined my toast.

I noticed one man separate from the crowd and advance towards me. Perhaps Pamela was right, it was not half as tricky as I thought. But then I saw it was the Swiss model agency director, of all people. I nearly dropped my glass.

'Do you mind if I join you?'

Hadn't I had left him for dead on the footpath days ago? Was he going to press charges?

'Oh, I probably won't be here for very long. Just until the rain stops. You shouldn't really bother.'

'This rain? This rain goes on until June. You may have a long time of it.'

He smiled as I frowned. Again, I caught a whiff of his woody, pleasant body smell. I scolded myself for taking note, sharpening my memory of the public *frisson* with the ethereal sylph.

'Well? Are you going to allow me to sit down with you?'

I looked behind him, expecting his tetchy girlfriend to emerge from the loo wiping her mouth. Surely this was a sleazy move to claim the window table.

'Oh, you can have this table if you like.'

I half-rose and saw his eyes look down. His arm extended and his hand quickly removed a white fleck from my hip.

'I apologise,' he said as the arm returned to its Swiss orbit. 'A bad habit from working way too long in the fashion industry. You had a fleck on your dress. Do sit down. That dress looks made for you.'

I sat down sedately. 'Look, about the other afternoon. I don't usually run off like that.'

'You don't usually leave collapsed men on the side of the road? I wouldn't be so sure about that. Don't worry, I have an angina problem, aggravated by what I have been going through lately. It was quite quickly resolved.'

'Oh, thank God. I am so sorry.'

'No, there's no need to be sorry at all. It's been a very timely wake-up call. You'll join me for another drink?'

I had guzzled down the *cabernet* and craved another to offset my unease. He had a driven, sleepless look.

'Okay, yes thanks. Where's your, er, that lovely woman you were with the other time? Will there be enough room for her?'

'You mean Estelle? My nineteen-year-old Latvian ex-wife? I don't think she'll be joining us,' he said calmly, waving two fingers to the waiter and pointing to our empty glasses.

'Oh,' I said, shocked into silence. 'That's a shame.'

He looked at me sternly and probably for the first time I looked into his face. In truth he looked like many older men I saw here – tanned and overconfident, plus a multitude of forehead wrinkles he didn't have to give a hoot about. But, unusually, his eyes were velvet grey. And the whites looked bothered, as though he had an eye complaint or he had been crying. 'I've been a grand fool,' he said emptily. 'And I daresay you and the world have been witness. I've thrown away twenty years of hard work. For an insouciant and ghastly cretin. Just what do you think of that?'

I sat there, my smile dangling.

Then he jerked back and looked embarrassed. 'I'm desperately sorry to impose upon you. I'm just a shambolic mess and you were the only face familiar to me and far from the agency. I'm afraid I've bothered you far too unreasonably.' He rose to leave and although I had wanted him to vanish the moment I set eyes upon him, I watched my hand snatch across and grab him by the coat sleeve.

'Do stay, don't go,' I tugged. 'Your shambles can't be any worse than mine.'

He paused and laughed softly through his wounds. We both allowed ourselves to smile. We sat there in silence until we remembered to lift our glasses, making a wordless toast. Then the Swiss model agency director gave himself a name. He was Arnaud Bertrand, originally of Lausanne.

'So, shall we skip the rest of our collective shambles and move onto regional weather conditions?' he ventured almost happily. 'I've heard the first snows have fallen in the mountains now, and they are expecting a very good winter season. Snow is always a metaphor for renewal I find. Winter is so cleansing. I have spent the past five winters in the Caribbean sipping *caipirinha*.'

'Some of us wouldn't complain about that.'

He looked at me oddly. 'I can't see you on a boat. I don't imagine you have sea legs.'

I didn't know if he were dressing me down or isolating an original quality of mine. All I knew was that – with his career choice – he had sized up innumerable quantities of women, each one judged in a matter of moments. I saw him on a boat deck surrounded by topless anorexics.

'I imagine you think I am some Svengali who deserves being brought down to earth with a crash.'

'I don't really think anything,' I murmured, trying not to see Estelle snaking around him. 'I thought we were going to put aside our shambles.'

I heard the beginnings of a hearty trapped laugh. 'You have the skin of someone who should breathe winter and the snow. Do you think people are designed for certain seasons? You know I grew up in a village that was the essence of simplicity. Perhaps I will take you there someday.'

I sipped my wine and grimaced, thinking the conversation had taken a sharp downturn. Perhaps such a charred pick-up line worked on fourteen-year-old Latvians. Outside I noticed an ephemeral white-faced vision walking steadfastly in the rain, pulling together the folds of an astonishing white coat. It was the insouciant Estelle, and I waited for his eyes to fall upon her.

Next, his face went from jaunty speculation to a mask of absolute calamity. He lurched up, combating the urge to stay at the table making small talk with me. I could see his eyes gnashing from one side to the other as his demons tightened their noose.

'I am so sorry.' He clutched my hand. 'Forgive me.' He threw himself outside towards her and I could just hear his muffled cries over the bar music.

Barking mad.

9. LONDON B

Late that night I was alone watching the same eighties soft focus porn show Federico had interrupted on his first nocturnal visit. The heroine in shoulder-pads had been called up again by her exacting boss, the older raven-haired woman who sat at her black lacquered desk. This time, halfway between them lay a shiny riding crop. Just as the camera cut to a vase filled with crisp orchids, my mobile rang. It was Vanessa. I snapped the TV off.

'Mum, are you all right?'

'Yes, of course. Why are you calling so late? What's wrong?'

'You'd better come back quickly, I think.'

'What? What's happened? Is Eddy okay?' I was in free fall, convulsing. I couldn't help thinking: Federico, my lover, my lovely sweet Federico. *I would never have sex again.*

'Yes Mum, we're okay. It's just that Dad and Danielle have split up and we are all back at the house. Dad's drunk and in bed so I waited, but please will you come back?'

What? And soothe that scum because his girlfriend couldn't handle my children? Pick up all the damned pieces?

'Oh Vanessa, I can't take any more of this. Why didn't your father call?'

'Dad's pathetic, he's been calling her all night. She's taken off. He's gone loony.'

I sat in my negligée with tears streaming down my cheeks. The bastard. Was he going to take away this, too?

'Mum? What's wrong? You don't want us anymore, do you?' Vanessa was about to cry.

'Oh God,' I sobbed. 'Of course I do. Well, you and Eddy I do. Not your father. But let's leave that.'

'Mum, I know you're having a good time in Milan. You can go back. Just come and get him sorted. Eddy's been crying. Please, Mum?'

As I listened to my daughter's voice I felt a deep emotion moving inside of me. It was part of my being and it uncoiled softly and with strength. How could I have hesitated? How had I become so selfish and despicable?

'Of course I will, darling. I'm so sorry. I miss you both so much. I'll be there when you come home tomorrow, I promise.'

I took the plane out the next day, leaving a note for Federico on the sofa in my best Italian. I didn't want to pass by the bar to see him in case he decided to chain me to the bath tap, and also because I hated the idea of a Peter-determined cadence further punctuating my life. This would be a damage control mission, strictly for the children.

I caught a taxi from Stansted to the house. After the glamour of Milan's boulevards the passing villages looked grey and glum. Traffic crawled along without the horn-tooting and the suave, staring men. I imagined I felt a touch of what Jean might feel when she flew in: mild shock at the frumpy clothing of people in the streets; a continental haughtiness.

I needn't have worried that a rush of homesickness might overwhelm me, I felt nothing more than irritation that my much more valid life had been interrupted by Peter's unfair play. I even wore the same dress that crazy Arnaud had removed the white fleck from yesterday evening, so I strode up the untidy front path with detached finesse.

Inside, the hallway was in chaos, with shoes and bags and jackets strewn all over the floor. I stepped into the living room, where the grainy curves of the Henry Moore sculpture were back in the middle of the rug. I felt a smile of triumph expand on my face. Peter's road had turned out to be rockier than he'd thought. Then Peter's shabby figure sat up on the couch in a pair of chocolate brown silk boxers.

'Danielle?' he called as he tried to focus. 'Oh my God! Marilyn darling, you're back!' He lunged at my thighs and sunk his destroyed face between them. I could smell his unwashed hair like a pet I remembered having loved once.

'She won't have me. It's over. My God, what have I done?'

I tried to pull myself away from his grip. 'Peter, get your face out of my dress and put some clothes on.' I stepped back and shook out the red fabric, staring at him on his knees. '*Che casino!* The house is truly a mess.'

Peter slumped on the couch, moaning. 'I tried so hard to make it work, God knows I tried.' He looked up at me with the same cruel eyes that had briskly told me to 'move on' and 'savour life', and had sparked with relief when I had booked the singles bus trip. These eyes were now bloodshot and glassy, like a spaced-out ghoul. I knew Danielle would never take him back like this. But did I want this monster?

I shrieked at him. In Italy I had really learned how to use my vocal cords. 'You *tried* to make it work? You *tried* to make your sordid little affair *work?*'

I had half a mind to bring in Fiona's name and really set the ball rolling, but I saw his pathetic hairy legs sticking out from the chocolate boxers and thought that these were the limbs that had wrapped around Danielle, Fiona and myself. How disgusting. I walked out to begin tidying the kitchen, ignoring his sobs in my wake. Every pan I had ever possessed was stacked in the sink, while the stove area was splattered with a radius of orange grease. I saw egg cartons thrust into the tiny disposal bucket I used to keep so clean, and a stack of pizza boxes on the floor. Pinned under Pamela's fridge magnet from Greece was a photo of Peter and Danielle on a windy beach. She clasped his arm, her frizzy hair blown across her face. Peter preened next to her in middle-aged disbelief. Beneath this was a post-orgasm shot, showing Danielle's blurred cheek and ear crushed into the mole on Peter's chest. I had never seen such rubbish. I crumpled them both amongst the egg cartons and pizza debris where they belonged.

I thought grimly of the advantages of living on coffee and grappa as I tied on an apron and rolled back my sleeves. I refused to remove my heels and heard them tapping the linoleum with a remote grace. It was the singsong of my other life. I stopped and breathed in deeply, trying to block out my crying husband in the other room. I saw the other Marilyn Wade sweeping down a Milanese footpath in a trench coat. I saw her looking wistful in the window of a bar. I turned back to my cleaning with gusto and popped on a Pavarotti give-away CD I found in a pile of newspapers. The music drowned out Peter and elevated my spirits. As I cleaned I glanced out to my neglected garden. As if Danielle would have a clue about roses. In all the hoo-ha no one had even given them their autumn prune. But the roses would have to wait at least until term finished. I wasn't hanging around on this battlefield once my job was done.

I called out to Peter, 'What about your job then, Peter? Had any time to get to work lately?'

I walked back out to the living room and began with the rubbish and clothing there, tapping his foot with my shoe. His body odour made me nauseous.

'Wake up, you witless dope.'

'I am not a witless dope,' he whined. 'I gave the car to Danielle while hers is in the garage. I can't find the keys to yours.'

'Well, get up and I'll take you to the station. You might just have to move on and learn to *savour life* again,' I said smartly. 'I know this great singles trip to the north of France.'

He jerked up, putting a new silk cushion between his overused member and the ruthless outer world. 'Marilyn.' He'd caved in. 'There is just no need to be like this.'

I revved the car on the driveway until he finally stumbled out of the front door in a messy suit with a God-awful tie. I supposed it was a gift of Danielle's. He blundered down the front path and got into the car, which soon began to reek of his Rambo-style aftershave.

He began to stare at me. 'You know, you look super. You've taken years off. I'm so grateful you've come to help sort things out. I really am, Marilyn.'

I frowned and told him I would be sleeping in the spare bedroom for a couple of days, and that there was no need to come home if he couldn't keep himself together. I told him I wasn't here to hear about his bloody breakup.

'Hop out, will you,' I said as I pulled up at the station. 'I have to shop. I don't know what you've been feeding those children on, there's not a scrap of food in the house.' He stumbled off clutching his mobile.

I parked in the huge lot behind the supermarket and breezed around to the trolleys at the entrance. Already I missed Milan: the avenues of stone façades with glowing cafés tucked below, the G-strings on revolving dummies and the dense traffic of good-looking men. Here, I bumped into a fuggy red-faced gent walking with a woman wearing a big white plaster on her cheek. I passed a cake shop with racks of buns each seamed with a fat cord of cream. I longed for a *prosecco* trill to set my heart singing.

Outside the supermarket I glanced at a woman taping a notice to the glass. As she stepped back to see if it were straight I nearly tripped over my feet. It was Jean Harper herself. She was wearing a fitted woollen skirt and cropped jacket. A dark-haired baby with ringlets sat on her hip.

It was years since I'd laid eyes on her, but it could only have been Jean. A small black bow tied back her hair in the Italian fashion and there were silver knots on her patent leather shoes. The pair of them looked like envoys from another planet. I stood marvelling as people roamed in and out of the supermarket. I wanted to rush over and grasp her hand. I wanted to touch her little black handbag and feel the texture of the baby's hair.

Jean packed away her adhesive tape and kissed the contented child on the forehead. I stood open-mouthed as she walked away, unlocked a parked car nearby, loaded the baby into a child seat, and drove off.

I hurried up with my trolley to read the sign.

'ENGLISH TEACHERS WANTED IN GLAMOROUS MILAN, ITALY.'

There was a brief blurb and a two different telephone numbers written on tear-off tabs.

This was the second time I'd seen Jean's notice calling me to Milan. My destiny was insistent. I shook as though I had consumed a bucket of espresso.

Thankfully Peter was waylaid on his return from the office, no doubt while collecting the family vehicle from poor, stranded Danielle. I learned this from a vague and barely audible message left on the answering machine towards the end of the afternoon. He sounded exhausted – perhaps the reconciliation with his hussy had taken it out of him. I was pleased, however, that Danielle had relieved us of his presence. This cleared the way for me to face the children.

They came in on the afternoon bus, grins widening as I opened the front door. Hugs all around. In three weeks they had already grown taller and sturdier. I hoped it wasn't from the crash course in sex education from Peter and Danielle. Vanessa almost cried. Eddy, for once, switched off his iPod and followed me into the kitchen with his bag, watching me steadily with hope. I was nervous. I made them ham sandwiches and we sat in the clean kitchen. I recognised their adolescent smells of smoke and sweat and chewing gum steeped into their clothes and hair.

As we sat there I felt a surge of maternal love, a warm tightness that made the years of wretched chores spin aside as their births came reeling back with all their agony and immeasurable bliss, and the evolution of another being within my own reassumed its miraculous and privileged status. I remembered their soft unfinished skulls in my nervy hands as I looked over Eddy's red-headed Mohawk and Vanessa's shorn asymmetrical haircut. I remembered their pulsing baby rib cages as I looked over their crooked school blazers. I thought how they had once shared my blood.

'So what's Italy like then, Mum? Did you go to the football?'

'Oh, like sure she did. Can't you see her get-up?'

'Did you bring us anything?'

'I have football passes for when you come out at Christmas.' I figured Federico could deal with that.

'Gee, I like your bag there.' Vanessa had spotted Fiona's old leather handbag I was still using. She was right, it was a rich woven thing, like a species of small deer. 'And those shoes.'

I wasn't sure how to steer the conversation so just let it run. I'd found some *prosecco* at the supermarket and cleverly uncorked one without piercing the ceiling. I poured myself a fluted glass and gave Vanessa a generous nip in a tumbler.

'No, I want a glass like you, Mum,' she said. Then Eddy demanded one too. Vanessa insisted, 'Go on, you've no idea all the new things we've been trying out.'

I blanched. Apart from the interminable shagging, then what?

'Oh, you should see what she cooks. It's fine for a while. All rice and things, and then after a few days she flakes out and buys soup in cups and won't wash the dishes. Dad tried to help, I mean he bought pizzas and that, but gawd then they'd just fight and go away to shag.'

'Yeah,' complained Eddy.

'In my bedroom?'

'On your flipping bed, Ma.'

'Good gracious.' I gulped. 'Noisy?'

'Oh yeah,' Eddy giggled. 'She shags him something stupid.'

They both snorted into their drinks and I threw back mine, picturing the bedroom quilt I used in winter and feeling its pale blue diamond pattern under my hands. I had made that bed a zillion times.

Vanessa winked, 'Bet the Italian chaps are quite something, hey, Mother? You look like you've been getting some.'

I blushed, but below felt a great clanging of pride. After all the years of Lego bits and nappies and fevers, wet beds, ironing and mud on the carpet, my daughter had returned me my sexual rights. I felt like an endorsed, recalibrated product.

They went off to do their homework and I prepared some simple pasta which was much appreciated. I cooked it *al dente* and spoke a few words in Italian to show off. Then we all plonked ourselves in front of the television and I told them how the sitcom actors spoke in Italian with their mouths out of sync, and that every five minutes a woman in hot pants appeared on the screen to revive the male audience. Peter's name was not mentioned again and we all trailed off to sleep.

I had a wild *prosecco*-induced dream, or rather a series of dreams running into each other, given I woke more than once to drink water. Each time I clicked on the bedside light in the spare room I struggled to comprehend where I was, and this confusion pervaded my subconscious. I saw myself with Peter in Milan; together we caught a train to the park to look for my stolen underwear. Then Danielle, whose face was never entirely revealed to me, was in Fiona's apartment watching Federico and I making love.

Just before dawn I woke again. I drank from the glass next to my bed and the chilly water rushed down my throat. After that I slept until morning. I dreamt I was on a slow train crossing a mountain valley, watching banks of swaying yellow flowers.

I saw Pamela's Bentley careering down our lane as I carried the rubbish bags across the front lawn. She beeped and waved, rearing the old car up the drive behind mine, rushing over to pinion me in her arms.

'I've been thinking so much about you,' she said. 'It's lovely to see you in the flesh.'

I realised how close to me she had been all along as we stood glued on the overgrown lawn, rubbish bags collapsed on the grass.

'There'd better be a bottle of something inside,' she said.

'But it's only nine o'clock.'

'Don't try and fool me. You've been sloshing that grappa stuff into your coffee every morning.'

She marched me inside and I put on the coffee pot and she sat down admiring my curves.

'You're wearing a G-string. I don't believe it! After all these years. Eric tried to get me into one and I felt like a sumo wrestler. And what's with the hiked-up boobs? You look scrumptious.'

I was wearing a grey knit dress I'd found rolled up in the washing basket at Fiona's. It fell in lovely pearly folds.

'It's called underwear, Pamela. A friend made me revamp. They have underwear shops over there like we have Indian restaurants. How are Eric and the kids?'

'Well, Sally lost the baby, so I guess that's fine. The father was about to do a runner and her career is getting on the move. I just did the breakfast slot with that cow again. She's got the clap and hasn't bonked in two weeks. Serves her right. Eric's been picked up for putting car batteries over the fence. He'll never learn.'

'Oh, dammit, I'm sorry. Grappa?'

'Don't be a twit.'

I moved across like an old hand just before the coffee percolator bubbled. I covered the bottoms of two espresso cups and let the cheap supermarket grappa flow.

'You know that smells like Polish bleach?'

'My friend calls it rocket fuel. You just wait for take-off.'

I swirled in a little sugar and we both sat back. 'So how's Our Lady of Milano? What was all the bluffing for the other day?' Pamela began. 'I for one have never seen you look better.'

I went back to the beginning. I told her how meeting Fiona had kick-started it all: how I'd been wandering about the station and Fiona had taken me home; how we'd gone shopping together and she told me about Peter's affairs, including the one she'd had with him herself.

'Oh yes,' Pamela said doubtfully. 'I'd watch that Fiona if I were you. And she said she was off to Korea? Korea my eye. Camden Town more likely.'

'And so what? She's really a lovely girl. She's given me her apartment and the rent is paid up. I'm wearing half her clothes. And I'm ....'

'Shagging her boyfriend?'

'Yes. Federico is just divine. He studies agronomy and he is teaching me Italian and he has a gorgeous ....'

'Irrigation pump?'

'It's enormous. It truly has a life of its own. And he is teaching me Italian. Pamela, you won't believe how.'

And then I couldn't stop laughing. I couldn't tell her.

'It's okay, I saw you wince when you sat down. Jolly good. You've got the language under wraps.'

I tipped back my cup but the liquid was long gone and I was looking at black coffee grounds and smelling a bouquet of industrial-grade grappa. It was indecently early, but I plucked the *prosecco* from the fridge and we adjourned to the living room.

I felt the rocket fuel pulsing behind my eyeballs and wanted to tell her more. Pamela lit up a skinny cigarette and I filled our glasses. 'Oh yes,' she said when I told her about losing my shoes in the park. 'I thought I saw an African chap. Decent fellow, wasn't he?' And then, 'That's right, I remember a group of Asians and that evil woman. A smoker, with awful burnt red hair, right? She had it in for you, eh?'

That was when I told her about the Koreans at the *fiera*, and Federico's noxious aunt. I noticed a tattoo frond escaping on Pamela's wrist as she listened to my tales and the bump of her nipple-piercing through her shirt. I suddenly launched myself over the coffee table and gave her a huge Italian-style embrace with hot tears running down my face.

'There, there.' She rubbed my back. 'It's all been such a journey already, hasn't it? You really have been so brave. Now I think you should stick to your guns.'

'You do?' I pulled back. 'You mean, try to bring the kids out and get a job?'

'Of course I do. I would ride that young man until you get a taste of something more your style. I'm certain it's in the air for you. Work is going to be a little trickier but you'll get there, probably in the most unlikely sector.'

'So what exactly *is* in the air for me?'

Pamela looked away and shook out another cigarette. It was a dodgy moment and we both knew why. In all our years together this was only the second time I had ever asked her what she could see. When we were teenagers, my mother fell ill and was taken to hospital. I asked Pamela. Pamela hadn't been able to look me in the face. For a while I was angry at her for announcing there was no hope. After my mother died I developed a deep aversion for what Pamela could see. Even when I took up with Peter, I never asked her if he were the right man to marry or whether my marriage would fall to bits. Back then, it would have killed me to know that Peter would betray me over and over, and that I would be discarded in my own kitchen on a quiet Sunday afternoon.

'Do you really want to know?' Pamela brandished her fag, pulling back. 'I know I should shut my trap sometimes.'

I sank into my seat. I took up one of her cigarettes and began inhaling ten to the dozen, the nicotine influx colliding with the grappa in my head.

'No, I don't suppose I really do.' For I already knew that Federico could only leave me. I also knew that I would never travel to the Andes and follow Jean's love path. And I was terrified Pamela could already see me back here, watching television in a pair of track suit pants.

'Hey,' Pamela urged. 'How about cracking open that bottle before it warms up, and telling me what the Australian girl has in her bottom drawer? I think it's time I put Eric on his toes.'

We drank ourselves silly after that. I described the contents of Fiona's bottom drawer, remembering each item I had tried and telling her about my favourites. I showed her the little travel item I had packed in my handbag and we both watched its strenuous buzzing. Around midday we went to the Italian restaurant down the road, where a young Italian waitress with worried brown eyes took our orders. It was her first day on the job and her second in the country. Just short of being tremendously drunk, I spoke to her in my survival-book Italian. Pamela looked on impressed. The young woman was an architecture student from Vicenza, over here trying to improve her English. She relaxed and showed relief when she heard I was learning Italian in Milan. It was as if I were part of an inner circle. I felt blessed.

The food was copious and mediocre, and as we ate I told Pamela about my strange interlude in Rome, where the mysterious Leonardo had taken me on a Vespa spin and then out to eat food fit for the gods. I told her how there must have been something between Leonardo and Fiona, but I hadn't been able to put my finger on it. And that Leonardo had put me up at the hotel behind the Pantheon and I had spent the day walking along cobbled ancient Roman streets.

'It must be such a beautiful city,' Pamela said dreamily. 'I can see myself coming to visit you there one day.'

I squinted.

By the time the children came home again my vision for the future had panned out. I would go back to Milan and seriously apply for a job at Jean Harper's language institute. In the month or so before Christmas I would sort out my rent situation with Federico, even if it meant revealing to him that perhaps Fiona would never be his bride. Jean and I would become firm friends and she would definitely have some tips about putting my children into English schools in Milan, and being employed myself would help me financially articulate the big change. I remembered the waitress at the restaurant that afternoon and called up to ask if she would be willing to coach Vanessa and Eddy in exchange for a meal in English once a week. She seemed overjoyed. At dinner over *al dente* pasta I asked Vanessa and Eddy what they thought of the idea of them moving out to Italy with me.

Understandably, both worried about losing their school friends and I knew they had wanted me to say that I would come back to England, and that our lives would resume as they had been before. But, I said with difficulty, I could no longer be the same mother as I had been when I was Peter's wife, and that I could no longer live in the house where Danielle and Peter had shagged like cats.

They sniggered, then looked at me with eyes that wanted to trust and believe and I wondered if I had sounded too tough. I could see Vanessa's eyes severely weighing me up and expected an angry comment to escape.

'It's all right. We know you're right to clear out of here, Mum. You don't need to worry about Eddy. I'll see to him. We'll be out at Christmas time to see you.'

135

I felt small and foolish before her brave twinkling eyes. I saw that she was going to be a stronger, wiser woman than I had ever been. I hugged her warm body madly.

After they had gone to bed I sat in the living room with a nip of grappa and looked over the curves of the Henry Moore sculpture. I already felt removed from this house with its long path of memories dwindling into the distance. I looked at ornaments and photographs on the shelves, at Peter's three awards for record-breaking shows and at the ranks of novels I had sifted through in my calm, suppressed state. Peter and I arrived here as novice parents brandishing tins of paint and gardening catalogues. Exactly when he had started duping me, I no longer cared to know. I realised this life was ending. Ahead lay a broad new landscape I would have to furnish. A catch of fear snagged in my throat. What would I make of my freedom? What if nothing came of it? What if Jean Harper had set the bar a mile too high?

As I sat there I heard a rapping on the front door. It was Peter's knock. I dropped my head back on my shoulders and closed my eyes. However his knock sounded more like his regular self than he had been yesterday, so eventually I pulled myself upright.

He started fumbling with his front door keys and I heard him call out to someone behind him. Then I jumped to the door, petrified he might have his lover with him and the three of us might have to mingle under the same roof.

'Peter?' I called out loudly and heard the keys jar.

'Oh no, wait,' I heard him say to someone.

I opened the door and saw a groovy, upmarket Peter under the lights. He had shaven, but someone had run a hand through his styled fair hair. The lights in his blue eyes were switched on.

'Oh, Marilyn, it's you! So glad to have caught you before you left. I'm not staying so don't panic. Danielle's out in the car there.

Although her own seems to be running again. I thought we'd just check everything was okay.'

'Why don't you bring her in?' I said dourly, the grappa hitting base.

'Oh no, she's a shy thing. Another time perhaps. We'd best be moving. The children are okay? Danielle was worried the, er, split might have confused them. We're back together again now, as you might have guessed. Everything back on track. Perhaps we can all have a drink in the New Year. Mind if I come in to, er, collect something? Just be a second.'

He strode up the hall to the main bedroom and I heard him rifling through papers. He dashed out again, closing the door behind him, with an armful of books and one-hour photograph envelopes. Now I understood. Danielle and Peter didn't wish me to stumble upon their home porn. I felt doubly queasy.

'How about a quick drink of grappa with your ex-wife?' I said, pushing a full tumbler into his hand. Hopefully he would have the mother of all hangovers tomorrow morning.

'Well, just a quick one, so you're not sitting here on your own.' He plonked down the papers and tossed the grappa back. 'Shite! What is this stuff?'

'It's grappa, Peter. It'll help you sleep. Ease your conscience.'

Peter ignored that. 'Well, you're off then tomorrow, that's right? How did you find the children? Don't believe half of what they say. I've caught the pair of them out on some amazing garbage. They can be quite cruel to Danielle – but she's done so much for them. You just wait and you'll see yourself, Marilyn, when the time comes around and your children have to accept your new partner. It's no bag of apples. By the way,' he said cheekily, 'when are we going to meet the new Mediterranean man? It's obvious somebody's been loving you up. I was telling Danielle this afternoon, the change is just remarkable. Going to Italy has done you wonders. We're all awaiting the next step.'

There was another knock on the front door and I saw Peter's facial muscles brace. He leapt up, opened the door and stepped outside. I couldn't understand what they were saying, not even the timbre of her voice. Nor was I game enough to tear open the curtains. Peter's pile of evidence sat on the coffee table and a small photo jutted out of the papers, catching my eye. It was their two bare feet entwined, his yellow and immediately recognisable, hers browner, looking slightly pudgy with a silver toe ring and accurate black nail polish. Somehow this slow, tingling intimacy threw me off more than the corny shots on the fridge.

Peter dashed in, hovering protectively near his pile, pushing the toe composition back to safety.

'We really must be moving on, Danielle has an early meeting tomorrow morning. It's been lovely to sit down with you, Marilyn. All the best.'

He gave me a peck on the cheek and closed the front door, his footsteps pacing quickly down the front path. I heard the car starting up and switched off the lamp so I could open the curtains unseen. A woman with Peter's hand in her frizzy hair put on the indicator and drove off. I pulled back, watching his head cram against her neck.

10. MILAN B

I felt the most extraordinary relief as I finally marched down the aeroplane aisle and looked for my seat. The distracted Italian businessmen on the shuttle bus, the whirring of the turbines on the tarmac, the synthetic smell of the upholstery – these were enough to send me back into a state of unfathomable bliss. I had retrieved my path.

It was a full flight and 11A was a window seat over the wing. I hadn't caught enough planes to have seat number preferences but I knew well enough how to count, so I was quite flustered when I saw someone was already sitting in 11A, and even more taken aback when I recognised a bristly head of grey-black hair. It was Brett, my internet date from London and hat-buyer, reading a Chinese newspaper. I had a briefcase brushing my bottom and turned around to see a tanned Milanese businessman with silvery locks.

'*Mi scusi, signora. Mille scuse,*' he trilled smarmily.

I called to Brett.

'Brett?'

'Yes, Madam?' He smiled. 'I'm sorry. Am I in the wrong seat?'

'Yes, excuse me. I think I have 11A. The window seat.'

He looked at his tab. 'Oh, I do apologise, you're correct. It seems I'm 11B. Have we met before?'

This time the briefcase rammed into my bottom. 'Do you mind?' I squawked.

'*Ma non vuole spostarsi? Non è il momento giusto per fare una chiacchierata,*' he said harshly, saying this was hardly the time for chit-chat. '*Puttana inglese,*' he muttered, shoving past.

Brett changed seats and I manoeuvred my rear past him as every head craned around to watch. 'Where's Roderick?' I asked quickly, using Fiona's handbag as a shield.

'Roderick's back in Provincetown picking up a client. I'm going over to Italy to see some more samples. Then on to Berlin. Have I seen you in a bar some place? Or are you a performer? I have the feeling I know your face.'

'A performer? You must be joking.' I laughed, acting out the bemused Milanese traveller. I pulled away from him slightly as the bucket seats pitched us rather too close together. But Brett plunged over to me breathily. His lips were a violet colour framed with a delicate brown outline. As a young man he must have been irresistible.

'Then where? Do keep me guessing, I love a good hunt.'

I folded my rather large arms and stared off the nosy woman across the aisle. 'So, you gentlemen run a hat shop, I understand?'

Brett chuckled. 'Out the front, yes. Did Roderick tell you that? Out the back we sell equipment.'

'Equipment?' I was honestly thinking horse saddles and stirrups; or fishing tackle and bait.

'Oh, come now,' he said. He drew across the Chinese newspaper and there was a magazine with two men in leather studded Balaclavas wearing tight black trousers with the buttocks cut out. 'Interesting samples. Although between the Germans and the Dutch, it's always a hard choice. But you'd be surprised what you find in unexpected places. Mexico, for example, where I travelled last year. However, I do find that the English use abominable leather. What do you think of this?'

He swung over to a woman whose buttery curves sprang out of a black, laced-up bodice. I giggled.

Brett paused reflectively. 'You know, I seem to remember you now, despite your wish to remain mysterious. It was Hamburg, wasn't it? That club by the port. I don't recall quite everything, but Roderick claims we had a wild time.'

I pulled the Chinese newspaper over the image. A hostess wheeled up the drinks trolley. I hadn't even noticed the take-off.

'Mmm?' He peered like a detective. 'Could I be right?'

'Well,' I said, ordering a gin and tonic, 'these days so much has been happening I'm afraid my memory is quite like a sieve.'

'It was a three-way, wasn't it? In one of those booths out the back with that darling Finnish boy. There *are* some moments of pure clarity that one never forgets, isn't that so?'

I sat there stunned, gulping my drink. I thought a three-way was a sort of bypass on the M25.

Brett had ordered a Bloody Mary, which he looked at unhappily for some seconds. 'Bad choice Brett,' he announced to no-one in particular. 'You should have followed the lady's example and taken a gin and tonic.' He called the hostess, but in her place came a fluffy-chinned steward with a pimple close to his lip. 'I'm sorry, son. Could you whiz this into a gin and tonic for me, please?'

As the steward took Brett's drink, his eyes landed on a young hooded man on his knees in handcuffs. He turned crimson. I wondered with shock what might have lurked behind the orange ducks in the Cantonese restaurant in Soho. I sat there aghast.

'A little young, but interested. How Roderick chastises me for my wandering eye.'

Involuntarily I stammered, 'Can you doubt he's not doing the same thing?'

'Of course,' he admitted. 'Men being such confounded buggers.'

An older, beefy attendant brought Brett his drink and peered at the innocuous Chinese newspaper now draped over his lap. He stared at me accusingly. Brett smiled with wide, perfect teeth and the broad-shouldered man backed off.

We drank in silence. After the damp and rainy lowlands, there rose the icy pinnacles of the Alps. Intoxicated by gin, we both looked down. The sunlight caught on webs of ice while towns thinned along the green folds of the earth. I remembered someone had recently spoken to me of snow as a metaphor for renewal, and then I recalled it had been the crazy Swiss man, whose head was full of it. Presently we began to drift down towards the industrial plains of northern Italy, with their factory boxes and silvery roads traversed by determined beetles.

'At last. Touchdown time nears,' said Brett happily. 'I have quite a programme over the next few days. You're in Milan, aren't you? Care to join myself and a couple of friends for drinks? I could have you try out some samples for us. Roderick is not very multilateral but I tend to be utterly democratic.'

'Oh,' I gasped. 'I couldn't possibly. I'm off to Lausanne tonight. I – I have an engagement.' What on earth was I saying?

'Lausanne? I'm afraid I can't abide the Lausanne set. Is it private?'

I nodded.

'Well, do take our card, dearest. In London I work behind my cousin's restaurant in Soho. We run trials and do product selection and sometimes host the type of events you know well.' He winked. 'With *your* credentials and talent you'd be more than welcome. And by the way, don't mind Roderick, his deep dislike of the English is due to his mother abandoning the roost for a young baron Roderick was smitten with as a child. Roderick's pique knows neither logic nor depth.'

We touched down smoothly. I almost tugged his sleeve, about to tell him that this was a huge mistake, that I was a small-minded divorcée he had picked up on the internet who had never been to Hamburg, let alone seen people wearing buttock-free leather pants. But I said nothing. He helped me on with my coat and we walked along the airbridge off the plane into the terminal. As we headed for passport control I was petrified his tongue would invade my mouth again as on our Soho date. However Brett gave me two respectful pecks on the cheek and disappeared into the crowd.

This was the second time I'd passed through Malpensa Airport in a month. I thought back to the distraught woman leaning against a pilaster a few weeks ago, wishing for a nuclear meltdown between her legs. I remembered her intimidation before the Sophia Loren official with her lavish eyebrows and tanned breasts. I pulled out my passport for the same feisty brunette and levelled her in the eye. She stared back like a storm trooper on battle alert, glancing quickly at my hair, my accessories and makeup, even lifting her chin to see what she could of my elegant woollen dress. This time there was no snide comment to the sexy young guard, who was too busy checking me out in any case. I saw that I had cleared both hurdles and collected my passport.

Out in the luggage hall I looked around for the young policeman from my first trip. I remembered how bereft I had been on my arrival that afternoon; how I had shuffled over the gleaming marble in a trance; how he had administered my first miraculous cup of espresso while distractedly caressing the wolf-like dog. Suddenly I saw him parting the crowd and heading towards me, the same animal pulling the leash taut. I beamed with pleasure until the dog's nose plunged into my groin and began vigorously sniffing my handbag. Then I saw the steely glint in the young officer's eyes. I started to swoon.

'*Venga con me, signora,*' he said as people stopped in their tracks. I saw his grip tighten on the leather leash and felt a hot trigger burst between my thighs. He thrust his other hand under my arm and closed his fingers assertively on it, sweeping me along.

He pulled me into a different room this time and softened his grip, indicating I should sit at a huge, beige-topped table. Impressed by his dashing ploy, I waited for his grin to break out. Instead he unclasped a radio from his belt and began to murmur. I became concerned. The creaminess of my arousal suddenly curdled.

'What's wrong? *Cosa succede?* Why am I here?' I tried to think again, willing myself to reason. It was the dog. The dog had sniffed something in my bag. Had Brett planted drug samples on me? Holy shite! I would be locked away with *mafiosi* and my children would touch my fingertips through greasy panes of glass. The officer said nothing and stood to attention by the door. His full lips were pulled downward and his arms folded like a bodyguard. I clasped my bag to my chest and wept.

Presently, a second officer came into the room with a jacket bearing more braids and stripes, clearly more senior. My head was running through who I should call: Peter? Federico? Jean Harper? That was great. My future employer would learn I had been sprung for running drugs. And then Peter would get custody of the kids while I lived on gruel in pyjamas.

The senior officer sat down, grimacing, and then his face eased. I had seen enough police shows to know that everything I said would work against me, and realised that even my great blobs of tears on the table had already done their share.

'*Signora, gentilmente, vuole consegnarci la sua borsa? Mi capisce?*' he said kindly. 'Would you pass the bag, please?'

I placed Fiona's handbag on the table expecting to notice for the first time the five pound bag of cocaine Brett had sandwiched inside. I saw myself trying to explain: *He is from Hong Kong. I met him online the first time. They have a hat shop in Provincetown, you know, with a sort of leatherwear section out the back.* I started to feel short of breath as the officer opened up the zipper and began to pull items out onto the table. I saw the last condom packet I had opened with Federico, Fiona's phone, an emergency G-string, photos of my two kids as babies, my wallet and documents and the small lilac travel vibrator of Fiona's I thought I might have needed on the trip. The junior officer's eyes widened. His colleague calmly opened up the device and popped out the two batteries, shaking it to his ear.

'*Hai visto, Martino, cosa ci regala la tecnologia?*' he said to the young man. (Martino, have you seen what technology has given us?) '*Sì, signore.*'

Martino gulped.

His boss placed the vibrator on the table and began feeling through the interior of Fiona's small deer bag. Very soon his eyes hardened. I saw Martino's face tense. The senior officer pulled out a tiny surgical knife and made an incision in the lining where he extracted a roll of coloured pills twisted in plastic and what looked like a sachet of hemp. I blanched rather than cry again, having been no closer to recreational drugs in my life than I had to Brad Pitt in his underwear.

'This is not mine! *Questo non è mio! Voglio chiamare un amico,*' I said as distinctly as I could manage. I needed Federico to tell them the bag was Fiona's. Federico's girlfriend was the one they should be looking for, and she had taken off to Seoul.

'*Sì, sì, signora.*' The officer sighed. '*Dicono tutti così.* Everybody say this one.'

He pushed the phone my way and I desperately scrolled down to Federico's name. It rang and rang for ages and I had a vision of him toying with the blond girl's hair while she dreamily read a book. Finally he answered and my eyes squirted tears of relief.

'Where you go, baby? I have big toy to give you. You never learn *italiano* if you disappear. Are you with Fiona?'

'Darling. I'm at the airport, the *aeroporto di Malpensa*, and I went to England for my children and now they have found drugs in Fiona's bag. I need to you help me.'

'*Che cazzo dici? Ma vai proprio in cerca o sbaglio?*'

'Federico, I don't understand you, please come here.'

'*Madonna che pasticcio!*' he said angrily. 'I no understand why you always find mess. Here I wait to fock you bad and teach you *italiano* and you go to England and buy drug!'

'I didn't buy drugs.'

'I tell you, you have red *culo* after this.' He clicked off and I didn't know whether it meant he would come to my aid or not, so I told the senior officer my friend was coming to explain everything and I began to pray. I watched him make an incision in the plastic roll of pills and put a couple on a stainless steel tray. He did the same with the sachet of hemp, although the substance he removed looked like a sprig of brown grass. I saw the dog's ears lift and a look of contentedness came onto its face. Stupid mutt. The officer snapped open my passport and frowned at the dowdy post-divorce photograph I had taken for the trip to Rouen. That was when my hair fell flat around my broad shiny face and my eyes were tight and hurt. He looked back sceptically.

'*È lei, questa donna?*' (Is this woman you?)

I nodded as he shook his head.

'*È sicura?*' (Are you sure?)

I could have wept again. I had moved mountains.

The senior officer left the room with his samples and Martino walked up to the coffee machine at the end of the room. He pulled out two tiny cups from a long stack and slotted them under the two spouts. I thought of Federico and prayed he was dodging through traffic, hoping he hadn't abandoned me for the young blond. The coffee aroma pervaded the room and I inhaled. He placed the cup by the refuse from my bag, avoiding any contact with the lilac vibrator lying naked next to my wallet.

'*Quanto zucchero?*' As he glanced at the open passport I saw his face twang with recognition.

'*Ma lei è già stata qui, vero?*' (You've already been here, haven't you?)

He remembered me. Though my liberty hung by a thread I was thrilled to the back teeth that the young stud had recalled my existence. He mimed the two of us drinking coffee together and pointed in the direction of the other staff room, the one where they didn't bring criminals. I was enchanted. His hand swept down my body, indicating there had been a miraculous change.

'*Italia, vero?*' he asked proudly.

'*Sì, sì,*' I said like a dumb cow. '*Italia, sì.*'

He then pointed disapprovingly at the vibrator. '*Ma questo, in Italia, no, no! Non ce n'è bisogno.*' He was telling me there was no need for it in Italia. He then vaguely indicated his nether regions, and put his hands apart in the air like a fisherman describing the one that got away. I showed that I was impressed. He shrugged his shoulders and smirked.

He leant across. '*Posso?*' He reinserted the batteries and I showed him how to clip on the top and wind it around to vary the speed. He frowned at the buzzing machine and went from the first to the fastest velocity. '*Però!*' he said, like a guy with a new gadget. '*Bello?*'

As he looked over enquiringly and I was agreeing with a happy nod, his boss re-entered the room with another policeman. Both of their eyes landed upon the lilac member whizzing in the young man's hands.

'*Tenente Michelini!*' shouted the officer. The young man leapt to attention against the wall. The little machine buzzed on merrily until the senior officer reached out and switched it off. He looked at me sternly. He moved to the table and dropped my drugs onto the rest of my paraphernalia.

'This drug is *caramella*, it is sugar. And your *erba* is grass from somewhere out of *Italia*, maybe Australia. You are very stupid woman doing stupid *barzelletta* to *polizia*. Go now.' He then began to yell at Martino, indicating the dog cringing on the floor.

A knock sounded and Federico was ushered into the room by a policewoman.

'*Carissima!*' he cried, rushing to me. The officer stared in bewilderment at my young robust lover pinioned against my

147

generous Hungarian bones. 'Say notin,' Federico whispered in my ear while wailing loudly.

Then the yelling started on all fronts. The officer began to yell at Federico, who yelled back soundly. Martino added his two pennies' worth and I know something insulting was said about the cheeky lilac thing, as I saw Federico's eyes glance at it, blazing. The policewoman piled my things into my handbag and urged me outside while the men argued.

Moments later Federico burst out of the room. He stormed through the building while I half-jogged behind him all the way to the car park. He unlocked the car and floored the accelerator, screeching onto the autostrada in a matter of instants. His hand travelled over and rummaged in my handbag. He pulled out the vibrator and shook it at me.

'This, does it look like my *cazzo?*' He was furious.

'No, no, darling. Not at all.'

'*Rispondimi in italiano!*'

'*No Federico, non è come il tuo c-cazzo.*'

He threw the object out the window and it bounced merrily under an oncoming truck.

11. CRUEL BLISS, HARD-CORE SPECIALITIES

Late one morning after my return from England I was awoken by an angry rapping on the door. I worried it was Federico calling in for an untimely grammar lesson after a night on the town, or that the wife of my sleazy neighbour was beating down the door in search of her husband. I rolled my negligée down my thighs and glanced at my face in the mirror by the coat rack. I'd had my first facial two days ago and brought home a selection of silky creams. For an old hag on her second wind, I thought I still cut the mustard. I shook out my bangs and thought of the raven-haired woman with the riding crop up in the Hollywood hills. I wondered if Fiona had a riding crop and a pair of thigh-high boots stashed somewhere.

Probably the last person in Milan I expected to see was Alberta, my vicious *fiera* boss, but there she was on the landing wearing a temporary greeting smile and a woven Chanel suit, several heavy necklaces layered over her flat chest like chain-mail. I saw she was in city warfare mode, with gold cluster earrings and a swab of scary red lipstick. Unable to form words, I cringed behind the door as her eyes swept into the shuttered half-dark. She marched in and I pulled my negligée further downward. My suitcase still lay on the living room floor after my trip to London and I had barely managed to hand wash some lingerie. The dry cleaning lay sprawled out on the divan where Federico and I usually studied so diligently. I wondered if there was a whiff of red ass in the air.

Alberta went shamelessly into the bedroom. She jerked up the blind with her bracelets clanking and a bar of milky morning light seeped into the room. In an instant my eyes were buzzing and I knew I had tumbled into some sort of family black hole, even before Federico's name showed on my phone which started ringing on the dresser.

'*Amore?*' I answered.

'*È venuta mia zia Alberta da te?* My aunt Alberta? She is? *Quella stronza?*'

'*Er, sì-sì,*' I stammered. Whatever happened to the simple times, when we looked ahead to the big family wedding party and enjoyed an in-house prenuptial fock?

'Look, I speak *inglese* to be faster. Alberta want apartment for her *figlia* and *gemelli*, I think you say her daughter and twin *bambine*, who come from *Venezia*. Now they all make peace and come to live in *Milano*. My father talk to Gustavo for apartment and they have big fight.'

'But Fiona said the rent is paid for three months. You people can't do this to me. What about my ....'

I was about to say my *life*. Already I saw myself back at home in dumpy clothes, trimming roses and smoothing the Danielle-soiled quilt. I felt a monstrous rage flare up inside of me.

'Look, my baby,' Federico said. 'I can do nothing. I find you another place just like, even better with big television screen. I fock you with Fiona toy all day and let you give me sexy massage.'

I cut off the call and turned to Alberta's smug yellow face. She stood there savouring my agony as the wintry air from the open front door wove through the apartment and seized my bare legs. I shivered as the goose bumps travelled over my skin. Then I heard shoes clattering up the stairs below. They were children's feet. A little girl's voice called out '*Nonna?*' and two identically dressed ten-year-olds burst into the apartment.

They began to stare with incredulous eyes at the half-dressed woman frozen in front of their grandmother. What if my own children saw me dressed like this, about to be thrown onto the street in a silk negligée?

It didn't take me long to pack my belongings. I found my old suitcase tucked in a broom cupboard and stashed in as many dresses and shoes as I could. Alberta's nameless daughter finally puffed up the stairs. She was broad and out of shape, unlike her razor-edged mother. Her head had broader bones too, more like Federico's, but her small and noxious eyes were tilted at the same severe angle as her mother's. Her hair was dyed an unnatural racy blond, and her fawn skin had been coloured in a tanning cubicle, so that inside her billowing fur coat she looked like an overweight Venetian hobbit. Mother and daughter began to speak as though I were a Polish painter in the room, unable to understand their language. But I knew enough of what they were saying to want to crawl under the bed and hide.

'*È quella che sta dietro il tuo cugino.*' (She's the one who's been running after your cousin.)

'*Guardala, nuda così, si vede subito che non si vergogna di niente.*' (Look at her, naked like that, you can see straightaway she doesn't have a scrap of shame.)

I knelt down to Fiona's bedside cabinet and took out my favourite vibrators, remembering that first night when Federico had picked one up from the floor and I had cracked his chin. My eyes blurred with tears. One by one I took down the damp items of lingerie hanging in the bathroom and placed them in an empty shopping bag. I peeled off the negligée and put on some steamy black underwear, throwing on Fiona's grey dress. I remembered to pack my new collection of creams and a handful of Fiona's condoms. I wasn't going to leave them for Alberta's little squirts.

When I came out to look for my shoes I heard Alberta already at work in the kitchen while the twins had turned on the TV set and thrown themselves on the divan. I stumbled over to Fiona's sparse bookshelves and took down her dictionary and the grammar book I'd been studying. Savagely, I grabbed the signed George Clooney picture. Alberta's hobbit daughter looked across

151

at me, tugging a chunk of gold on one of her ear lobes. Like Alberta, she smelt of smoke from a mile off and looked as though she hadn't been undressed by a man in a decade. She stared as I gathered my suitcase and shopping bags together at the door and began pulling on my coat. As soon as I was outside I paused, blubbering on the landing, and she quickly slammed the door behind me.

My life had come apart again after just a few days. How could I have thought that I could step into Jean Harper's blessed shoes by teetering around in Fiona's tacky heels? What on earth had I been putting into my morning coffee? Sobbing, I dragged the suitcase downstairs, landing by landing. At each one, I puffed back to collect the shopping bags, so that by the time I reached the street I was a wreck. I pushed onto the footpath feeling like the local bag lady in high heels. Familiar faces and shopkeepers watched my laboured progress. Gobsmacked, the girl in the underwear shop doorway dropped her cigarette and shook her head.

But I staggered away from Federico's zone and hauled myself onward. I trundled over pedestrian crossings and stumbled over tram tracks and kerbs. I craved a *caffè corretto* with every step. All around me shoppers and mothers and old women watched my efforts with detachment. Young men glanced at me as their dogs urinated on trees. Filipino nannies frowned as they pushed their four-wheel drive strollers. By midday I noticed shopkeepers in aprons using their hooked steel rods to yank down their front rollers for lunch. Suddenly the bus stops were full of staring, smoking teenagers on their way home from school.

Finally what had happened this morning began to seep in. I realised I wouldn't ever be returning to Fiona's house. Never again would I sit on her couch watching Charles Bronson or Bruce Willis speaking out-of-sync Italian. Never again would I greet the formidable George Clooney as I waltzed into the living room. That was when I sank down on my suitcase and began to weep. I hadn't a clue where I was going. I hated Milan. I knew I should never have come here.

Then, across the road, I noticed an older man with a shiny head standing in the doorway of a bar. I realised he'd been watching me for some time. His head was cocked to one side and he had a pleasant half-smile. He checked the traffic, stepped onto the road as a fine rain began to descend, and walked towards me. I was overwhelmed. I wiped my smudged eyes. He took hold of my suitcase on its shoddy wheels, lifted the bags, and looked at me, the half-smile spreading.

He led me across the road and into the bar, where he settled me by the window and took my luggage out the back. Wordlessly, he served me a full glass of red wine. I rubbed my cheeks, looking at my reflection in the glass: my nose was glowing bright red and my hair was a mess; my hands were burning from the cold.

It took a long while to thaw, three or four glasses to be exact. The bartender brought over a couple of tuna *tramezzini,* the first food I had touched that day. He smiled as I struggled to swallow. Outside, people had begun to push onto the footpath after the long lunch break, unfolding umbrellas or beeping the alarms of parked cars. A barber across the road rattled up his metal shutter and stood in the doorway rubbing his hands. Young boys went off to football practice with big sports bags thrown over their shoulders.

The man began upending chairs and drew a bucket and mop onto the floor. I made a motion to leave and he urged me to sit down as he lit a cigarette. He said he didn't mind if I stayed. He turned up the radio and I watched him, mesmerised by the swishing of the mop. I was about to think it might be the perfect occupation for me when he passed me a business card he picked up from under my table.

The card read:

CRUEL BLISS
HARD-CORE SPECIALITIES
BEHIND CLOSED DOORS
SOHO, LONDON
PROVINCETOWN, MASS.

At first I shook my head and handed it back to him. Then I realised: it was Brett's card, the one I had pocketed at Malpensa as I prayed his tongue wouldn't enter my mouth. That day I had imagined Brett was walking away from me into oblivion. Now he had turned around and was striding back.

There was a string of telephone numbers with different country codes from all over the world. Some of them I recognised: Switzerland, Hungary, Germany, Poland, perhaps Australia and Japan. I found a Milan number. As I punched in Brett's number on Fiona's mobile I was astonished how the work of the alcohol made this feel like the most logical course of action.

On the other hand, I knew it was the most insane thing I had ever done.

'*Pronto?*' Brett said curiously. 'Hello there? Surely this must be my sculpted friend with the stunning facial bones?'

How could he know? I felt utterly ghastly and went to hang up. Brett must have registered my hesitation. 'Now, now, no need to be shy with me. I heard what happened at your Swiss do. Unremarkable, wasn't it? Well, don't say you weren't forewarned. And no doubt you've heard about Roderick's bash upstairs tonight? So glad you've decided to touch base and stop being so *elusive*. There's a bed made up for you. Just throw out that devilish hand of yours and find yourself a cab. Here's our address.'

I looked over to the gentle man rinsing the mop. It made me ache to see something so straightforward occurring before my eyes. Outside the rain had thickened. It splattered off the car windscreens and people huddled past with umbrellas. The bartender opened the door one more time and a rush of damp cold air grasped my ankles. Whatever Roderick's bash might entail, it was going to be better than hauling all my belongings around looking for a hotel, and spending the night watching a pair of go-go girls on TV.

Ten minutes later Brett threw open the front doors and tried gallantly to shield me from the rain. He pushed some money at the driver and made no nonsense of carrying my stuffed suitcase and bags inside off the street. In the foyer a young Oriental man came out immediately to help him. They both looked at my dishevelled state kindly.

'Well, my damp beaver friend, there was no need to run yourself into the ground, was there?' We stood dripping on a woven mat under a modern light fixture made of gold planets. He rolled his eyes as I stared up.

'Roderick's taste. He's a friend of the designer. Now do follow me.' He gave me two pecks on the cheek and began leading me down a broad hallway with several closed doors. I paused. Never had I so recklessly followed a man down the garden path. I remembered Brett's catalogue on the aeroplane, with all the faceless models in leather suits. But I was so desperate and cold I told myself didn't care. Brett opened a door to the right and a warm welcoming smell came over from the darkness. I listened hard: I couldn't hear any whips or squeals.

Brett switched on the light and I followed him into a room where Jane Austen might have felt at home. There was a silk canopy draped over a wooden bed that ended in twin carved scrolls. It must have been oak or chestnut, a lovely warm wood. On the walls there was an array of antique prints. They were

Greek perhaps: big-chinned warriors with shields and knobbly legs. I exhaled. Brett had morphed into another of my Milanese saviours.

'Let me introduce the very trusty Lam.' Brett winked as his assistant wiped down my suitcase and placed it on an old chest. Lam tried to arrange my drenched plastic bags.

'Why don't you rest yourself for a short while before this evening's delights?' Brett suggested as the pair withdrew. 'An indulgent afternoon nap.' I dropped my wet clothes to the ground and crawled under the covers.

I shook and tossed in the bed thinking of crafty Alberta and her hobbit daughter pawing through my things back at Fiona's place. But then I must have fallen into a deep, wounded sleep. At some point my ex-husband Peter was conjured up in my dream. Even as I dreamt I was shocked. He was standing in Fiona's kitchen and I came to him in my new black negligée. We stood staring at each other. Then Peter's hand caressed my thigh. For an instant I parted my legs, absurdly wanting his fingers to travel north.

My dream was interrupted by a chuckle.

A dark, shirtless figure was standing over me. 'Honestly,' it said as the hand withdrew, 'if I didn't have Roderick in such a stew over the sound system I assure you I'd welcome the distraction. How about seeing if this is your size?'

It was Brett, standing over me holding a black item that twisted on itself like a snake skin. I saw that I was in a naked tangle with his silk sheets. 'Good God!' I gasped. I remembered I had consigned myself to Brett's house. And now Brett had almost consigned himself to me.

He held up the black thing, which I realised was one of the garments from his magazine, complete with double-stitched air vents and peep-holes. I jerked to the other side of the bed, clutching the sheet.

'You must be joking,' I whispered.

'That's of course if you haven't packed anything more startling yourself,' he said, glancing at my demure pile of goods. 'I'm certain it's your size. You know I have a knack for perusing people's dimensions. Let us see if I have understood you.'

He reached over and squeezed my ankle, but this time he was like a long lost girlfriend I couldn't disappoint. Had Brett really laid his hand on my naked thigh? He left the room as I lay under the covers hyperventilating.

Shortly afterwards the handsome Lam entered with a tray of tea. I peeped out from the bedclothes. Then I stared into the canopy over the bed until my eyes started to waver. There had to be a way out of this. Perhaps I should have tried to get along with Alberta's daughter. Perhaps the mopping barman could have given me a job. I felt for my lifeline, Fiona's mobile. I looked at my incoming calls and saw with satisfaction that Federico had called *twenty-seven times*. I started punching in Pamela's number and then I stopped. I knew what Pamela would tell me. Pamela would laugh herself silly and tell me to squeeze into Brett's gear.

I looked down at the leather outfit lying on the bed. Surely if I pulled some dry clothes out of my bag I could do a runner. But I knew I couldn't face walking out into the rain again. I gripped my teacup, staring at the antique prints framed on the walls. I realised they were half-naked Greek wrestlers in combat, each one with a long bouncy penis like a banana.

Cazzo!

When the last tea in the pot was stone cold I straightened the covers and had a long shower in the bathroom. Afterwards I massaged my skin with the rich cream by the sink until it felt buttery and smooth. I walked over to the outfit on the bed. Brett was right, the leather quality was astonishing. The substance rippled in my hands and the stitching was extraordinary.

I worked out where the trousers began and started to wriggle into them, my thighs turning into two black-skinned sausages. As I tugged at the waist I realised there were two round punctures over my buttocks, whose flesh squeezed out into the cool air. Shocked, I ran my hands over my naked bottom. All around me the Greek wrestlers lunged in their frames, bananas wriggling. I picked up the leather top and began straining into the tight sleeves, lacing my trembling breasts into the bodice. My skin broke out into a fine sweat as I heaved.

At this point Lam slipped into the room with a fitted leather cat mask, which he guided over my head. I tried not to shriek, pretending this was the type of gear I tossed on every other day of the week. When he left I stood back and gazed at the sleek busty feline before my eyes. Staring back at me, I saw a cross between Suzi Quatro and Sarah Ferguson.

I slipped into the heels awaiting me and picked up the first riding whip I had held since my one unfortunate riding lesson, when I fell off the horse. I whirred it through the air, feeling a thrill. Then I noticed a bucket of champagne had replaced the teapot by the bed. I extended my leather-bound arm and threw down the first flute. The room became grainy and soft-edged as I prowled around hearing the swish of my black sausage thighs.

Outside I saw a light was on down the hallway, beckoning towards an internal lift. I walked up and stood in front of it. The doors opened. I felt a wave of human warmth expelled and heard an echo of thumping music. I took the lift up to the top floor where the doors opened onto a spectacular triptych of writhing bodies.

For a second I stood pinned in the light. Then I groped my way into the densest shadow I could find. As my eyes adjusted I grabbed onto wet limbs, and horribly, some of them grabbed back. I tumbled onto a gritty couch bearing three or four people in a monstrous embrace. Tearing away, I elbowed through onlookers with glazed eyes and dodged a man wearing nothing but a studded collar with a chain dangling down his back.

Then, as I stood wondering how to escape, a warm hand spread over my tender left buttock and I swung round to deliver a slap. But I saw that it was Brett himself, bare-chested, in leather trousers. The kohl around his eyes made him look like an ageless eunuch.

'Have you ever felt a softer product?' He came close to me, panting with slightly unpleasant breath. 'I'm convinced this is the range for the season. From Mexico, would you believe?'

He handed me a glass of champagne from a passing tray and I guzzled it straight off. Brett studiously ran a finger along the seams restraining my uplifted bosoms.

'This stitching is just marvellous. Just look at these borders. I believe we can enter the Japanese market with this product, don't you think?'

'Gosh, I love this song!' It was some old hit from the eighties and I took a running leap onto the dance floor. A bank of smoke passed over the crowd. Purple lights picked out a couple clamped together like rabbits under a bush and a British pop has-been wearing a dog collar and leash. What was it with dogs tonight? I grabbed another glass of champagne, swinging my riding crop into the air and starting to lash out the words. The wild disco girl trapped inside of me had decided she wanted to break loose.

Three songs later I collapsed onto a divan in a wheezing lather. Brett was right: the outfit neither chafed nor felt uncomfortable, though the heels were killers. If they played Blondie again I would have to pass.

I lazed back, noticing an older man sitting not too far away. He also wore a silly cat mask and the skin of his bare shoulders rippled comfortably against the cushions. He tilted his head to watch two young women getting deep down and racy together. Any moment now I expected him to stride off and join them, performing some lurid act I would revisit in my crinkly old age. Instead he turned to me and I could see a pair of jaded grey eyes.

We inched closer. A shirtless waiter wearing chains passed with a full tray of drinks, so my leather-bound companion grabbed a pair. We gulped these down and he took two more. A pleasant, woody scent came my way.

We turned to each other and stared through our silly masks. Quite slowly, he placed his considerable hand behind my neck and cupped my head, approaching my mouth with his. I threw away my glass and kissed him. I couldn't remember feeling a man's lips dissolve into mine so rapidly, and a tongue that tasted so good. I clambered onto his lap and threw my leather arms around his neck. We squashed noses and my catsuit squeaked against his. His arms travelled down my back, finding the gap above my waist and squeezing my bare buttocks.

I opened my eyes and realised both of our masks were askew. Holy Greek wrestlers! I had seen this man before. It was crazy, barking mad Arnaud Bertrand.

Arnaud tore off my mask and put his hands into my hair. 'Oh my God! It is you, I can hardly believe.'

Immediately the alcohol wore off and I tried to jump away but Arnaud Bertrand gripped my thighs with force.

'What are you doing here?' he yelled over the music.

I shrugged, not very convincingly given the tautness of the suit. I bent close, inhaling him with greedy shock. 'I know Brett,' I shouted. 'The guy organising this. Not so very well though.'

'It is of no importance.' He nuzzled my ear, then gripped me even tighter, crushing his face into the leather lattice over my belly, muffling his words. Despite realising he was a total crackpot I felt a hot rush through my innards.

'Arnaud?' I pushed him away. 'Perhaps there's been some mistake. I'm Marilyn, the Englishwoman, the one you left sitting in the bar the other night. I think we are both very drunk.'

He frowned up at me, pulling down my face so that I felt a click in my neck. 'I know very well who you are.' His face grew serious, it was the same face that had been reading the newspaper the first time I had addressed him weeks ago at the bar. 'Despite the painful death of my foolish marriage, I was aware of you from the very first moment, when that stupid waiter asked if you wanted olives and you asked me for a translation. You drank a *prosecco*. You were wearing a dove grey dress.'

I had nowhere else to look but over his worn skin flashing in the disco light, his scruffy eyebrows and the ridge between them, along the contours of his nose with its open pores, to the mouth I had just been kissing with the ring of stubble that had ground into my face. I didn't know what was happening to me. Rich coils of warmth were flooding my belly.

I put my hand out and braced it against his chest.

'Hold on. Perhaps you and your wife should work on getting back together.'

He frowned. I thought he hadn't understood. But he pulled me to him once more. 'How I love your English pragmatism, it is more foolish than my own. My young wife finds me old and stringy, that I like stupid music and long-winded conversation. She in turn is discovering the voracity of her powers.'

'Oh,' I mouthed when he released his grip. Then he pulled me back again.

'Estelle has taken my two properties and virtually melted down my company. She is expecting some rock prodigy's baby and they have moved down to Monte Carlo and I have lost everything, *everything*.'

I crawled off Arnaud Bertrand and this time he didn't resist. My naked buttocks plonked onto the velvet sofa. Arnaud turned to me. He looked appalled.

'You must excuse my dreadful behaviour.' He pushed the words into my ears before he stood up quickly and shambled off into the dark, his two bare bum cheeks bearing the furry imprint of the velvet.

I sat there in a vacuum, irrational tears filling my eyes. I felt around for my cat mask and tied it around my head. In that time Arnaud disappeared and a surge of bodies thriving to Metallica covered his tracks. A topless waitress passed with a tray of drinks and I nearly tripped her up as I grabbed another glass of champagne. I wanted to erase what had happened. Or I wanted to savour the sensation of Arnaud Bertrand's woody tongue linked with mine as long as I possibly could.

But then Brett slid next to me, the kohl around his eyes smudged. He stretched his arms out along the back of the divan and relaxed his head, spreading his legs wide apart. I saw with horror that he was wearing cowboy trousers like the ones my brother had as a boy, which were two long leather flaps. Of course that could only mean one thing: that I wasn't hanging around to see Brett walk away.

'Christ,' said Brett. 'Have you found anything worth taking home? I find there is far too much youth tonight, too much glitter. Us old whores. I saw you with that Swiss wallflower, believe me you won't get far with him. Far too orthodox for you, my dear.'

I felt a vast and confusing sadness, followed by the eddying of the drink. They were playing Blondie again. I watched the dancers with their erratic, chemical passion. Then I snuggled under Brett's shoulder where there was a faint smell of tea.

Although Brett flew out to Sao Paolo the following morning he left a precise list of tasks for me to carry out. I panicked, put on my reading glasses, and began to read. It seemed I had been hoovered up into the business – the 'Behind Closed Doors' business. I put the sheet of paper down in disbelief. Brett had summoned me to model his wares at one o'clock.

Around half past twelve, I nervously met Brett's group of models in the stock room, where they came to collect their costumes. They were an odd ensemble: a petite Brazilian woman with bad skin; a perfectly proportioned Senegalese man; a broad hairy Italian who went by the name of Chester. They were very welcoming and set about chatting as though they were rehearsing for the school play. Brett's assistant Lam brought pots of aromatic tea while breasts and bottoms were fitted into double-stitched leather peep-holes.

At one o'clock some distinguished Japanese clients arrived to see the merchandise. The models paraded in silence, the occasional whip was flourished. The session went off pleasantly and a substantial order was placed. Afterwards Lam handed me a discreet envelope full of fresh hundred euro bills.

12. IO AMO ARNAUD

In the days that followed I tried hard to embrace my new life. If one turned a blind eye to content, I was just an older saleswoman hawking Mexican handicrafts. Not that I had ever sold a tin of biscuits in my life. But after the fiasco of the trade fair and having been thrown onto the streets, I couldn't refuse employment of any sort. Besides, Brett's payments were generous. I had never seen such wads of cash. I stacked it in a lilac-scented box in my antique dresser, humming in my room at night.

Around twice a week Lam brought in a fresh fax from the US with the arrangements for an afternoon showing. We had a group of cheerful Russians, some very serious Norwegians who bought very little, as well as the usual well-behaved Japanese. It appeared Brett had effectively broken into his target market. I watched their stern faces from behind my mask as they perused our products, in some cases making small diagrams in notebooks, or nodding with intercontinental finesse. Afterwards I returned to my room and felt immense satisfaction. Lam brought me a cup of smoky tea and another reviving envelope of bills. Only occasionally I snuggled into bed thinking of my children catching the train in their school uniforms, and then I cringed with shame. How they would laugh if they saw me in my get-up.

The days were shorter and colder now. In the evenings I dressed in the new overcoat I had bought and walked along the boulevards. The lights glowed in bars and I missed Federico's kooky English. But I kept away from my old neighbourhood. I didn't want to run into crazy Arnaud. Then I would have to admit how often the he resided in my thoughts. Instead, each evening I hobbled further and further afield, crippled by my new patent leather boots. I tried to erase my ten minutes of passion in Arnaud Bertrand's arms with glass after glass of blood-red *barbera*. Often before I slept I had a vision of him on a yacht with the breeze ruffling his hair, surrounded by fifteen topless anorexics.

Some evenings I would go back to the bar where I had taken refuge with my bags. The bartender would salute me kindly and offer my first drink on the house. In time the bar filled with workers with unshaven faces, or old women with shocking teeth. I listened to conversations with the sharp Milanese inflection, and was sometimes asked for an opinion, or referred to as *La Bella Straniera*. I ordered *prosecco* and olives some nights, and I could tell the *prosecco* was cheap and the olives had been swilling in nasty jars at the cheapo supermarket.

One evening I saw Estelle shimmering on the cover of a magazine someone had left and quickly reached across to read it. Inside there were spreads of Arnaud's Latvian ex-wife surrounded by urchins, modelling next spring's fashions in an African fishing village. There was a brief accompanying article with Estelle showing off her baby bump, grinning inside a small jet. There were two smaller photos, one with the dazzling half-naked model embracing a tattooed musician whose grimy hand rested on her belly. The other showed an old grumpy man I had seen before. I read: *Ex-marito, Arnaud Bertrand.*

Ex-marito, Arnaud Bertrand? Then it was true what Arnaud had told me at the nightclub. Estelle had really taken off to Monte Carlo with the musician. Arnaud was a single, broken man. I stared into the photograph of Arnaud Bertrand shuffling down a chic Milanese street. Dressed in a shabby coat, his grey eyes downcast in pain, he looked like an old tramp. How I longed to pull his front to mine and smell his woody scent. I wanted to stroke his ravaged cheeks. I felt my heart somersault with delight and ordered another drink.

I don't know how I tottered home that evening. I remember the bartender helping me into a taxi, driven by an aloof Sikh who pretended not to understand my jokes. Halfway home I called Pamela, ready to tell her I was falling in love, but Pamela's voicemail came on and by then we were at Brett's front door. I remember tumbling onto the street and swaying up the hall to my room, Fiona's phone still clutched in my hand. I looked down and saw my thumb squashed on the screen. Two new text messages had just bounced onto it:

Il tuo prof non respira più senza i tuoi bacini. (Your teacher cannot breathe without your kisses.)

Sono durissimo, solo tu puoi aiutarmi. (I am really hard, only you can help me.)

No! I didn't want Federico. I deleted them immediately in cold blood. I tossed away my clothes and threw myself under Jane Austen's crisp canopy. Steadily, the pleated fabric began to spin, joined by the bouncy Greek wrestlers. As the bed rocked I thought of the way Arnaud's face had rubbed against mine as his hands trembled through my hair. I thought of his two vulnerable bottom cheeks textured by the velvet couch as he walked away. I had never felt so fond of a man's bottom.

Hours later I awoke with a sledgehammer hangover to the sound of yodelling from somewhere in the apartment. Brett and Roderick must have come home in the night. After a long silence I heard them reefing into each other, or whatever it was that they did. I gulped down the water next to my pillow as noisily as I could. I rolled away and threw my sick head under the covers.

Moments later my mobile started ringing. I saw Pamela's name flashing and took the call.

'Hello darl, what's up this morning?' she said cheerfully. 'Got ourselves in a fix have we?'

I cowered. 'A damned hangover is more like it.'

Pamela chortled. 'I'll have you know I did another piercing. Down *there*. Although quite tame compared to what you've been up to. And I thought he was a cheap Chinese businessman.'

'You mean Brett?'

'If that's the gentleman in question. It seems you've fallen on your feet.'

'What the hell do you mean?' I hissed. 'Will you stop being so bloody cryptic for once?'

'Marilyn? Is that you speaking? I've never quite heard the rage in the machine before. It becomes you.'

'Look, I'm sorry. But things are getting, well, quite out of hand here.'

'How now? I thought you'd cleared the first hurdle. What was that noise?'

It was Roderick or Brett emitting wild jungle sounds.

'Oh, nothing,' I said tiredly. 'Just my flatmate's dog. Do you think I should persevere with this, Pamela?'

'You know, I was up past your place the other day. Saw Peter's damsel with a trowel on her knees in your garden.'

'In my garden?'

'She was looking very stretched – a little dowdy even. Peter brought out two glasses of wine and I believe she threw hers at him. Delightful scene. I wouldn't rush back, dearest.'

I was brought back to my new reality as Lam walked in with a tray of tea. I heard a snatch of the lovers sighing.

'What about the other fellow then?' Pamela continued.

But I didn't want to speak about Arnaud. Not this morning. What if I never laid eyes upon him again? Milan was a big pushy city with hoards of hopeful teen models ready to shimmy up an old toad like him. What if it was just a very kinky party, a drunken kiss and a pair of bottomless pants?

'Of course, I quite understand,' she said. 'It may all appear a bungle but it seems you have never been as blessed as this.'

I rolled my eyes and thought that the piercings were sending her dotty. No wonder the breakfast show executives had sent her packing. I said goodbye and hobbled towards the shower. As the steaming water poured down I heard Pamela's words over and over: *It may all appear a bungle but it seems you have never been as blessed as this ... Saw Peter's damsel with a trowel on her knees in your garden.* Damn Pamela! I slumped against the shower wall. I turned off the water and looked at the big wet woman in the mirror. She was busty and round and her eyes were sharp. She wasn't the woman I thought I was moaning to on the inside. She tweaked her dark apricot nipple. We looked at each other as I dried my hair.

I don't know who winked first.

I put on a tailored suit and walked outside into the street. It was nearly midday. The rain had stopped and the sky was peeling away to its crisp autumn hue, the colour of bright blue paint. I walked along the footpath with no destination in mind, glad to have left the house before Brett and Roderick pulled me into an international threesome.

Brett's neighbourhood was far more classy than Fiona's neck of the woods. That meant broad shop fronts with top brands and women walking dogs in tartan jackets. I strolled on, feeling the chilly wind chasing my heels. I pulled into the first bar I saw and shivered. I asked a bartender dressed in a white bib for a double espresso. As the liquid trickled into the white cup I inhaled. The headache had started to clear in the biting air, but what I would have given for a fried egg and a round of bacon. I poured in my diet *zucchero* and took up a newspaper. There was a half-page advertisement plugging a famous photographer's exhibition in the city centre. Today might be a good day to put in some local culture.

Back on the busy street I skirted around some dim-wit leaning into a window making frames on the glass like a photographer. As I stared lovingly at a frock a few metres on, I felt a shiver along my spine. It wasn't a dim-wit I had just passed, it was Arnaud Bertrand on a possessed photo shoot. Except that poor Arnaud was minus his camera and his marbles.

I turned back but he had shambled on behind me. A woman with a pushchair curved around him and stared in distaste. It was true, every one of the pale thin dummies looked like an extrusion of Estelle. Every one of their gaunt faces looked like a fawn trapped in snow. I strode back towards him as his hands framed shot after shot of his plastic wife.

'Arnaud!' I grabbed his coat sleeve and he turned. His face looked calm and concentrated, swept up in his work. He looked at me pleasantly. But then recognition and something uglier crossed his face. He clutched his heart and sagged, his grey-blue eyes swimming upward as a tortured saint. As I laced my strong arms under his armpits and whipped out my mobile, I had to fight off a vision of skinny Estelle straddling him like a beached walrus.

Hours later Arnaud was discharged from the hospital with two more vials of pills. He was exhausted and dishevelled and conscious of everything that had happened.

'I am astonished by my behaviour. I have never behaved like a madman in my life. I can't think of what was going through my mind. But ever since they took away the keys to the agency ....'

He broke down and I hugged him. I told him to keep calm and offered to take him back to his apartment. Stunned, Arnaud agreed. My stomach was rumbling after hours sitting by his bed and I hoped he couldn't hear it. I hailed a taxi. As he gave directions to the driver he looked at me with lucid eyes.

'I don't know you in the slightest,' he said. 'But you are the only person I wish to be with now.'

He looked back out of the window as Milan filed by. We went to the most glamorous streets of the city. I sat there, startled, not knowing whether I was a new lover or the nurse who would dab his wounds. I very much wanted to hold the hand quivering slightly on his knee.

Arnaud slipped his key into a set of fancy glass doors on the street. He insisted I should go inside. We caught the lift up as far as it would go, walking directly into an open-plan apartment with an almighty panorama. At first I thought we had made an enormous blunder and Estelle was standing in the hall waiting for her ex-husband, but it was a life-sized nude photograph which Arnaud breezed past without a glance. I followed awkwardly, avoiding her arresting body, pretending I had hardly noticed. All over the walls there were huge glossy photos in the Helmut Newton style, where despite being a thin waif she seemed like a chiselled predator. I lowered myself onto a divan. On the coffee table there were even more Estelle mementos: a stack of Estelle-covered magazines and a batch of Polaroid photos of the bewitching young woman, taken upon this very chocolate couch.

Arnaud reappeared from the kitchen with a jug of water and two glasses. He pushed away the naked photos as if they were fishing magazines and poured me a drink. He had smoothed back his unruly hair and put on a fresh shirt. This Arnaud looked awfully efficient after the bumbling one in the street.

'You can see …' He threw his arm around apologetically. '… I haven't had the time to throw away any of this.' He looked over at one of the shots near the kitchen entry, shaking his head slowly. 'I don't even know if she wants them. Some gallery in Berlin has offered a mint to have them for an exhibition.'

Then he leaned over and slid his warm tongue into my mouth. It was so warm, so delicious.

'Ahh!' he cried, as his hands gently reached out to touch me.

But I turned from his mouth and sprang backwards like a nun. I removed his hands from my breasts.

'What on earth is the matter?' he barked. 'What has gotten into you?'

I sat glued there, knees rammed together. 'I can't. Not here.'

'What?' He was irritated. His frown deepened. I wondered if all the heart drugs would make his moods like a snakes and ladders game, all jolty ladders and slippery scales.

'It's her,' I pointed behind him. 'She's *naked.*'

Arnaud looked back with an irate twist of the head. 'Well, of course she is. What is this show of prudery all of a sudden?' he looked me over with puzzled eyes. 'Rather tall from a woman I met in leathers at Milan's local Sodom.'

'How dare you!' I felt faint.

He came over and as he crouched next to me his knees cracked loudly. He touched my back, rubbing as my eyes filled with tears. 'Yes but how divine you looked, my darling. I have never seen a riding crop wielded with such abandon.'

'Oh.' I blushed and squirmed away but his hands spread over my thighs.

'And now you must forgive me. I should never have brought you here amongst all these demonic photographs. Believe me, I am putting this place up for rent next month. Look at me, my sweet saviour.'

'I am not your saviour.'

He lifted my chin and looked into my face. 'Oh, but you are.'

I resisted his smell by trying to hold my breath as long as I could. But it was useless. As I inhaled his lips drew towards mine and their salty softness made contact with my skin. We kissed without opening our mouths like small children, savouring and shy. Then Arnaud rose and went out to the kitchen. I heard a kettle boiling and he brought out a pot of strong tea and two china cups. He sat down and sighed.

'If you'd be kind enough to listen, I'd like to tell you about all of this. Right now.' He leaned forward and grew businesslike. 'You see, I invested my best energy over the last few years into that woman. Her father and I even became friends of a sort, despite not sharing a word of common language. I took the first photographs of her here on this divan,' (he tapped the place next to him) 'When she was fifteen.'

'Good God, Arnaud,' I whispered. 'I don't want to know this.'

'No, please. Just hear me out. I did not make love to her. At that time I was married to another model.'

'*Another* model?'

'Yes, a French-Canadian model, you may have heard of her. I got Estelle into her first shows on the strength of those photos. I got her out of her post-Soviet hinterland and a future of unemployment and potato farming. Then, when eighteen, I touched her.'

Here his face sparkled. 'She was so beautiful. It was like touching life itself. Every cell of her was perfect. And she was clean, her skin smelt clean. She had grown up on the most rudimentary farm and her skin had not been marred by life or pollution or even the sun as we know it. Her limbs were endless and her sex was ....'

'Arnaud.' I stood up angrily. But Arnaud locked his arms around my legs, so I would topple before I could storm off.

'Please don't leave.' He gripped tighter. I saw that tears had gathered in the corners of his eyes.

'Why not?' I cried.

'Just hear me out. You see, I believe I know a little of who you are, and it is only fair that you know a little of myself, no? Much is said about this industry, but Estelle, you see, became my wife and I loved her. And now I have been emptied, I am an emptied man, and everything that I can give to you comes after this.'

As he spoke I heard alarm bells clanging so loudly I didn't know if they were in my head or if it was the fire alarm downstairs. This was the nasty man with a heart problem, the kook who framed plastic dummies in shop windows.

'Please,' he said, drawing back as I sat down again. 'Can you not see? For a great many years I have been stumbling towards saturation point, and marrying Estelle put everything on fast-forward, while also providing me the rope to hang around my neck. Estelle wanted all of this.' He indicated the wall of photographs, the glamorous views. 'I wanted to get out a long while back. If I see another topless anorexic I think I will choke.'

I knocked my cup over on the pile of magazines and the tea drowned poor skinny Estelle. Arnaud watched the wet cover crinkling without moving a muscle.

Then he spoke softly. 'Listen to me, I have an old feisty mother who is a sculptor, living in the mountains not too far from here. Tomorrow she is opening an exhibition of her work in Venice. Margarethe would be very pleased to meet you. I would be grateful if you would come.'

He was finished. Arnaud leaned over and laid his head in my lap. He exhaled. His whole body seemed depleted. I looked down at his wild grey hair and the unfamiliar turns of his ear.

We made love. Arnaud took me to a stylish hotel around the corner where he was recognised and given the works. My eyes traced over him in the hotel lift, watchful and wary. This time it mattered. It wasn't like Federico tearing away my shirt as we watched the eighties porn film, or Fiona's vibrators bouncing along the floor. The suite Arnaud led me into begged the most elaborate and refined sex. For a minute I worried Arnaud had brought lovers here, wooing them with gorgeous underwear and priceless champagne, but I swept away the thought as I opened the floor-to-ceiling curtains. Milan blinked at me and in the corner of my eye I saw Arnaud neatly fold his trousers. He was naked. I was thrilled.

In the morning we clung together stroking one another's skins. I looked into Arnaud Bertrand's eyes as we kissed, and they

173

were full of wonder. I felt that I had found a closeness beyond comprehension. The room service girl brought us an ample breakfast for five and I found myself pouring tea for my lover. We began touching again across the croissants and jam sachets, ending up halfway out of our plush dressing gowns on the floor. Afterwards I stretched out on the carpet, turning to the deep smile on Arnaud's face.

As we showered together, Arnaud finally convinced me to accompany him to his mother's exhibition in Venice. We were to travel there by train, Estelle having taken his Mercedes to Monte Carlo. We dressed, polishing off the last of the croissants and the pot of tepid coffee. I felt naughty, as though I were about to be discovered. I didn't quite know who by, but seeing Arnaud's grumpy photo in a celebrity magazine made me think we had done something scandalous.

Arnaud nuzzled my neck as a taxi was summoned and we waited in the lobby. A doorman came over and tapped Arnaud on the shoulder as we kissed. Arnaud reluctantly drew away, pulling strands of hair from my face. I blushed.

On the way to the station we detoured via Brett's apartment so I could collect a small bag of clothes. I unlocked the door, praying Brett & Co were out flexing at the gym. I heard nothing, not even Lam at work in the kitchen. On the hall table under Roderick's baubly chandelier I scribbled a quick note to Brett and hurtled down to my room. I packed a change of underwear and a supply of makeup, adding a slinky dress and one of Brett's printed silk scarves. I heard the taxi beeping as I charged towards the front door. For an instant I thought, What if it is all a dream? What if he's gone and left me?

Then I saw the pair of them. Arnaud was half-dozing on the window and the cranky foreign taxi driver was gesticulating.

As we drove I stole glances at my new lover. I studied his weary shoulders and the speckles on his hands. The verve of last night had taken its toll, leaving a relaxed smile even as he dozed. It was a far cry from the manic devotion in his eyes when the white goddess had appeared at the bar window. I couldn't stop myself wondering what would happen the next time she crossed his path. Would he tense and charge off as he had before? I looked at him frowning. I wasn't going to kid myself, I knew he was still in her thrall.

The train pulled away from Milan in gaunt winter light, crossing the factory belt and ranks of colourless apartment blocks. Exhaust fumes rose from cars waiting at traffic lights and the factories released trails of smoke. Gradually the city dissolved and the air was rinsed clean and a ridge of mountains came clear to the north. We rocked along plains criss-crossed by rows of bare poplars. Small towns smudged past. The train stopped and people stood dressed in scarves and coats, staring or talking into their mobiles. After a long while we passed a single hill crowned by cypresses, overlooking a lake that stretched towards the mountains. I saw Arnaud's hand waver and the way his eyes gazed out over the water. What had happened here? Was this Lago di Garda? My heart quickened as I wondered whether he had been here on a yacht with his young ex-wife, or at one of the villas dotted along the shore. I turned away painfully and saw a middle-aged woman across the aisle staring at me, the Sophia Loren type I used to fear. She was dressed to the hilt. By her side sat a small bald man. I swept the worried look from my face and laid claim to Arnaud's long thigh in a dishevelled pair of designer jeans. Arnaud turned to me with a look of love and in the corner of my eye I could see Sophia Loren's face tighten. Arnaud's head fell upon my shoulder and I looked back at her in triumph.

At Verona the river twisted over icy stones and I wondered when Arnaud was supposed to take his next pills. My lover shifted in and out of wakefulness. I wanted to slam his cheeks with kisses.

'Was that Verona?' Arnaud's eyes suddenly sprang open. 'I haven't passed through here for years. We were married there. She had just studied Romeo and Juliet at high school and was too embarrassed to invite her parents. What an amusing ceremony that was.'

I don't think he could have hurt me more had he slapped me on the face. His eyes roamed over the city as I sat there beginning to shake. I was such an insider now that he hadn't even needed to say the name *Estelle*.

'Perhaps if you had produced some offspring along the way,' I said coldly. 'You would have been too embarrassed to marry a child.'

I got up from my seat and ran off towards the toilets. Sophia Loren caught wind of the change in temperament and her *Hello!* magazine banked downward. I pushed past the drinks trolley at the head of the carriage. An Indian man with a strong accent was offering Pringles and iced tea in a falsetto voice. Arnaud sat there peering up at him with a blank expression.

I sat on a bumping window ledge with miles of vineyards sliding past at my back. After Peter had left me, I didn't think another man could make me feel such outrage. I braced myself, staring at the yellow sticker with the emergency brake instructions in four languages.

'What on earth is the matter with you?' When the drinks cart moved along Arnaud staggered up the rocking aisle. 'Do you know where I left my twelve o'clock pills?'

It was sickening. Despicable as he was, just the sight of him made me want to throw my arms around his neck. Two young women passed with low-cut jeans and exposed midriffs so ripe you could smell them. I stood my ground and scowled at him.

'Did any of your models give you children?'

Arnaud looked at me gruffly. 'Not at all. There was no time for them. I never wished to have children.'

I didn't feel cruel enough to mention the rock baby his ex-wife was now expecting, but I thought I saw a shadow of discomfort cross his face. I turned away from him. Arnaud sank against the wall of the toilet cubicle. 'Okay. Carole and I produced a daughter. She was my first wife.'

'Oh?' So here it was, the hidden child in a Swiss boarding school. And the discarded first wife.

'I was an art history student in Lausanne, far too young to be parenting. Renée would probably be the age of your eldest now. Carole remarried and had other children. She was just pregnant when she found out that I was fooling around with a Swedish girl. We rarely communicated after that. Meret, my Swedish girlfriend, wanted to model. We left Lausanne for Milan, and that's when I started this wretched business.'

I felt an enormous convulsion struggling through me, bursting to get out.

He stared at me, looking perplexed. 'What is wrong with you? We don't all lead lives without mistakes.'

But all I could see was the statuesque trail of underage waifs Arnaud had courted for the planet's magazine covers. I saw them writhing over him like a pile of snakes with blond thatches and biscuit-sized breasts.

'Why me then?' I moaned theatrically. 'What the hell are you doing with me?'

'This I cannot explain,' he said with a baffled look. 'It is as though you have some gnawing quality that excites me. I cannot understand. I have never looked at a woman like this, the way that you are.'

'You mean *old*, I take it?'

'Yes. That is it. I have never wanted an *old* woman.' He stared at me, frowning. 'You know, I want you to understand just this. I have treated many women very badly. I have sent them away because they are too fat, because their eyes are too close, because I don't like their ears or their knees, or their arses did not have the right curvature and their nipples were not fine. I have traded in women like a slave runner, never considering a woman over the age of twenty-three.'

'Arnaud,' I said firmly, while shaking all over. 'Don't come to me for therapy for your obsessions.'

I was about to add more – I was just getting started – when I saw I had an audience. A line of people waiting for the next station had formed behind Arnaud. 'Let's go and sit down,' he said nervously and began to squeeze back towards our seats.

But as I watched him move I clutched my handbag and stayed at the head of the line. When the train creaked to a halt at Padua I pushed the door release and thudded onto the platform. I hurtled past people queuing with suitcases and saw Arnaud's face aghast at the window. He looked beyond forlorn. I didn't know whether I had saved myself or smothered my lover in his sleep.

I emerged from the station building and took the main drag into town. It was peopled by Moroccan men and Chinese women with pushchairs, and Italian women wearing printed autumn tights. I bought a bottle of water at the first bar on the corner and drank quickly, letting it drip onto my shirt and welcoming its coolness. Dirty old bastard. And fancy trying on the heartfelt self-analysis while reminding me I was a fat old broad. I ordered an espresso and stood there heaving as I tried to calm myself. I asked for a well-deserved grappa and watched the colourless liquid slosh into my tiny cup from a huge cheap bottle. But then I took a dizzying step backwards. What was I doing here, after such a fragrantly composed night? I glanced at a pair of drinkers downing their pink aperitifs and setting off to lunch. I looked at the bartender with her heavy green eye shadow and plump shuddering arms. But how could I want a man who collected stick figure women the way I collected bulges on my thighs? The bartender laughed as the men headed off to lunch and she began to wipe the counter in front of me. I paid and swished around, nearly banging into the glass door.

Outside on the footpath I suddenly thought of Vanessa, who was just over the age Estelle had been when he had photographed her on the couch, rescuing her from her post-Soviet future. What if Vanessa fell for a man who wanted her to be thinner and flat-bellied and breastless like a fish? I had to speak with her right now.

'Hello? Is that you Vanessa darling?' I called.

'Hi Mum! How is Milan treating you? You're lucky we're off this afternoon. Nikki and me are on a diet. We're just having lettuce and so forth, you know? We found this great salad bar just up from the mall.'

I nearly tripped on the footpath. I should have been there with her, feeding her shepherd's pie and borscht soup. It was all my fault.

'Diet? What do you mean? You've never lasted longer than thirty seconds on a diet. Remember that crème caramel you used to ask for? Vanessa?' I heard her laughing with her friend. I already saw the clothes hanging off her knobbly shoulders. 'Just wait till you come to Italy, love. There'll be all that wonderful pasta and pizza. I'm just going to have some for lunch.'

'Bollocks, Mum. You told me yourself you've given up carbohydrates.'

'Did I? Well, that was just for a week. I really eat like an absolute horse here, you've no idea how scrumptious the food is.' I was trying to sound jolly but the words stuck in my mouth.

'Mum? What's wrong? You're not sounding normal. Is it all working out? Your visit was grand, you know. Eddy and I finished off the bottle of *prosecco* after you left.'

I had to cut her off. I realised I was staring into a Chinese restaurant window with musky green slats and a porcelain lion sitting in the dust. People were veering around me the way I had veered around Arnaud in Milan. There was a young Chinese girl standing in the doorway and snatches of sad wailing music came from inside. She looked at me kindly and I slipped my mobile into my pocket.

I sat down and she gave me a small cup of jasmine tea. The walls were covered in bamboo panelling and there was a picture of a man on a sampan made out of grains of rice. What if my daughter became a topless anorexic, the type of female whose gruelling efforts a man like Arnaud could cancel out in seconds? The girl handed me the menu and I suddenly felt like wallowing in a dish of greasy spicy food. Just as I was trying to work out what 'stir-fry' was in Italian, Arnaud Bertrand tumbled through the doorway tearing chairs apart.

Arnaud marched up to me like a big Swiss bear, as wild-eyed and messy-haired as ever, making Estelle's grungy rock star look like a boy who'd raided the costume box. The waitress and the smeary-aproned cook ran out from the kitchen. Arnaud seized me and I fell into nuclear meltdown, burning nuggets dragging me through the earth.

'I am terrified of losing you,' he gasped. 'You must believe me. You have driven something into me.'

We adjourned to a two-bit hotel on the station road run by North Africans and made love until we collapsed. Later in the evening I woke him twice to take his pills and each time watched him drink a full glass of water. I squeezed myself to his nutty-smelling chest and couldn't stop inhaling the skin there.

13. IN VENICE

I didn't think Venice was a city for lovers. Although modern postcards would have us see couples in gondolas under the Bridge of Sighs, or romantic vistas threading through the canals, as a young movie buff's girlfriend my first visions of the city were films of seedy decay. I remembered the typhus epidemic in *Death in Venice* that brought makeup-daubed Dirk Bogarde to his end as he swooned over that perfect boy, played out to Peter's gloomy Mahler. And then Donald Sutherland's slasher finale in *Don't Look Now*, despite the adorable love scene and Julie Christie's retro beauty. After my previous life spent raging in discothèques, Peter had avidly tried to draw me into the world of cinema, before his destiny in television became concrete. But after those two films Venice made my skin crawl. I thought I saw sly figures lurking in the low doorways, or faces watching us over the gloomy water. I thought the façades needed a good scrub down and that the sellers should remove the slight sneers from their smiles. The frenzy of the *carnevale* frightened me – the masks made me think of a manic world of courtesans with syphilis – and though Peter filmed us as if we were lovers on location I remembered counting the days until we took the aeroplane. I had never wanted to see Italy again.

I felt some of that unease creep back as the train left the industrial mainland and slowly rocked along the spit into the lagoon. Ruddy, crammed Venice loomed as an unavoidable encounter. The church spires pricked the sky. A long punt advanced as a line of standing men dug poles into the water. Arnaud clutched my hand and I felt uncomfortable, his hand was heavy and hot. I felt that Venice was pulling me towards her exquisite trap.

The train snuggled into the terminus and the first passengers started to descend. It was early afternoon and we had missed

Margarethe's opening last night. Arnaud assured me the gallery was nearby, although I knew that 'nearby' in Venice could mean a two-mile hike over bridges. For some reason I imagined Arnaud's mother would be a refraction of Estelle. A slim, almighty goddess, barely traced with age. After all, why would he be drawn to shimmering sylphs if not programmed at birth?

'Why the grim expression, my dearest?' Arnaud nudged me. 'You're filling with doubts again, aren't you? I assume in this moment – no matter the string of pleasures I gave you last night – that you are struggling between Good-Arnaud and Bad-Arnaud, weighing up every single factor. Tell me, who is winning after my efforts this morning? On which team should I lay my overvalued Swiss francs?'

I was charmed by Arnaud's vigilance but laughed it off. It was true though. I still wondered how far Estelle had chewed into his brain and, despite the delights of the morning, I still saw her draped on the chocolate brown couch in Milan, unfurling her mesmerising beauty while Arnaud genuflected before her.

I looked back at him, trying to stamp out that image. Bad-Arnaud again. The carriage was empty and Good-Arnaud came to the fore, kissing me with tingling purpose. I felt my toes straining in my shoes. We tumbled out of the train onto the platform and as we marched arm in arm through the station people glanced warmly at us. We were a handsome couple.

'Are you enjoying this?' He smiled. 'You realise I used to be asked if I were her grandfather?'

Again, I couldn't help remembering their *frisson* in the bar. And how Arnaud had declared: *This woman became my wife and I loved her.* I smiled and fought down my queasiness.

We strode outside to the marble stairs above the chaos below. Opposite us, on the other side of the busy canal, stood the same streaky stone cupola that had astonished me when I had come here with Peter. I hadn't known it was to be the first of hundreds.

A ferry boat pulled into the *vaporetto* stop making white ribbons on the dirty water. Seventeen years later and here I was with a new man on my arm. My marriage had collapsed and the children I had produced were far away from me – possibly starving themselves to death – and another woman was digging up my garden. Arnaud heard the catch in my throat and softly brought his lips to the skin there. I was so grateful, so disarmed. We walked up the steps and onto the first of many arched bridges. At the top we paused and he brought me over to lean on the railing where we kissed deep and hard.

'There,' he said. 'Feel that murky breeze on your face. The best from the refinery.'

I laughed and we moved on. For the next half hour we walked through alleyways crammed with glass trinkets and painted masks, with tourists fingering merchandise and Senegalese vendors hawking their fake bags. I wandered on with Arnaud, occasionally noticing the green water ruffling mossy walls, or a string of very human washing. 'Thank you,' I said, clutching him. 'For what?' he replied. He urged me onward, linking his arm through mine. 'Let us pass this way,' he said, and we emerged into the wide and dramatic Piazza San Marco with its restaurant tables, pigeons and meandering tourists.

'Isn't it marvellous?' He peered into my face as the unfettered sea air crossed the expanse of pigeons and chic café tables to caress the pair of us. 'I am sorry for marching you along so swiftly, but I couldn't wait to see your expression. I quite wanted to be the first to bring you here. Is this so?'

I didn't have the heart to tell him Peter had done the same thing. Peter with his silly striped beanie and concertina map, while I had dragged my feet behind him, trying not to throw up into a canal.

'Oh yes,' I lied. 'This is the very first time, Arnaud. I'm speechless. It's all too much.'

He explained the mottled history of the Byzantine basilica while I gazed up open-mouthed. He drew a sketch of the Venetian Republic and walked me past the sweeping Doge's Palace with its chequered pink façade and the scalloped loggia looking out over the glittery water. We walked through the tourists feeding pigeons and little stands with straw hats and football shirts, and past the line of shiny black gondolas tended by men in striped T-shirts. Over on the Giudecca opposite, he pointed out, was the ancient Jewish ghetto and on the far left was the isolated San Giorgio Maggiore on its salvaged lip of land, which had issued blessings to sailors as they left on their long ocean voyages. He explained how the whole place had been built on tree trunks wedged into the marshes to reproduce solid ground, hence the crooked alley-ways and tilting floors.

'I was an art history student in Lausanne, before passing through numerous other phases. Please forgive me if I go on. *On fait la révolution pour arriver où on a commencé.'*

'What was that?' I was utterly entranced.

'My native tongue, my dear. About how we travel in circles back to where we began. Of course under the current circumstances I refuse to take the analysis any further.'

Cazzo! Hearing Arnaud speaking French made me hot. It also opened up a new range of learning techniques in the new tongue. I grabbed him and kissed his surprised mouth. If this were my circle, then I wanted to savour Venice properly the second time around. He looked back amused and we strolled along the shoreline. Then he threaded his arm through mine as I glanced at his firm brows above his relaxed grey eyes. His skin was lined from too many Caribbean cruises while his quick temper had left incisions at the bridge of a nose which was long and well-drawn, probably indicating the architecture of the family. I quickly stamped out the thought of Estelle's glowing skin next to the age spots I could have outlined with a marker.

When the wind became too chilly we slipped into a bar by one of the *vaporetto* stops. Arnaud ordered two glasses of red wine and hung up my coat, shepherding me to a table in the corner. Born on the continent, he was not bothered by the cranky bartender with his dirty cloth. But I also saw he glanced around at the clutch of regular drinkers and made sure every one of them was watching the curvy woman he settled in her seat. Arnaud sat back and raised his eyebrow slightly, which made me wonder how much more ample the thrill must have been when he paraded around with a famous top model, so shockingly young and divine.

I sat there shaking my head and flipped through an old sports newspaper while Arnaud went off to the bathroom. Whether it lasted or not, I began telling myself, I had no intention of falling in love with Arnaud Bertrand. I had passed the age where one stepped blindly into a vacuum-sealed box called 'Love' and came out a mangled tortured mess. That was for Estelle and Vanessa. Whatever came about, I had to ensure it would be a measured, fruitful thing, born of a long acquaintance with the substance of life. After Peter's turn-about, I thought I owed myself that.

But then, even if we did manage to cling together until we were both using walking frames, how would we survive without decades of whittled domestic history behind us? How would I know what toothpaste to buy and whether he farted in bed? After all, I had been with Arnaud for two days so far, and I had only barely decided he was not a lunatic. I closed the newspaper and slumped back.

'I see you have your thinking cap on again.' Arnaud sat down and leaned towards me. 'Let me inform you that while these drunkards are staggering home I will be undressing you again. My plan is to get you quite drunk and as frisky as this morning. Now, let us finish this bottle before we go to poor Margarethe.'

We raised our glasses and despite the vast amount of worry rising from the idea of meeting Margarethe, the idea her son had just put forth had me very, very turned on. Outside the window at the other end of the room the sky rouged and the island across the shipping channel became a long silhouette of bell towers and roofs against the turmoil of colour.

'Why *poor Margarethe?*' I asked.

'Margarethe has not been enjoying good health lately. She will not heed her doctor's orders to slow down. Putting together this show could possibly be the end of her.'

Suddenly I was on alert. The delicately-aged Margarethe had become a cantankerous pensioner.

'Really?'

'Let me explain. Margarethe has moved around many lives. I left our home soon after our father died, ostensibly to study in the city, but it was because my mother was driving me to insanity. She broke down after Pierre died. They had been a very united couple. She survived breast cancer, which I believe was the fallout from my father's loss, and bore down on my sister in New York for several years until Portia could have no more of her. She went to India to follow some guru for years, then suddenly she was studying sculpture in New Mexico. After that she decided it was time to join me in Europe.'

Arnaud paused to reflect and began slowly shaking his head. I guessed that these were around the same years I was breastfeeding and becoming a duped housewife. He began to speak again. 'Of course Zoë, my second wife, hated Margarethe, and I believe it was quite mutual.' He said the name Zoë with a type of candour and surprise in his voice, and it sounded as though it was a name he had not spoken for a long time. My heart spiralled into a nosedive. I could listen no more.

'No, my darling, now is not the moment to turn away from me.' He tilted my chin back in his direction. 'Then, over ten years ago now, Margarethe met a mountaineer while hiking and now lives in a tiny mountain village near here, where she collects bits of wood and has honed herself into a credible sculptor. You see her work fell into the right hands with my sister's people and sells quite handsomely. She has all manner of American clientele flying into Venice. It has truly taken decades, but I believe she is living her intended life now. You know how they say that some people burn out brightly, whilst others save their flare to the end.'

But I was too flustered by the ex-wives to focus on Margarethe's burning and the precious American clientele. We were outside again, veering into a bitterly cold alley-way without light. I realised I would never be able to shoo away Arnaud's ex-wives. They would always be there, the women he had cherished. Small oily tears flared out over my cheeks. Then, without warning, Arnaud pressed me into a doorway and kissed my face.

'What are you doing?' I gasped. Somehow, he raised my tight skirt beneath my coat and touched my skin with cool fingers. He whispered something in French, which I thought might have been 'Sorry my fingers are so cold', given he circled his hand in the fabric until his fingertips felt warmer. He opened his trousers, skilfully reaching my parts. Further along the alley-way I heard footsteps and smelt the filthy water. I heard a game show gong from an upstairs television. Then I heard myself moaning to a vanishing point.

'*Tu vois,*' he said as he kissed me softly. 'You are making an even crazier man of me.' He held me tightly as I shook with pleasure as much as disbelief. I didn't know how to evaluate what he had just said. He pulled my skirt down and I listened to his breathing as it slowed and softened again.

We walked up and over the next series of bridges in silence. I felt the weight of his arm and heard our tired shoes trudging together. The mauve night closed around us and I felt a sense of bottomless peace pervading my being.

After hesitating once or twice Arnaud came to a stop before a brilliantly lit window along one of the canals. We peered into the warm world inside, making two fog patches on the glass. Tall twisted sculptures were arranged on blond planes of wood. Highlighted in the window was a tilted cone shape with meticulous twigs and thrusting boughs entwined in gleaming ascension. Arnaud nodded slowly. In the corner of the gallery a silver-haired woman was bent over beneath a reading lamp. A couple were looking at one of the works.

The sculptress lifted her head the moment a buzzer rang as we crossed the doorway. She knew the smell and presence of her son the way every mother did. I could feel her nimble eyes running over me from yards away but I stood tall. This was the woman who had driven her son to wed teenagers and knock back young models according to the angle of their noses. But I had just made love to this man and could still feel his touch burning on me.

Arnaud stepped towards her and they hugged. She would have been the same height as her son but had shrunken in stature. Suddenly I was out of control, worrying about Arnaud's heart condition and not wanting him to die whilst I hadn't even begun to love him. Tears filled my eyes. The couple parted and stopped murmuring in French to turn to me.

'I am so sorry we missed your opening night. We were held up.' He extended his arm to me. 'In Padova.'

I smiled uncertainly and stepped forward. Their smiles were identical. As were the firm brows and the sweeping nose, the wide worried foreheads. Perhaps I was unsteady after the recent sex, but I was filled with emotion.

'*Maman*, this is *Marileen.*' Though he pronounced my name with an irresistible French accent he gave me no title – girlfriend or special friend – and I felt an enormous pang, like a car crashing into a wall, and gave my hand to the strong woman. Her grip was kinder than I could have imagined. I felt guilty for having seen her as a priestess from Estelle's world. She had some sort of power, like Pamela in a way, and there was a clear resonance between her and the circle of works. Their woody smell was beginning to affect me, as well as the airlessness of the warm room. Suddenly my eyes fissured white and I was aware of my head bouncing on the wooden floor.

I woke up as they were arranging my limbs on a *chaise longue* at the back of the gallery. Arnaud pulled a rug over me. Margarethe brought over a steaming cup of tea. Arnaud touched my cheek while he and his mother spoke softly in French. I remembered enough from high school to understand *'manger'* (to eat) and *'fatiguée'* (tired) but the other words ran too fast together for me to comprehend anything other than their concerned tone. I thought I heard Margarethe ask about my family origins or something along those lines, to which Arnaud had no real reply. I had barely spoken of Peter and Danielle, Vanessa and Eddy, and the much more sedate life that was part of me. As I drifted I thought I heard him say, *'La seule chose que je sais, c'est que je ne veux pas la perdre.'* (The only thing that I know is that I don't want to lose her.) But I was the last person to be trusted with a foreign language, plus I had just collided with a very hard floor.

I listened to their voices weaving together thinking, *this is the woman who first spoke to my lover, this is the woman who taught him sounds and watched the joy on his tiny infant face.* It was a strange but blessed inroad, sensing his person refracted through the woman who had loved him before anyone else. I could have listened all night to Arnaud's relaxed comfort as he talked on, while distractedly caressing my cheek. Heaven could not have been a more perfect place.

Reluctantly I opened my eyes and sat up. I drank Margarethe's tea and apologised for scaring away her customers.

Margarethe patted my thigh and said I must not venture out again into the cold night. She had a pot of soup in the kitchenette at the back of the shop where we ate, crammed together on a bench for starved artists, and the two of them finished a bottle of wine. She said there was a single bed next door where I could rest but Arnaud insisted that she remain there, that we would bundle up somehow in the gallery.

After our simple dinner he settled me under Margarethe's warm covers and kissed me a careful goodnight. He unrolled a blanket on the floor next to me and grinned up from the wooden floor like a kid on a camping adventure. Moments later he was snoring. Sometime afterwards, when Margarethe stopped pottering about, her snores too could be heard reverberating in the hallway. I smiled, listening to snatches of Venice outside. Occasionally the water lapped up against the walls of the canal. Or footsteps marched up and over the bridge and tapped into the distance.

I must have broken my fall with my knee and hip, so during the night I began to feel a trail of tender points along one side. I crawled down onto my lover's body, dragged the covers over the pair of us and held him tightly. I was feeling too blissful to sleep. My fatigue had turned itself inside out and the night progressed steadily, each half hour marked by gentle chimes from nearby churches, until the dawn wended down through the canals and into Margarethe's sculpted forest. I heard water pulled along the canal walls as gurgling punts brought produce to the market. Women's heels clattered past and over the bridge. The early church bells tolled more vigorously and Arnaud whispered my name. I had been waiting all my life to be living moments as perfectly scripted as these.

We made love slowly and quietly in the stillness, enclosed by Margarethe's magical trees. When we heard her movements in the kitchen, we arose. Arnaud looked about for his discarded clothes and I savoured him dressing. Never had I seen a more rudimentary and erotic spectacle. I marvelled over his spent member and the old curve of his buttocks in the raw winter light, and the persistence of his youthful musculature under his loosened, aged skin.

'Up you get, *ma cherie*, before Margarethe's American clients come knocking. I shall put the coffee on.'

Margarethe joined us looking refreshed and prepared for the day. She had said she had some wealthy Americans arriving in their boat this morning, who wanted to take her out on the lagoon. Margarethe tut-tutted, 'You young lovers must go out on the boat, not me with my wooden mountain legs. Arnaud, with all your vacuous winters in the Caribbean ....' She paused and winked at me, while I tried to fade-out my vision of Arnaud surrounded by topless anorexics on a yacht. I gulped down my coffee, swilling some of Margarethe's home-made aniseed grappa into the grounds. It flared down the centre of me and again I remembered how much history I still had to reckon with. A first wife. A second wife. And then Estelle, yet to reach her prime, who until a minute ago had been able to yank Arnaud's strings.

'Now *Maman*, we are in healthier company and those days are long gone,' Arnaud said a little self-defensively.

'I don't at all mean to pry,' said Margarethe, pressing her bullet black coffee to her plum lips. 'But surely you have a family? A fine woman like yourself can't have been left idle.'

I saw Arnaud's eyes retreat slightly and couldn't understand why. He began efficiently unscrewing the coffee percolator, just as I used to do at Fiona's place when I was nervous and in raptures over young Federico. I slid my arm around his waist.

'You once told me you were certain I had no sea legs. Do you remember?' I asked him.

Now it was my turn to wink at Margarethe and she left off her enquiries. Arnaud's smile returned. 'I most certainly do. You were wearing an astonishing red dress which confirmed everything I had initially thought of you.'

'Which was?'

'That you, like myself, were embarking upon a new life.'

Margarethe left the kitchenette to respond to the buzzer sounding in the gallery and I sat there speechless. We kissed, his coffee tongue mingling with mine and his hand reaching under my skirt. I thought I would faint again, then I heard Margarethe's voice very distinctly in the gallery, followed by an enthusiastic American woman. A man spoke and I had the oddest sensation I had heard his voice before. Arnaud pulled the tiny door closed. Paralysed, I couldn't believe his daring.

He murmured, 'You are like a child in the morning. And a woman in the night.'

Though breathless again, I was disturbed by the corny line. Was this a reference to Estelle and his need for juvenile flesh? Or was I only allowed to be old when the lights were low? Down under my skirt Arnaud was chuckling. He rose and seized me, 'I know what you are thinking,' he chided. 'That was in no way a reference to my ways of the past. You must believe this,' he declared a little desperately, making me recall the crazy man in front of the shop window.

We went into the gallery and met Margarethe's clients, Greta and Roderick from Provincetown. I nearly hit the floor in another dead faint. It was Brett's better half with a groomed horsey-looking woman dressed in a mannish suit. They were buying for Greta's posh waterfront restaurant. Greta spoke in a loud, demanding voice as Roderick, glancing coolly at me, turned to Margarethe's art. I was sure Greta possessed a fine horsewhip.

Outside their boat was tied to a pair of docking posts painted in a blue and white candy swirl. Greta had suggested Arnaud and I go out for a spin while she considered Margarethe's works. The driver was a young Venetian beauty with long red-blond locks and the traditional striped T-shirt despite the chill morning. 'Keep your eyes off him,' Arnaud warned before the young man hoisted me on board. The pair of us snuggled at the back of the vessel while the engine spluttered in the green water. Soon enough the craft pushed under arched bridges and surged around corners, exploring the narrow gorges between astonishing palaces. The early sunlight crossed over us, occasionally highlighting a tourist in baggy shorts taking photographs. We lay locked together like a pair of nobles, Arnaud's hands under my hair feeling for the bump from last night, our faces slowly warming in the mild sun.

Finally we broke free of the citadel into the *Canal Grande* with her traffic of red-cushioned gondolas manned by elegant *gondolieri*, and the chugging *vaporetto* filled with camera-wielding travellers. The sunlight fell upon the brilliant white façade of San Giorgio Maggiore and flashed on the creamy pink bricks of the Doge's Palace. From afar, Piazza San Marco milled with colourful enthralled crowds and soon diminished in our wake as we headed for the islands.

As I gripped Arnaud after a series of larger waves, my mobile rang inside my bag and I half-crawled into the cabin so I could hear. 'Peter? Peter is that you? I'm in Venice, it's wonderful.' And then, given this was a flawless perfect day I exclaimed, 'I think I've met him, the man of my dreams, we are on a boat in the lagoon.'

I heard Peter stammer. Then he began to sob. He said my name, then repeated it madly. I cut the line. I didn't want to hear that Danielle had left him again and caused even more chaos. I called Pamela quickly and she answered with a tight voice. I wondered what the hell was going on in England this morning.

'Hello you,' she said flatly.

'Hello Pamela, I just had Peter with his usual rubbish,' I burst out. 'I expect she's left him again. Pamela, it's divine! I'm here with him in Venice. You know, Arnaud. I do believe I am letting go finally. We love each other.'

Pamela didn't reply immediately. 'Oh really?' she said. I was beginning to feel annoyed. 'I think I should be calling you back love, I've got Sally here raising the roof. Do watch out for yourself.'

I closed the phone, flabbergasted, entirely convinced that my life was now rooted here, with Arnaud, wherever he would take me, and that these two miserable elements of my past would soon be languishing in my wake. I looked out to my gorgeous lover sitting on the white upholstered seat with Venice shimmering at his shoulders. He grinned back at me, pulling off his shoes and socks as he basked in the sun. Then I saw him pull out his own phone from his jacket and flip it open. His face tensed and he sat up straight. I thought of Margarethe. Then Estelle.

I came out onto the deck and Arnaud pushed past me into the curtained cabin where he sat hunched up with his head away from me. The boat tossed over the wake of a huge cruiser that had crossed our path. A tall, slim woman came out onto the stern deck in a skimpy top and a pair of jeans and peered over towards Venice. She lost interest and turned back inside the glass doors of the rumbling vessel. I glanced at Arnaud still clenched over, his hand running through his hair until it all stood on end. The hard sun and wind cut into my face and I felt myself age a year each second that passed. My perfect moments skittered away on the dirty foam.

Arnaud heaved himself up the cabin steps and outside onto the deck. I read his face. I knew what he was going to say.

'It was Estelle,' he announced, holding onto a chrome railing, his face like chalk. 'I am so abominably sorry. I am fully responsible for all of this but believe me, *Marileen*, I am compelled, I cannot abandon her. I brought her to this. I loved her.'

It was over, I knew it was over. I had known it the moment I heard the glitch in Pamela's voice. I couldn't even speak to him.

'She was losing blood and they ran a series of tests. They found it wasn't even his child and now he's dumped her. The rock star. Estelle said the baby is mine.'

He collapsed onto the white plush seat and I began to stare at his bare toes, each one of them, the worn wrinkled skin and the nails plunged into them, each one at a different angle like a weird musical instrument. The skin of his heels was white and dry. Ten minutes ago I would have bathed his feet with my hair. Now they were the feet of a monster. I could never touch them again.

If I were a better swimmer I would have leapt out into the frothing wake behind the boat. But I didn't have the courage to jump into the cold green water and ruin my hair. Arnaud moved up behind the driver and cupped his mouth to the red-headed man's ear. Then the boat turned back on its own wash and made for the shore. Arnaud tried coming out to me but he couldn't. He stayed in the curtained cabin where he held his head in his hands. When the boat slowed minutes later and the Venetian shoreline loomed like a shoddy movie set, he came out next to me but I was furled away, it would have killed me to feel his hands. My throat was dry as cement.

Oblivious, the driver with his curly locks lined the boat alongside the jetty by San Marco. I clambered over the white upholstery onto the deck and clattered towards the piazza, tears squirting down my face.

I did not turn back. I knew Arnaud would not follow me.

14. 'ENGLISH NOW'

I did not run directly to the station, although I could not stand to be in Venice a moment longer. Its hazy air was suffocating and I did not wish to repeat last night's fainting episode surrounded by a ring of American tourists with their fake Prada bags. I walked around haphazardly with no idea where I was headed. I would have liked to have said goodbye to Margarethe, with whom I sensed some sort of warm and natural bond. But I was ashamed. I was ashamed that her son who had loved me last night had now gone back to his pregnant wife. (Just wait till Estelle's succulent skin bore a few stretch marks and the fatigue of breastfeeding set in – if her biscuit-sized knockers could produce any milk. No more photo shoots among African urchins for a while.)

But I wasn't really feeling vicious. For the first fifteen minutes I was in shock. I felt a dizzy displacement as a shark victim must feel, before they realise a leg is gone and their blood is colouring the water. Then I began to feel torn into, my skin was shredded and my organs released a stupefying pain. I didn't think I could bear anything this intense. I ran into a park, found a secluded bench, and howled. After I could howl no more I floated above my body and watched myself sitting all alone, my red face in tatters. Far off, I heard a plane scoring the sky and realised Arnaud would have caught the first flight back to Milan. There was no danger of running into him at the station now that he had rejoined the jet set.

What the hell had I been thinking? Hadn't I seen the fanaticism back at his apartment? And the madman in the street? How on earth had I diverged from Jean Harper's mild-mannered romantic path to become involved with this obsessive, cradle-snatching lunatic?

I tried to breathe deeply and think back to calm, successful Jean Harper and the path she had mapped out for me. I saw the clip in Jean's neat hair. I had a vision of the windswept Andes. But it was no use. My thoughts roved back to last night after I fainted, when I listened to Margarethe and Arnaud speaking softly over my head, when I had imagined I was as close to heaven as I could be. I thought of my blissful sleeplessness as Venice murmured outside, and how we had made love with such slow transfixing power. I began to choke. I saw Estelle's flimsy rib cage pressed against Arnaud's far-from-firm belly, and his old grizzly probing her dainty crevice. I threw up into a small bush.

As evening fell I headed back to the station. I bought a ticket for the slow train to Milan and let my head fall against the dusky views beyond the window, not caring whether the businessman with a newspaper opposite saw the tears pouring down my face or not. The train rattled across the same plains I had crossed with Arnaud and I couldn't help looking back to the past. Two days ago the rock star still loved Estelle. And the phone call that would turn my lover's toes into poisonous sea creatures had not yet occurred. I tried to quieten my sobs. The businessman flexed his newspaper in irritation, as if I were disturbing the fringes of his world; as though women like me were a pest.

The train pulled into the great hooded expanse of the *Stazione Centrale* and the businessman sped off, pulling up his coat collar and stashing the newspaper into a bin. I walked down the long platform a different woman, a thousand years older than the one whose husband had sat her down in the kitchen to tell her he was in love with a woman from Shepherd's Bush.

Outside the station the wind blew grit into my face and I looked at the mass of buildings and lights. Arnaud and Estelle were out there in the city, reunited. I saw Arnaud pouring her water from a jug, massaging her spindly white thighs. I saw Estelle dumbstruck on the divan. Her lover had left her, and now she knew she was carrying this old and boring man's baby in her belly. Would she have hated him, or be relieved to run back to

197

Daddy? Try as I might, I couldn't hear their small talk.

'Hey, Madam, you no hear me?' An African man waving red scarves came over with a smile. 'You looking fine. I see you have new shoes. Here, take one scarf from me. Do you remember me? I am Christian from Lagos.' He handed me the blood-red scarf that bore my darkest thoughts. 'Where you coming from?'

'From Venice.'

'Ah, Venessia. I sell bags there, but police beat you up. Milano is better. Where you going now?'

It was a good question. When I had left with Arnaud I had no idea what would happen and couldn't have cared less. I had watched Milan fold away behind me and followed him to Venice like a lost sheep. Had I forgotten that my children were coming in a few weeks? How was I going to show them that my life was almost on track? I knew I had no choice but to crawl back to Brett's house before he recruited another kinky stray.

'I think I am going to a friend's house. Thank you so much for your shoes the other day. You really saved my life.'

'Oh no, Madam, it is nothing. I see that you no belong in this city, you be too fine for this city. God bless you and your family.'

I walked on to the taxi rank and gave the driver Brett's address. The taxi rumbled over Milan's uneven flagstones, each bump felt like a punch in my gut. An orange tram shook along in front of us and I imagined the vehicle plunging into its side. I was stunned by this new reckless way of thinking. Even in my bleakest hours with Peter I had never had such a violent thought. The taxi driver sped up at a broad intersection and left the tram trundling in its wake.

I unlocked Brett's door again. Even in the silence I could sense that he was out and there was only Lam cooking in the kitchen alone. The smell of food reached into my belly and I realised I hadn't eaten since my sexy aromatic breakfast in Arnaud's arms. Tears spurted down my cheeks again as I steadied myself in the hall. Lam's face rounded the corner and he calmly led me into the kitchen. He lowered me into Brett's rattan chair and I clutched my hands to my face. I sat there in the soundless room while he prepared some noodles for me. Would Arnaud have taken her to some chintzy restaurant to eat? Would they clasp each other naked in bed? What would Arnaud say to her as he caressed the bump where their small child lay? Would he spare a thought for me? Would he ever think of me again?

Later I stripped and crawled into the Jane Austen bed. I thought of how nasty Mr Darcy had been and how nobody even knew whether he and Elizabeth Bennet had lasted longer than three months. I listened to Lam padding down the hall. Then there was a silence which became a huge, rabbit-like thumping. I worked out it was my heart. I knew I had to stop thinking of Arnaud and Estelle before I killed myself. I decided that in the morning when I woke up I would never think of my beastly Swiss ex-lover again. I let my fingers trace the swelling on my head and the trail of bruises down my side. They were Arnaud's beautiful, sensuous tracks, and they had led me nowhere.

In the morning I arose briskly and made myself a pot of powerful coffee. I dressed in a tailored grey suit and coiffed my hair. My status as a woman who had been double-dumped was not going to be written on my person. If the children were coming I needed a plausible job – not in the leather industry – although I wasn't sure how I was going to ease away from Brett's comforting flow of cash. I found a telephone directory in a cabinet in the hallway and looked up Jean Harper's English Now Language Institute. I asked Lam if he knew the address. Lam frowned and pointed around the corner. I didn't think he had understood, and thought I had better check with someone in the street. I went back to my room and sat down on the bed. I observed the Greek wrestlers with their hilarious bananas. I looked at the flutes carved into the oak. I reminded myself I had stepped off the Arnaud roller-coaster onto solid ground again. If anything, I had loved a man perfectly for a day in creepy old Venice, but he had left me and I had slammed into the dust.

Jean's small school facility was indeed in a street parallel to ours, as Lam had said. I walked up to the snazzy sign above the glass doors, indicating that the English Now Language Institute was on the second floor. There was a bar at street level with posters for the school taped up inside the window. I forced myself to walk closer. I heard some loud music playing in a classroom upstairs. It was an old U2 song that used to be my favourite. I stood still and took a few breaths to contain my excitement. For over a year now Jean Harper had been my icon. I had heard her boots trudging in the Andes. I had imagined her erotic nights in a wind-lashed tent. I could hardly believe that I had flown out to Milan on the strength of Jean striking it lucky on a singles trip and getting herself pregnant somewhere after forty. And here I was, finally about to meet the woman who had become a beacon in my shipwrecked life.

I watched a couple of students come out onto the footpath. They headed into the bar and ordered espressos. I thought I could use one of those too. As I stood there Jean herself waltzed in with a secretary or assistant and ordered a cappuccino in loud imperfect Italian. She wore a ruffled shirt that did not become her, and looked like she had taken the Milanese act a tad too far. The students greeted her and I saw a flash of chunky gold earrings, the type that babies like to rip from your ear lobes. She looked tired and spent beneath her salon tan, with her bright blond hair harshly pulled back. I didn't remember Jean smoking, but she held a fancy slim cigarette.

'Christ,' she said in pure London tones. 'Andrea's off to the football again this weekend. Just like last weekend and the one before. He's left me all the accounts to do, and his mother claims she's coming around to help with the baby, which means she'll be checking on what I've been feeding him all week.'

'Come on, Jean,' said her companion in Italian-accented English. 'Andrea is a good cook. You say he cooks for you, no?'

I thought it might a good moment to introduce myself, before the conversation went too far and she might think I had been listening in. I moved a few chairs noisily.

'Hello, excuse me. My name is Marilyn Wade. Would you be Jean Harper?' I tried to upgrade my accent slightly, given my non-existent teaching experience.

Jean frowned. I remembered that was why I had never particularly liked her: first the judgemental frown, then a cursory smile. My visions of our Milanese sisterhood trembled.

'Can I help you at all?' she said.

'Well, you probably don't remember me. We had toddlers in the same playgroup. An age ago, of course. At home. We were almost neighbours.'

'I'm sorry, I don't recall.'

'And, er, recently I saw you putting up a notice in the supermarket at home asking for English language teachers for the school.'

'What are your qualifications? You see this is a serious school. The government runs certain checks.' Her Italian friend gave her a quizzical look. 'I'd have to give you a formal interview.'

Qualifications? What qualifications? 'Fine, er, when would that be?'

Then she spoke in horrific Italian to the other woman. *'Allora Stephen ha detto che parte sabato, proprio questo sabato?'* (So did Stephen say he is leaving Saturday, this Saturday?)

The woman nodded.

Jean pressed her lips together. 'On the other hand perhaps you can help us out immediately.'

I followed the pair upstairs to Jean's office. There was an odd selection of photographs and posters on the walls, presumably reflecting what Jean thought her students perceived of our grand old country. David Beckham half-naked in Dolce e Gabbana; Prince William and the friendly Kate Middleton waving from Buckingham Palace balcony; John Lennon and Paul McCartney with their moptops and hourglass guitars. Jean fussed with papers on her desk and lit a thin cigarette before looking my way.

'We're in a slight state of upheaval here at the moment. My brother Stephen has been helping me manage, and also taught several classes. But Stephen,' she said with a touch of acid, 'has decided that *Milano* is not for him. He has rather left us in the lurch. I have a class for you at two o'clock this afternoon, they are on page twenty-seven of the Ranger Series. You do know it, don't you?'

'Of course, I don't have my copies here though, my books are yet to arrive,' I lied quickly.

'Never mind, you'll find one on the desk. If not just do conversation. Talk about pop stars and Kate Moss, anyone you can think of. Okay, I think that's all. I must leave now, my mother-in-law has just called the secretary to say my son is running a fever.'

Jean snapped open her mobile which pealed out some atrocious Italian love song and excused herself as she took the call. I wondered if it would be the lover Jean had discovered in the Andes and I would hear their molten tones. I wondered if Andrea were a better lover than Arnaud, but then my heart closed into a tiny clutched fist, the fist that had been plugged into my bawling eyes. Arnaud was having a baby with Estelle. Jean and Andrea had produced the miracle baby with ringlets. And lucky Marilyn Wade would be winging it with the Ranger Series.

'*Carissimoo!*' Jean's voice became breathy, I guessed for my benefit. 'How are you, darling? Yes, I've heard about the baby.

Your mother told me. Yes, I am going there right now. Yes, *non ti preoccupare,* I have found a replacement for Stephen.'

She then sat there listening for a while as a continuous noise came from her phone. He had quite a lot to say. And I didn't think it was lovey-dovey from the way Jean's forehead crinkled.

'*Certo, certo,*' she said, glancing at her nails. 'I will.'

She snapped the mobile closed, lit another slim fag and stood up straightening her tight skirt.

'Excuse me, that was my husband Andrea. Such a dear, though he worries far too much about the business. Two o'clock then, are we all right about that? You might have some more classes tonight and tomorrow so you'd better leave your details with Francesca.'

She extended a chilly hand my way and snatched up her bag, checking her hair clip and pony-tail in the mirror on the way out. I frowned, thinking of Jean in a baggy pair of trousers down at the duck pond, her dyed hair with its split ends, the little roll of tummy fat we all carried after our kids. I hadn't seen the turn-about coming, but come it had. She looked like she had spent the past two years in grooming school. And I was puzzled by the phone interlude. Had baby and family tarnished the Andes glow? Had the solicitor in hiking boots revealed that he was bossy and attached to his mum?

I wrote down Brett's address and Fiona's mobile number in Francesca's book. I heard some students moving into classrooms off the main hall and suddenly felt terrified. I would have to figure out Jean later on, right now I needed to work out how to teach the Queen's English without breaking into a hyper sweat. I went back downstairs to the bar and ordered a double espresso with grappa, letting it tear into my chest. I immediately felt lucid and able to conjugate my verbs.

But then a woman left a celebrity magazine open on the next table. I reached across and grabbed it, devouring the faces of

Europe's jet set. I saw women with almighty breasts and trout lips and carrot tans, men with Buddhist tattoos and wet-look hair and ridged abdominals. My eyes filled with tears as I scoured the pages for them.

And there they were. Estelle was smooching the rock star who was about to abandon her, sitting in his grungy lap as his tattooed hands cupped her belly. This time I read the captions of Estelle's Latvian-accented English: 'We are so happy together. I can't wait to see our child'. The tears ran down my face. I saw another stern *ex-marito* shot of Arnaud. I looked at last week's date printed on the edition. These facts were all about to change. Soon everyone would know that Estelle had swapped the grungy rock star for her ancient husband, and that cranky Arnaud Bertrand was the real father of her child. There would be romantic reunion shots, and the glowing nude belly displayed on a chaste cover for a vast sum. Next, there would be the blessed pink baby in a designer sling and Estelle's tips for immediate weight loss, along with beaming Arnaud pushing a stroller and circling her newly microscopic waist. I closed the magazine, ordered a shot of sheer grappa and began to rebuild my face.

At ten minutes to two o'clock I climbed the stairs to the school offices and began to bolt through the Ranger Series textbook. There were basic conversations structured to demonstrate easy grammar points, which I thought I could capably rattle off. The students began shuffling into the classroom and immediately asked where Stephen was, unsettling me somewhat. Their English was jolty and hit-and-miss like Federico's, and I realised they were entirely unimpressed with my neat clothing and recent manicure. Stephen, from what I could recall from neighbourhood talk years back, had been in a New Romantic band and never really shaken the Duran Duran look, something that might have come in handy with the current eighties revival.

'Stephen, he go?'

'But why Stephen go?'

'We want Stephen again!'

I smiled grimly at their stroppy faces. The girls were like a team of junior Sophia Lorens with scalloped breasts and voluptuous eyebrows.

'Well then. Now let's turn to page twenty-seven of the Ranger book. I was told you finished up here. Who would like to volunteer for the part of Penny?'

As I looked over them I realised they were frightfully different from English adolescents. They had not been raised on chips and Tesco Indian dishes and soggy shepherd's pie. Rather, they ate risotto while sipping *merlot* and weren't afraid of *carpaccio* sitting half alive on their plates. They had probably learnt how to make coffee at the age of five.

The class continued staring until a boy at the back made a comment and they burst into laughter. I stood there detesting every one of them, about to crumble, wishing I had my riding crop in my hand. I took a deep breath and considered walking out the door and never coming back. I still had a job as Brett's unlikely leather model for the Japanese and Norwegian buyers passing through town. But my children were coming out for Christmas, so I had only a few short weeks left to cobble a life together and look normality in the eye.

As they laughed, I walked around the desk and sat down, closing the textbook and giving it shove onto the floor. They became silent. I figured I had about thirty seconds to contain their interest.

'Anybody heard of *la mia nipotina* Kate Moss?'

After a string of lessons I found myself light-headedly walking down the street. My various students drove off on Vespas like the one I had straddled in Roma with Leonardo. After my scrawny niece Kate Moss, we had talked about Madonna (who used to live up the road from me), the Beckhams (who sometimes shopped at the same supermarket) and Prince William's Kate Middleton (who I'd bumped into at the local Zara shop). I found I was a splendid knitter of garbage and their attention was undivided. I even worked the same trick with the next class and the one after that, diverging a little into the Princess Diana legend and mentioning Pink Floyd with an older class full of lacklustre businessmen. I had each group reel out their favourite songs which caused a pleasing pandemonium in shocking English.

I'd gone into an interesting-looking bar on the next block, feeling quite chuffed and thinking that my life might be back on track, when my mobile started to ring. I hoped it was Pamela so I could tell her my suspicions about Jean Harper. But I saw with annoyance that it was Peter's number.

'Thank God you've answered. I just needed to hear your voice,' Peter gasped.

I rolled my eyes and purred my favourite word – *prosecco* – to the handsome grey-haired barman. I headed towards a table at the back.

'Darling!'

Darling?

'Yes Peter, I'm with you. What's up today then? Has your missus trimmed my roses? Are you ready to wallpaper?' I said smartly as I removed my coat.

'Oh, my darling Marilyn!' my ex-husband gasped again. 'I just want you to forgive me for all of this. We were meant for each other. I knew it the moment I saw you back at the house.'

I had a vision of Peter's face crammed into Danielle's neck. 'Well, you could've fooled me,' I responded.

The waiter brought me my drink and casually winked at me. It was a refined, non-vulgar wink that hit me deep in the belly. I winked back and returned to my aggravating phone call.

'Darling!' Peter cried. 'It's all been a mistake. I knew it all along. You are the woman of my life. You've supported me through all this. No other woman could have done that. When I look at our children ....' He began to cry and my irritation burst its banks. What had this woman done to reduce him to this?

'Peter, did you go to work today? Peter?' I asked firmly.

'Marilyn,' he begged. 'We could make it work again. I know we could. Marilyn, I desire you. I want you to come back.'

I nearly tumbled off my chair. It was years since I had heard Peter speak like this.

'What did you say?'

'I said I want you back. I want to make love to you. I want your smell in my mouth.'

In spite of myself, I felt a hot spur between my legs. Then there was silence. I could hear him breathing jaggedly, as though this were real, but I knew it wasn't. I felt an uncomfortable sensation stirring beneath my consciousness and my will. It was my old love for Peter, murmuring in its sleep.

I shook my head, gulping down my drink.

Peter took off again. 'Marilyn, you don't know what I want to do to your body. I saw what you've become. I want to make you howl. I am coming to you now. I just have to make love to you tonight.'

'No!' I shrieked. 'I mean, thank you, but not now Peter. You have been seeing another woman and I ....'

'Oh God, I know you've met someone Marilyn. That's why I have to act now. Please darling, just give me the chance to love you again. I can't live without holding you again. I've been such an egotistical bastard to you. I've known it all along. It's *you,* Marilyn. You're the woman I want.'

I motioned for another *prosecco* and sat drumming my fingers until the drink came. The barman stood poised a little too long by my shoulder, his aroma lingering on the air. It was alarmingly good. But I frowned at him to go away, wondering why the hell Peter had turned around like this, and why in my loins I suddenly felt a stumbling, illogical arrest. Thoughts of our dutiful spousal intercourse of the last decade fell away and I remembered the hours we had spent lunging into each other on every surface of our new freshly-painted house, how on summer nights we had made love on the wet grass while the neighbours drank themselves stupid.

'Just let me come and see you, Marilyn. Just one night together. The kids will be fine here, I'll tell Elizabeth next door. You know how deeply we need each other.'

It was all too much. I felt tears welling in my eyes. I knew I wanted my life to make sense and so far, it did not. I knew that I loved my house and I missed my sloppy gardening clothes and the calluses on my hands. I missed the children bickering outside on the porch and, after dinner, emptying the rubbish bin under the moon. That had been my life, and it had been taken from me. All of a sudden I smelt Peter's scent at the back of my nostrils with a sting of longing.

'Look Marilyn, the truth is I'm at the airport. I'm booked on a flight out in half an hour. I've organised everything. I'll be in Milan in around nine o'clock. I'll take you to a hotel, anywhere will do. Just let me love you again, Marilyn. I know we can make it work,' he said weakly. 'Marilyn darling, did you hear all that? Will you be there?'

But I was lurching to my feet, throwing my money on the counter, hurtling outside.

'Okay,' I whispered, pacing madly.

'You'll see, my darling,' he crooned. 'Everything will be better from now on. I know we were meant for each other.'

But I was not okay. I felt spasms of shock along my body and my nerves were alight. The fact that I had allowed myself to acknowledge my love for Peter was like giving birth to a monster with five heads. I had another lesson in an hour, and after this I could almost make it to the airport on time. But did I want to go to the airport? Did I want to kiss and make up with Peter after everything he had done?

And yet perhaps I owed it to him. I had been grumpy and unattractive all those years, more interested in gardening than sex, so it was no wonder he had searched elsewhere. And I didn't want the kids to come from a broken home, and who could tell how it would pan out if they had an inkling of my indecent escapades in Milan?

After my lesson I rushed to the station and caught the airport bus, feeling bubbly and weightless. I would have a lot to tell Peter, much of which he would hardly believe. Despite the traffic the bus arrived just as Peter's plane touched down and I made my way to the arrivals hall, watching the first passengers with briefcases and the pink financial newspaper tucked under their arms. A tear came to my eye as a young black husband was reunited with his white wife and their small honey-coloured child. I remembered Arnaud's words in French – *On fait la révolution pour arriver où on a commencé* – about how, despite everything, one always returned to the way one had been at the start. These now seemed words of irrefutable wisdom, and perhaps even Arnaud had been right to carry out his own words.

I waited over an hour, checking each face, waiting for each middle-aged man to morph into my ex-husband. None of them did. The last passengers dribbled to nothing and the doors remained closed. There were no more flights from the UK.

15. MORE GRAMMAR

That night I slept as though drugged. Then, the next morning, I could hardly face what had happened the night before. I recalled the wave of heat Peter had planted between my legs on the phone yesterday. And how, despite the distance between us, I had wanted him. I felt repulsed. The pair of them were probably shagging this very minute. I thought of the frizzy-haired woman I had glimpsed under the magnet on my fridge. She was now moaning under my ex-husband.

Thankfully I had another eleven o'clock lesson that morning so there was a reason to shower and dress. I greeted Lam in the hall. He handed me a cup of steaming smoky tea. The next time Brett flew by I would have to find a way to tell him the truth – or as much as he agreed to hear – and find more realistic lodgings for the duration of the children's visit. I didn't want Peter and Danielle applying for custody when social services tracked me down. Nor did I fancy my teenagers seeing me in leather cut-out pants, with my lily-white bottom they had barely glimpsed since they were in nappies.

The day was bright and no-nonsense and I sailed into the café below the school and ordered my cappuccino. My icon Jean was there scowling into her coffee. I tried hard to hear the roaring silence of the Andes around her, but Jean looked sleepless and depressed.

'Hello Jean,' I said brightly.

'Oh, hello there. Marion wasn't it?'

'Marilyn. Marilyn Wade.'

'Oh, I'm sorry. So how did it go yesterday? I'm sorry I didn't make it back. My son's *motorino* was hit by a car outside our apartment. Andrea was furious. The idiots just drove off.'

'That's not good. My own children are coming out in a few weeks.'

'And Robertino – that's our baby – just hasn't been himself lately. My mother-in-law says it's the *sesta malattia*, you know, the one the doctors can't diagnose. I must say they pick up children's illnesses I didn't even know about over here. But he's been pooing all right. Maria, my mother-in-law, sees to that. I think she prepared him that spinach with parmesan again last night. Just *full* of iron.'

Jean waved at some young students entering the bar before their lessons. She had perked up somewhat after the baby talk and asked the barman for another coffee. I remembered the winking bartender from last night when Peter was making his drastic pleas, and thought I might have a port of call on the way home.

'So where did you and your husband meet, Jean?' I wanted to hear about some of the magic at least, in Jean's own words. 'I understand you left England quite a while ago now.'

Jean glanced at me harshly. 'Well, my first husband married a woman he chatted up on the train. Ukrainian, I think. She was after immigration papers. I met Andrea at my dentist's. His mother lost a denture when he was taking her around the sights.'

'You mean you didn't meet him in the Andes?'

'I beg your pardon?'

'The Andes, you know, the mountains in South America. I thought you went on a trek over there. A singles trek.'

'You must be joking, I've never been to South America in my life. And with Andrea's high blood pressure he can hardly do two flights of stairs.' She gave me a dirty frown and released her coffee cup. 'And a singles trek? How awful.' She gave me one more look that said I was completely loopy and strode away.

I took a deep breath and looked up at the clock. The barman collected Jean's empty items and I saw the lipstick where her mouth had sipped. I slumped against the bar, flabbergasted. My vision of naked feet melding inside a wind-whipped tent

211

vanished. Instead, I smelt dental disinfectant and saw pastel walls dotted with five-pound Van Gogh prints.

I climbed the stairs. I remembered how the entire neighbourhood had been abuzz with Jean Harper's new lease upon life, her love affair born in the exotic Andes. Those of us who had been uncertain had looked it up in the atlas. Others pushed trolleys in a distracted stupor at the supermarket, or spent months drifting to sleep thinking of the furnace of a man's clasping thighs, while the wind whistled beyond a skein of high-tech canvas. Who on earth had come up with such an awesome rumour?

I stumbled into the classroom and opened the Ranger Series textbook as the students filed inside, chatting too fast and with too much slang for me to understand. I glanced at a young man who had Federico's profile and began to think nostalgically of the nights we had spent together. My buttocks began to prickle as I realised it was indeed Federico at the back of the room, looking sad and disinterested as a blond girl began to speak to him. I blundered into the first grammar exercise and Federico turned to me, staring open-mouthed. I found a volunteer to read Penny's part in the dialogue on page twenty-nine. Federico threw up a hand and volunteered to read Ben's part, his face breaking into a grin.

Penny: *'Shall we go to the supermarket, Ben? What do we need to buy today?'*

Ben: *'Yes, let's go to the supermarket, Penny. But first I want to make love to you. It's a long time I don't make love to you.'*

The class burst into laughter and I turned the colour of my grandmother's beetroots.

'Please, ah, Ben. I don't think that's what is written there. Could we have another Ben please?' I begged the class.

'But why, *signora o signorina?'* said Federico. 'Mister Stephen he let us make our own words. He say is good for us to invent. Something make me very, very hard here and I can only think of my ….'

'Okay, Penny,' I addressed the young brunette with pencilled eyebrows at the front. 'How about you think of another discussion to have with Ben, or anyone else? But please keep to the topic. Shopping and food, please.' I tried to sound crisply British despite feeling warm between the thighs.

'Oh, I know this one,' shouted Federico at the back. 'Penny, let us go to shop. I need to buy rubber toy for my girlfriend. She like colour purple, like light or dark purple.'

The brunette turned around and as far as I could tell, started swearing at Federico. The class was in fits. I maintained my beetroot colour. I heard Jean's heels clicking up the hallway.

'Please, everyone. *Io perdo il lavoro se non state zitti.'* I begged them to be quiet, singling out Federico who showed me his tongue. 'After the lesson, you will all be free to talk about whatever you wish. But right now I want you to pay attention to me.'

Somehow it worked. Federico turned on his star pupil behaviour. I had each student introduce themselves to me and tell me the attribute of themselves that they liked least. When Federico's turn came I held my breath but he looked mournfully in my direction and declared that he didn't treat his friends well enough and he had a pretty rotten temper. I saw some of the girls looking hopefully his way and kept my gears in check, but I wanted to think he was apologising to me for exploding at the airport and not salvaging Fiona's apartment from the dastardly Alberta. After the lesson was over he came up to me shyly, all of his bold talk dissolved.

'I never think I see you again, Fiona sister. When we marry, Fiona and me, you know I love you like real family. I miss you so much baby. Do you hear Fiona? She call me, you know, from Korea. She say she coming back. I ask her to marry me and she say maybe. So I have to learn English better, you know, for when we go to Australia. You know that?'

I looked at him doubtfully and touched his cheek. If this was what he wanted to believe, then I would be up there with the bridesmaids.

We kissed deeply with lashings of tongue. It felt so juvenile in the empty classroom. Federico interrupted to say, 'You know I love Fiona. Fiona she understand me. But you have help me so much.'

We wandered outside and had drinks in a bar around the corner from the school. I saw Jean herself striding past, pouting in a shop window when she thought no one could see. She wore a high-belted trench coat which before discovering about the Andes I might have stared at with envy. But now I frowned at her, seeing a dental nurse with dyed blond hair and a nose piercing and a pile of stale magazines. I shook my head and turned to Federico whose finger was stroking my forearm.

'You know,' he said to me. 'Before I marry your sister, you have to teach me about Australia. I wanna know your country. Now you be my teacher.'

'That should be no problem,' I smirked, remembering Federico's teaching methods and thinking of my riding crop back home. 'I will teach you everything I can think of. When shall we start?'

After a quiet dinner we wandered back to Brett's apartment and I invited Federico inside. There were no lights on and I hurried my lover down the hallway. We entered my austere bedroom. Curious, Federico looked around. He peered at the Greek wrestlers on the walls with their jerky bananas. He ran his fingers along the oak flutes of the bed.

Very quickly however, the role of disciplinarian passed into my hands. I pulled out my riding crop and sliced the air. Federico froze on the cushions.

'What happen to you, Fiona sister?' he cried fearfully. 'I want geography lesson, not how to ride horse.'

I brandished the riding crop in the air a little longer, enjoying the whooshing sound and noting the dryness of his lips. Federico seemed to have entirely forgotten my suffering in the name of Italian grammar. I crawled over him and told him he was a bad, forgetful boy. I demanded that he name the highest mountain in Australia.

After the lesson, I allowed him a few sips of the grappa I had stashed under the bed. Federico stopped sweating and lay there panting.

'*Va bene così,* my baby,' he sighed. *'Ti prego,* your geography lesson is killed me.'

Then he fell asleep in my arms as I wound my fingers through his curls. It was so different from the bliss I had felt with Arnaud, but beautiful nonetheless. I wondered how Federico had gotten it into his silly head that Fiona would give him the time of day, let alone drag him to Australia. I held his salty body tighter and drifted to sleep.

Somewhere in the night I awoke and found Federico calmly looking at me. Our skins were seamed together.

'You leave Swiss boyfrenn, don't you?'

'*Didn't* you.' I pinched his thigh.

'Eeeii! You hurt me. *Didn't* you?'

'Yes, he left me. He went back to his ex-wife.'

'But you love him, no?'

I didn't answer.

'You see, when I get Fiona, your Swiss fock he come back to you.'

Yeah, and camels might fly. And yet the wound Arnaud had left was healing fast and I found I rather liked being with Federico again. I had missed the playfulness and Arnaud's big talk and fabulous history had worn me down.

'Of course, darling. Now lie back and roll over.'

He obliged and I lazily ran my fingers along his spine, up across where his shoulders fanned out, then down to his firm buttocks. I thought briefly and curiously of Arnaud's speckled hands doing the same to Estelle's luminous bottom, and how the couple would struggle to find lovemaking positions as her body changed shape. But even these thoughts tumbled away as I turned to what I had been missing.

Brett flew in several days later from Copenhagen. One evening I saw him walking through the apartment in a sarong and bare chest, wearing a pair of thick glasses. I followed him into the kitchen and watched him stretching, his grey cropped hair like a toilet brush as he rolled his head on his shoulders.

'Ah, there you are.' He smiled warmly as he set his glasses on the table. 'Our wonderful lodger. I'm very sorry this week has been so slow. Lam tells me we have had manufacturing problems in Mexico. I might just have to fly out there. Of course, Roderick won't stop saying I-told-you-so, given his preference for the Dutch. I believe he's just helped Greta buy some handsome art in Venice, where he said he glimpsed you sampling the locals. How have you been then? Who was that piece of good fortune I saw stumbling onto the footpath when I came in this morning?'

'Oh,' I stammered, 'that's my, er, my lover.' It was the first time in my life I had ever used a label of the sort and it cancelled out the ugly memory of seeing Roderick and the horse-faced woman in Margarethe's gallery. I felt myself lift several inches from the floor.

'Mmmm. I must say I've enjoyed my student-come-barman types. Highly recommended.'

Lam came into the kitchen with a bowl of scented oil and Brett pulled over the worn rattan chair. He sank down, throwing his sarong open to the heavens, while I stared rigorously at the kitchen shelves. Lam began to knead Brett's honey-coloured shoulders. Gradually, a kind of smile crinkled Lam's face and I saw he was not the young exquisite boy I had always thought but, rather, he was a middle-aged man with glowing skin. I stood in shock as my eyes wandered towards the bulge in Brett's lap. I grasped the kitchen table. It was enormous.

'Isn't it marvellous?' Brett said blurrily. 'You must let him take your body to bits. There is not a thing like it. How fatigued I am by all this travel.' He sighed. 'How about joining me on the trip to Mexico? I do know some interesting spots, tequila you'll probably dream about for the rest of your life. You know I met a Mexican woman once on the internet. I never thought I would fall for such a folly. We corresponded pure blunt sex for months and months and I went there to discover she was a hairy old taxi driver. It was so delightfully unlikely. What a badly signposted warren this world has become.'

Lam's fingers dug deeper and deeper into Brett's left shoulder, as though he were realigning the tendons themselves. Brett's forehead occasionally tensed or a ripple ran into his cropped hair. I wondered if this could be the moment to address my personal issues, as I pulled my eyes away from Brett's one-man nature show.

'Brett, I was wondering, I mean, I am ever so grateful to you. This has been the most difficult and confusing time in my life and now, well, the truth is I am divorced and my children are coming out in a few weeks for Christmas.'

'You have children?' Brett exclaimed. 'Why that's fantastic. What ages are they?'

I stammered, 'Vanessa is sixteen now and Eddy is fourteen.'

'Marvellous! They're around the same ages as my own,' he told me. 'Percy just turned seventeen on the sixteenth of last month, while young Oliver is eleven and darling Katie is almost nine.'

'You have children too?' I said, aghast, as Lam gently bent Brett's arm like a rag doll. He then began on the articulation of Brett's fingers. I heard knuckles crack.

'Why, of course. Percy is an excellent student and hopes to study chemistry in Glasgow. I just had him on the phone.'

'I never thought.'

'I also thought Scotland was an unlikely choice but he seems quite determined. How about Vanessa, what are her study plans?'

'Vanessa? Vanessa has no idea, I don't think.'

'Well, certainly you must have them out here for Christmas. My family being in Hong Kong, I've yet to speak to their mother. She is a tremendous worker and it is almost impossible to tear her away from her bank.'

I watched Lam drape Brett's arm across his body and over the opposite shoulder, pulling slightly. It felt like a piston had popped in my brain.

'You must take the apartment in Via Contini then, it would be inappropriate to stay with us. I'm not sure who Roderick will be bringing here over the break and, frankly, I was hoping for a spot of real recreation. I have a recurring fishing dream, can you imagine that? Utterly inexplicable for a man who grew up on the twenty-first floor without a whiff of the harbour.'

The two men exchanged a sheer glance and Lam placed Brett's arm across his thickening belly. Soundlessly, he walked around to Brett's other side and began to knead his right shoulder.

'Lam will give you the keys to the apartment. It's a quick walk from here and I am sure you and Vanessa and Eddy will be more than comfortable.'

I walked barefoot down the hall leaving the two men in the kitchen. I had a feeling Brett's mysteries would run deeper still. As I stood in my room something about the men's closeness or the scented oil made me feel an unwelcome pang for Arnaud. I curled up under the covers and clasped myself. Was he still in Milan? Would that pregnant nymphet remember to make him take his pills?

That last week before the children were to arrive my worries made me anxious and cruel and I kept Federico on a short leash. His geography lessons were scorching. Each time the thought of Arnaud returned I was harder on him still, asking him useless questions about rivers and marsupials as I tried to recall what I had studied at school. Afterwards, I consumed him with a loveless fever.

One night Federico grabbed my shoulders and shook me with manly, exasperated force. I had overstepped the line. I began to sob and sob, collapsing in his arms. I was so worried about the children arriving in a matter of days. My fury with Peter had started to return in bursts. And I was angry at Jean Harper because I had been stupid enough to believe she had found everlasting love with a tawny solicitor in the Andes. Though I had tried and tried, my life made less sense than it ever had.

'What you have Fiona sister? You want to kill my children?'

Federico soothed me for hours. We lay on the bed under the canopy and I thought of the first time he had seen me naked, when I had cracked his chin in Fiona's bathroom. I plastered his face with grateful kisses. The next morning we moved my considerable collection of garments and shoes to the Via Contini apartment.

16. VIA CONTINI

In a matter of moments it seemed, I was back on the airport bus staring out at the factories and apartment blocks filing past. The children were arriving at Malpensa in an hour. Vanessa had called me with the flight details. Peter hadn't had the courage to speak to me since he had double-dumped me at the airport and scuttled back to his harlot. I looked back to those moments when he had moaned *Marilyn, I desire you! I want to make you howl* and I had grown aroused. Had I really wanted him back? How had I been such a pushover when they had shagged mercilessly on my diamond-patterned quilt?

I returned to the many and lingering pleasures I had enjoyed with Federico last night. That morning I rinsed him in the shower and he dragged himself off to his last exam on ancient Roman aqueducts. He was almost as excited about the children as I was. But while Federico was desperate to take Eddy to the football, I was desperate to package my young lover for my wary, emotionally-ravaged kids. Having ridden the Peter-Danielle roller-coaster for six months, I didn't want them to see their mother spiralling into a sexual freefall with a randy barman, let alone have them discover my leather career over on Brett's block.

The bus pulled up before one of the airport entrances and I hobbled down the aisle in my high heels. A rush of cold air flew up the steps from outside and lifted my dress over my black *autoreggenti*. The bus driver saw fit to make a cheeky remark, to which I lacked the wherewithal to reply. I must have looked like an East European whore picking up afternoon customers. I struggled down the steps but at the bottom my ankle bent the wrong way and I fell sideways onto the footpath. My first thought was Arnaud. *Why wasn't Arnaud by my side?* I wanted to cry. The bus driver chuckled in his seat and a young African man swept over to help me to my feet.

'Sorry, Madam. *Stai bene?*'

'Yes, thank you so much,' I gushed as he pulled me up with strong arms. 'Christian? Is that you?' He looked so much like my saviour from the park.

'Of course it be me, Madam. I come to meet my brother from Lagos. Why you crying?'

'Oh God, I have to stop.'

'You come inside and I get you coffee. Where be your bag, Madam?'

'Please don't call me Madam, my name is Marilyn. I'm meeting my children. When is your brother coming?'

'Tomorrow. My friend give me ride this morning, he go collect his sister from Abuja. I go sleep here tonight.'

'Are you crazy? You can't sleep here. Take this for the bus and come back tomorrow.'

'No, no, sister. Just you stop your cryin' and don't worry.'

He helped me inside and after the coffee I rushed down to the arrivals section where the children would appear. I was sweating. It took an age for people to funnel out through the doors.

Then I saw them: Vanessa's face, bright and snappy; Eddy, lagging behind with a big trolley bag. What on earth had they brought? I thought with a shock how it would have been if Peter and I had polished off a dirty weekend in Milan, and were now standing here ready to tell our children that their lives were under control again. But I stood alone on the empty marble, hugging myself, waiting until their eyes found me. I was so glad Peter had abandoned me. I never wanted him by my side again.

Vanessa pounded into my arms and Eddy swung around the pair of us. I burst into tears, as did they. We wandered outside and I waved to Christian hunched in the cold and hailed the first taxi my eyes fell upon. The three of us snuggled into the car and we headed back into Milan.

'Mum, you look grand. But what happened to your leg? Did you take a spill?'

'I did, I fell out of the bus.'

Eddy giggled. 'When are we going to the football?'

'Are you all right then?'

'Yes, I am certainly. How about pizza?'

It was almost lunch-time so we left their bags at the apartment and set out on foot through the neighbourhood. Vanessa's eyes lingered on the shop windows. They were both dressed like English children and their rosy complexions shone. People glanced at the odd trio we made: Vanessa with her pink and black asymmetrical hair and face piercings; Eddy's red-headed Mohawk, and myself in a black leather trench coat Brett had brought back from Denmark.

'Mum, they have underwear shops on every corner.' Vanessa giggled, looking at yet another G-string twirling on a limbless dummy.

After they'd consumed a fair amount of pizza, they relaxed and started to tell me everything:

'And you should see her when she gets up in the morning. We won't get out of bed and she shouts and screams and Dad's onto her, trying to get a shag out of her before she takes off to work. They fight in the bathroom.'

'My bathroom?'

'Course. And once Dad ran down the front path to her in the car in his boxers.'

'The chocolate silk ones?'

'No, the orange ones, they're worse … and she drives off … and he just sits there crying on the frost.'

'And then,' Eddy added. 'In the night-time they come in really, really late, and Dad checks if we're asleep and then they smoke pot in the sitting room with music on and you can hear them.'

Vanessa frowned at me, worried. 'Is it all right Mum, if we tell you this? You're not mad, are you?'

'How can I be? I don't know how you put up with it.'

'Well, we put laxative in the coffee tin. She's a coffee freak.'

'And we put her knickers in the rubbish. She goes barmy!'

I glanced out the window as I brought my wine to my mouth and noticed a couple strolling into view. I couldn't believe who I saw. It was Arnaud and his young wife, parading in the afternoon light. Arnaud's fingers were laced with hers and her face glowed with perfect beauty. I nearly passed out. Vanessa followed my gaze and her eyes squinted.

'Isn't that that model, what's-her-name? From Russia?'

'I think her name is Estelle. I heard she's from Latvia,' I mumbled as I stared.

Vanessa frowned at me, but her excitement took over. 'Oh wow! Only two hours here and we're already seeing famous people. Isn't she having a baby with Stevie Hollow from The Rotters? Who's that old creep holding her hand?'

I gripped the poor waiter's arm and begged for a whole carafe of wine. 'Who knows?' I stammered. 'Probably her grandfather.'

'What about that coat? Did you see it, Mum? Fur all the way to the ground!'

I had seen. Creamy fawn fur from a dozen skinned rodents. I also saw the small but now prominent belly, fruit of their joint sexual labours. I cringed as Arnaud passed by me on the other side of the glass. A path had opened for the glamorous couple and people craned around as they moved on. I took one last glance at Estelle's divine face and wondered what she really thought about carrying Arnaud's long-winded genes, now that the duped rocker had sent her home to Daddy. She had cuckolded them both.

Still, I thought that today Estelle wore a trace of hurt at the corners of her mouth, while I had to admit Arnaud seemed safely besotted. Smile girl, I thought bitterly, if it weren't for him you'd be pulling up potatoes.

I guzzled down another glass of wine and tried to clear my face for the children. I ignored the footpath in turmoil and took off to the bathroom. As I dodged chair backs and waiters I couldn't help remembering how Arnaud's face had changed on the boat in Venice.

It was Estelle, Arnaud had murmured, *Estelle said the baby is mine.* Our eyes had never crossed paths again.

'You okay, Mum?' Vanessa came in while I was drying my hands. 'You know that old fellow, don't you? It came up like something on your face.'

'Please don't tell Eddy. Don't tell your father. I've been rather foolish.'

'Well, it looks as though *he* is acting the fool out there on show for all.'

'You're right there.'

'He was rough on you, wasn't he?'

'Nothing I can't keep in check. It is odd after you've been married seventeen years. Your father just went out and had a fling. I can't do that. I don't know how. I just seem to be doing everything stupidly.'

'But you're having sex, aren't you?'

'What?'

'Mum, you left a jumbo bag of condoms in the cabinet in the spare room and some pretty saucy underwear. Danielle put Dad through the wringer and I'm certain he told you he wanted you back again, didn't he?'

'Yes, he did.'

'Bloody idiot.'

'Vanessa, that's your father you're talking about.'

'And you're defending him? I've had enough of him. And so should you. He should just eff off and leave us in peace.' She turned away and I saw her lovely long eyelashes were blotted with tears. 'We'll be okay Mum, and we'll sort you out. That's what we're here for.'

I didn't see Federico for the next few days in class and I was beginning to grow faint with waiting. Then I came home one afternoon, tired of Jean's stroppiness, and Federico was sitting in the living room with the children, speaking his nonsensical English. I was immediately on edge, having been unclear about whether or not they should all meet. Federico heard me enter and was swiftly on his feet planting a kiss on my cheek.

'This is my English teacher. Very good English teacher.' As I hadn't thrashed out my Fiona story I knew the inevitable bumble into uncharted territory was coming, so I headed out to the kitchen to prepare a drink. Federico was at my heels.

'*Perché sei venuto qui?* Why are you here?' I hounded him as his hands entered my dress.

'This is the why,' he gasped into my hair as I shook against the table.

'*Federico non puoi!* You can't! And the children? *I ragazzi?*' I said desperately. They had turned on a game show on the television, the one with the girl in the silver hot pants. I heard the audience of perverts clapping.

'You're right, Mum!' screamed Vanessa from the other room. 'She's actually wearing silver hot pants. Can you believe this?'

Federico pushed me into the bathroom and hoisted me powerfully onto the sink. I was trying to work on my Fiona story, but Federico was intent upon his task. I twisted around and flushed the toilet three times to drown his groaning and tried to curdle my yelps. I felt a small explosion travel along my spine and through my legs. Afterwards I washed my face and Federico opened a welcome bottle of *prosecco*, coolly pouring glasses for all of us.

'I have wine from when I am this high.' He drew a line in the air and Eddy looked thoroughly puzzled.

Vanessa was glued to the television frowning. 'I just can't believe a woman would do this. Did you see her?'

'Oh yes,' said Federico, and I became increasingly embarrassed about what might be coming next. 'She get undress on television so all the husbands at home have something to think of when they make love to fat wife. You know, like pornography. Then women can relax and tidy kitchen while the men watch television.'

Vanessa's eyes widened and she looked over to me. 'You mean women don't mind parading around like that?'

I was worried they were going to seriously clash and didn't know whether to change topic or wait for the fallout.

'No, I don't think. Look at.' He started zapping around all the channels. It was mid-evening and the quiz shows were in full swing as people sat around their dinner tables supplying answers. On each channel there was a booby female holding up a card with a letter or spinning a wheel. On one channel two girls were doing a go-go dance.

'You see? It is always like this.' Then he switched to a news channel with an older woman announcer. Her skin had been stretched across her face and her lips were fat and shiny. 'And then they get like this.' He shook his head, glancing for a split second in my direction. 'But this is awful. This woman she not know who she is anymore. She is like *carnevale* mask, very scary. But this is Italy now, everyone afraid to get old except short bald man, you see him?'

He was pointing back to the game show announcer, a bald man with a paunch, who was pointing to the girl in the hot pants and reading from his cue card. Then he turned off the television and said, '*Basta!* My new Australian family will think Italy crazy place! Tonight I take you out to trattoria.'

226

The children stared at me and I shook my head at him. 'That's not necessary, Federico, even though you might think my family seems lost. I think it's better we catch up at *scuola* tomorrow, no?'

'No, no, no. *Non se ne parla nemmeno. Vi offro io la cena.* I know good place around corner.'

'Federico, *no.*'

'Marilena *sì*,' he insisted. I was shocked. It was the first time Federico had ever addressed me by my name and I wondered what the hell he had been playing at all these months of pretending to be the obsessed brother-in-law. I liked the way he said Mary-lena, it sounded fetching and foreign. I felt a residual tingle between my legs and told the kids to grab their jackets.

As we were walking along the street people couldn't help but look at us. My smart English teenagers, myself in Brett's leather coat and stocky Federico lacing his arm around my waist while I quickly snatched it off. I was terrified of traumatising the kids any further by looking like a hell-bent cradle-snatcher. The last shops had closed and the bars were full of people. Trams rattled across intersections beneath Christmas lights twinkling in long arcs above the streets.

'It's so lovely,' exclaimed Vanessa, and I was thrilled to see the smile on her face. She folded her arm through mine and we strode together. Eddy bundled along looking this way and that, rather more guarded, and I saw Federico walking behind proudly. He steered us into a restaurant and found us impressive seats by the window, swiftly ordering a round of *prosecco* before our coats had found their way to the rack.

'Eddy, are you sure you want that?' I asked.

'He wants it, Mum,' said Vanessa.

Federico left the table and I felt I should quickly test the waters. 'Federico's been a great friend, you know. I was staying at his girlfriend's flat a while back – she left to work in Korea – and the flat actually belongs to Federico's family. He's obsessed with this girl, her name is Fiona and she's Australian. Poor guy, he sometimes gets so mixed up. He's really helped me with my Italian and now he is trying to improve his English. He is odd but he's all right.'

Vanessa rolled her eyes as she opened a packet of *grissini*. 'Cut the bull Mum, he looks like a fine shag.'

'Vanessa!' I gasped. Eddy giggled and they calmly shared the breadsticks out as they had been doing since they were kids.

'What Mum? Innit?' she grinned.

'Your father behaves like that. I don't.'

'Come on, we heard you at it in the bathroom. We don't mind if you have a boyfriend. It's okay, Mum.'

'He's not my boyfriend! He's getting married to this Australian girl.'

'Yeah and I'm buying silver hot pants.'

Federico returned to the table and we settled down. He ordered plates for all of us, including delicate langoustine for myself, safe spaghetti for Eddy and saffron risotto for Vanessa. I was delighted. Federico said the owners were remote cousins and I worried that I might see Alberta brandishing a knife, but I didn't see any sign of her nor the witless Gustavo and his lap dancing sidekick. Throughout the meal I waited for Federico to start asking about kangaroos and Bondi beach but he behaved magnificently, answering all of Eddy's questions about Italian football players and the last European Cup. In fact, most of the evening was spent remembering goals and foul play, or team-swapping by players or who was better, Ronaldo or Rooney. I saw rapture in Eddy's eyes when Federico promised to take him to a big match at San Siro while Vanessa and I shopped *in centro* the next day. Vanessa laughed with glee. Federico escorted us to the front door in Via Contini and gave us all chaste kisses on the cheeks. It was one of the most perfect evenings I had ever spent.

The truth was that Jean Harper paid shite. I couldn't believe my first pay packet when I opened up the cheap brown envelope the next morning. I went back to Francesca and asked if there had been some mistake. I had been doing four or five lessons a day for almost a month and Brett paid me more for walking around in leathers for a couple of hours.

'But you have no *partita IVA*. Signora Jean cannot pay you the full rate.'

'How am I supposed to pay rent and feed myself?'

'Teach more lessons. I have a new class every Wednesday morning if you want it.'

'Teach more? Why don't you pay more?'

Jean walked out of her office looking drawn and severe. To my shock I saw she had two melons filling up her plunging shirt. My eyes homed in. New lover plus new baby plus new breasts.

'Hello?' she squawked.

'Oh, I'm sorry, I noticed your, er, your change.'

'Well,' she snorted. 'It's more or less obligatory these days. I flew to Spain the other weekend. Now, what were you saying to Francesca?'

'Well, it's the pay. I was hoping for a little more. It's a very expensive city.'

'What? More than London? You must be joking. Living costs are certainly less. You should see the running costs I have. And the taxes.'

'Oh, I'm certain.'

'If you feel you have to complain then perhaps English Now is not the right place for you. There are plenty of university students who'd be grateful for the experience of living over here. And who wouldn't be whingeing about their pay packets.' (I saw Francesca nodding adamantly.) 'And given your lack of qualifications, I don't see that you have a leg to stand upon. Will that be all?'

I glanced at Jean's plump melons again, and noticed the contrast with the train tracks on her neck. She still had a few weekends in Spain ahead of her.

'Hmmm?' she said staring harder.

I turned down the hall and went to my classroom.

I took Vanessa on a mother-daughter shopping spree that afternoon while the boys went to San Siro. I was furious. I did what every woman worried about her financial situation does: I spent more. We caught the *metropolitana* as far as the Duomo and came into the piazza teeming with lights. But I ignored the massive cathedral façade and steered Vanessa into the Galleria Vittorio Emmanuele with its spectacular shops. We walked into one of the big names, Vanessa wincing as we trod onto malt-coloured carpet with six-foot shop assistants shaking their locks. I tried on some divine heels and had the girl bring me a matching handbag. Vanessa fell onto a pouf and exclaimed, 'Shite!'

I strode in front of the floor-to-ceiling mirror and decided in a matter of minutes that I couldn't live without the ensemble. Vanessa blanched. I turned to the exquisite young woman and rather harshly told her to put them in a bag. Her freshness and beauty made me think of Estelle who, on her days off, probably made desultory purchases like this. I pulled out the credit card that wound back to Peter's account.

'Gawd, Mum,' oozed Vanessa as the doorman cranked open inch-thick glass. 'Stuff Zara.'

As we walked back across the freezing piazza carrying my glossy shopping bag I felt that things were partially back in place. Jean wasn't going to belittle me with her thin salary and melon breasts. I would be turning up dressed like a goddess while she caught the cheap flight down to Spain. We passed the little bar where I had insulted the Chinese man and I quickened my pace. We trekked into the underwear boutique where the girl had wrapped up my red brassiere just before I was robbed in the park.

Inside there were ranks of young women examining shreds of underwear as though they contained the meaning of life. Vanessa began browsing, finding an emerald green set she liked and I stood at the curtain while she tried it on. Standing there, my mind kept going back to pregnant, flawless Estelle, rescued from her potato-farming future and chosen to make every woman feel chubby and unkempt. I thought of Jean Harper under the knife, trying to win back the years she had lost. My hands were gripping the tasselled gold cord of my shopping bag in a hot sweat and I felt a wave of dizziness, just as I had in Margarethe's studio before I crashed to the floor. Vanessa called out for me to come in. I felt a deep panic, pushed inside and sat on the tiny stool throwing my head between my knees. Vanessa, poor love, bent over me in her shocking green knickers and bra.

'What is it, Mum? What's the matter?'

'It's nothing,' I said groggily. 'These shops are so overheated. I just feel a little faint, that's all. I shouldn't have spent so much money.' I wanted to tell her about Arnaud and how in Venice I had loved a man perfectly for twenty-four hours, and how all I wanted to do was go back to that feeling of crystalline completeness. Was it wrong to desire that? But as I looked at her perfect rounded body in the super underwear I wanted to protect her from the worst. I wanted desperately to tell her she would never face pain, and that good things would always come to her.

'Mum, take your time.' She kissed me on the forehead. 'There's no rush, is there?'

She gave me a squished hug, difficult in the changing booth, and I was not certain if she had crossed over and read my thoughts or if she was referring to the amount of time we still had left to blow Peter's cash. I breathed deeply until my panic evaporated and I felt a stinging light-headedness.

I bought her the emerald underwear and we continued down the boulevard collecting shopping bags.

In all, the children stayed only two weeks. Federico passed by every few days. One evening he cooked *spaghetti con le vongole* which the children looked at doubtfully. The grey *vongole* lay seamed through the pasta like tiny eyeballs. However after a series of football matches Eddy was ready to eat from Federico's hand, and he soon gobbled down the meal. Federico kept a respectful distance from my body, which I couldn't quite fathom apart from family decorum, and he made no more bewildering references to Australian flora or fauna. I relaxed. The children made hilarious commentaries on the local television programmes and avidly watched the same dubbed American cop shows I had watched back in Fiona's apartment. We had a great old laugh.

The English Now Language Institute closed for a week and I took them to the Christmas party held in one of the classrooms. Jean herself handed out cheap *prosecco* in plastic cups. Her transformed English teenagers came along too, dressed in preppie clothes with bobbed hair. Vanessa and Eddy pissed themselves laughing. *Did you see that effing vest? Did you see the belt on those jeans?*

I looked around and saw the love-child with ringlets buried in the bosom of a staunch Italian matron. Did that mean Jean's new husband had appeared for the turnout? I scoured the room for Jean's lover, no longer the faceless tawny athlete who had writhed with her in the wind-lashed tent, but a pick-up from the dental surgery who couldn't do two flights of stairs. Then Jean flitted up to an anxious-looking man under a Duran Duran poster and gave him a smooch. Overweight, with grey skin and two tufts of hair above each ear, the man my entire neighbourhood had dreamt about puckered up and kissed Jean Harper's tanned forehead. I watched painfully as my vistas of the Andes folded away.

She saw me watching and waltzed over. 'Hello Marion, so glad you could come. Are these your, er, children? Well, of course. They certainly don't seem very Italian. I'm not sure they would want to mix with Pietro and Giovanna over there. They're so fluent in Italian they've changed their names. Just over for a visit, are we?' She grimaced at Vanessa and Eddy. 'Let me introduce my Milanese husband, Andrea. He's likely to become the life of the party.' She gave a small laugh.

We walked over and Jean introduced us. Andrea's hands were clammy and he smiled in a business-like way without meeting my eyes. Jean's face broke into crisp, wrinkled pleasure.

'Pleased to meet you. Jean speaks the world of you,' I said. But Jean manhandled him away to one of the desks where a purple salami waited to be sliced. I looked at his baggy trousers and soft bottom, shaking my head. A legion of housewives back home would be weeping into their aprons.

I looked around for Federico thinking we could escape for a drink and share a grammar lesson or two. But Federico hadn't turned up. Vanessa looked over to me, crossing her eyes. Andrea was wolfing down the salami while Jean reminded him of his blood pressure, pawing his arm. Later, the traditional *panettone* was sheared to bits.

An hour into a Beatles medley we left. Outside, an uneven sleet covered the footpath. It was trying to snow. I wondered if Arnaud were clutching his lover in their lush pad with Milan twinkling along the horizon. Or if they had already taken off to bask in the tropics. I felt the rain dribbling down my face. Eddy saw an Irish pub on a corner and we knocked back a plate of greasy potato chips before going outside and facing the cold hike to the house.

On Christmas day it snowed. It was dry, ragged snow that quickly built up along the footpaths. The more it snowed, the more the city seemed like a big soundless village. It made me think of Arnaud's childhood town he had wanted to show me, when he was still trying to break into my skirt.

By New Year's Eve all the snow had turned to dirty frills along the streets and we persevered out to a fireworks display in one of the piazzas. Brett called me up to invite me to a party in Helsinki. He was in a wild mood and I heard shrieking and laughter in the background. Peter telephoned from New York and Eddy took the call in the kitchen while Vanessa and I watched a spaghetti western with a scorching Clint Eastwood. Long after midnight we crawled into bed and I cried alone for hours. Days later Federico's disappearance had begun to ache, the children had departed and the Via Contini apartment was depressingly empty.

17. IN LATVIA

I went back to Brett's place. Roderick's friend Greta, who'd bought the sculptures from Margarethe, had returned after New Year in Gstaad. She had broken her hip falling off a ski-lift and missed her flight back to Boston. Roderick hadn't known where to put her and it was decided that the Via Contini apartment would be best. Brett still hadn't flown in from Finland and Lam silently helped me rearrange my clothes in the antique dresser next to my Jane Austen bed.

January classes started at Jean's and I went back to work. I made it my new policy to forget about the Andes and be as friendly as possible to my ex-icon who had given me a job. Perhaps there was another way to work the sisterhood. I smiled at Jean's tired face and fearsome boobs, and drank a cappuccino with her in the morning before work.

At night I fell asleep, snuggling up to Lam's hot water bottle against the cold. I didn't know why Federico no longer wanted me. Perhaps he had seen through the Australian ruse. Perhaps the older children scenario had thrown him off. I couldn't put my finger on it. Nor could I be bothered about Fiona's toy collection residing in my bottom drawer. One morning when I had no lessons I asked Lam to give me a massage rather than think it all through again. He pulled over the old rattan chair in the kitchen and bade me to sit down. I let my gown slip away and felt his fingertips warm my skin. He massaged my shoulder, easing the tendons. He soothed my spine, loosening the vertebrae. Thoughts of my marooned children, my disobedient student lover and the man I adored (probably lounging on a yacht by now, fawning over his treasure) finally meandered away.

I met Roderick in the hall outside and he cut through my dreamy state. Until now Roderick had hardly even registered my presence in the flat.

'You speak Italian, don't you? That stuff that Greta bought in Venice last month hasn't come through and she wants to check they have the shipping details right. She says there is some man who either can't or won't speak English at the gallery. Would you be a dear and go over there and help her out?'

I froze. That was Margarethe's gallery.

'Did you hear me?' he looked at me.

'Yes. Of course.'

'Here, take the keys. The woman's got us all running around while she's parked in front of the television. I just bought another dozen DVDs. It'll be hell until she gets on that plane, I assure you.'

I wandered over to Via Contini later in the afternoon and unlocked the front door. Inside Greta, the horse-faced woman, was immobilised on the divan with an array of cushions. She sat there zapping the television.

'Hello, are you the nurse? Roderick said he would send a nurse. You do speak English, don't you? Tell him there is no satellite connection whatsoever. I'm just not reading it and for God's sake my brother owns a telecommunications company.'

I smiled and trod forth. 'No, I'm not the nurse. Roderick said you needed some calls made to Venice in Italian.'

'Christ, yes. I wanted the pieces cleared next week and so you think these wise guys have even got them packed? With the airport all of two miles away? Huh? Let me give you that number.' She pulled out her Blackberry and scanned. 'Here it is. Here's the phone. Now go.'

She handed me the phone and I made the call. I'd been hoping for a little composure gap before speaking to Margarethe as I had a severe case of butterflies. Greta just stared at me as though I were a halfwit sent to help her out.

'Hello?'

'*Si, pronto.*'

236

I nearly fainted. It was Arnaud. My voice cracked away to a whisper.

'*Marileen, c'est toi?* Is that you?' he gasped.

'No – I mean yes, it is. I'm not calling for me, I'm calling for Greta ….'

'Scarsdale,' Greta provided.

'For a Miss Scarsdale. An American client of Margarethe. Of your mother.'

'Jesus, I know Margarethe is my mother,' he said impatiently.

My stomach jumped. 'Miss Scarsdale says she can't get into contact with anyone who speaks English. She needs to have her sculptures sent to the US.'

'Margarethe had a stroke two days ago.'

'Oh no, that's terrible.'

'What the hell is going on?' barked Greta, banging the television remote on the coffee table.

'It's not a serious one. She'll probably get everything back if she is lucky.' He broke down. I wanted to throw my arms around him.

'Is Estelle with you?' I made myself say.

'I demand to know what the hell is going on. Do you know this jerk?' Greta yelled from the couch.

I paced to the far end of the room and indicated that she pipe down. But this set her yelling more. I cupped the phone to my ear.

'Who on earth is that yelling?' asked Arnaud.

'It's Margarethe's client, the one who sent us out on that boat, and she's furious.' I didn't know why I had needed to mention the boat but I was glad that I had. My chin started to wobble and I could hardly hear him talk.

'You know, I sent her away. She's gone home to Latvia. I spoke to her father.'

'I thought you had no language in common.'

'We do not.'

'Then what about the baby? It's yours.'

'Children require some sort of family. Not a set of nutcases and rock stars. Estelle had started down a nasty spiral and unfortunately I brought her there. Christ! It's been so long since I held you in my arms.'

'Oh no, no, no.' I shook my finger in the air towards him, glancing over as Greta threw the television remote in my direction and it clipped me on the shoulder and hit the floor.

'I think you should be with her in Latvia,' I said coldly. I could hardly believe my words.

'I am begging you, *Marileen*,' (once again, the French pronunciation had me ready to crumble). 'In Venice I lost my head. I did not know what to do but return to her. She needed me then. In many ways I was her ….'

'Father? That's disgusting. You should be ashamed of yourself.' I realised my shoulder was stinging while Greta was looking white-faced and clutching her side. Her baseball pitch must have popped her pelvis out of kilter. 'Arnaud, I'm afraid this is a business call. Ms Scarsdale has paid a lot of money for those sculptures to be shipped out. Just when are you thinking of taking them to the airport?'

'*Je n'en sais rien!* Arturo will pack them today. It will be a matter of days, I think. Can I call you back?'

'You'll find Ms Scarsdale on this number and she'll be very happy to speak with you in English. I'm sorry, I'll have to go now it appears she has had a turn of some sort.'

Greta was livid and in pain. I helped her to ease back on the cushions and as soon as she started swearing I knew no damage had been done.

'You stupid foreign ignoramus! I just asked you to make a phone call, not crank up my medical bill. I swear I'll get my lawyers onto you and you'll be eating your left thigh for breakfast. I swear, you all have shit for brains here. Now pass me that God-forsaken remote control I need to watch a film to forget your dopey face.'

I stepped back from her fury, watching a blood vessel pumping in her neck. I was fighting back the tears Arnaud had set off behind my eyes. I turned to where the remote lay on the floor after she had thrown it at me. I stared at it for a moment, then left the room and locked the apartment.

It was early evening, *prosecco* time. I walked hard against the cold. Each time the hot tears leaked from my eyes the freezing air sent them back. I must have covered four blocks. The harder I walked, the easier it was to pretend that Arnaud was still lounging in the Caribbean, and that he had never told me he was alone in Venice and Estelle had been sent back to Latvia. I shook my head like a madwoman, stamping out his voice every time it flared up in my brain.

– *Marileen, c'est toi?*

– *You know I sent her away.*

– *It's been so long since I held you in my arms.*

I pulled into a trendy-looking bar with deep purple décor and low lights. Inside it was tremendously warm and I slung my coat on the rack and patted down my dress. Sultry jazz music was playing and I could see the place was neither a local football den nor an under-thirty-five hang-out. Lovely! Finally everyone was acting their age. I could get drunk and spend the night obliterating my treacherous ex-lover.

I sat on a velvet bar stool and ordered the cocktail of the evening, a syrupy Campari with whatever. Within moments it had lined the pit of my stomach like a small animal with a growl.

I looked around, suddenly feeling fantastic. Three grey-haired men in suits were grouped around an attractive woman in a tailored jacket. I realised I had more to show off than what she or poor Jean could afford in a month of weekends in Spain. The men's eyes drifted my way, and soon enough one of them turned around and took a few steps over to me.

'*Buona sera.*' His smile made George Clooney look slightly jaded. My feathers ruffled at the genteel greeting.

'Good evening,' I said cheekily in English.

'*Vuole sedersi con noi? Mi chiamo Alessandro.* Would you like to join us?' he added in flawless English. I was introduced to the small party and handed a glass of the robust red wine they were drinking.

'I do apologise,' Alessandro said to me. 'We have the very bad habit of speaking of work even when we have escaped the office. Tell me, what has brought you to our difficult city?'

I saw that he and I were making a slightly separate group and he had casually placed his arm along the counter. No wedding ring. His hand twirled the stem of the glass and he studied the wash the wine made inside, while I studied his handsome good looks. For the first time in my life, this felt very, very easy.

'I wouldn't call *Milano* so difficult,' I said throatily, the first drink having oiled my tongue.

'That's not what I've heard most foreigners say. Or most Italians themselves. Does your husband have a job here?' he asked with discretion.

Here I couldn't contain a slight laugh. 'No, I'm divorced. I'm from England. My husband ran off with a woman with frizzy hair.' My laugh turned into a giggle, although I wished it hadn't escaped. I wondered what Alessandro's tongue tasted like.

'I am very sorry. But as you know, this is life.' He refilled my wineglass. I obliged by throwing back another mouthful and playfully watching the liquid slither back to its pool.

Alessandro leant in. 'You know Italian men are rumoured to be very good lovers. Do you believe this rumour? I imagine you've had the opportunity to try.'

I giggled again. 'Of course I do. It's no rumour. Not at all.'

The alcohol was sloshing around inside of me. It had hit my bloodstream like girls out on Friday night. And yet I had an inkling something in the Alessandro-Marilyn equation was not quite right.

'I find you an extremely attractive woman.' His gaze moved over me. 'I can't understand how your husband could have left a woman like you. Did you fail him in some way?'

All of a sudden my understanding of the situation abandoned me and I could only produce my blankest look. I went back to numb, sexless Marilyn on her knees weeding the garden. Yes, I *had* failed my husband.

Alessandro pulled back to say something to the woman in the tailored jacket. Then he joined in the group's laughter. It sounded like an unkind, conspiratorial laugh.

'I apologise. My colleagues were convinced you were a woman of the night. I informed them you were an English divorcée with Italian lovers. If you'll excuse me, my partner is expecting me at home. We have just had twins,' he said proudly.

He was gathered up by the leaving group and gave me a wink from the door. My feet dangled in heels from the velvet bar stool like a woman who had been hung. *We have just had twins. Did you fail him in some way?*

Sometime later I was still watching the wine pooled in my glass. I was imagining Alessandro, Arnaud and Peter lost in a blizzard in Latvia, the snowflakes slowly burying their blurred shapes. I watched the cold agony in their faces and their clenched, frostbitten fists. Then I heard sleigh bells. A couple passed behind me and bells jangled on the woman's wrist. I glanced up and saw Federico leading Fiona to the back of the bar. They threw themselves onto a purple couch and began canoodling.

Cazzo! I wanted to check it really was them but I was too terrified to turn my head. Now I knew why Federico's visits had tapered off over the last two weeks. Then it was true that she had called from Korea. Could it be true that she was thinking of marrying him?

I thought back to Fiona's note scribbled on the kitchen table an age ago. *Federico (owner's son, works in bar down the road) wants to marry me and it is really out of the question.* That was before Federico discovered me trying out Fiona's sex toys, and before I opened up my nightshirt to Federico on her divan. Holy flip! What if Federico had told her about that?

I looked desperately at the rows of drinks above the bar, my eyes lolling with alcohol and fatigue, my heels banging against the bar stool. I was stone drunk. I made myself count the piercings on the barman's face and found I couldn't keep a steady tally. I had a vision of my body plonked on the floor, brought back to consciousness by the young student who had thrashed my bottom more than either of my parents. I turned around just an inch. My eyes met Federico's as he rushed towards me.

'Hey, big sister! You look more drunk than my *zia Alberta* at *Natale!'* He gave me a big bear hug, devoid of any sexuality. 'My woman she come back. My Fiona, my lovely wife. We gonna have a hundred babies! You gonna come to our beautiful wedding. I love her. I love my Fiona baby!'

He whisked me to the back of the bar, saving me from falling off my heels. I saw our hours of devastating copulation evaporate in nanoseconds. Fiona sat on the purple couch beaming.

'Hel-lo there,' Fiona said with a grand smile. I had no way of reading her. I could have been wrong but I thought she looked thinner and a little tanned. I tried standing up straight and finding a focus point. This was still the woman who had slept with my ex-husband.

'Fiona! What a surprise. How was, er, Korea?' I asked cautiously. I was fully prepared to beat around the bush until I understood what was going on here.

'Have a seat, darling. It was all a bit tricky. The show didn't really take off. I might have to go back there but right now …' She gripped Federico's arm possessively while Federico looked like an addict back on drugs. '… I decided it was time to come back to my darling here. I understand he's been languishing.'

'Most probably. Yes, certainly.' I blushed all the way to my innards and slithered into my seat. 'Poor thing's been lost. Though I've hardly had the time to catch up with him.'

Federico, rather than erase any conniving from his face, sat there swooning. I felt a pang of jealousy bolt along my thighs.

'Fede told me there was a bit of upheaval at the apartment.'

'Sorry?' Surely he hadn't told her about our conjugations?

'His cousin moving in and so forth. Sorry to put you out. Fede says you've found a rather nice set-up.'

I couldn't tell if there was any irony in her voice or whether Federico had effectively led her astray. But they were so busy kissing now, hands fumbling, his fingers in her hair. Fiona pulled back and wiped her mouth, 'Sorry to be so indecent in front of you, but you understand it's been a very *very* long time.'

She rolled her eyes and plunged back in again. The barman brought a trio of red cocktails, looking in my direction. I picked mine up and guzzled. Federico handed Fiona her drink and then hungrily watched her lips part over the glass. I had never seen him so transfixed.

'And what about you? We really have so much to catch up on. Federico tells me you have a Swiss boyfriend. How wonderful. I do hope he's not too kinky.'

They began kissing again, hands interlocked between her thighs, the bump in Federico's trousers apparent. I could taste his smell rising on the air.

'Ahh,' I mumbled. 'I must be off now. I have an early, er, lesson tomorrow morning.' Neither of them looked up as I threw some money down and set myself on course for the glass doors.

I waved down a taxi and and went back to Brett's. Thankfully the apartment was quiet. Brett was taking an awfully long time in Finland. What if Federico was dumb enough to tell Fiona we had slept together? Surely he wouldn't tell her. I rocked into my room feeling queasier by the minute, nursing my sodden liver. I undressed and threw myself down, pulling over the covers as the bedposts swam.

For hours I turned over and over, wrestling with the sheets. I saw suave Alessandro holding a pair of babies, leering at me. I saw Federico and Fiona clasped naked together, waving at me from a couch in a bar. I saw crazy Arnaud Bertrand smoothing his mother's hair in a mouldy Venetian hospital, and world-famous Estelle in a grey high-rise watching snowy swirls on the window.

18. LEATHER BOUNDARIES

I woke up with a groan. Lam handed me a mug of reviving tea. He said the Peruvians were in the showroom.

'What Peruvians?' Then I remembered the fax from last week and this morning's clientele. My eyelids unfastened. I tried to think of the real money rolling my way – not Jean Harper's thin envelopes – and threw off my covers.

After the Peruvians, my work colleagues set out to other jobs in the city and I lingered over a coffee in the kitchen. That was when I heard Brett and Roderick burst into the apartment arguing. I had never heard them with raised voices, although I did not rule out this being some sort of sophisticated foreplay. I hurried off to my room and lay low, dreading a bout of yodelling or the crack of a whip.

But their voices grew more and more aggravated. I began to worry that it was about me, that Roderick had finally declared what I had sensed all along, that he hated me and wanted me to push on. I kept hearing the word *she* bandied about. I waited for Roderick to come thumping to my door with his tetchy ultimatum. Then I heard the door slam on the room they shared and their angry voices carried on inside. I rushed down to the kitchen to consult Lam, who was standing almost in a position of prayer.

'What is it, Lam? What's going on?'

'Mister Brett's wife Sandra is very sick in Hong Kong.' He turned away and began polishing the already gleaming sink.

'And why doesn't Brett go there? Why is Roderick so mad?'

Lam shook his head slowly as he began wiping the spotless benches.

I rushed back down the hall and braced behind my bedroom door. They were still shouting, although it was mostly Roderick now. Then there was a lull.

I shrank away from the door handle. Oh gosh! I didn't want to be around when the other sort of shouting began. But then I heard thrifty steps – they were Roderick's – coming towards my room. I swung around a picked up a book on Tudor botany.

Roderick rudely tore open the door and exclaimed, 'He wants *you*.' I saw him back off in distaste, toss a leather jacket over his shoulder and shortly after I heard the front door slam.

I stood there quaking. Was there a way out of this? After a spot of contemplation I realised there wasn't. Brett had given me a roof over my head when I was a bedraggled beaver dragging her suitcase across Milan. He still believed we had that three-way in Hamburg. And he had told me about his children Percy, Oliver and darling Katie, with Percy being the eldest who wanted to study in Scotland. I trod out into the silent hallway.

This was the first time I had ventured anywhere near the room their jungle cries came from. I nudged open the door and saw a gory red wall like a giant open artery. At its centre was a lavish painting with gold cornices. I made out a group of naked figures cogged together and quickly looked away. In the half-dark, at the end of the broad and sinful double bed, I saw Brett crouched against a lacquered oriental chest. I walked over and bent down, wondering how I could possibly deliver him any comfort. I put my hand out towards his stiff grey doll's hair.

'Brett? Are we okay?' I remembered his tongue fishing into my mouth in Soho, and how I had charged off up the street. 'Shall we head off to the kitchen then?'

Brett looked up at me with swollen eyes. He turned away and sobbed. After a minute or so I slid my hands under his armpits and tugged him to his feet. He allowed me to walk him to the kitchen where Lam was waiting with a pot of smoky tea. Lam and I eased him onto the rattan chair.

He looked around glassily and began mumbling like a madman. 'They've given her weeks. They've suspended all treatment. I'm pulling out of this run and transferring back to London. There's the children to think of next.' He looked over at Lam. 'Unfortunately Roderick's on another wavelength. All dressing and shoes and jawlines here. Roderick's become far too pampered in this environment. As soon as they're all settled I'm looking back to the east – not our East – I mean Poland and Hungary. Lots of repression. Well-made boots. I think we have to shift from Mexico. What do you think, lovely lodger?'

He reached out a hand towards mine. Single tears tracked down from each of his eyes. When I'd first met him in London I thought he looked like a detective. Now he reminded me of a cop who had discovered the culprit, but had been fatally wounded in the shoot-out.

'I know you are dismayed. But this is far from our first conflict. However, our rugged friend has worn me down this time.'

He took my hand in both of his and began to stroke it with fine, chilly fingers. 'I'm feeling slightly better now, thanks to you. You've brought me such delight. We've travelled quite a way together now, haven't we?'

I stared at the lifeless thing in his hands that was still attached to my arm. What was he talking about? Our sleazy internet date in Soho when I ran screaming up the street? Or when we bonded over his leatherwear magazine on the flight back from England?

'Don't speak, I know exactly where your thoughts lie. I promise you, we have not yet shared our most fruitful time together.'

I eased my hand away and stepped backwards, trying not to stare at the enormous bulge under his sarong. I stood still, eyes wandering over the kitchen shelves. Lam moved in with his scented oil and thankfully Brett's eyes closed.

Back in my room I bundled away my roll of cash for the morning's work. I tried to picture Brett and his wife in happier times, eating breakfast at a round table. I saw his fine-boned children in school blazers. I saw the harbour in deep pockets between city buildings. Try as I might, I couldn't picture the strong-willed merchant banker he had married, who was now slipping into the abyss.

I set out to school wearing a grey dress I made sure did not belong to Fiona's collection. I knew there was a good chance Federico might drag her into the classroom, where I was afraid some sort of showdown might take place. What would I say if she asked me in her point-blank way whether Federico and I had made love?

Federico? Are you mad? Federico wouldn't touch an old bird like me.

Federico? Well, yes, we did shag that one time. I had a spat with my Swiss boyfriend, and he was so lonely without you. Very brief and quite embarrassing really.

Downstairs, I bumped into Jean at the bar. I knew my face was tense and haggard. My hangover headache was starting to dig in claws.

'Hello, Marion. Aren't we looking a little off-key this morning?' she said jauntily after she ordered her cappuccino. Today by contrast her fine skin looked tight and honey-toned.

I frowned at my old icon. She would have left me in peace had she seen me parading for the Peruvians three hours back. 'I'm sorry, I had a rough night. And a rather eventful morning.' I begged the barman for a *caffè corretto*.

'Don't tell me you've been having *sex*.' She stared curiously, jumping to her own conclusion. 'At your age! Come on Marion, in every magazine the cut-off age is thirty-five and after that we cease to exist. Let alone have the right to prowl. For God's sake, you'll pick up something. And after childbirth you can scarcely believe a man can sincerely want to draw into your berth, can you? I'm both relieved *and grateful* if I can get Andrea to keep his needs to one evening a week. Anything else would surely be a bore,' she cackled.

I drank my coffee and turned on her. The woman was intent on erasing the trail of sex that had blazed from South America to Milan. 'But don't you two ever, you know?'

'Don't we ever what? Come on girl, grow up now. It's over for all of us. Who dreams of a forty-five-year-old centrefold? Or even further down the road? Tell me? I'm telling you, whatever the hell they say, you'll never be anybody's first choice. This is why I can't understand your little *singles* escapade in Milan. What in God's name do you think you'll find out over here?'

I stood staring at her. If the silly woman ever knew what we had all imagined. But I could never tell her any of that. Of the chasms rolling with mist. Of how the thought of Jean and her Italian lover in the wind-lashed tent had made me touch myself at night.

'Er, my husband left me and my life fell apart. I just wanted to get away.'

Jean tut-tutted. 'Just believe me Marilyn, it's over. And don't let anyone fool you otherwise. In fact, I'll let you in on our little secret. His mother takes the baby on Tuesday night, which is when the championship is on, the older children go to friends' houses to study, and Andrea likes me to bend over cleaning at half-time. In my underwear, of course, like something from bloody Benny Hill. If I'm lucky he's passed out by the end of the match and that's it for the week. Last night he fell asleep, so I tried this new face mask. Isn't it lovely?'

I didn't think I could stand it any longer. 'What happened to his first wife?'

'There was no first wife,' Jean replied. 'He lived with his mother. Only son and so forth. His father had a heart attack at thirty-nine. That's also why I've had to, well, let Maria be quite present with us. We're all she has.' Jean clutched her unlit cigarette. 'I've been lucky. But you have no idea what I have to go through. Well, that's it for me, I expect you're here for your lunch-time Conversation Brush Ups, no?'

'Yes, I am,' I replied.

'In case Francesca forgets to tell you, one of your afternoon students is bringing in his Australian girlfriend who wanted to sit in on the lesson. Apparently they're getting married shortly. You probably won't even remember the lad. Filippo or Federico, I think. The girlfriend is older, seems terribly keen, the usual sex kitten. You know these Australians – just about anything goes. So, you've been at it then?'

'At what?'

'Sex. You know, *carnal* relations.'

I said nothing.

'Ever thought of having those lines around your mouth filled? They do a marvellous job these days. Can you believe the Italian word for them is *solchi*? Which translates as *furrow*, as in what a farmer ploughs across a field. Whatever happened to poor, innocent *wrinkle*, I'd like to know.' She looked at her watch dramatically while putting down coins for her drink and quickly glanced at the mirror behind the bar. 'Must have my roots retouched. I'm starting to look like the wreck of the Hesperus – my dear old grandmother used to say that.'

I found myself frowning at her, and then quickly smoothed out my forehead. I paid for my coffee then dragged myself upstairs.

After lunch Fiona did indeed turn up for Federico's lesson. The other class members were eyeing her curiously as she and Federico kissed at the back desk. When I entered they all turned questioningly to me. Federico had spent the last weeks of term wooing me from the back of the room, hassling me to talk about vibrators, masturbation and the translation of every sexual term under the sun. I suspect they all knew we had been sleeping together, though I swear I had never even grazed his hand in class.

Federico and Fiona unglued and I tried to contain my blushing. Federico introduced his Australian fiancée to the class. The students followed our exchange of greetings like a tennis match. Then Fiona stood up and swanked down the aisle. As she passed me she whispered, 'Today's lesson is on me. They all want to know about Oz-Tray-Lia. You just sit down and take it easy,' she smirked. 'Old bin-liner face down the hall will never know.'

'But what about the Ranger series?' I said frantically.

'Don't be silly. Who gives a flying fuck about the Ranger series in this room?' She turned brightly to the class and I saw Federico swooning at the back, his face drowning in love. I sat there devastated, listening to Fiona's flat and endearing voice rattle on about spiders, surfboards and kangaroos.

After the lesson Federico took off to work and Fiona saluted the rest of the class while I stood at the doorway holding my briefcase. Her manner had been engaging and she had won everyone's hearts. She used the same Kate Moss trick that worked for me week after week. When a young man put up his hand and asked if she knew Nicole Kidman, Fiona crossed her legs on the teacher's desk and looked out to the distance magnificently. 'Of course,' she cried, 'we were at North Sydney Girls' High School together. Has anybody else heard about my friend Nic who won the Oscar?' She sounded pretty convincing and I had a quick shot of tall gawky Nicole in a school tunic, walking along with perky Fiona. At the end of the lesson she invited the whole class to the wedding party. Everybody cheered. She and Federico united in one last gripping kiss before he took off and Fiona turned herself over to me. She clattered down the steps in a new pair of fancy heels.

'Sorry if I stole your thunder,' she said. We stepped outside into a light rain. I was glad to get her away from the place before she started telling tales about Russell Crowe and Kylie Minogue. 'I bet she pays you chicken-feed right?'

'Oh, the pay's not so bad.'

'Bullshit!' She looked at me. 'I was worried you would end up in a hole like this. Let's have a drink. Do you *realise* I just asked them all to our wedding party? I can't even believe I'm getting married. My mates will never believe this one. Talk about a beggar for punishment.'

'Sorry?' Already the wedding bells scenario had blown me away. I couldn't believe Federico's desire for me had been so neatly transferred to another woman, albeit his original girlfriend. Rapidly, it seemed, poor old bin-liner face was making sense. When Peter wanted to come flying back to me it was because his lover had ditched him and I was second choice. Then when Arnaud had succumbed to my charms it was only because his true, pearly-skinned love had fallen for the grungy rock star. And now Federico, my grammar staple, had merely been sharpening his pencil while Fiona had pushed the pause button.

'I'll have a double vodka thanks.' We had reached the same snazzy purple bar where Alessandro had told me about his twins last night. I climbed onto a bar stool and ignored the staring bartender. Fiona chattered on compulsively, ordering drinks and sending a text message to Federico. I decided I would be on vodka-speak all night.

'So I've told my parents. They won't make it to the ceremony but we'll probably have another one in Sydney, next summer when it's hot. I really want Fred to see the beaches and the coast. You know, try surfing and sailing if he likes.'

'Fred?'

'It's a pet name. He *loves* it. So you don't mind being bridesmaid? I mean it's not a bridesmaid technically, as it's just in the *comune* not the church. Great excuse to buy a new dress though. Do you think your Swiss guy will come? By the way I had no idea Fred's cousin was going to turn up and kick you out of my place. Sorry, that must have really stressed you out. Drink?'

'Yes, darling. Hair of the dog. Do you say that down under?' Already the fresh alcohol had begun to sooth my shredded nerves and I wasn't so daunted by having Fiona buzzing before me. 'So whatever made you come back? You sounded like you wanted to drop Federico like a hot iron. I thought he was just a great shag.'

'And how!' she said, putting her hand to her crotch. 'Don't even go there or I'll wet the carpet!'

I winced. 'But surely you can't just marry a man for his, you know, his thingy.'

'Thingy? We're talking about a piece of architecture here! I swear to you Marilyn, I've never seen anything like it. You can't imagine!'

Oh yes I could.

'Look, I don't want to go on about it, but if you knew what I was talking about, you'd understand. I want him inside of me. I want to have his babies. I want to spend the next five years on planet orgasm.'

I frowned, a genuine frown with wrinkles. 'And then what?'

'Who knows? He still wants me, or he doesn't. I still want him, or I don't. And we work on what happens with the kids.'

'What about the long term? What about Till-Death-Do-Us-Part?'

'Who believes in that any more? Look at you and Peter. He's screwing around with Danielle and your kids are eating frozen pizzas. Don't start crying! I didn't say it's your fault. But you two really ought to organise what's up ahead for the pair of them.'

'Who are you to tell me what to do with my children?'

'Calm down, Ms Plunging Neckline. Fred told me they were out here and they were lovely kids. I'm just saying, every girl needs a five-year plan. Otherwise you'll end up like bin-liner face on the plastic surgery bandwagon. When I'm that old I want to be on my banana plantation stoned out of my wits. Not checking my boob bounce in the mirror.'

'But she's only few years older than you are.'

'That's what I mean. You can tell she's as un-shagged as they come. Where the hell is she going with it? I don't mind going downhill, but I want my *perversion* first.'

Here there was a glint in her eye that I didn't like. I felt my underarms irrigated with sweat. Darling Freddy had probably told her every damned thing.

'Perversion?' I said a little off-key. 'Who's talking about perversion?'

Fiona swept her phone up to her ear and sat there beaming, her eyes opened wide. 'Oh God, yes, oh my God, Fred. You're joking, you can't be bloody serious. With what? Oh, I will baby, you too, sweetheart.' She switched off the phone and her eyes rolled backwards. 'That was him. Oh God! He told me what he's going to do to me tonight. It's just electrifying. I think I have to go and wet my pants in the bathroom.'

I sat there chugging down vodka. I had a hunch Fiona was making me pay for utilising Federico's skills, and wondered how much longer I could pretend. Did she want me to break down and confess? Or were we going to beat around the bush throughout her next five-year plan?

Fiona rushed out again and resumed chattering without missing a beat. 'Federico of course doesn't know I haven't been completely faithful. It's just not in my nature. But now that we've decided to tie the knot I don't want to go breaking his heart. Hell, I really did not see this coming. Although let's get real here, a guy like that's probably been swinging his donger around, don't you think?'

'Er, well, I can't really say.'

'But that's just the thing with us, I suspect. Nobody else really hits the spot. Okay, I shagged my way to Korea and back. I was even in London on my back in Peter's office, do you believe? I think I just wanted to get at her on your account. Bloody piece of work he is. He would screw the garden tap.'

'You mean you *shagged Peter*?' I remembered the warm trickle of his voice in my ear when I'd been using Fiona's phone.

'I just wanted to rock the boat. Peter's always treated you like a dim-wit. Never let you shine. And then he falls for that trollop who's probably done the whole corporation. I'm just curious to know who Federico's been doing. You haven't seen him with anyone? Not that it could make any bleeding difference now.'

'Fiona ....' I just couldn't bear it anymore and decided to take the plunge. 'Federico actually gave me some grammar lessons, just a couple or so, well no, perhaps quite a few, and we, er, we had sexual intercourse.'

'With the cane? On your arse? That's hilarious.'

I wasn't really thinking along the lines of hilarious. 'You mean you don't mind?'

I couldn't tell if there was a hitch in her smile or not. 'Are you joking? I told him to look after you. It's the only way to learn a language. Just don't come asking for a threesome.' She turned to the menu and starting flipping through it. 'I'm famished.'

I felt quite put off. 'You're not going to mention it to Federico, are you? I mean it was just grammar, you know?'

'Sure,' she mumbled, eating *grissini*. 'What goes on tour, stays on tour.'

I called over the bartender and ordered more drinks. I realised this is where Fiona had been driving the conversation ever since I had laid eyes upon her last night. Fiona sat there mulling over the menu.

'So,' she said distractedly. 'When are you handing over my vibrators?'

I sat there absolutely stumped. The bartender's face shot over to us. 'Er, soon – tomorrow. Is tomorrow morning all right?' I stammered.

Fiona fixed me with her green-flecked eyes. 'Did you really think you were going to get away with this? I mean, moving in on my man while I was slaving my arse off on another continent? I know he was up for grabs, but how could you do it? Why all the bullshit about telling him you were my sister?'

'I – I didn't! I never did, it's what he wanted to think. Believe me, he never stopped talking about you, not for a second! I swear, he was devastated!'

She kept staring at me, her stare becoming deeper and nastier as I floundered. 'Did he ever shout my name when you guys were doing it?'

'Well, um, yes.'

'Often?'

'Often,' I said, looking away, remembering the times I had wanted to slap him. 'Quite a lot.'

The ferocity left Fiona's eyes and her face cleared. She leaned over and gave me a tight hug, so that I felt her narrow muscly shoulders and perky breasts. Her hair went up my nose as I inhaled her scent.

'Thank you so much.' She started to cry. 'For keeping him on track for me. You've been great, you really have. All is forgiven, Marilyn. Don't you just love what he can do with that cane? Let's just have one more drink for the road. And by the way, the vibrators are yours, every single one of them.'

19. HOT PANTS

The next afternoon I was crossing one of Milan's heel-unfriendly streets when I noticed a man with a camera sneaking between the parked cars. He bobbed up and aimed a fat black lens in my direction. I immediately swung around looking for the famous person the man was trying to snap. But the street was empty, just two rows of cars in front of gracious apartment buildings. I stepped between two shiny BMWs onto the kerb, keen to show myself at my best. I swanked my backside just that little bit more, which came naturally with the tottery boots I was wearing, thinking that perhaps every woman had an Estelle or a Claudia Schiffer tucked deep down inside of her. The photographer whistled. I dodged a mound of dog pooh on the footpath and set off to work chuckling. Why would anyone waste film on an old thing like me?

Several days later Jean Harper called me into her office with the sternest look I had ever seen on her face. She threw a magazine towards me on the desk. It was *People* or *Hello!* in bright clashing colours. I saw a carved stone Venetian bridge crammed with Senegalese vendors and tourists. The buildings and sky were crisp with winter light. At the centre a couple were locked in an embrace, kissing for all they were worth. It was Arnaud Bertrand and myself.

Cazzo! According to my translation from Italian the headline read something like 'Mogul Trades In Top Model For Older Sex Tramp'. Alongside there was a smaller photograph of Estelle in one of her clear-faced teen shots. There was another of her cupping the innocent and betrayed belly. Then – how on earth – there was a shot of me in my leather catsuit parading before the group of Peruvians.

I glanced across at Jean, whose face remained livid. 'Open it,' she spat. 'Page five.'

I turned to page five and shock travelled through me like cold water. There I was, strutting my stuff for the photographer, who must have used some digital device to amplify my rump, which looked impressive. There were other shots: me with students outside the language school, the 'English Now' sign clearly visible. It said 'Here Signora Wade speaks with Italian students unaware of her secret life'. There were more shots taken at Brett's party, including the pop star on a dog leash. I saw another image with an Arnaud-shaped man in a black mask.

Further down the page there was a box where Estelle's interview began. I read the desolate headline: *'Era tutto per me'* (He Was Everything to Me). Translucent Estelle was photographed between two short and heavily-dressed parents holding hoes in a muddy allotment patch. I was too shocked to go on. I turned the page and saw with horror that the article continued. There was another insert framed in Union Jack regalia with a photograph of Jean Harper at her desk. Jean's new breasts nestled together in her ruffled shirt, her pose reeking of righteous pique: *'Pensavo di conoscerla. La consideravo un'amica.'* (I thought I knew her. I considered her a friend.)

I sat back in disbelief. 'It's not true.' I shook my head dizzily.

'How dare you!' Jean boomed, rising to her feet and throwing her pen against the wall. 'You bring your filth into a respectable place and try to tell me these are lies. Are these lies, Marilyn? Are they?' She grabbed the magazine and held up the cover between her white-knuckled hands, pointing her shaky finger at the catsuit shot with the Peruvians. 'This! *This!*' she shrieked. 'Is this a lie? What the hell do you think I am? An idiot? Do you know what they all think of me now? One of your students told the journalist you gave them a lesson in masturbation – in the Queen's English. You read this!' She shook the magazine at me. 'I've read every word and you are the lowest creature in the world I have ever come across. Get out of here before I strangle you.'

I hurried away. The magazine hit my back and I heard her screaming into her phone to the secretary. A group of students stared at me open-mouthed in the hallway. Downstairs, outside the café, two men leaning against a wall sprang to life as I came outside, one removing a camera from his coat. I turned away, pulling up my collar, and ran.

I bumped into people as I tore into a crowded street. Looking upward, I saw magazine covers pegged on a news-stand. On two of them I saw pictures of myself. Another celebrity magazine had a searing close-up of the wronged supermodel clasping her belly before a snowflake-encrusted window, while the brazen older couple snogged in Venice above. I zigzagged onward. At a bus stop I saw a woman reading avidly, a man peering over her shoulder. An elderly lady in a fur coat pointed at me as I walked.

I scrambled down the street and swerved into a bar, ordering a straight grappa which I downed instantly. Then I became afraid I might collapse on the spot and the photographers would be onto me, immortalising my strife-seeking G-string as my skirt flew to the heavens. I moved to a back seat in the shadows, heaving uncontrollably, ready to hug the greasy table surface and weep.

I sat out the rest of the afternoon at the cinema watching an action film. I huddled low in my seat, hoping none of the popcorn-scoffing teenagers had seen this week's *Hello!*. I wished I had never come to Milan. What was I doing on the cover of a magazine, when all I had wanted to do was repair my life? Why hadn't I tried harder on the singles trip to Rouen, or booked the Coastal China Cruise?

I caught a taxi back to Brett's house, making the driver criss-cross Milan to shake off any followers. The driver turned around to me and swore, then his eyes flared open with recognition. I saw the *Hello!* magazine with dog-eared corners on the passenger seat. I threw him some cash and tore into the house.

I had just taken off my coat when I heard the door buzzer ringing wildly. I picked up the outside phone and listened. Nobody replied. I knew it was the photographers again, presumably trying to snap me in my negligée.

Then I thought I heard a muffled voice say, 'It is Arnaud.' He sounded out of breath.

Without thinking I pressed the buzzer that opened the door onto the street. Arnaud pushed it open and in a moment was standing in front of me, holding his chest.

'Why do you drive like a maniac across the city?' he puffed.

'They've been following me, taking pictures,' I blurted out.

'Give me some water,' he said, falling into one of Brett's neoclassical chairs. 'It has been thirty years since I have ridden a bicycle.'

But I wasn't getting Arnaud Bertrand any water. I stood there staring at the cruel man who had dumped me on a motorboat in Venice.

'*Et alors?* There is no water in this house?' he looked up and grimaced at Roderick's baubly chandelier.

I shook my head, fuming. I pulled off my shoe and started beating the life out of him. That he sat there shielding himself only made me hit harder. When I'd finished I dropped the shoe and slapped his face. The skin was soft and cold and my hands made a wet whacking sound on his cheeks.

Arnaud finally swung up and clutched my wrists. '*Putain! Mais tu es devenue folle? Tu sais ça fait mal!*'

'How dare you come here after what you did to me!' I screamed.

We stared at each other, enraged. I have never spat at a living creature but I spat into my former lover's face, watching the dribble smear down over his nose and cheeks.

But as I stood there, I began to smell him. A deep draught of his smell made its way into the centre of me. I forgot what I was doing and my instincts took over, softening as his injured eyes reached into mine. By the time his mouth reached my lips our bodies were crushed together.

'*Je t'en prie*, calm down, my sweet saviour. I am taking you away from this place,' he whispered, inhaling my hair. 'We have both had enough.'

It was so hard to think while kissing. Somewhere I still wanted to fight back, and I reminded myself that I was furious while I tongued the inside of his mouth.

Then I braced my hands against his chest, pushed myself away and cried, 'I cannot come anywhere with you. You are bound to another woman. Do you think I am just going to fall into your arms?'

Arnaud stepped back. 'You are entitled to reject me,' he said mournfully. 'I have been unfair, inconsistent, as well as a brute. You have every right to remain with your able student lover rather than a poorly equipped ex-Svengali with a shabby heart.'

'Federico's getting married.'

'My sweet, are you marrying that youth?'

'Not at all. His girlfriend came back from Korea. That Australian girl with the reddish hair, surely you have seen her.'

Arnaud shook his head. 'Truthfully, I only ever saw Estelle, and then yourself.'

'Okay.' I stopped him short. 'I don't need another Estelle session.'

'But I am cured of her,' he pleaded. 'I have emptied out the apartment. It's ready to be rented out next week. I shall never go back there.'

'Arnaud, you forget that you and Estelle are having a baby that has to be loved and raised.' As I said the words I realised their terrible logic. Arnaud Bertrand would soon become the father of a famous and photographed baby. The man I wanted to love was entirely spoken for. 'Don't you see?'

He took one of Brett's silk scarves and wove it around my shoulders. The smell of his skin came over in warm drifts.

'Then you won't come away with me tomorrow? I was planning to escape,' he said sadly. 'What will you do in this wretched city?'

He had a point. I had no respectable job and my face had been plastered on news-stands with a cat suit underneath. What if the *Hello!* shots went to England?

We walked silently to my room, arms laced together. We undressed. I sat on my haunches on the bed and watched Arnaud do the same. For a long while we sat without speaking. On the walls, the ancient Greek wrestlers played tag.

Slowly and cautiously our worn faces approached one another. This was knowing, this was living. I thought I would never feel this again.

Brett and Roderick had left for Moscow. I read this in the brief note Lam handed me in the kitchen the next day. It also said that as Lam would be closing the apartment, I could have the keys to Via Contini as long as I wished. It appeared Greta had been sent on her way. Brett had left me his business card again, with a thick red line under the Soho address. I put his card in my gown pocket and took the two cups of Lam's tea along the hall to my lover.

I pulled down the sheets and plastered myself against Arnaud's body.

'So who was the "older sex tramp" you were caught kissing in Venice?' I whispered to him.

Arnaud raised an eyelid. 'I believe that is my best cover shot yet.' He kissed me. 'For once I share the cover with my woman. And the photograph was inadvertently artful, alive and heartfelt, not all acid and bony joints. I think the paparazzi have done us a wonderful favour in providing the licence to be utterly carefree, selfish and debauched. Let us do our best to confirm what the public now believes of us.' He kissed me hungrily.

I laughed and laughed, rolling under him again, reaching my arms above his shoulders and tying them around his head.

'I'll have you in hot pants before the end of the month,' he murmured.

We looked at the train timetable together and Arnaud called a taxi while I went off to shower and do my hair. Margarethe had just left the hospital and he wanted to take me up to the mountains to see her, high in the Dolomites where she lived. I was reluctant, worrying that Margarethe would witness another of our breakups. I realised I had already installed an Arnaud Bertrand panic button within my body. But when he saw me tense he gripped my shoulders and kissed my hair, then placed a massive hand on my heart.

'My beauty,' he said, 'you will love Margarethe's village up there. And my mother is truly looking forward to seeing you.'

We saluted Lam and the taxi pulled away from the kerb. I saw one photographer focusing a zoom lens far away down the street. As we passed him Arnaud gave a regal wave and the man went into a snapping frenzy, leaping onto a Vespa that had revved up behind him. Arnaud promptly had the taxi driver stop near a traffic policeman writing out a parking fine, handed over a hundred euro note and had the Vespa pulled up while we sped away. I felt a novel sense of breaking rules and escaping to my freedom, which made my heart rock inside of me. As the sun-warmed buildings unfolded I saw they were shifting into my wake, and that should I ever walk down them again, it would be as a different woman once again. I looked at Arnaud, wondering whether he was feeling anything close to the same thing, and if men ever thought with all the desperation and naked hope that women did. He smiled at me, shook my chin, and said, 'Yes my love, it will all be different now.'

As the train was late, we sat nibbling pistachio nuts, leaning together on a bench. Both of us slept when we finally pulled away from Milan and her hinterlands onto the busy plains we had traversed together weeks before. Occasionally I awoke and my eyes fled to his face. Arnaud slept. I saw the same towns streaming past. I saw the deep blue lake with its cypress-crowned hillocks where we had begun to argue the last time. I drank water and forced my eyes to close. But then I couldn't help but remember the morning on the boat in Venice, the way he had pulled off his shoes and socks, and how his face had dropped during the phone call when he had become Estelle's husband again, the father of Estelle's child. How foolish was I to live with this hanging over my head. I needed Pamela's gut feeling on this and this time I wanted her to tell me the truth.

We changed trains and travelled north. The train moved through tunnels slinking beneath the first sudden hills, thrusting into the edgy light. Arnaud breathed deeply, occasionally shuddering awake, his eyes moist. I wondered if, for a moment, he had forgotten the life he had fallen into and the very different woman he now had by his side. But he relaxed into the headrest and whispered, 'I have just had the most indecent dream about you.'

I crammed my face to the window feeling as though I were a mischievous schoolgirl. There was a church spire with an onion top covered in black shingles, on the edge of a broad town filling the valley. The fields had already been turned for the summer crop. Some were bright green with young barley that swept this way and that, caressed by the wind. At the end of the valley the real mountains commenced in ice-topped triangles like the drawings of a child. The train banked, curving into another tunnel. We came out of the darkness to a field of yellow blossoms bursting in the sun.

At the sleepy little station, we were collected by a friend of Margarethe's who owned a hotel in one of the ski villages. After the initial talk about Margarethe's health and the duration of a welcome rain-free spell, we began our ascent. The van chugged around sharp turns sliced from the rock, climbing above valleys where pines clutched the slopes. Feeling woozy, I opened my window. I smelt streams bearing their melted snows downward in a noisy rush. I turned my head to Arnaud who was staring out of the window. Was he thinking about his new child? And what if Margarethe desired a rapport with her grandson or daughter? What if Margarethe craved a tiny yoghurt-smelling dangly-limbed sliver of herself?

Arnaud looked out over the valleys and then I knew he was thinking of other things. He smiled at a little house perched improbably on a bald peak, its façade preening in the light. He watched two old women resting on a wooden bench outside a tall shuttered house, its walls built of hewn stones. I dared to ask myself: could he be thinking how we might age together in a gabled cottage, warming our creaky joints in the sun?

'*Si va per di qua,*' said the driver as we turned at the bottom of an enormous valley, and headed towards even higher peaks. I looked at Arnaud but he was grinning at the massive mountain rising to the skyline, the sun mercurial on its icy pleats, a tuft of cloud pushing away into the vast panel of blue.

'How I marvel to be back up here. You will love this place. I see you already with thick stockings and a strong walking cane.'

I saw withered thighs and a set of dentures in a glass. 'It must be cold in winter,' I said brainlessly.

'Well, my dear, you will have to chop wood or enjoy the services of some off-season ski instructor, I expect. There is no need to look at me so foolishly, I will be off herding the cows. How would that suit you, woman-without-sea-legs, early retirement at 1500 metres? The air could be a little thin for you, used as you are to your rolling English plains barely above sea level. And you would have to adjust your wardrobe slightly.'

Suddenly, as though Arnaud's point required reiteration, round the next bend a deer stood in the middle of the road. It turned its head enquiringly. The driver slowed, the deer moved its huge ruddy haunches and delicately slipped over the guard-rail into the forest.

'There, it's you! Such a marvellous rear and a look of absolute apprehension. But nevertheless leaping over the guard-rail into the unknown,' Arnaud said. I had never even imagined such words, let alone a man would say them to me. 'No need to look so disturbed, I shall not turn you into a wizened old woman collecting berries in the woods. Most likely we will head south.'

I looked away from him to where the deer had chosen her path. There was nothing but tree trunks and ferns. Was he making fun of me? How could he even contemplate a life by my side? Somehow, I felt undermined. I thought of Vanessa with her asymmetrical dyed pink hair and I worried that the path of my life had forked in two. I didn't know how to turn back, or whether I wanted to. My chest hurt as we rose steeply, heading towards a small village where the houses lay pitched into the mountainside, every gabled façade turned to the sun.

'My mother lives in the last house to the right, the one that stands slightly detached from the town. I imagine she is sitting on her terrace watching the van's progress, and wondering if I have been brave enough to bring you.'

'Your mother really remembers me?'

'My mother found you a fine woman. You have no idea how we have clashed in the past.'

So I wasn't the only one who detested topless anorexics.

'And her companion?'

'Mother lives with a man called Mauro. Don't be shocked, his age lies somewhere between hers and my own. He must have been rather wild in his youth but, like her, he sculpts. He rarely leaves the valley. Naturally, he worships her.'

The van shunted along the village's single narrow road, several walkers saluting the driver and peering inside, recognising Arnaud and waving cheerfully. Margarethe stood in the doorway as we arrived, looking paler than before, but her eyes were bright with recovery. She hugged the pair of us, beaming at her son as they disengaged, then taking me with a gentle force in her arms.

'I am overjoyed to see you again, Marilyn. Just thrilled. I see Arnaud is trying his best to accelerate my recovery. Mauro is off on his walk and will be back soon enough. In the meantime, I have prepared us some food. Please, do come in.'

We entered a pine-walled room just off the street, whose windows looked out over the valley. An open door led onto a terrace with astounding views. Margarethe's chair sat there in the warmth, arranged with cushions and rugs. Arnaud pulled me outside. He plonked me onto a carved chair and bent over me. 'Close your eyes first, then the view will hit you harder, I used to do it when I was a child. Hold your breath for as long as you can.'

I opened my eyes and gasped. Over the balcony the peaks jostled into the cobalt sky seemingly at arm's reach, while the valley careered downward frilled with incandescence. I felt my heart fly out and begin to soar.

I spent the next few days in a silky trance. On the one hand I was certain that it would come to an abrupt end as it had in Venice, after which I would select a peak from which to throw myself. On the other hand my wrestling demons – perhaps slowed by the altitude – occasionally took a rest and allowed me to relax. In the mornings I awoke sensing the alpine chill beyond Margarethe's embroidered covers. Birds twittered in the woods nearby and the cool sun trickled over sculpted knick-knacks on the wall. I lay within Arnaud's embrace pinching myself, watching his mobile on the commode, certain it would buzz to life with needy Estelle's voice in her Latvian kitchen, as their baby twisted and hiccupped in her taut white belly. This thought came to sicken me several times each day, and even when that day closed and moved on to night, and then another day passed without Arnaud leaving me, I fully expected the phone to trill during the night and feel him pull away as he had in Venice.

But it did not. Margarethe's companion Mauro was usually up by the time we rose, banging or sawing away in the workshop downstairs. He was a large, loose-boned man with long arms and a hairy unshaven face, his skin ruined by sun and wind. I could see why Margarethe loved him. He was jovial enough, but most of his language came through his striking blue eyes. I had never seen eyes like his before. Mid-morning, Margarethe fitted on her sun-glasses and sat out on the terrace in the hazy light. I joined her there, sunning my arms and legs. Arnaud sauntered off to the newsagent and bought the local newspaper, *Il Corriere delle Alpi*, which he pored over, recounting stories of honey production and trout fishing. After lunch, he and I walked along a trail to a *malga* in a grassy clearing above the village, where spring flowers swayed in the cool wind. He told me that, in summer, the stone hut was open to walkers who drank mulled wine and ate local cheese. Though it was damp, he lay me down in the grass and we made love strenuously, alert for voices but hearing only cowbells.

On the last night, as we held one another close to sleep, Arnaud's telephone rang. His arm left my belly and I felt a cold stain on my skin. I knew he knew that it was her. I wondered if he had ever called her when he walked off to fetch the newspaper. Of course he had, *he had been everything for her.* I waited for him to leap up and for the tension in his voice to rise. I waited for him to start rubbing his forehead as he did when he was worried, pushing the hair back so that it all stood on end. I eased away to show I was ready to give him his space. I wanted him to see that I was no fool, I had seen this coming.

But he gripped me tighter, kissing my temple.

'No, I'm not alone Estelle, I'm with Marilyn. Yes, well, thanks to you and your photographer friends, most of Europe now knows Marilyn is my new partner. We're up here at Margarethe's in the mountains. Yes, the bothersome mountains you always hated. I've rented out the flat to a couple from Berlin, very well-referenced with no children or dogs.'

My eyes filled with tears. His voice was caring but firm. There were no traces of the old angst I had seen governing his actions. I almost heard her distant teenage voice sounding morose and whiny. It was strange: I had never associated her immense beauty with such a mean, high-pitched voice.

But then he closed the phone, sighed and rose from the bed. He went into the next room where our bags were stored and there were cupboards of old clothes. I heard him opening drawers and boxes. I lay there paralysed, convinced that their talking had been some sort of code and that he was preparing his gallant return to her.

Arnaud came back into the room, switched on a small lamp and held out an article of clothing towards me. It was a pair of soft leather lederhosen with embroidered borders of *stelle alpine*. To me it looked like a pair of mountain hot pants.

'Please, my dear, this is a fantasy of mine, and I know I have now found the only woman in the world who can carry it out. Will you put these on for me?'

I frowned. He pulled back the covers and I lay there naked. I stood up, taking the leather straps with their Heidi-style buckles, touching the coarse bib with its stitched pocket. The stars outside teased and twinkled on their black velvet as I stepped into my first pair of hot pants. My lover came towards me, dusting his hand through my hair.

269

20. COFFEE AND BLOSSOMS

We had almost reached Milan and were dozing in the train when I received a frantic phone call from Fiona. I'd been so drunk when we met at the bar that I couldn't remember whether I had to hand over her vibrators or not. I tried to prise open my mind.

'Marilyn! Oh my God, I'm so glad I've got you. Where the hell are you? Jean said you'd been sacked. I saw your photo on a magazine cover. Way to go girl! I'm marrying the bloody bartender and you've got yourself a mogul. Look, what are you doing on Friday? There's a spot at the *comune* for the marriage – somebody's got cold feet – we've brought everything forward. Fred's given up university and he's dying to go to Australia. Are you up for it? We'll have a great bash afterwards, just a few of us. Why don't you take us to one of your leather haunts?'

I flushed and Arnaud looked across at me, eyebrows raised. 'Oh, I don't think so. That's all been misinterpreted. It must have been photoshopped. It could have been Peter's people.'

'Bollocks, Marilyn, I've heard what you're like. And when Peter lays his eyes on the English edition you can be sure he'll be over here like a tomcat smelling you on heat.'

'What?'

'Yeah, Fred said someone brought the British *Hello!* into school the other day. They were reading the text in class. Bit weird, hey? And now Jean's trying to turn herself into some sort of martyr, a real Joan-of-Arc. By the way, Fred's quit now and I'll finish off his English education. And I'm expecting.'

'What?'

'A kid, you know, a baby. I can't think of any other way to call it.'

'Oh my, what a surprise. I mean, congratulations. Federico does seem to have good ....'

'Good sperm going down? Well, you ought to know about

that. So will you turn up on Friday? Mum's the word on the kid though. Otherwise his family will never let us go to Oz.'

'Of course. Yes, I will. Of course I will.'

I turned to Arnaud and saw my hand was gripping his thigh. Arnaud spread apart the pages of this morning's *Corriere delle Alpi* and moved my hand somewhere else.

An hour later we drove up to the Via Contini apartment. It had begun to rain. Brett's gloomy, formal sitting room stared back at me and I couldn't believe I had left such crystalline happiness behind me. What was going to happen to us? Arnaud looked at me a little strangely. Was he thinking the same thing?

We were too tired to eat. I wandered into the bedroom but Arnaud didn't follow me. I showered and crawled under the covers. Then, I heard him speaking on the phone for a long while in French. I was certain it was his contact in New York and they were laying the bones for a new model agency. Surely that was what they were talking about. Soon he would have a hundred fourteen-year-old Russians on his books.

Arnaud called me. I walked out to him in the half-dark. He was sitting on the edge of the divan smoking. I hadn't even known he smoked before.

My lover extinguished his cigarette and held onto my hips. Then he peered up at me with concentration and I was certain this was the end. I waited for him to tell me the affair was over and his plans had shifted again. I waited to hear about the new agency he was launching in New York.

'That was Rory, my love,' he began. 'Rory is a very good friend. He also has his own unusual situation.'

Unusual situation? Another nineteen-year-old wife? Another 'older sex tramp' in the woods?

'*Marileen*, I am a thrice-divorced man soon to become a father,' he said. 'You are a once-divorced woman with two teenage children.'

'Yes,' I whispered.

'I don't rule out marriage, but I can't marry you now. I want to breathe the way we are breathing. Let us be scandalous and unkempt. Live with me. Rory, for a variety of reasons, wishes to alter his life here. He leaves from Trieste next week to sail around the world.' Arnaud paused. 'I've told Rory about you from the beginning. He wishes us to stay in his apartment in Rome for the duration of his trip. I think it could be a good starting point for us. I need to consider my work situation and see to your needs. It may not be evident, but I can think of nothing better than moving there for a while. Perhaps, in the future, you might invite your teenagers over to see the sights and examine your monstrous old lover. I admit I'm quite wary of this. What do you say, *Madame Marileen?*'

He began to trace the skin exposed beneath my nightshirt. I placed my hand in his ragged grey hair.

The rain poured even harder on Fiona and Federico's wedding day. *Sposa bagnata, sposa fortunata*, people in the crowd kept repeating. Wet bride, lucky bride. It was hard to believe that Fiona had found her match in Federico, whose talents seemed singular and restricted to me. Now that he no longer had a future as an agronomist in Milan, perhaps he could branch out into his uncle's banana plantation in Australia.

The small group huddled under umbrellas outside the *comune* building, and I couldn't help wondering if Fiona were marrying the wrong person to offset everything that should have gone right the first time around, when her husband had cheated on her and she had lost her baby. Now, in any case, her bump had started to show and I saw what had perhaps drawn her back from Korea. For a shocking moment I worried that the baby may have been Peter's, and we may have shared offspring from the same dastardly man, but then I looked into Federico's adoring eyes and knew that the baby could only have been issued from, well, Fred's piece of architecture.

Fiona came over to me after the speedy ceremony. 'Well, you must be next up on the chopping board. Do you think anyone noticed my tum?'

The photographer broke through the crowd and she folded her hands over it. I pulled down my dark glasses.

'You must be getting used to this, now that you've graced a couple of magazine covers. Give those anorexics a run for their money. Well? What's it to be?'

'Arnaud's not going to marry me. Or not just yet. I think we're both still too traumatised.'

She looked at me doubtfully, 'Just up for the ride, are we? I suppose he's had three underage supermodel brides. I don't know how you hauled him in, given what they say about him.'

'But you mustn't believe that. It's all exaggeration. He's really just a businessman.'

'Businessman come pimp, my ass. And don't get all shirty. Anyone can see you're all he cares about.'

'We're going to live in Rome. We're moving next week.'

'Rome?'

'A friend of his is sailing around the world and has left us his apartment. Hang on, do you know a guy called Leonardo? He called on your phone when you were in Korea. I even went down to see him in Rome. He was very insistent that I go.'

Fiona's eyes sprang open. 'Leo? He called you? Why didn't you tell me this?'

I remembered how fondly he had spoken of her. *This is Fiona's favourite street. This is Fiona's helmet, the one she likes. This is the restaurant she prefers.* All along, even when I had been trying to impress him myself and he had told me the story about being an old childhood friend of hers, I had realised that Leonardo was the man Fiona had always loved.

She shook her head. 'If I'd have known I would have gone down there. He said he never wanted to see me again. I don't understand. Why now?'

Her hand dropped to her belly and I wished I hadn't mentioned Leonardo. Then Federico appeared at her side and his large beautiful hand covered hers.

'Fred, kiss me will you?' She reached up to him. 'You're my man.'

They kissed full-on and the crowd cheered. Federico pulled back, his eyes glistening. Fiona threw her little posy which went too far and landed in the gutter next to a parked car. Then Federico led her away and sat her in the back of a black Lancia driven by one of the uncles. On his way back to salute his parents he stopped in front of me. It was the first time we had been alone together since his visits when Eddy and Vanessa were in Milan. I remembered him making love to me on the bathroom sink as I flushed the toilet. Now, I felt a mix of treachery and embarrassment for all I had let happen. Fiona wouldn't have let him skip a single detail.

'I know I promise you wedding party fock,' he said gravely, remaining absolutely true to form. 'But now we have quiet party, not big family thing with kids in trattoria. Maybe if we stay in Italy and my wife *pancia* get too big and she no fock me, I come to you *sorella*. But now my Fiona she have my baby inside and we fly to Australia and ride camel and grow banana. When you come to see your *nipotino?*'

'Soon,' I smiled, 'Very soon. You must send me photographs.'

'Your Swiss boyfrenn', he too old, you need young guy who stay hard long time, *come me.* He need medicine?'

'No Federico, he requires no medicine.'

The crowd waved them off down the rainy city street. I saw cranky Alberta under an umbrella, her makeup smeared, and

Gustavo with his thin greased hair eyeing a teenage cousin with her midriff exposed. I saw the grey-faced uncle who had leered at me out of his bathroom window. He was being kept on a short leash by his grey-faced wife. I was glad when Arnaud appeared back by my side after his wander through the streets. Arm in arm, we hailed a taxi away from Fiona's new family.

We made love slowly in the warm apartment. Arnaud teased me about my ex-lover Federico, demanding I compare their erotic skills. I was embarrassed Federico had meant so much to me, but confessed to Arnaud that after the long stale years with Peter, he had been the first man to touch my skin. Arnaud feigned jealousy and managed to arouse me once more. This time I couldn't believe how far I went spiralling. I nearly cried, but I didn't want him to see my tears. I stroked his face as his breathing relaxed on my chest.

Around two in the morning I was woken by someone banging the shutters of the living room which faced the street. It sounded as though a man were being beaten to death. I rushed to the hall window further down which had security bars rather than closed shutters. I picked up my mobile, ready to call the police.

Outside, wailing on the footpath, I saw my ex-husband Peter. I saw lights snapping on in apartments across the street. I dreaded the arrival of more paparazzi on bikes.

I opened the window and called, 'Peter, shush!'

'Marilyn,' he howled.

'What's wrong, *cherie?* Who is that idiot out there?' Arnaud appeared, the pair of us still pleasantly sticky and naked.

'Arnaud, I'm so sorry, it's my ex-husband Peter. I have to let him in or he'll wake the neighbourhood.'

'Must you?'

He looked so gorgeous and worried that we resumed lovemaking on the spot. Peter's cries fell on deaf ears.

'This is what happens when you leave my side,' he said as he eventually pulled away. 'Now I am returning to bed. Do come back quickly.'

I pulled on one of Arnaud's shirts and told Peter to shut up again. He was pounding on the front door now. I buzzed it open and ushered him inside. One of my neighbours upstairs shouted into the stairwell. I looked at my ex-husband's dishevelled desperate state and knew I still had a long night ahead of me.

'Oh shit!' he wailed. 'I can smell it! He's been shagging you while I've been pacing outside. How callous of you, Marilyn. How could you, when you can hear I'm in agony over you? Where is he? I'll blow his brains out!'

'He's not here,' I snapped. Then I lowered my voice. I didn't want Arnaud to hear me speaking like this. 'There's no one here. I don't know what you're talking about.'

'Marilyn.' He came close to me and I backed away. 'Just look at you. Look at your hair. I can see your mouth. Don't let him do this to you. Filthy bastard. I know you've just shagged that man.'

Somewhere inside of me I felt the emotion that used to yearn for that voice. I heard its echo. But as my silence extended I worried that Arnaud, listening from the other room, would think I were yielding to the man I had once loved.

'Peter, you forget we are divorced. I can shag who I want.'

He grabbed me. I was not prepared, nor strong enough to push him away. I was terrified Arnaud would stumble out, find me in this man's arms, and it would destroy everything.

'There,' he said. 'I can feel you still want me. Danielle always said you wanted me back. And setting up that magazine photograph, nothing was as obvious as that. She and I both knew you were crying out to have me. I've dealt with everything now. We'll be on our own forever. It's been a long twisted path and how metaphorical that we find ourselves in Italy once again, the country of lovers and saints,' he declared.

He made to take me in his arms again. I arched backwards, tripping over the coffee table and falling sprawled over it, Arnaud's ashtray digging into my lower back. Peter leapt on top of me and I shrieked.

At first Peter failed to see an incensed Arnaud filling the doorway next to him. As I stopped screaming, staring at him, Peter finally turned to the Swiss ex-model agency director.

'Shit!' he shouted.

'Get off my fiancée,' Arnaud said coldly.

'Fiancée?' Peter stuttered. My ex-husband dropped off me like a dead fly and, for once, words failed him. Arnaud stepped forward to help me from the table. My back throbbed. He saw what had happened and said, 'I'll get some ice for that. Just let me show this man the door.'

Peter stood there, gaunt and spent. In my eyes, he ceased to exist. I had never thought less of him. Perhaps in the first months of his romance with Danielle, when he used to come to the house with the aura of sex about his body, and he had grafted our children so readily onto his new life. Then the hurt had been driven in so deeply it had been better to let the wound close over. But that night my marriage to Peter truly ended. I saw Arnaud escort him to the door then turn back to me with concern.

I fell in love with Rome this time around. The city stirred the love of my soul. Perhaps it was because I was so abundantly full of love myself. Blossoms cascaded over the terraces above the streets, as cafés released their rich aroma of morning coffee. The air was warmer and looser. Palm trees and sea pines fanned into the sky alongside Baroque façades with their ornamental crests.

Rory's apartment was a treasure. The building jutted into a small piazza and so the apartment had two walls of windows that charted the sky and sun. A broad terrace was tucked between his and the next block, where he had bougainvillaea in pots and bamboo hedges blocking the neighbours' view. We ate our lazy lunches out there and I sunbathed in secret in the afternoons. At night the orange street lamps lit up a small church façade with a ridge of gentle scrolls against the purple sky. We leant over the street, watching people meet up in the piazza and Vespas whirring past with pretty long-thighed girls.

I quickly grew used to the long salty nights stretched out next to Arnaud, and the spring-scented mornings before feisty traffic filled the streets. As the weather warmed I took to having a long siesta – it was the only time the neighbourhood grew quiet – after which we strolled several blocks down to the broad Piazza del Popolo where cars swirled around the obelisk Mussolini had carted off from Africa.

In time Arnaud began looking into business interests, most of which he shelved immediately: opening a Swiss bar; an art gallery specialising in northern European art; a designer furniture outlet. I dreaded the day he would come home and say he had to return to the modelling business. For a long while I lived with that terror. I imagined I would end up teaching English to a class of Roman Federicos, while Arnaud would be sorting through fifteen-year-old Somali girls for his next international icon, all of them eager and willing as Estelle to bend over on the couch.

But in the end he seemed keen on joining a luxury boat dealership with Rory, our sailor landlord, and I found a part-time job as a physiotherapist in a sports centre around the corner. I worked with a C-grade rugby team drawn from internationals working in the city. My English was very useful with the Kiwis and South Africans, although Arnaud looked very disturbed when I told him about loosening thigh tendons in a Maori player's leg. I saw a side of Arnaud I hadn't seen. His lapse in confidence was so charming. To calm him down I opened up the trunk with Brett's squeaky leather gear and gave him some specific reassurance. Other times I donned the mountain hot pants and both of us inhaled the soft embroidered leather as though it were a field of fresh alpine grass.

At Easter, I asked Arnaud if he were ready to meet Vanessa and Eddy. I yearned to see them again. Vanessa was sceptical on the phone when I told her the famous supermodel's ex-husband was now the man of my life. She told me she didn't care to meet him and I had no idea how to dismantle the hard distrust in her voice. I was worried I would lose them if I waited any longer so I booked them tickets and prayed I would find a way to make Arnaud palatable to a pair of London teenagers.

The children arrived at Fiumicino Airport and after the train ride into the city we caught a taxi to our place. Though there had been hugs and splutters at the airport, I noticed both of them were holding themselves in check. It wasn't shaping up to be a fun visit like the last. They asked about Federico and I told them he had married his girlfriend and gone to Australia. Neither of them wanted to know about Arnaud. The silence in the car lasted until we reached Rory's front door.

After we pulled their bags onto the footpath Vanessa looked at me squarely, her brother close by her side. 'So has Arnold stopped trafficking teenage anorexics and dragging you to orgies?' she burst out. That was when I realised they had both pored through Jean's celebrity rag. I was mortified.

'Er, it's Arnaud darling, not Arnold. It's a French name. And Arnaud is now dealing with boats, not models,' I said to them uncertainly. 'We, er, only went to that place once.'

'What a joke, Mum. Do you really believe he's not going to run back to his top model wife with the baby he's abandoned?'

'I do, Vanessa. Yes, I do.' But my daughter had hauled out the biggest fear of my life.

We stood at the base of the stairs as Arnaud quickly appeared at the curve on the landing above. Vanessa sprang back, recognising him. Then she flushed all the way to the back of her neck.

'I heard your voices out in the street,' Arnaud said cheerfully. 'I see I wasn't fast enough to help you out of the taxi. But what a curious conversation. I do apologise if I listened.'

He took Vanessa's bags and she turned to me, still violently red. I was annoyed at Arnaud.

'Don't be embarrassed, Vanessa,' he said. 'Your concerns are entirely valid and I am very glad of your interest.' He talked on as he led her upstairs. Eddy ambled after us, his ears pricking up. 'The baby will be in fine hands and Estelle and I were totally unsuited to one another. Yes, my name is Arnaud, a fairly regular name given to me by my parents. Over the years I've grown reasonably fond of it. I'm sorry, I'm afraid I really couldn't answer to the name *Arnold*. Far too *Hasta la vista, baby.*'

Inside, I saw the redness fading from her face, replaced by a mild smirk. Arnaud turned and shook Eddy's hand. Eddy glowered. 'I saw you pashing with my mother in a magazine, I did. All the kids in my class saw it. You're much older than my father.'

My knees went to water.

'And your mother is the finest kisser I have ever come across,' Arnaud replied without missing a beat. 'Shall we go out onto the terrace and look at this splendid city?'

It was a tentative week. I took them through the ruins of the Forum. We ate the best pizza I had ever eaten in my life, followed by a glorious ice-cream. Arnaud borrowed a Vespa and took Eddy for spin late in the night. They went screeching around the piazza below us and I believe they rounded the Coliseum three times. Vanessa began to sunbathe on the terrace but, plump and chesty, she was shy of Arnaud. One afternoon she caught us kissing out there, when I thought they were watching a DVD inside.

She stared and spoke to Arnaud, 'How can you love my mother if you've spent your life doing this?' She held up a fashion magazine with a stringy brown model jumping in a designer dress. Unlike his frozen deer-eyed teens, Arnaud had begun to realise that Vanessa's tongue could be venomous.

Arnaud squinted. 'Isn't that Naima? She was once with my agency. Poor thing, she came from a village in northern Somalia.'

'Arnold.' Vanessa rolled her eyes. 'Now do you see what I mean?'

'A-r-n-a-u-d,' Arnaud and I chorused.

'Whatever,' slurred Vanessa. 'Mum, don't you realise he's part of this whole stupid world? How can you stand it? What do you think he sees in you?'

'Well, that's a fair enough question,' Arnaud said, detaching from me and shrugging in his endearing French way. A single bougainvillaea flower freed itself from the cloud above and strayed along Arnaud's cheek, coming to rest in his lap. He studied its bright fuchsia petals and its odd boxy form. He looked across at me for a moment, then cupped the flower and transferred it to my lap. I sat there waiting for my desensitized daughter to jump upon his reply.

'You know, Vanessa, the strangest thing is that I don't wish I had met her before, when she was young and raising yourself and your brother. I want her now, like this, the way she is sitting in the sun listening to me so gullibly. Isn't she beautiful?'

Vanessa sat down on one of Rory's iron chairs and met his eyes. Arnaud made no move to draw me onto his side. This was between the pair of them.

'You'd better mean it,' she said. 'Otherwise we'll be onto you.'

Just before the end of the children's visit Arnaud left for Latvia to see how Estelle was faring. Despite his copious reassurance I was convinced he would never return. It was painful to have Vanessa and Eddy see my discomfort. Initially, I had thought it would have been super to have a few days with them on my own, but this was the first time Arnaud had left me to go to *her* and I was a mess. I started pouring vodka into my tonic around midday, and sloshed it into almost everything I drank throughout the afternoon. I thrashed in the bed sheets all night, no longer used to being alone and not making love. The morning after I nursed monster hangovers and despised the light searing through the shutters. I went to work stumbling over the cobbles and wept on a Maori footballer's shoulder.

Unexpectedly, Vanessa took stock of the situation.

'Look Mum, I have already dealt with a lunatic father for nearly a year now. I am not letting you start. The man loves you, it's completely obvious, and wants to be by your side. He'll be back in two days, he calls you every other hour, and I won't even contemplate studying in Rome if it's going to be like this. Grow up, Mum.'

I slumped in the tiny kitchen in one of Arnaud's shirts and Vanessa stormed outside. She was right. Arnaud was coming back and we would string our life together. The kids weren't all over him as with Federico, but their cool disrespect might just turn into something warmer.

I watched her walk outside and unscrewed the coffee percolator, rinsed it in the sink and crammed in as much aromatic powder as possible, putting it on the burner. Down in the piazza I watched an older, straight-backed woman wheeling a shopping trolley full of vegetables. I breathed deeply, suddenly thinking I would buy some fresh zucchini and eggplant at the market for Arnaud's return, and prepare some fish. I put out cups, the sugar bowl and teaspoons, and waited for the pot to gurgle. Outside, I watched my lovely daughter musing in the sun with Rory's fuchsia bougainvillaea blossoms cascading behind her.

EPILOGUE

Arnaud returned. Prematurely, Estelle gave birth to a baby girl named Sasha. Arnaud didn't like the name, he told me, but it was Estelle's decision. He said the child looked like Estelle's father.

Brett called several times from Hungary, wanting me to work as a consultant. I knew one word in Hungarian: *Nem.* However Arnaud and I flew there for a few dirty weekends, if only to stop our leathers going mouldy. Brett's wife died in the summer and his children now live with a nanny in London, where he frequently stays. I finally visited the Soho outlet and went behind the Peking Duck façade. There were no surprises for me. Roderick spends most of his time in London, as I understand, but still jets over to events in Milan. Lam appears to like Budapest.

Rory never came back. He fell in love with a local woman in Polynesia. The woman already had nine children and bore him twins. The boat dealership fell through and Arnaud befriended an aged Lithuanian antiques dealer two streets away who acquires icons, which Arnaud loves. He now works there much of the time. I drink coffee with him at the back of the shop and on slow afternoons we make love on a Napoleon 3rd day bed resting on four lion paws. For two tall people, the bed is quite short.

Pamela was here in August. We sat out on the terrace drinking cocktails. She wore a silly shoestring-strapped top with sunburnt shoulders, her nipple piercing making a bump under the fabric and her tattoo fronds on show. As usual, she kept mum about what is coming next for me, but I caught her looking at me with a satisfied smile as we took in the view from the apartment.

'When I see you here,' she said. 'I remember a dream I had the very first time I saw you, just after he left with that gorgeous young bird and I told you it wouldn't last. I swear I saw you here. I saw that little church. I saw a big man surrounded by thin women. That was the bit I didn't get though. I thought I had my wires crossed and that it was Peter coaching gymnastics.'

Pamela also told me the latest about my ex-icon Jean Harper. Her kids had left Milan and gone home, covering every inch of themselves with piercings and tattoos. They were jobless, on welfare, living with their grandparents. Jean had a plastic surgery mishap and went into a coma in Spain, and then woke up asking for her ex-husband. Apparently the English Now Language Institute is booming and she is branching out into Turin and Padua and Venice. The smutty celebrity magazine article about her famous ex-employee has put her on the map.

The other day an envelope arrived from Australia. Inside, there was a photograph with a few lines scrawled on the back. It showed three people sitting on a camel in front of what looked like a banana plantation, all wet earth and glossy green leaves. I squinted. There was a spaced-out woman with cropped red hair wearing a tiny T-shirt that did not cover her newly pregnant belly. Behind her there was a tanned, swarthy-looking man holding up a naked brown baby that looked about six months old. I finally made out the words.

This is Tilly in Fred's arms. I'm four months gone with the next. I am never coming back. I am so where I want to be it's not funny.